THE PURSUIT OF LOVE

LOVE IN A COLD CLIMATE

The Pursuit of Love

&

Love in a Cold Climate

TWO NOVELS BY

Nancy Mitford

MODERN LIBRARY · NEW YORK

To Gaston Palewski

FOREWORD

"The Mitford Industry" is a phrase cleverly coined by the odious London *Evening Standard* (ever the bane of our family) circa 1979, when the English reading and telly-viewing public were subjected to an unprecedented barrage of Mitfordiana: Harold Acton's memoir of Nancy, David Pryce-Jones's book about Unity, Diana's book about Diana, mine about me.* BBC produced two hour-long documentaries about Nancy and me, soon followed by Thames Television's six-part dramatization of *The Pursuit of Love* and *Love in a Cold Climate.* As I write this the Industry rolls on with Ned Sherrin's and Caryl Brahms's musical show, *The Mitford Girls,* featuring six dancing and singing actresses who alternate period songs of the twenties and thirties with snippets of conversation from the aforementioned books. My sister Deborah has cruelly dubbed this show "La Triviata."

It was, of course, Nancy who started it all. Without her, there would be no Mitford industry. If only she could have lived to see the unlikely fruits of her early endeavors! "*How* I shrieked," she would have said.

And how *I* shrieked when I first read *The Pursuit of Love,* which clattered into my postbox in California some time in 1945. Because there we all were, larger than life, Mitfords renamed Radletts, reliving our childhoods as seen through Nancy's strange triangular green eyes.

Some contemporaneous family reactions: My mother (*alias* Aunt Sadie in the book) wrote to say *she* thought it very amusing, but she doubted if anybody outside the family would want to read it because they wouldn't understand the jokes. (In the event she was proved wrong. According to Harold Acton, it has sold over a million copies.) My sister Deborah (*alias* Vicky) was vastly annoyed at Nancy's saying that she and I (*alias* Jassy) had called our secret society "The Hons" because we were Honourables, when in fact the name derived from the sweet hens we used to keep, whose eggs were the mainspring

---

* *Nancy Mitford: A memoir,* Harold Acton. Harper & Row, 1976. *Unity Mitford: An Inquiry into Her & the Frivolity of Evil,* David Pryce-Jones. Dial, 1977. *A Life of Contrasts,* Diana Mosley. Times Books, 1978. *A Fine Old Conflict,* Jessica Mitford. Knopf, 1977.

of our personal economy: we sold them at a slight profit to my mother, and then ate them for breakfast. This distortion persisted in translation; in the French edition, the Hon's Cupboard is "la Cave des Nobles." Debo was pleased when later I made a public correction (in *Hons and Rebels*)* of wicked Nancy's misrepresentation.

To what extent, then, are the characters in these novels drawn from life? Almost entirely, I would say, with, of course, the novelist's propensity to merge and distill characters: Linda, for example, seems to me to be a composite of my sisters Diana and Deborah, with a splash of Nancy herself thrown in.

Before the war, Nancy had written three novels, all pretty much based on family and friends. Her first was *Highland Fling,* in which our father is felicitously named General Murgatroyd, later to become the terrifying Uncle Matthew of *The Pursuit of Love* and *Love in a Cold Climate*. His distinctive argot—"Damm sewer" or "Stinks to merry hell"—his violent outbursts against those unfortunates to whom he had happened to take a dislike, are drawn to the life. In fact, so accurate was Nancy's portrayal of my father that after his death in 1958, even the London *Times* obituary writer seemed confused as to whether he was describing Lord Redesdale or "the explosive, forthright Uncle Matthew" of her novels.

To supply further clues to the reader: Lord Merlin is Lord Berners, who really was a neighbor of ours and who really did have the cable address of "Neighbour-tease." Lady Montdore is partly drawn from Violet Trefusis, of whom Harold Acton writes: "One can almost hear Violet remarking, like Lady Montdore, 'I think I may say we put India on the map. Hardly any of one's friends in England had ever even heard of India before we went there, you know.' "

But—what of Nancy herself? Ah, that was the real puzzler. To what extent did that intensely private character let down her comedian's mask to reveal herself in these novels?

As soon as I had finished reading *The Pursuit of Love,* in which Linda after many a false start finds true bliss with a hero of the Free French resistance movement, I sat straight down and wrote to Nancy: "Now Susan [we called each other Susan—why, I can't remember], we all know you've got no imagination, so I can see from yr. book that you are having an affair with a Frenchman. Are you?" She wrote back, "Well, yes, Susan, as a matter of fact I am."

Jessica Mitford
November 1981

* Published in this country as *Daughters and Rebels* and now available in paperback from Holt, Rinehart and Winston.

CHAPTER 1

THERE is a photograph in existence of Aunt Sadie and her six children sitting round the tea-table at Alconleigh. The table is situated, as it was, is now, and ever shall be, in the hall, in front of a huge open fire of logs. Over the chimney-piece plainly visible in the photograph, hangs an entrenching tool, with which, in 1915, Uncle Matthew had whacked to death eight Germans one by one as they crawled out of a dug-out. It is still covered with blood and hairs, an object of fascination to us as children. In the photograph Aunt Sadie's face, always beautiful, appears strangely round, her hair strangely fluffy, and her clothes strangely dowdy, but it is unmistakably she who sits there with Robin, in oceans of lace, lolling on her knee. She seems uncertain what to do with his head, and the presence of Nanny waiting to take him away is felt though not seen. The other children, between Louisa's eleven and Matt's two years, sit round the table in party dresses or frilly bibs, holding cups or mugs according to age, all of them gazing at the camera with large eyes opened wide by the flash, and all looking as if butter would not melt in their round pursed-up mouths. There they are, held like flies in the amber of that moment—click goes the camera and on goes life; the minutes, the days, the years, the decades, taking them further and further from that happiness and promise of youth, from the hopes Aunt Sadie must have had for them, and from the dreams they dreamed for themselves. I often think there is nothing quite so poignantly sad as old family groups.

When a child I spent my Christmas holidays at Alconleigh, it was a regular feature of my life, and, while some of them slipped by with nothing much to remember, others were distinguished by violent occurrences and had a definite character of their own. There was the time, for example, when the servants' wing caught fire, the time when my pony lay on me in the brook and nearly drowned me (not very nearly, he was soon dragged off, but meanwhile bubbles were said to have been observed). There was drama when Linda, aged ten, attempted suicide in order to rejoin an old smelly Border Terrier which Uncle Matthew had had put down. She collected and ate a basketful of yew-berries, was discovered by Nanny and given mustard and water to make her sick. She was then "spoken to" by Aunt Sadie, clipped over the ear by Uncle Matthew, put to bed for two days and given a Labrador puppy, which soon took the place of the old Border in her affections. There was much worse drama when Linda, aged twelve, told the daughters of neighbours, who had come to tea, what she supposed to be the facts of life. Linda's presentation of the "facts" had been so gruesome that the children left Alconleigh howling dismally, their nerves permanently impaired, their future chances of a sane and happy sex life much reduced. This resulted in a series of dreadful punishments, from a real beating, administered by Uncle Matthew, to luncheon upstairs for a week. There was the unforgettable holiday when Uncle Matthew and Aunt Sadie went to Canada.

The Radlett children would rush for the newspapers every day hoping to see that their parents' ship had gone down with all aboard; they yearned to be total orphans— especially Linda, who saw herself as Katie in *What Katie Did*, the reins of the household gathered into small but capable hands. The ship met with no iceberg and weathered the Atlantic storms, but meanwhile we had a wonderful holiday, free from rules.

But the Christmas I remember most clearly of all was when I was fourteen and Aunt Emily became engaged. Aunt Emily was Aunt Sadie's sister, and she had brought me up from babyhood, my own mother, their youngest sister, having felt herself too beautiful and too gay to be burdened with a child at the age of nineteen. She left my father when I was a month old, and subsequently ran away so often, and with so many different people, that she became known to her family and friends as the Bolter; while my father's second, and presently his third, fourth and fifth wives, very naturally had no great wish to look after me. Occasionally one of these impetuous parents would appear like a rocket, casting an unnatural glow upon my horizon. They had great glamour, and I longed to be caught up in their fiery trails and be carried away, though in my heart I knew how lucky I was to have Aunt Emily. By degrees, as I grew up, they lost all charm for me; the cold grey rocket cases mouldered where they had happened to fall, my mother with a major in the South of France, my father, his estates sold up to pay his debts, with an old Rumanian countess in the Bahamas. Even before I was grown up much of the glamour with which they had been surrounded had faded, and finally there was nothing left, no foundation of childish memories to make them seem any different from other middle-aged people. Aunt Emily was never glamorous but she was always my mother, and I loved her.

At the time of which I write, however, I was at an age when the least imaginative child supposes itself to be a changeling, a Princess of Indian blood, Joan of Arc, or the future Empress of Russia. I hankered after my parents, put on an idiotic face which was intended to convey mingled suffering and pride when their names were mentioned, and thought of them as engulfed in deep, romantic, deadly sin.

Linda and I were very much preoccupied with sin, and our great hero was Oscar Wilde.

"But what did he *do*?"

"I asked Fa once and he roared at me—goodness, it was terrifying. He said: 'If you mention that sewer's name again in this house I'll thrash you, do you hear, damn you?' So I asked Sadie and she looked awfully vague and said: 'Oh, duck, I never really quite knew, but whatever it was was worse than murder, fearfully bad. And, darling, don't talk about him at meals, will you?'"

"We must find out."

"Bob says he will, when he goes to Eton."

"Oh, good! Do you think he was worse than Mummy and Daddy?"

"Surely he couldn't be. Oh, you are so lucky to have wicked parents."

I stumbled into the hall blinded by the light after a six-mile drive from the station. Aunt Sadie and the children were having tea, under the entrenching tool, just like in the photograph. It was the same table and the same tea-things, the china with large roses on it, the tea-kettle and the silver dish for scones both kept hot over flickering flames; the human beings were five years older. That is to say the babies had become children, the children were growing up. There had been an addition in the shape of Victoria, now aged two. She was waddling about with a chocolate biscuit clenched in her fist, her face was smothered in chocolate and was a horrible sight, but through the sticky mask shone unmistakably the blue of two steady Radlett eyes.

There was a tremendous scraping of chairs as I came in, and a pack of Radletts hurled themselves upon me with the intensity and almost the ferocity of a pack of hounds hurling itself upon a fox. All except Linda. She was the most pleased to see me, but determined not to show it. When the din had quieted down and I was seated before a scone and a cup of tea, she said:

"Where's Brenda?" Brenda was my white mouse.

"She got a sore back and died," I said. Aunt Sadie looked anxiously at Linda.

"Had you been riding her?" said Louisa, facetiously. Matt, who had recently come under the care of a French nursery governess, said in a high-pitched imitation of her voice: "As usual, it was kidney trouble."

"Oh, dear," said Aunt Sadie, under her breath.

Enormous tears were pouring into Linda's plate. Nobody cried so much or so often as she; anything, but especially anything sad about animals, would set her off, and, once begun, it was a job to stop her. She was a delicate, as well as a highly nervous child, and even Aunt Sadie, who lived in a dream as far as the health of her children was concerned, was aware that too much crying kept her awake at night, put her off her food, and did her harm. The other children, and especially Louisa and Bob, who loved to tease, went as far as they dared with her, and were periodically punished for making her cry. *Black Beauty*, *Owd Bob*, *The Story of a Red Deer*, and all the Seton Thompson books were on the nursery index because of Linda, who, at one time or another, had been prostrated by them. They had to be hidden away, as, if they were left lying about, she could not be trusted not to indulge in an orgy of self-torture.

Wicked Louisa had invented a poem which never failed to induce rivers of tears:

"A little, houseless match, it has no roof, no thatch,
It lies alone, it makes no moan, that little, houseless
match."

When Aunt Sadie was not around the children would chant this in a gloomy chorus. In certain moods one had only to glance at a match-box to dissolve poor Linda; when, however, she was feeling stronger, more fit to cope with life, this sort of teasing would force out of her very stomach an unwilling guffaw. Linda was not only my favourite cousin, but, then and for many years, my favourite human being. I adored all my cousins, and Linda distilled, mentally and physically, the very essence of the Radlett family. Her straight features, straight brown hair and large blue eyes were a theme upon which the faces of the others were a variation; all pretty, but none so absolutely distinctive as hers. There was something furious about her, even when she laughed, which she did a great deal, and always as if forced to against her will. Something reminiscent of pictures of Napoleon in youth, a sort of scowling intensity.

I could see that she was really minding much more about Brenda than I did. The truth was that my honeymoon days with the mouse were long since over; we had settled down to an uninspiring relationship, a form, as it were, of married blight, and, when she had developed a disgusting sore patch on her back, it had been all I could do to behave decently and treat her with common humanity. Apart from the shock it always is to find somebody stiff and cold in their cage in the morning, it had been a very great relief to me when Brenda's sufferings finally came to an end.

"Where is she buried?" Linda muttered furiously, looking at her plate.

"Beside the robin. She's got a dear little cross and her coffin was lined with pink satin."

"Now, Linda darling," said Aunt Sadie, "if Fanny has finished her tea why don't you show her your toad?"

"He's upstairs asleep," said Linda. But she stopped crying.

"Have some nice hot toast, then."

"Can I have Gentleman's Relish on it?" she said, quick to make capital out of Aunt Sadie's mood, for Gentleman's Relish was kept strictly for Uncle Matthew, and supposed not to be good for children. The others made a great show of exchanging significant looks. These were intercepted, as they were meant to be, by Linda, who gave a tremendous bellowing boo-hoo and rushed upstairs.

"I wish you children wouldn't tease Linda," said Aunt Sadie, irritated out of her usual gentleness, and followed her.

The staircase led out of the hall. When Aunt Sadie was

beyond earshot, Louisa said: "If wishes were horses beggars would ride. Child hunt tomorrow, Fanny."

"Yes, Josh told me. He was in the car—been to see the vet."

My Uncle Matthew had four magnificent bloodhounds, with which he used to hunt his children. Two of us would go off with a good start to lay the trail, and Uncle Matthew and the rest would follow the hounds on horseback. It was great fun. Once he came to my home and hunted Linda and me over Shenley Common. This caused the most tremendous stir locally, the Kentish week-enders on their way to church were appalled by the sight of four great hounds in full cry after two little girls. My uncle seemed to them like a wicked lord of fiction, and I became more than ever surrounded with an aura of madness, badness, and dangerousness for their children to know.

The child hunt on the first day of this Christmas visit was a great success. Louisa and I were chosen as hares. We ran across country, the beautiful bleak Cotswold uplands, starting soon after breakfast when the sun was still a red globe, hardly over the horizon, and the trees were etched in dark blue against a pale blue, mauve and pinkish sky. The sun rose as we stumbled on, longing for our second wind; it shone, and there dawned a beautiful day, more like late autumn in its feeling than Christmas-time.

We managed to check the bloodhounds once by running through a flock of sheep, but Uncle Matthew soon got them on the scent again, and, after about two hours of hard running on our part, when we were only half a mile from home, the baying slavering creatures caught up with us, to be rewarded with lumps of meat and many caresses. Uncle Matthew was in a radiantly good temper, he got off his horse and walked home with us, chatting agreeably. What was most unusual, he was even quite affable to me.

"I hear Brenda has died," he said, "no great loss I should say. That mouse stank like merry hell. I expect you kept her cage too near the radiator, I always told you it was unhealthy, or did she die of old age?"

"She was only two," I said, timidly.

Uncle Matthew's charm, when he chose to turn it on, was considerable, but at that time I was always mortally afraid of him, and made the mistake of letting him see that I was.

"You ought to have a dormouse, Fanny, or a rat. They are much more interesting than white mice—though I must frankly say, of all the mice I ever knew, Brenda was the most utterly dismal."

"She was dull," I said, sycophantically.

"When I go to London after Christmas, I'll get you a dormouse. Saw one the other day at the Army & Navy."

"Oh Fa, it *is* unfair," said Linda, who was walking her pony along beside us. "You know how I've always longed for a dormouse."

"It is unfair" was a perpetual cry of the Radletts when young. The great advantage of living in a large family is that early lesson of life's essential unfairness. With them I must say it nearly always operated in favour of Linda, who was the adored of Uncle Matthew.

Today, however, my uncle was angry with her, and I saw in a flash that this affability to me, this genial chat about mice, was simply designed as a tease for her.

"You've got enough animals, miss," he said, sharply.

"You can't control the ones you have got. And don't forget what I told you—that dog of yours goes straight to the kennel when we get back, and stays there."

Linda's face crumpled, tears poured, she kicked her pony into a canter and made for home. It seemed that her dog Labby had been sick in Uncle Matthew's business-room after breakfast. Uncle Matthew was unable to bear dirtiness in dogs, he flew into a rage, and, in his rage, had made a rule that never again was Labby to set foot in the house. This was always happening, for one reason or another, to one animal or another, and, Uncle Matthew's bark being invariably much worse than his bite, the ban seldom lasted more than a day or two, after which would begin what he called the Thin End of the Wedge.

"Can I bring him in just while I fetch my gloves?"

"I'm so tired—I can't go to the stables—do let him stay just till after tea."

"Oh, I see—the thin end of the wedge. All right, this time he can stay, but if he makes another mess—or I catch him on your bed—or he chews up the good furniture (according to whichever crime it was that had resulted in banishment), I'll have him destroyed, and don't say I didn't warn you."

All the same, every time sentence of banishment was pronounced, the owner of the condemned would envisage her beloved moping his life away in the solitary confinement of a cold and gloomy kennel.

"Even if I take him out for three hours every day, and go and chat to him for another hour, that leaves twenty hours for him all alone with nothing to do. Oh, why can't dogs read?"

The Radlett children, it will be observed, took a highly anthropomorphic view of their pets.

Today, however, Uncle Matthew was in a wonderfully good temper, and, as we left the stables, he said to Linda, who was sitting crying with Labby in his kennel:

"Are you going to leave that poor brute of yours in there all day?"

Her tears forgotten as if they had never been, Linda rushed into the house with Labby at her heels. The Radletts were always either on a peak of happiness or drowning in black waters of despair; their emotions were on no ordinary plane, they loved or they loathed, they laughed or they cried, they lived in a world of superlatives. Their life with Uncle Matthew was a sort of perpetual Tom Tiddler's ground. They went as far as they dared, sometimes very far indeed, while sometimes, for no apparent reason, he would pounce almost before they had crossed the boundary. Had they been poor children they would probably have been removed from their roaring, raging, whacking papa and sent to an approved home, or, indeed, he himself would have been removed from them and sent to prison for refusing to educate them. Nature, however, provides her own remedies, and no doubt the Radletts had enough of Uncle Matthew in them to enable them to weather storms in which ordinary children like me would have lost their nerve completely.

CHAPTER 2

IT WAS an accepted fact at Alconleigh that Uncle Matthew loathed me. This violent, uncontrolled man, like his children knew no middle course, he either loved or he hated, and generally, it must be said, he hated. His reason for hating me was that he hated my father; they were old Eton enemies. When it became obvious, and obvious it was from the hour of my conception, that my parents intended to doorstep me, Aunt Sadie had wanted to bring me up with Linda. We were the same age, and it had seemed a sensible plan. Uncle Matthew had categorically refused. He hated my father, he said, he hated me, but, above all, he hated children, it was bad enough to have two of his own. (He evidently had not envisaged so soon having seven, and indeed both he and Aunt Sadie lived in a perpetual state of surprise at having filled so many cradles, about the future of whose occupants they seemed to have no particular policy.) So dear Aunt Emily, whose heart had once been broken by some wicked dallying monster, and who intended on this account never to marry, took me on and made a life's work of me, and I am very thankful that she did. For she believed passionately in the education of women, she took immense pains to have me properly taught, even going to live at Shenley on purpose to be near a good day school. The Radlett daughters did practically no lessons. They

14

were taught by Lucille, the French nursery governess, to read and write, they were obliged, though utterly un-musical, to "practise" in the freezing ballroom for one hour a day each, when, their eyes glued to the clock, they would thump out the "Merry Peasant" and a few scales, they were made to go for a French walk with Lucille on all except hunting days, and that was the extent of their education. Uncle Matthew loathed clever females, but he considered that gentlewomen ought, as well as being able to ride, to know French and play the piano. Although as a child I rather naturally envied them their freedom from thrall and bondage, from sums and science, I felt, never-theless, a priggish satisfaction that I was not growing up unlettered, as they were.

Aunt Emily did not often come with me to Alconleigh. Perhaps she had an idea that it was more fun for me to be there on my own, and no doubt it was a change for her to get away and spend Christmas with the friends of her youth, and leave for a bit the responsibilities of her old age. Aunt Emily at this time was forty, and we children had long ago renounced on her behalf the world, the flesh, and the devil. This year, however, she had gone away from Shenley before the holidays began, saying that she would see me at Alconleigh in January.

On the afternoon of the child hunt Linda called a meet-ing of the Hons. The Hons was the Radlett secret society, anybody who was not a friend to the Hons was a Counter-Hon, and their battle-cry was "Death to the horrible Counter-Hons." I was a Hon, since my father, like theirs, was a lord.

There were also, however, many honorary Hons; it was not necessary to have been born a Hon in order to be one.

As Linda once remarked: "Kind hearts are more than coronets, and simple faith than Norman blood." I'm not sure how much we really believed this, we were wicked snobs in those days, but we subscribed to the general idea. Head of the hon. Hons was Josh, the groom, who was greatly beloved by us all and worth buckets of Norman blood; chief of the horrible Counter-Hons was Craven, the gamekeeper, against whom a perpetual war to the knife was waged. The Hons would creep into the woods and hide Craven's steel traps, let out the chaffinches which, in wire cages without food or water, he used as bait for hawks, give decent burial to the victims of his gamekeeper's larder, and, before a meet of the hounds, unblock the earths which Craven had so carefully stopped.

The poor Hons were tormented by the cruelties of the countryside, while, to me, holidays at Alconleigh were a perfect revelation of beastliness. Aunt Emily's little house was in a village; it was a Queen Anne box; red brick, white panelling, a magnolia tree and a delicious fresh smell. Between it and the country were a neat little garden, an ironwork fence, a village green and a village. The country one then came to was very different from Gloucester-shire, it was emasculated, sheltered, over-cultivated, almost a suburban garden. At Alconleigh the cruel woods crept right up to the house; it was not unusual to be awoken by the screams of a rabbit running in horrified circles round a stoat, by the strange and awful cry of the dog-fox, or to see from one's bedroom window a live hen being carried away in the mouth of a vixen; while the roosting pheasant and the waking owl filled every night with wild primeval noise. In the winter, when snow covered the ground, we could trace the footprints of many creatures. These often ended in a pool of blood, a mass of fur or feathers, bearing witness to successful hunting by the carnivores.

On the other side of the house, within a stone's throw, was the Home Farm. Here the slaughtering of poultry and pigs, the castration of lambs and the branding of cattle, took place as a matter of course, out in the open for whomever might be passing by to see. Even dear old Josh made nothing of firing, with red-hot irons, a favourite horse after the hunting season.

"You can only do two legs at a time," he would say, hissing through his teeth as though one were a horse and he grooming one, "otherwise they can't stand the pain."

Linda and I were bad at standing pain ourselves, and found it intolerable that animals should have to lead such tormented lives and tortured deaths. (I still do mind, very much indeed, but in those days at Alconleigh it was an absolute obsession with us all.)

The humanitarian activities of the Hons were forbidden, on pain of punishment, by Uncle Matthew, who was always and entirely on the side of Craven, his favourite servant. Pheasants and partridges must be preserved, vermin must be put down rigorously, all except the fox, for whom a more exciting death was in store. Many and many a whacking did the poor Hons suffer, week after week their pocket-money was stopped, they were sent to bed early, given extra practising to do; nevertheless they bravely persisted with their discouraged and discouraging activities. Huge cases full of new steel traps would arrive periodically from the Army & Navy Stores, and lie stacked until required round Craven's hut in the middle of the wood (an old railway carriage was his headquarters, situated, most inappropriately, among the primroses and blackberry bushes of a charming little glade); hundreds of traps, making one feel the futility of burying, at a great risk to life and property, a paltry three or four. Sometimes we would find a screaming animal held in one; it would take all our reserves of courage to go up to it and let it out, to see it run away with three legs and a dangling mangled horror. We knew that it then probably died of blood-poisoning in its lair; Uncle Matthew would rub in this fact, sparing no agonizing detail of the long drawn-out ordeal, but, though we knew it would be kinder, we could never bring ourselves to kill them; it was asking too much. Often, as it was, we had to go away and be sick after these episodes.

The Hons' meeting-place was an unused linen cupboard at the top of the house, small, dark, and intensely hot. As in so many country houses, the central-heating apparatus at Alconleigh had been installed in the early days of the invention, at enormous expense, and was now thoroughly out of date. In spite of a boiler which would not have been too large for an Atlantic liner, in spite of the tons of coke which it consumed daily, the temperature of the living-rooms was hardly affected, and all the heat there was seemed to concentrate in the Hons' cupboard, which was always stifling. Here we would sit, huddled up on the slatted shelves, and talk for hours about life and death.

Last holidays our great obsession had been childbirth, on which entrancing subject we were informed remarkably late, having supposed for a long time that a mother's stomach swelled up for nine months and then burst open like a ripe pumpkin, shooting out the infant. When the real truth dawned upon us it seemed rather an anticlimax, until Linda produced, from some novel, and read out loud in ghoulish tones, the description of a woman in labour.

"Her breath comes in great gulps—sweat pours down her brow like water—screams as of a tortured animal rend the air—and can this face, twisted with agony, be that of my darling Rhona—can this torture-chamber really be our bedroom, this rack our marriage-bed? 'Doctor, doctor,' I cried, 'do something'—I rushed out into the night——" and so on.

We were rather disturbed by this, realizing that too probably we in our turn would have to endure these fearful agonies. Aunt Sadie, who had only just finished having her seven children, when appealed to, was not very reassuring.

"Yes," she said, vaguely. "It is the worst pain in the world. But the funny thing is, you always forget in between what it's like. Each time, when it began, I felt like saying, 'Oh, now I can remember, stop it, stop it.' And, of course, by then it was nine months too late to stop it."

At this point Linda began to cry, saying how dreadful it must be for cows, which brought the conversation to an end.

It was difficult to talk to Aunt Sadie about sex; something always seemed to prevent one; babies were the nearest we ever got to it. She and Aunt Emily, feeling at one moment that we ought to know more, and being, I suspect, too embarrassed to enlighten us themselves, gave us a modern text-book on the subject.

We got hold of some curious ideas.

"Jassy," said Linda one day, scornfully, "is obsessed, poor thing, with sex."

"Obsessed with sex!" said Jassy, "there's nobody so obsessed as you, Linda. Why if I so much as look at a picture you say I'm a pygmalionist."

In the end we got far more information out of a book called *Ducks and Duck Breeding*.

"Ducks can only copulate," said Linda, after studying this for a while, "in running water. Good luck to them."

This Christmas Eve we all packed into the Hons' meeting-place to hear what Linda had to say—Louisa, Jassy, Bob, Matt and I.

"Talk about back-to-the-womb," said Jassy.

"Poor Aunt Sadie," I said. "I shouldn't think she'd want you all back in hers."

"You never know. Now rabbits eat their children— somebody ought to explain to them how it's only a complex."

"How can one *explain* to *rabbits*? That's what is so worrying about animals, they simply don't understand when they're spoken to, poor angels. I'll tell you what about Sadie though, she'd like to be back in one herself, she's got a thing for boxes and that always shows. Who else—Fanny, what about you?"

"I don't think I would, but then I imagine the one I was in wasn't very comfortable at the time you know, and nobody else has ever been allowed to stay there."

"Abortions?" said Linda with interest.

"Well, tremendous jumpings and hot baths anyway."

"How *do* you know?"

"I once heard Aunt Emily and Aunt Sadie talking about it when I was very little, and afterwards I remembered. Aunt Sadie said: 'How does she manage it?' and Aunt Emily said: 'Skiing, or hunting, or just jumping off the kitchen table.'"

"You are so lucky, having wicked parents."

This was the perpetual refrain of the Radletts, and, indeed, my wicked parents constituted my chief interest in their eyes—I was really a very dull little girl in other respects.

"The news I have for the Hons today," said Linda, clearing her throat like a grown-up person, "while of considerable Hon interest generally, particularly concerns Fanny. I won't ask you to guess, because it's nearly tea-time and you never could, so I'll tell straight out. Aunt Emily is engaged."

There was a gasp from the Hons in chorus.

"Linda," I said, furiously, "you've made it up." But I knew she couldn't have.

Linda brought a piece of paper out of her pocket. It was a half-sheet of writing-paper, evidently the end of a letter, covered with Aunt Emily's large babyish hand-writing, and I looked over Linda's shoulder as she read it out:

". . . not tell the children we're engaged, what d'you think darling, just at first? But then suppose Fanny takes a dislike to him, though I don't see how she could, but children are so funny, won't it be more of a shock? Oh, dear, I can't decide. Anyway, do what you think best, darling, we'll arrive on Thursday, and I'll telephone on Wednesday evening and see what's happened. All love from Emily."

Sensation in the Hons' cupboard.

CHAPTER 3

"But why?" I said, for the hundredth time.

Linda, Louisa and I were packed into Louisa's bed, with Bob sitting on the end of it, chatting in whispers. These midnight talks were most strictly forbidden, but it was safer, at Alconleigh, to disobey rules during the early part of the night than at any other time in the twenty-four hours. Uncle Matthew fell asleep practically at the dinner-table. He would then doze in his business-room for an hour or so before dragging himself, in a somnambulist trance, to bed, where he slept the profound sleep of one who has been out of doors all day until cockcrow the following morning, when he became very much awake. This was the time for his never-ending warfare with the housemaids over wood-ash. The rooms at Alconleigh were heated by wood fires, and Uncle Matthew maintained, rightly, that if these were to function properly, all the ash ought to be left in the fireplaces in a great hot smouldering heap. Every housemaid, however, for some reason (an early training with coal fires probably) was bent on removing this ash altogether. When shakings, imprecations, and being pounced out at by Uncle Matthew in his paisley dressing-gown at six a.m., had convinced them that this was really not feasible, they became absolutely determined to remove, by hook or by crook, just a little, a shovelful or so, every morning. I can only suppose they felt that like this they were asserting their personalities.

The result was guerrilla warfare at its most exciting. Housemaids are notoriously early risers, and can usually count upon three clear hours when a house belongs to them alone. But not at Alconleigh. Uncle Matthew was always, winter and summer alike, out of his bed by five a.m., and it was then his habit to wander about, looking like Great Agrippa in his dressing-gown, and drinking endless cups of tea out of a thermos flask, until about seven, when he would have his bath. Breakfast for my uncle, my aunt, family and guests alike, was sharp at eight, and unpunctuality was not tolerated. Uncle Matthew was no respecter of other people's early morning sleep, and, after five o'clock one could not count on any, for he raged round the house, clanking cups of tea, shouting at his dogs, roaring at the housemaids, cracking the stock whips which he had brought back from Canada on the lawn with a noise greater than gun-fire, and all to the accompaniment of Galli Curci on his gramophone, an abnormally loud one with an enormous horn, through which would be shrieked "Una voce poco fa"—"The Mad Song" from *Lucia*—"Lo, here the gen-tel lar-ha-hark"—and so on, played at top speed, thus rendering them even higher and more screeching than they ought to be.

Nothing reminds me of my childhood days at Alconleigh so much as those songs. Uncle Matthew played them incessantly for years, until the spell was broken when he went all the way to Liverpool to hear Galli Curci in person. The disillusionment caused by her appearance was so great that the records remained ever after silent, and were replaced by the deepest bass voices that money could buy.

"Fearful the death of the diver must be,
   Walking alone in the de-he-he-he-he-epths of
   the sea"
or "Drake is going West, lads."

These were, on the whole, welcomed by the family, as rather less piercing at early dawn.

"Why should she want to be married?"

"It's not as though she could be in love. She's forty."

Like all the very young we took it for granted that making love is child's play.

"How old do you suppose he is?"

"Fifty or sixty I guess. Perhaps she thinks it would be nice to be a widow. Weeds, you know."

"Perhaps she thinks Fanny ought to have a man's influence."

"Man's influence!" said Louisa. "I foresee trouble. Supposing he falls in love with Fanny, that'll be a pretty kettle of fish, like Somerset and Princess Elizabeth—he'll be playing rough games and pinching you in bed, see if he doesn't."

"Surely not, at his age."

"Old men love little girls."

"And little boys," said Bob.

"It looks as if Aunt Sadie isn't going to say anything about it before they come," I said.

"There's nearly a week to go—she may be deciding. She'll talk it over with Fa. Might be worth listening next time she has a bath. You can, Bob."

Christmas Day was spent, as usual at Alconleigh, between alternate bursts of sunshine and showers. I put, as children can, the disturbing news about Aunt Emily out of my mind, and concentrated upon enjoyment. At about six o'clock Linda and I unstuck our sleepy eyes and started on our stockings. Our real presents came later, at breakfast and on the tree, but the stockings were a wonderful *hors d'œuvre* and full of treasures. Presently Jassy came in and started selling us things out of hers. Jassy only cared about money because she was saving up to run away—she carried her post office book about with her everywhere, and always knew to a farthing what she had got. This was then translated by a miracle of determination, as Jassy was very bad at sums, into so many days in a bed-sitting-room.

"How are you getting on, Jassy?"

"My fare to London and a month and two days and an hour and a half in a bed-sitter, with basin and breakfast."

Where the other meals would come from was left to the imagination. Jassy studied advertisements of bed-sitters in *The Times* every morning. The cheapest she had found so far was in Clapham. So eager was she for the cash that would transform her dream into reality, that one could be certain of picking up a few bargains round about Christmas and her birthday. Jassy at this time was aged eight.

I must admit that my wicked parents turned up trumps at Christmas, and my presents from them were always the envy of the entire household. This year my mother, who was in Paris, sent a gilded bird-cage full of stuffed humming-birds which, when wound up, twittered and hopped about and drank at a fountain. She also sent a fur hat and a gold and topaz bracelet, whose glamour was enhanced by the fact that Aunt Sadie considered them unsuitable for a child, and said so. My father sent a pony and cart, a very smart and beautiful little outfit, which had arrived some days before, and been secreted by Josh in the stables.

"So typical of that damned fool Edward to send it here," Uncle Matthew said, "and give us all the trouble of getting it to Shenley. And I bet poor old Emily won't be too pleased. Who on earth is going to look after it?"

Linda cried with envy. "It *is* unfair," she kept saying, "that you should have wicked parents and not me."

We persuaded Josh to take us for a drive after luncheon. The pony was an angel and the whole thing easily managed by a child, even the harnessing. Linda wore my hat and drove the pony. We got back late for the Tree— the house was already full of tenants and their children; Uncle Matthew, who was struggling into his Father Christmas clothes, roared at us so violently that Linda had to go and cry upstairs, and was not there to collect her own present from him. Uncle Matthew had taken some trouble to get her a longed-for dormouse and was greatly put out by this; he roared at everybody in turn, and ground his dentures. There was a legend in the family that he had already ground away four pairs in his rages.

The evening came to a climax of violence when Matt produced a box of fireworks which my mother had sent him from Paris. On the box they were called *Pétards*. Somebody said to Matt: "What do they do?" to which he replied: *"Bien, ça péte, quoi?"* This remark, overheard by Uncle Matthew, was rewarded with a first-class hiding, which was actually most unfair, as poor Matt was only repeating what Lucille had said to him earlier in the day. Matt, however, regarded hidings as a sort of natural phenomenon, unconnected with any actions of his own, and submitted to them philosophically enough. I have often wondered since how it was that Aunt Sadie could have chosen Lucille, who was the very acme of vulgarity, to look after her children. We all loved her, she was gay and spirited and read aloud to us without cease, but her language really was extraordinary, and provided dreadful pitfalls for the unwary.

"*Qu'est-ce que c'est ce custard, qu'on fout partout?*"

I shall never forget Matt quite innocently making this remark in Fullers at Oxford, where Uncle Matthew had taken us for a treat. The consequences were awful.

It never seemed to occur to Uncle Matthew that Matt could not know these words by nature, and that it would really have been more fair to check them at their source.

CHAPTER 4

I NATURALLY awaited the arrival of Aunt Emily and her future intended with some agitation. She was, after all, my real mother, and, greatly as I might hanker after that glittering evil person who bore me, it was to Aunt Emily that I turned for the solid, sustaining, though on the face of it uninteresting, relationship that is provided by motherhood at its best. Our little household at Shenley was calm and happy and afforded an absolute contrast to the agitations and tearing emotions of Alconleigh. It may have been dull, but it was a sheltering harbour, and I was always glad to get back to it. I think I was beginning dimly to realize how much it all centered upon me; the very timetable, with its early luncheon and high tea, was arranged to fit in with my lessons and bedtime. Only during those holidays when I went to Alconleigh did Aunt Emily have any life of her own, and even these breaks were infrequent, as she had an idea that Uncle Matthew and the whole stormy set-up there were bad for my nerves. I may not have been consciously aware of the extent to which Aunt Emily had regulated her existence round mine, but I saw, only too clearly, that the addition of a man to our establishment was going to change everything. Hardly knowing any men outside the family, I imagined them all to be modelled on the lines of Uncle Matthew, or of my own seldom seen, violently emotional papa, either of whom, plunging about in that neat little house, would have been sadly out of place. I was filled with apprehension, almost with horror, and, greatly assisted by the workings of Louisa's and Linda's vivid imaginations, had got myself into a real state of nerves. Louisa was now teasing me with the *Constant Nymph*. She read aloud the last chapters, and soon I was dying at a Brussels boardinghouse, in the arms of Aunt Emily's husband.

On Wednesday Aunt Emily rang up Aunt Sadie, and they talked for ages. The telephone at Alconleigh was, in those days, situated in a glass cupboard halfway down the brilliantly lighted back passage; there was no extension, and eavesdropping was thus rendered impossible. (In later years it was moved to Uncle Matthew's business-room, with an extension, after which all privacy was at an end.) When Aunt Sadie returned to the drawing-room she said nothing except: "Emily is coming tomorrow on the three-five. She sends you her love, Fanny."

The next day we all went out hunting. The Radletts loved animals, they loved foxes, they risked dreadful beatings in order to unstop their earths, they read and cried and rejoiced over Reynard the Fox, in summer they got up at four to go and see the cubs playing in the pale-green light of the woods; nevertheless, more than anything in the world, they loved hunting. It was in their blood and bones and in my blood and bones, and nothing could eradicate it, though we knew it for a kind of original sin. For three hours that day I forgot everything except my body and my pony's body; the rushing, the scrambling, the splashing, struggling up the hills, sliding down them again, the tugging, the bucketing, the earth and the sky. I forgot everything, I could hardly have told you my name. That must be the great hold that hunting has over people, especially stupid people; it enforces an absolute concentration, both mental and physical.

After three hours Josh took me home. I was never allowed to stay out long or I got tired and would be sick all night. Josh was out on Uncle Matthew's second horse; at about two o'clock they changed over, and he started home on the lathered, sweating first horse, taking me with him. I came out of my trance, and saw that the day, which had begun with brilliant sunshine, was now cold and dark, threatening rain.

"And where's her ladyship hunting this year?" said Josh, as we started on a ten-mile jog along the Merlinford road, a sort of hog's back, more cruelly exposed than any road I have ever known, without a scrap of shelter or windscreen the whole of its fifteen miles. Uncle Matthew would never allow motorcars, either to take us to the meet or to fetch us home; he regarded this habit as despicably soft.

I knew that Josh meant my mother. He had been with my grandfather when she and her sisters were girls, and my mother was his heroine, he adored her.

"She's in Paris, Josh."

"In Paris—what for?"

"I suppose she likes it."

"Ho," said Josh, furiously, and we rode for about half a mile in silence. The rain had begun, a thin cold rain, sweeping over the wide views on each side of the road; we trotted along, the weather in our faces. My back was not strong, and trotting on a side-saddle for any length of time was agony to me. I edged my pony onto the grass, and cantered for a bit, but I knew how much Josh disapproved of this, it was supposed to bring the horses back too hot; walking, on the other hand, chilled them. It had to be jog, jog, back-breaking jog, all the way.

"It's my opinion," said Josh at last, "that her ladyship is wasted, downright wasted, every minute of her life that she's not on a 'oss."

"She's a wonderful rider, isn't she?"

I had had all this before from Josh, many times, and could never have enough of it.

"There's no human being like her, that I've ever seen," said Josh, hissing through his teeth. "Hands like velvet, but strong like iron, and her seat——! Now look at you, jostling about on that saddle, first here, then there—we shall have a sore back tonight, that's one thing certain we shall."

"Oh, Josh—trotting. And I'm so tired."

"Never saw her tired. I've seen 'er change 'osses after a ten-mile point, get onto a fresh young five-year-old what hadn't been out for a week—up like a bird—never know you had 'er foot in your hand, pick up the reins in a jiffy, catch up its head, and off and over a post and rails and bucking over the ridge and furrow, sitting like a rock. Now his lordship (he meant Uncle Matthew) he can ride, I don't say the contrary, but look how he sends the 'osses home, so darned tired they can't drink their gruel. He can ride all right, but he doesn't study his 'oss. I never knew your mother bring them home like this, she'd know when they'd had enough, and then heads for home and no looking back. Mind you, his lordship's a great big man, I don't say the contrary, rides every bit of sixteen stone, but he has great big 'osses and half kills them, and then who has to stop up with them all night? Me!"

The rain was pouring down by now. An icy trickle was feeling its way past my left shoulder, and my right boot was slowly filling with water, the pain in my back was like a knife. I felt that I couldn't bear another moment of this misery, and yet I knew I must bear another five miles, another forty minutes. Josh gave me scornful looks as my back bent more and more double; I could see that he was wondering how it was that I could be my mother's child.

"Miss Linda," he said, "takes after her ladyship something wonderful."

At last, at last, we were off the Merlinford road, coming down the valley into Alconleigh village, turning up the hill to Alconleigh house, through the lodge gates, up the drive, and into the stable yard. I got stiffly down, gave the pony to one of Josh's stable boys, and stumped away, walking like an old man. I was nearly at the front door before I remembered, with a sudden leap of my heart, that Aunt Emily would have arrived by now, with HIM. It was quite a minute before I could summon up enough courage to open the front door.

Sure enough, standing with their backs to the hall fire, were Aunt Sadie, Aunt Emily, and a small, fair, and apparently young man. My immediate impression was that he did not seem at all like a husband. He looked kind and gentle.

"Here is Fanny," said my aunts in chorus.

"Darling," said Aunt Sadie, "can I introduce Captain Warbeck?"

I shook hands in the abrupt graceless way of little girls of fourteen, and thought that he did not seem at all like a captain either.

"Oh, darling, how wet you are. I suppose the others won't be back for ages—where have you come from?"

"I left them drawing the spinney by the Old Rose."

Then I remembered, being after all a female in the

presence of a male, how dreadful I always looked when I got home from hunting, splashed from head to foot, my bowler all askew, my hair a bird's nest, my stock a flapping flag, and, muttering something, I made for the back stairs, towards my bath and my rest. After hunting we were kept in bed for at least two hours. Soon Linda returned, even wetter than I had been, and got into bed with me. She, too, had seen the Captain, and agreed that he looked neither like a marrying nor like a military man.

"Can't see him killing Germans with an entrenching tool," she said, scornfully.

Much as we feared, much as we disapproved of, passionately as we sometimes hated Uncle Matthew, he still remained for us a sort of criterion of English manhood; there seemed something not quite right about any man who greatly differed from him.

"I bet Uncle Matthew gives him rat week," I said, apprehensive for Aunt Emily's sake.

"Poor Aunt Emily, perhaps he'll make her keep him in the stables," said Linda with a gust of giggles.

"Still, he looks rather nice you know, and, considering her age, I should think she's lucky to get anybody."

"I can't wait to see him with Fa."

However, our expectations of blood and thunder were disappointed, for it was evident at once that Uncle Matthew had taken an enormous fancy to Captain Warbeck. As he never altered his first opinion of people, and as his few favourites could commit nameless crimes without doing wrong in his eyes, Captain Warbeck was, henceforward, on an infallible wicket with Uncle Matthew.

"He's such a frightfully clever cove, literary you know, you wouldn't believe the things he does. He writes books, and criticizes pictures, and whacks hell out of the piano, though the pieces he plays aren't up to much. Still, you can see what it would be like, if he learnt some of the tunes out of the *Country Girl*, for instance. Nothing would be too difficult for him, you can see that."

At dinner Captain Warbeck sitting next to Aunt Sadie, and Aunt Emily next to Uncle Matthew, were separated from each other, not only by four of us children (Bob was allowed to dine down, as he was going to Eton next half), but also by pools of darkness. The dining-room table was lit by three electric bulbs hanging in a bunch from the ceiling, and screened by a curtain of dark-red jap silk with a gold fringe. One spot of brilliant light was thus cast into the middle of the table, while the diners themselves, and their plates, sat outside it in total gloom. We all, naturally, had our eyes fixed upon the shadowy figure of the fiancé, and found a great deal in his behaviour to interest us. He talked to Aunt Sadie at first about gardens, plants and flowering shrubs, a topic which was unknown at Alconleigh. The gardener saw to the garden, and that was that. It was quite half a mile from the house, and nobody went near it, except as a little walk sometimes in the summer. It seemed strange that a man who lived in London should know the names, the habits, and the medicinal properties of so many plants. Aunt Sadie politely tried to keep up with him, but could not altogether conceal her ignorance, though she partly veiled it in a mist of absent-mindedness.

"And what is your soil here?" asked Captain Warbeck.

Aunt Sadie came down from the clouds with a happy smile, and said, triumphantly, for here was something she did know, "Clay."

"Ah, yes," said the Captain.

He produced a little jewelled box, took from it an

enormous pill, swallowed it, to our amazement, without one sip to help it down, and said, as though to himself, but quite distinctly,

"Then the water here will be madly binding."

When Logan, the butler, offered him shepherd's pie, (the food at Alconleigh was always good and plentiful, but of the homely schoolroom description) he said, again so that one did not quite know whether he meant to be overheard or not.

"No, thank you, no twice-cooked meat. I am a wretched invalid, I must be careful, or I pay."

Aunt Sadie, who so much disliked hearing about health that people often took her for a Christian Scientist, which, indeed, she might have become had she not disliked hearing about religion even more, took absolutely no notice, but Bob asked with interest, what it was that twice-cooked meat did to one.

"Oh, it imposes a most fearful strain on the juices, you might as well eat leather," replied Captain Warbeck, faintly, heaping onto his plate the whole of the salad. He said, again in that withdrawn voice:

"Raw lettuce, anti-scorbutic," and, opening another box of even larger pills, he took two, murmuring, "Protein."

"How delicious your bread is," he said to Aunt Sadie, as though to make up for his rudeness in refusing the twice-cooked meat. "I'm sure it has the germ."

"What?" said Aunt Sadie, turning from a whispered confabulation with Logan ("ask Mrs. Crabbe if she could quickly make some more salad").

"I was saying that I feel sure your delicious bread is made of stone-ground flour, containing a high proportion of the germ. In my bedroom at home I have a picture of a grain of wheat (magnified, naturally) which shows the germ. As you know, in white bread the germ, with its wonderful health-giving properties, is eliminated—extracted, I should say—and put into chicken food. As a result the human race is becoming enfeebled, while hens grow larger and stronger with every generation."

"So in the end," said Linda, listening all agog, more than could be said for Aunt Sadie, who had retired into a cloud of boredom, "Hens will be Hons and Hons will be Hens. Oh, how I should love to live in a dear little Hon-house."

"You wouldn't like your work," said Bob. "I once saw a hen laying an egg, and she had a most terrible expression on her face."

"Only about like going to the lav," said Linda.

"Now, Linda," said Aunt Sadie, sharply, "that's quite unnecessary. Get on with your supper and don't talk so much."

Vague as she was, Aunt Sadie could not always be counted on to ignore everything that was happening around her.

"What were you telling me, Captain Warbeck, something about germs?"

"Oh, not germs—the germ——"

At this point I became aware that, in the shadows at the other end of the table, Uncle Matthew and Aunt Emily were having one of their usual set-tos, and that it concerned me. Whenever Aunt Emily came to Alconleigh these tussles with Uncle Matthew would occur, but, all the same, one could see that he was fond of her. He always liked people who stood up to him, and also he probably saw in her a reflection of Aunt Sadie, whom he adored. Aunt Emily was more positive than Aunt Sadie, she had more character and less beauty, and she was not worn out with childbirth, but they were very much sisters. My mother was utterly different in every respect, but then she, poor thing, was, as Linda would have said, obsessed with sex.

Uncle Matthew and Aunt Emily were now engaged upon an argument we had all heard many times before. It concerned the education of females.

Uncle Matthew: "I hope poor Fanny's school (the word school pronounced in tones of withering scorn) is doing her all the good you think it is. Certainly she picks up some dreadful expressions there."

Aunt Emily, calmly, but on the defensive: "Very likely she does. She also picks up a good deal of education."

Uncle Matthew: "Education! I was always led to suppose that no educated person ever spoke of notepaper, and yet I hear poor Fanny asking Sadie for notepaper. What is this education? Fanny talks about mirrors and mantelpieces, handbags and perfume, she takes sugar in her coffee, has a tassel on her umbrella, and I have no doubt that, if she is ever fortunate enough to catch a husband, she will call his father and mother Father and Mother. Will the wonderful education she is getting make up to the unhappy brute for all these endless pinpricks? Fancy hearing one's wife talk about notepaper—the irritation!"

Aunt Emily: "A lot of men would find it more irritating to have a wife who had never heard of George III. (All the same, Fanny darling, it is called writing-paper you know—don't let's hear any more about note, please.) That is where you and I come in you see, Matthew, home influence is admitted to be a most important part of education."

Uncle Matthew: "There you are——"

Aunt Emily: "A most important, but not by any means the most important."

Uncle Matthew: "You don't have to go to some awful middle-class establishment in order to know who George III was. Anyway, who was he, Fanny?"

Alas, I always failed to shine on these occasions. My wits scattered to the four winds by my terror of Uncle Matthew, I said, scarlet in the face:

"He was king. He went mad."

"Most original, full of information," said Uncle Matthew, sarcastically. "Well worth losing every ounce of feminine charm to find that out, I must say. Legs like gateposts from playing hockey, and the worst seat on a horse of any woman I ever knew. Give a horse a sore back as soon as look at it. Linda, you're uneducated, thank God, what have you got to say about George III?"

"Well," said Linda, her mouth full, "he was the son of poor Fred and the father of Beau Brummell's fat friend, and he was one of those vacillators you know. 'I am his Highness's dog at Kew, pray tell me, sir, whose dog are you?'" she added, inconsequently. "Oh, how sweet!"

Uncle Matthew shot a look of cruel triumph at Aunt Emily. I saw that I had let down the side and began to cry, inspiring Uncle Matthew to fresh bouts of beastliness.

"It's a lucky thing that Fanny will have £15,000 a year of her own," he said, "not to speak of any settlements the Bolter may have picked up in the course of her career. She'll get a husband all right, even if she does talk about lunch, and *en*velope, and put the milk in first. I'm not afraid of that, I only say she'll drive the poor devil to drink when she has hooked him."

Aunt Emily gave Uncle Matthew a furious frown. She had always tried to conceal from me the fact that I was an heiress, and, indeed, I only was one until such time as my father, hale and hearty and in the prime of life, should marry somebody of an age to bear children. It so happened that, like the Hanoverian family, he only cared for women when they were over forty; after my mother had left him he had embarked upon a succession of middle-aged wives whom even the miracles of modern science were unable to render fruitful. It was also believed, wrongly, by the grown-ups that we children were ignorant of the fact that my mamma was called the Bolter.

"All this," said Aunt Emily, "is quite beside the point. Fanny may possibly, in the far future, have a little money of her own (though it is ludicrous to talk of £15,000). Whether she does, or does not, the man she marries may be able to support her—on the other hand, the modern world being what it is, she may have to earn her own living. In any case she will be a more mature, a happier, a more interested and interesting person if she——"

"If she knows that George III was a king and went mad."

All the same, my aunt was right, and I knew it and she knew it. The Radlett children read enormously by fits and starts in the library at Alconleigh, a good representative nineteenth-century library, which had been made by their grandfather, a most cultivated man. But, while they picked up a great deal of heterogeneous information, and gilded it with their own originality, while they bridged gulfs of ignorance with their charm and high spirits, they never acquired any habit of concentration, they were incapable of solid hard work. One result, in later life, was that they could not stand boredom.

Storms and difficulties left them unmoved, but day after day of ordinary existence produced an unbearable torture of ennui, because they completely lacked any form of mental discipline.

As we trailed out of the dining-room after dinner, we heard Captain Warbeck say:

"No port, no, thank you. Such a delicious drink, but I must refuse. It's the acid from port that makes one so delicate now."

"Ah—you've been a great port drinker, have you?" said Uncle Matthew.

"Oh, not me, I've never touched it. My ancestors——"

Presently, when they joined us in the drawing-room, Aunt Sadie said: "The children know the news now."

"I suppose they think it's a great joke," said Davey Warbeck, "old people like us being married."

"Oh, no, of course not," we said, politely, blushing.

"He's an extraordinary fella," said Uncle Matthew, "knows everything. He says those Charles II sugar casters are only a Georgian imitation of Charles II, just fancy, not valuable at all. Tomorrow we'll go round the house and I'll show you all our things and you can tell us what's what. Quite useful to have a fella like you in the family, I must say."

"That will be very nice," said Davey, faintly, "and now I think, if you don't mind, I'll go to bed. Yes, please, early morning tea—so necessary to replace the evaporation of the night."

He shook hands with us all, and hurried from the room, saying to himself: "Wooing, so tired."

"Davey Warbeck is a Hon," said Bob as we were all coming down to breakfast next day.

"Yes, he seems a terrific Hon," said Linda, sleepily.

"No, I mean he's a real one. Look, there's a letter for him, The Hon. David Warbeck. I've looked him up, and it's true."

Bob's favourite book at this time was Debrett, his nose was never out of it. As a result of his researches he was once heard informing Lucille that "The origins of the Radlett family are lost in the fogs of antiquity."

"He's only a second son, and the eldest has got an heir, so I'm afraid Aunt Emily won't be a lady. And his father's only the second Baron, created 1860, and they only start in 1720, before that it's the female line." Bob's voice was trailing off. "Still——" he said.

We heard Davey Warbeck, as he was coming down the stairs, say to Uncle Matthew:

"Oh no, that couldn't be a Reynolds. Prince Hoare, at his very worst, if you're lucky."

"Pig's thinkers, Davey?" Uncle Matthew lifted the lid of a hot dish.

"Oh, yes please, Matthew, if you mean brains. So digestible."

"And after breakfast I'm going to show you our collection of minerals in the north passage. I bet you'll agree we've got something worth having there, it's supposed to be the finest collection in England—left me by an old uncle, who spent his life making it. Meanwhile, what'd you think of my eagle?"

"Ah, if that were Chinese now, it would be a treasure. But Jap I'm afraid, not worth the bronze it's cast in. Cooper's Oxford, please, Linda."

After breakfast we all flocked to the north passage, where there were hundreds of stones in glass-fronted cupboards. Petrified this and fossilized that, blue-john and lapis were the most exciting, large flints which looked as if they had been picked up by the side of the road, the least. Valuable, unique, they were a family legend. "The minerals in the north passage are good enough for a museum." We children revered them. Davey looked at them carefully, taking some over to the window and peering into them. Finally, he heaved a great sigh and said:

"What a beautiful collection. I suppose you know they're all diseased?"

"Diseased?"

"Badly, and too far gone for treatment. In a year or two they'll all be dead—you might as well throw the whole lot away."

Uncle Matthew was delighted.

"Damned fella," he said, "nothing's right for him, I never saw such a fella. Even the minerals have got foot-and-mouth, according to him."

CHAPTER 5

THE year which followed Aunt Emily's marriage transformed Linda and me from children, young for our ages, into lounging adolescents waiting for love. One result of the marriage was that I now spent nearly all my holidays at Alconleigh. Davey, like all Uncle Matthew's favourites, simply could not see that he was in the least bit frightening, and scouted Aunt Emily's theory that to be too much with him was bad for my nerves.

"You're just a lot of little crybabies," he said, scornfully, "if you allow yourselves to be upset by that old cardboard ogre."

Davey had given up his flat in London and lived with us at Shenley, where, during term-time, he made but little difference to our life, except in so far as a male presence in a female household is always salutary (the curtains, the covers, and Aunt Emily's clothes underwent an enormous change for the better), but, in the holidays, he liked to carry her off, to his own relations or on trips abroad, and I was parked at Alconleigh. Aunt Emily probably felt that, if she had to choose between her husband's wishes and my nervous system, the former should win the day. In spite of her being forty they were, I believe, very much in love; it must have been a perfect bore having me about at all, and it speaks volumes for their characters that never, for one moment, did they allow me to be aware of this. Davey, in fact was, and has been ever since, a perfect stepfather to me, affectionate, understanding, never in any way interfering. He accepted me at once as belonging to Aunt Emily, and never questioned the inevitability of my presence in his household.

By the Christmas holidays Louisa was officially "out," and going to hunt balls, a source of bitter envy to us, though Linda said scornfully that she did not appear to have many suitors. We were not coming out for another two years—it seemed an eternity, and especially to Linda, who was paralysed by her longing for love, and had no lessons or work to do which could take her mind off it. In fact, she had no other interest now except hunting, even the animals seemed to have lost all charm for her. She and I did nothing on non-hunting days but sit about, too large for our tweed suits, whose hooks and eyes were always popping off at the waist, and play endless games of patience; or we lolled in the Hons' cupboard, and "measured." We had a tape-measure and competed as to the largeness of our eyes, the smallness of wrists, ankles, waist and neck, length of legs and fingers, and so on. Linda always won. When we had finished "measuring" we talked of romance. These were most innocent talks, for to us, at that time, love and marriage were synonymous, we knew that they lasted for ever, to the grave and far, far beyond. Our preoccupation with sin was finished; Bob, back from Eton, had been able to tell us all about Oscar Wilde, and, now that his crime was no longer a mystery, it seemed dull, unromantic, and incomprehensible.

We were, of course, both in love, but with people we had never met; Linda with the Prince of Wales, and I with a fat, red-faced, middle-aged farmer, whom I sometimes saw riding through Shenley. These loves were strong, and painfully delicious; they occupied all our thoughts, but I think we half realized that they would be superseded in time by real people. They were to keep the house warm, so to speak, for its eventual occupant. What we never would admit was the possibility of lovers after marriage. We were looking for real love, and that could only come once in a lifetime; it hurried to consecration, and thereafter never wavered. Husbands, we knew, were not always faithful, this we must be prepared for, we must understand and forgive. "I have been faithful to thee, Cynara, in my fashion" seemed to explain it beautifully. But women—that was different; only the lowest of the sex could love or give themselves more than once. I do not quite know how I reconciled these sentiments with the great hero-worship I still had for my mother, that adulterous doll. I suppose I put her in an entirely different category, in the face that launched a thousand ships class. A few historical characters must be allowed to have belonged to this, but Linda and I were perfectionists where love was concerned, and did not ourselves aspire to that kind of fame.

This winter Uncle Matthew had a new tune on his gramophone, called "Thora." "I live in a land of roses," boomed a deep male voice, "but dream of a land of snow. Speak, speak, SPEAK to me, Thora." He played it morning, noon and night; it suited our mood exactly, and Thora seemed the most poignantly beautiful of names.

Aunt Sadie was giving a ball for Louisa soon after Christmas, and to this we pinned great hopes. True, neither the Prince of Wales nor my farmer was invited, but, as Linda said, you never could tell in the country.

Somebody might bring them. The Prince might break down in his motor-car, perhaps on his way to Badminton; what could be more natural than that he should while away the time by looking in on the revelry?

"Pray, who is that beautiful young lady?"

"My daughter Louisa, sir."

"Ah, yes, very charming, but I really meant the one in white taffeta."

"That is my younger daughter Linda, Your Royal Highness."

"Please present her to me."

They would then whirl away in a waltz so accomplished that the other dancers would stand aside to admire. When they could dance no more they would sit for the rest of the evening absorbed in witty conversation.

The following day an A.D.C., asking for her hand——

"But she is so young!"

"His Royal Highness is prepared to wait a year. He reminds you that Her Majesty the Empress Elizabeth of Austria was married at sixteen. Meanwhile, he sends this jewel."

A golden casket, a pink satin cushion, a diamond rose.

My daydreams were less exalted, equally improbable, and quite as real to me. I imagined my farmer carrying me away from Alconleigh, like young Lochinvar, on a pillion behind him to the nearest smith, who then declared us man and wife. Linda kindly said that we could have one of the royal farms, but I thought this would be a great bore, and that it would be much more fun to have one of our own.

Meanwhile, preparations for the ball went forward,

occupying every single member of the household. Linda's and my dresses, white taffeta with floating panels and embroidered bead belts, were being made by Mrs. Josh, whose cottage was besieged at all hours to see how they were getting on. Louisa's came from Reville, it was silver lamé in tiny frills, each frill edged with blue net. Dangling on the left shoulder, and strangely unrelated to the dress, was a large pink silk overblown rose. Aunt Sadie, shaken out of her accustomed languor, was in a state of exaggerated preoccupation and worry over the whole thing; we had never seen her like this before. For the first time, too, that any of us could remember, she found herself in opposition to Uncle Matthew. It was over the following question: The nearest neighbour to Alconleigh was Lord Merlin; his estate marched with that of my uncle, and his house at Merlinford was about five miles away. Uncle Matthew loathed him, while, as for Lord Merlin, not for nothing was his telegraphic address Neighbourtease. There had, however, been no open breach between them; the fact that they never saw each other meant nothing, for Lord Merlin neither hunted, shot, nor fished, while Uncle Matthew had never in his life been known to eat a meal in anybody else's house. "Perfectly good food at home," he would say, and people had long ago stopped asking him. The two men, and indeed their two houses and estates, afforded an absolute contrast. Alconleigh was a large, ugly, north-facing, Georgian house, built with only one intention, that of sheltering, when the weather was too bad to be out of doors, a succession of bucolic squires, their wives, their enormous families, their dogs, their horses, their father's relict, and their unmarried sisters. There was no attempt at decoration, at softening the lines, no apology for a façade, it was all as grim and as bare as a barracks, stuck up on the high hillside. Within, the keynote, the theme, was death. Not death of maidens, not death romantically accoutred with urns and weeping willows, cypresses and valedictory odes, but the death of warriors and of animals, stark, real. On the walls halberds and pikes and ancient muskets were arranged in crude patterns with the heads of beasts slaughtered in many lands, with the flags and uniforms of bygone Radletts. Glass-topped cases contained, not miniatures of ladies, but miniatures of the medals of their lords, badges, penholders made of tiger's teeth, the hoof of a favourite horse, telegrams announcing casualties in battle and commissions written out on parchment scrolls, all lying together in a timeless jumble.

Merlinford nestled in a valley of south-westerly aspect, among orchards and old mellow farmhouses. It was a villa, built at about the same time as Alconleigh, but by a very different architect, and with a very different end in view. It was a house to live in, not to rush out from all day to kill enemies and animals. It was suitable for a bachelor, or a married couple with one, or at most two, beautiful, clever, delicate children. It had Angelica Kauffman ceilings, a Chippendale staircase, furniture by Sheraton and Hepplewhite; in the hall there hung two Watteaus; there was no entrenching tool to be seen, nor the head of any animal.

Lord Merlin added continually to its beauties. He was a great collector, and not only Merlinford, but also his houses in London and Rome flowed over with treasures. Indeed, a well-known antique dealer from St. James's had found it worth his while to open a branch in the little town of Merlinford, to tempt his lordship with choice objects during his morning walk, and was soon followed there by a Bond Street jeweller. Lord Merlin loved jewels; his two black whippets wore diamond necklaces designed for whiter, but not slimmer or more graceful necks than theirs. This was a neighbour-tease of long standing; there was a feeling among the local gentry that it incited the good burghers of Merlinford to dishonesty. The neighbours were doubly teased, when year after year went by and the brilliants still sparkled on those furry necks intact.

His taste was by no means confined to antiques; he was an artist and a musician himself, and the patron of all the young. Modern music streamed perpetually from Merlinford, and he had built a small but exquisite playhouse in the garden, where his astonished neighbours were sometimes invited to attend such puzzlers as Cocteau plays, the opera "Mahagonny," or the latest Dada extravagances from Paris. As Lord Merlin was a famous practical joker, it was sometimes difficult to know where jokes ended and culture began. I think he was not always perfectly certain himself.

A marble folly on a near-by hill was topped with a gold angel which blew a trumpet every evening at the hour of Lord Merlin's birth (that this happened to be 9.20 p.m., just too late to remind one of the B.B.C. news, was to be a great local grievance in years to come). The folly glittered by day with semi-precious stones, by night a powerful blue beam was trained upon it.

Such a man was bound to become a sort of legend to the bluff Cotswold squires among whom he lived. But, although they could not approve of an existence which left out of account the killing, though by no means the eating, of delicious game, and though they were puzzled beyond words by the aestheticism and the teases, they accepted him without question as one of themselves. Their families had always known his family, and his father, many years ago, had been a most popular M.F.H.; he was no upstart, no new rich, but simply a sport of all that was most normal in English country life. Indeed, the very folly itself, while considered absolutely hideous, was welcomed as a landmark by those lost on their way home from hunting.

The difference between Aunt Sadie and Uncle Matthew was not as to whether Lord Merlin should or should not be asked to the ball (that question did not arise, since all neighbours were automatically invited), but whether he should be asked to bring a house party. Aunt Sadie thought he should. Since her marriage the least worldly of women, she had known the world as a girl, and she knew that Lord Merlin's house party, if he consented to bring one, would have great decorative value. She also knew that, apart from this, the general note of her ball would be utter and unrelieved dowdiness, and she became aware of a longing to look once more upon young women with well brushed hair, London complexions, and Paris clothes. Uncle Matthew said: "If we ask that brute Merlin to bring his friends, we shall get a lot of aesthetes, sewers from Oxford, and I wouldn't put it past him to bring some foreigners. I hear he sometimes has Frogs and even Wops to stay with him. I will not have my house filled with Wops."

In the end, however, as usual, Aunt Sadie had her way, and sat down to write:

"Dear Lord Merlin,
We are having a little dance for Louisa, etc. . . ."

while Uncle Matthew went gloomily off, having said his piece, and put on "Thora."

Lord Merlin accepted, and said he would bring a party of twelve people, whose names he would presently submit to Aunt Sadie. Very correct, perfectly normal behaviour. Aunt Sadie was quite agreeably surprised that his letter, when opened, did not contain some clockwork joke to hit her in the eye. The writing-paper did actually have a picture of his house on it, and this she concealed from Uncle Matthew. It was the kind of thing he despised.

A few days later there was another surprise. Lord Merlin wrote another letter, still jokeless, still polite, asking Uncle Matthew, Aunt Sadie and Louisa to dine with him for the Merlinford Cottage Hospital Ball. Uncle Matthew naturally could not be persuaded, but Aunt Sadie and Louisa went. They came back with their eyes popping out of their heads. The house, they said, had been boiling hot, so hot that one never felt cold for a single moment, not even getting out of one's coat in the hall. They had arrived very early, long before anyone else was down, as it was the custom at Alconleigh always to leave a quarter of an hour too soon when motoring, in case there should be a puncture. This gave them the opportunity to have a good look round. The house was full of spring flowers, and smelt wonderful. The hot-houses at Alconleigh were full of spring flowers too, but somehow they never found their way into the house, and certainly would have died of cold if they had. The whippets did wear diamond necklaces, far grander ones than

Aunt Sadie's, she said, and she was forced to admit that they looked very beautiful in them. Birds of paradise flew about the house, quite tame, and one of the young men told Louisa that, if she came in the daytime, she would see a flock of multi-coloured pigeons tumbling about like a cloud of confetti in the sky.

"Merlin dyes them every year, and they are dried in the linen cupboard."

"But isn't that frightfully cruel?" said Louisa, horrified.

"Oh, no, they love it. It makes their husbands and wives look so pretty when they come out."

"What about their poor eyes?"

"Oh, they soon learn to shut them."

The house party, when they finally appeared (some of them shockingly late) from their bedroom, smelt even more delicious than the flowers, and looked even more exotic than the birds of paradise. Everybody had been very nice, very kind to Louisa. She sat between two beautiful young men at dinner, and turned upon them the usual gambit:

"Where do you hunt?"

"We don't," they said.

"Oh, then why do you wear pink coats?"

"Because we think they are so pretty."

We all thought this dazzlingly funny, but agreed that Uncle Matthew must never hear of it, or he might easily, even now, forbid the Merlinford party his ball.

After dinner the girls had taken Louisa upstairs. She was rather startled at first to see printed notices in the guests' rooms:

OWING TO AN UNIDENTIFIED CORPSE IN THE CISTERN VISITORS ARE REQUESTED NOT TO DRINK THE BATH WATER.

VISITORS ARE REQUESTED NOT TO LET OFF FIREARMS,
BLOW BUGLES, SCREAM OR HOOT, BETWEEN THE HOURS
OF MIDNIGHT AND SIX A.M.

and, on one bedroom door:

MANGLING DONE HERE

But it was soon explained to her that these were jokes.
The girls had offered to lend her powder and lipstick,
but Louisa had not quite dared to accept, for fear Aunt
Sadie would notice. She said it made the others look
simply too lovely.

As the great day of the Alconleigh ball approached, it
became obvious that Aunt Sadie had something on her
mind. Everything appeared to be going smoothly, the
champagne had arrived, the band, Clifford Essex's third
string, had been ordered, and would spend the few hours
of its rest in Mrs. Craven's cottage. Mrs. Crabbe, in con-
junction with the Home Farm, Craven, and three women
from the village who were coming in to help, was planning a supper to end all suppers. Uncle Matthew had been
persuaded to get twenty oil-stoves, with which to emulate
the caressing warmth of Merlinford, and the gardener
was preparing to transfer to the house every pot-plant
that he could lay his hands on. ("You'll be dyeing the
White Leghorns next," said Uncle Matthew, scornfully.)
But, in spite of the fact that the preparations seemed to
be going forward without a single hitch, Aunt Sadie's
brow was still furrowed with anxiety, because she had
collected a large house-party of girls and their mammas,
but not one single young man. The fact was that those

of her own contemporaries who had daughters were glad to bring them, but sons were another matter. Dancing partners, sated with invitations at this time of year, knew better than to go all the way down to Gloucestershire to a house as yet untried, where they were by no means certain of finding the warmth, the luxury and fine wines which they looked upon as their due, where there was no known female charmer to tempt them, where they had not been offered a mount, and where no mention had been made of a shoot, not even a day with the cocks.

Uncle Matthew had far too much respect for his horses and his pheasants to offer them up to be messed about by any callow unknown boy.

So here was a horrible situation. Ten females, four mothers and six girls, were advancing from various parts of England, to arrive at a household consisting of four more females (not that Linda and I counted, still, we wore skirts and not trousers, and were really too old to be kept all the time in the schoolroom) and only two males, one of whom was not yet in tails.

The telephone now became red-hot, telegrams flew in every direction. Aunt Sadie abandoned all pride, all pretence that things were as they should be, that people were asked for themselves alone, and launched a series of desperate appeals. Mr. Wills, the vicar, consented to leave Mrs. Wills at home, and dine, unattached, at Alconleigh. It would be the first time they had been separated for forty years. Mrs. Aster, the agent's wife, also made the same sacrifice, and Master Aster, the agent's son, aged not quite seventeen, was hurried off to Oxford to get himself a ready-made dress suit.

Davey Warbeck was ordered to leave Aunt Emily and come. He said he would, but unwillingly, and only after the full extent of the crisis had been divulged. Elderly cousins, and uncles who had been for many years forgotten as ghosts, were recalled from oblivion and urged to materialize. They nearly all refused, some of them quite rudely—they had, nearly all, at one time or another, been so deeply and bitterly insulted by Uncle Matthew that forgiveness was impossible.

At last Uncle Matthew saw that the situation would have to be taken in hand. He did not care two hoots about the ball, he felt no particular responsibility for the amusement of his guests, whom he seemed to regard as an onrushing horde of barbarians who could not be kept out, rather than as a group of delightful friends summoned for mutual entertainment and joyous revelry. But he did care for Aunt Sadie's peace of mind, he could not bear to see her looking so worried, and he decided to take steps. He went up to London and attended the last sitting of the House of Lords before the recess. His journey was entirely fruitful.

"Stromboli, Paddington, Fort William and Curtley have accepted," he told Aunt Sadie, with the air of a conjurer producing four wonderful fat rabbits out of one small wine-glass.

"But I had to promise them a shoot—Bob, go and tell Craven I want to see him in the morning."

By these complicated devices the numbers at the dinner-table would now be even, and Aunt Sadie was infinitely relieved, though inclined to be giggly over Uncle Matthew's rabbits. Lord Stromboli, Lord Fort William and the Duke of Paddington were old dancing partners of her own, Sir Archibald Curtley, Librarian of the House, was a well-known diner-out in the smart intellectual world, he was over seventy and very arthritic. After dinner, of course, the dance would be another matter. Mr. Wills would then be joined by Mrs. Wills, Captain Aster by Mrs. Aster, Uncle Matthew and Bob could hardly be counted as partners, while the House of Lords contingent was more likely to head for the bridge table than for the dancing floor.

"I fear it will be sink or swim for the girls," said Aunt Sadie, dreamily.

In one way, however, it was all to the good. These old boys were Uncle Matthew's own choice, his own friends, and he would probably be polite to them; in any case they would know what he was like before they came. To have filled the house with strange young men would, she knew, have been taking a great risk. Uncle Matthew hated strangers, he hated the young, and he hated the idea of possible suitors for his daughters; Aunt Sadie saw rocks ahead, but this time they had been circumnavigated.

This then is a ball. This is life, what we have been waiting for all these years, here we are and here it is, a ball, actually going on now, actually in progress round us. How extraordinary it feels, such unreality, like a dream. But, alas, so utterly different from what one had imagined and expected; it must be admitted, not a good dream. The men so small and ugly, the women so frowsty, their clothes so messy and their faces so red, the oil-stoves so smelly, and not really very warm, but, above all, the men, either so old or so ugly. And when they ask one to dance (pushed to it, one cannot but suspect, by kind Davey, who is trying to see that we have a good time at our first party), it is not at all like floating away into a delicious cloud, pressed by a manly arm to a manly bosom, but stumble, stumble, kick, kick. They balance, like King

Stork, on one leg, while, with the other, they come down, like King Log, onto one's toe. As for witty conversation, it is wonderful if any conversation, even of the most banal and jerky description, lasts through a whole dance and the sitting out. It is mostly: "Oh, sorry—oh, my fault," though Linda did get as far as taking one of her partners to see the diseased stones.

We had never learnt to dance, and, for some reason, we had supposed it to be a thing which everybody could do quite easily and naturally. I think Linda realized there and then what it took me years to learn, that the behaviour of civilized man really has nothing to do with nature, that all is artificiality and art more or less perfected.

The evening was saved from being an utter disillusionment by the Merlinford house party. They came immensely late, we had all forgotten about them in fact, but, when they had said how do you do to Aunt Sadie and taken the floor, they seemed at once to give the party a new atmosphere. They flourished and shone with jewels, lovely clothes, brilliant hair and dazzling complexions; when they danced they really did seem to float, except when it was the Charleston, and that, though angular, was so accomplished that it made us gasp with admiration. Their conversation was quite evidently both daring and witty, one could see it ran like a river, splashing, dashing and glittering in the sun. Linda was entranced by them, and decided then and there that she would become one of these brilliant beings and live in their world, even if it took her a lifetime to accomplish. I did not aspire to this. I saw that they were admirable, but they were far removed from me and my orbit, belonging more to that of my parents; my back had been towards them from the day Aunt Emily had taken me home, and there was no return—nor did I wish for it. All the same, I found them fascinating as a spectacle, and, whether I sat out with Linda or stumped round the room with kind Davey, who, unable to persuade any more young men to take us on, gave us an occasional turn himself, my eyes were glued to them. Davey seemed to know them all quite well, and was evidently great friends with Lord Merlin. When he was not being kind to Linda and me, he attached himself to them, and joined in their accomplished chatter. He even offered to introduce us to them, but, alas, the floating panels of taffeta, which had seemed so original and pretty in Mrs. Josh's cottage, looked queerly stiff beside their printed chiffons, so soft and supple; also our experiences earlier in the evening had made us feel inferior, and we begged him not to.

That night in bed, I thought more than ever of the safe sheltering arms of my Shenley farmer. The next morning Linda told me that she had renounced the Prince of Wales.

"I have come to the conclusion," she said, "that Court circles would be rather dull. Lady Dorothy is a lady-in-waiting and look at her."

CHAPTER 6

THE ball had a very unexpected sequel. Lord Fort William's mother invited Aunt Sadie and Louisa to stay at their place in Sussex for a hunt ball, and shortly afterwards, his married sister asked them to a shoot and an Infirmary Ball. During this visit, Lord Fort William proposed to Louisa and was accepted. She came back to Alconleigh a fiancée, to find herself the centre of attention there for the first time since the birth of Linda had put her nose for ever out of joint. This was indeed an excitement, and tremendous chats took place in the Hons' cupboard, both with and without Louisa. She had a nice little diamond ring on her fourth finger, but was not as communicative as we could have wished on the subject of Lord (John now to us, but how could we remember that?) Fort William's love-making, retiring, with many blushes, behind the smoke-screen of such things being too sacred to speak of. He soon appeared again in person, and we were able to observe him as an individual, instead of part, with Lord Stromboli and the Duke of Paddington, of a venerable trinity. Linda pronounced the summing-up. "Poor old thing, I suppose she likes him, but, I must say, if he was one's dog one would have him put down." Lord Fort William was thirty-nine, but he certainly looked much more. His hair seemed to be slipping off backwards, like an eiderdown in the night, Linda said, and he had a generally uncared-for middle-aged appearance. Louisa, however, loved him, and was happy for the first time in her life. She had always been more frightened of Uncle Matthew than any of the others, and with good reason; he thought she was a fool and was never at all nice to her, and she was in heaven at the prospect of getting away from Alconleigh for ever.

I think Linda, in spite of the poor old dog and the eiderdown, was really very jealous. She went off for long rides by herself, and spun more and more fantastic daydreams; her longing for love had become an obsession. Two whole years would have to be made away with somehow before she would come out in the world, but oh the days went dragging by. Linda would flop about in the drawing-room, playing (or beginning and then not finishing) endless games of patience, sometimes by herself, sometimes with Jassy, whom she had infected with her own restlessness.

"What's the time, darling?"

"Guess."

"A quarter to six?"

"Better than that."

"Six!"

"Not quite so good."

"Five to?"

"Yes."

"If this comes out I shall marry the man I love. If this comes out I shall marry at eighteen."

If this comes out—shuffle—if this comes out—deal. A queen at the bottom of the pack, it can't come out, begin again.

Louisa was married in the spring. Her wedding dress, of tulle frills and sprays of orange blossom, was short to the knee and had a train, as was the hideous fashion then. Jassy got very worked up about it.

"So unsuitable."

"Why, Jassy?"

"To be buried in, I mean. Women are always buried in their wedding dresses, aren't they? Think of your poor old dead legs sticking out."

"Don't be such a ghoul. I'll wrap them up in my train."

"Not very nice for the undertakers."

Louisa refused to have bridesmaids. I think she felt that it would be agreeable, for once in her life, to be more looked at than Linda.

"You can't think how stupid you'll look from behind," Linda said, "without any. Still, have it your own way. I'm sure we don't want to be guyed up in blue chiffon, I'm only thinking what would be kinder for you."

On Louisa's birthday John Fort William, an ardent anti-quarian, gave her a replica of King Alfred's jewel. Linda, whose disagreeableness at this time knew no bounds, said that it simply looked like a chicken's mess. "Same shape, same size, same colour. Not my idea of a jewel."

"I think it's lovely," said Aunt Sadie, but Linda's words had left their sting all the same.

Aunt Sadie had a canary then, which sang all day, ri-valling even Galli Curci in the pureness and loudness of its trills. Whenever I hear a canary sing so immoderately it recalls that happy visit, the endless flow of wedding pres-ents, unpacking them, arranging them in the ballroom with shrieks of admiration or of horror, the hustle, the bustle, and Uncle Matthew's good temper, which went on, as fine weather sometimes does, day after unbelievable day.

Louisa was to have two houses, one in London, Connaught Square, and one in Scotland. Her dress allowance would be three hundred a year, she would possess a diamond tiara, a pearl necklace, a motor-car of her own and a fur cape. In fact granted that she could bear John Fort William, her lot was an enviable one. He was terribly dull.

The wedding day was fine and balmy, and, when we went in the morning to see how Mrs. Wills and Mrs. Josh were getting on with the decorations, we found the light little church bunchy with spring flowers. Later, its well-known outlines blurred with a most unaccustomed throng of human beings, it looked quite different. I thought that I personally should have liked better to be married in it when it was so empty and flowery and full of the Holy Ghost.

Neither Linda nor I had ever been to a wedding before, as Aunt Emily, most unfairly we thought at the time, had been married privately in the chapel at Davey's home in the North of England, and we were hardly prepared for the sudden transformation on this day of dear old Louisa, of terribly dull John, into eternal types of Bride and Bridegroom, Heroine and Hero of romance.

From the moment when we left Louisa alone at Alconleigh with Uncle Matthew, to follow us in the Daimler in exactly eleven minutes, the atmosphere became positively dramatic. Louisa, enveloped from head to knee in tulle, sat gingerly on the edge of a chair, while Uncle Matthew, watch in hand, strode up and down the hall. We walked, as we always did, to the church, and arranged ourselves in the family pew at the back of it, from which vantage point we were able to observe with fascination the unusual appearance of our neighbours, all tricked out in their best. The only person in the whole congregation who looked exactly as usual was Lord Merlin.

Suddenly there was a stir. John and his best man, Lord Stromboli, appearing like two jacks-in-the-box from nowhere, stood beside the altar steps. In their morning coats, their hair heavily brilliantined, they looked quite glamorous, but we hardly had time to notice this fact before Mrs. Wills struck up "Here comes the Bride," with all the stops out, and Louisa, her veil over her face, was being dragged up the aisle at double quick time by Uncle Matthew. At this moment I think Linda would gladly have changed places with Louisa, even at the cost—the heavy cost—of being happy for ever after with John Fort William. In what seemed no time at all Louisa was being dragged down the aisle again by John, with her veil back, while Mrs. Wills nearly broke the windows, so loud and so triumphant was her "Wedding March."

Everything had gone like clockwork, and there was only one small incident. Davey slipped out of the family pew almost unobserved, in the middle of "As pants the hart" (Louisa's favourite hymn) and went straight to London, making one of the wedding cars take him to Merlinford station. That evening he telephoned to say that he had twisted his tonsil, singing, and had thought it better to go immediately to Sir Andrew Macpherson, the nose, throat and ears man, who was keeping him in bed for a week. The most extraordinary accidents always seemed to overtake poor Davey.

When Louisa had gone away and the wedding guests had left Alconleigh, a sense of flatness descended upon the house, as always happens on these occasions. Linda then became plunged into such despairing gloom that even Aunt Sadie was alarmed. Linda told me afterwards that she thought a great deal about killing herself, and would most likely have done so had the material difficulties not been so great.

"You know what it is," she said, "trying to kill rabbits. Well, think of *oneself*!"

Two years seemed an absolute eternity, not worth ploughing through even with the prospect (which she never doubted, just as a religious person does not doubt the existence of heaven) of blissful love at the end of it. Of course, this was the time when Linda should have been made to work, as I was, all day and hard, with no time for silly dreaming except the few minutes before one went to sleep at night. I think Aunt Sadie dimly perceived this fact, she urged her to learn cooking, to occupy herself in the garden, to be prepared for confirmation. Linda furiously refused, nor would she do jobs in the village, nor help Aunt Sadie in the hundred and one chores which fall to the lot of a country squire's wife. She was, in fact, and Uncle Matthew told her so countless times every day, glaring at her with angry blue eyes, thoroughly bloody-minded.

Lord Merlin came to her rescue. He had taken a fancy to her at Louisa's wedding, and asked Aunt Sadie to bring her over to Merlinford some time. A few days later he rang up. Uncle Matthew answered the telephone, and shouted to Aunt Sadie, without taking his mouth away from the receiver:

"That hog Merlin wants to speak to you."

Lord Merlin, who must have heard, was quite unmoved by this. He was an eccentric himself, and had a fellow feeling for the idiosyncrasies of others. Poor Aunt Sadie, however, was very much flustered, and, as a result, she accepted an invitation which she would otherwise most probably have refused, to take Linda over to Merlinford for luncheon.

Lord Merlin seemed to become immediately aware of Linda's state of mind, was really shocked to discover that she was doing no lessons at all, and did what he could to provide some interests for her. He showed her his pictures, explained them to her, talked at length about art and literature, and gave her books to read. He let fall the suggestion, which was taken up by Aunt Sadie, that she and Linda should attend a course of lectures in Oxford, and he also mentioned that the Shakespeare Festival was now in progress at Stratford-on-Avon.

Outings of this kind, which Aunt Sadie herself very much enjoyed, soon became a regular feature of life at Alconleigh. Uncle Matthew scoffed a bit, but he never interfered with anything Aunt Sadie wanted to do; besides, it was not so much education that he dreaded for his daughters, as the vulgarizing effect that a boarding-school might have upon them. As for governesses, they had been tried, but none had ever been able to endure for more than a few days the terror of Uncle Matthew's grinding dentures, the piercing, furious blue flash of his eyes, the stock whips cracking under their bedroom windows at dawn. Their nerves, they said, and made for the station, often before they had had time to unpack enormous trunks, heavy as though full of stones, by which they were always accompanied.

Uncle Matthew went with Aunt Sadie and Linda on one occasion to a Shakespeare play, *Romeo and Juliet*. It was not a success. He cried copiously, and went into a furious rage because it ended badly. "All the fault of that damned padré," he kept saying on the way home, still wiping his eyes. "That fella, what's 'is name, Romeo, might have known a blasted papist would mess up the whole thing. Silly old fool of a nurse too, I bet she was an R.C., dismal old bitch."

So Linda's life, instead of being on one flat level plain of tedium, was now, to some extent, filled with outside interests. She perceived that the world she wanted to be in, the witty, sparkling world of Lord Merlin and his friends, was interested in things of the mind, and that she would only be able to shine in it if she became in some sort educated. The futile games of patience were abandoned, and she sat all day hunched up in a corner of the library sofa, reading until her eyes gave out. She often rode over to Merlinford, and, unbeknownst to her parents, who never would have allowed her to go there, or indeed anywhere, alone, left Josh in the stable yard where he had congenial friends, and chatted for hours with Lord Merlin on all sorts of subjects. He knew that she had an intensely romantic character, he foresaw much trouble ahead, and he continually urged upon her the necessity for an intellectual background.

CHAPTER 7

WHAT could possibly have induced Linda to marry Anthony Kroesig? During the nine years of their life together people asked this question with irritating regularity, almost every time their names were mentioned. What was she after, surely she could never possibly have been in love with him, what was the idea, how could it have happened? He was admittedly very rich, but so were others and surely the fascinating Linda had only to choose? The answer was, of course, that, quite simply, she was in love with him. Linda was far too romantic to marry without love and indeed I, who was present at their first meeting and during most of their courtship, always understood why it had happened. Tony, in those days, and to unsophisticated country girls like us, seemed a glorious and glamorous creature. When we first saw him, at Linda's and my coming-out ball, he was in his last year at Oxford, a member of Bullingdon, a splendid young man with a Rolls-Royce, plenty of beautiful horses, exquisite clothes, and large luxurious rooms, where he entertained on a lavish scale. In person he was tall and fair, on the heavy side, but with a well-proportioned figure; he had already a faint touch of pomposity, a thing which Linda had never come across before, and which she found not unattractive. She took him, in short, at his own valuation.

What immediately gave him great prestige in her eyes was that he came to the ball with Lord Merlin. It was really most unlucky, especially as it happened that he had only been asked at the eleventh hour, as a stopgap.

Linda's ball was not nearly such a fiasco as Louisa's had been. Louisa, a married London lady now, produced a lot of young men for Aunt Sadie's house-party, dull, fair Scotch boys mostly, with nice manners; nothing to which Uncle Matthew could possibly take exception. They got on quite well with the various dull dark girls invited by Aunt Sadie, and the house-party seemed to "go" very nicely, though Linda had her head in the air, saying they were all too impossibly dreary for words. Uncle Matthew had been implored by Aunt Sadie for weeks past to be kind to the young and not to shout at anybody, and he was quite subdued, almost pathetic in his wish to please, creeping about as though there were an invalid upstairs and straw in the street.

Davey and Aunt Emily were staying in the house to see me come out (Aunt Sadie had offered to bring me out with Linda and give us a London season together, an offer which was most gratefully accepted by Aunt Emily) and Davey constituted himself a sort of bodyguard to Uncle Matthew, hoping to stand as much as possible between him and the more unbearable forms of irritation.

"I'll be simply wonderful to everybody, but I won't have the sewers in my business-room, that's all," Uncle Matthew had said, after one of Aunt Sadie's prolonged exhortations, and, indeed, spent most of the week-end (the ball was on a Friday and the house-party stayed on until Monday) locked into it, playing "1812" and the "Haunted Ballroom" on the gramophone. He was rather off the human voice this year.

"What a pity," said Linda, as we struggled into our ball dresses (proper London ones this time, with no floating panels), "that we are dressing up like this, and looking so pretty, and all for those terrible productions of Louisa's. Waste, I call it."

"You never know in the country," I said, "somebody may bring the Prince of Wales."

Linda shot me a furious look under her eyelashes.

"Actually," she said, "I am pinning great hopes on Lord Merlin's party. I'm sure he'll bring some really interesting people."

Lord Merlin's party arrived, as before, very late, and in very high spirits. Linda immediately noticed a large, blond young man in a beautiful pink coat. He was dancing with a girl who often stayed at Merlinford called Baby Fairweather, and she introduced him to Linda. He asked her to dance the next, and she abandoned one of Louisa's Scotch boys, to whom she had promised it, and strutted off with him in a quick one-step. Linda and I had both been having dancing lessons, and, if we did not exactly float round the room, our progress was by no means so embarrassing as it had been before.

Tony was in a happy mood, induced by Lord Merlin's excellent brandy, and Linda was pleased to find how well and easily she was getting on with this member of the Merlinford set. Everything she said seemed to make him laugh; presently they went to sit out, she chattered away, and Tony roared with laughter. This was the royal road to Linda's good books; she liked people who laughed easily more than anything; it naturally did not occur to her that Tony was a bit drunk. They sat out the next dance together. This was immediately noticed by Uncle Matthew, who began to walk up and down in front of them, giving them furious looks, until Davey, observing this danger signal, came up and hurried him away, saying that one of the oil-stoves in the hall was smoking.

"Who is that sewer with Linda?"

"Kroesig, Governor of the Bank of England, you know; his son."

"Good God, I never expected to harbour a full-blooded Hun in this house—who on earth asked him?"

"Now, Matthew dear, don't get excited. The Kroesigs aren't Huns, they've been over here for generations, they are a very highly respected family of English bankers."

"Once a Hun always a Hun," said Uncle Matthew, "and I'm not too set on bankers myself. Besides, the fella must be a gate-crasher."

"No, he's not. He came with Merlin."

"I knew that bloody Merlin would start bringing foreigners here sooner or later. I always said he would, but I didn't think even he would land one with a German," Uncle Matthew bellowed.

"Don't you think it's time somebody took some champagne to the band?" said Davey.

But Uncle Matthew stumped down to the boiler room, where he had a long soothing talk with Timb, the odd man, about coke.

Tony, meanwhile, thought Linda ravishingly pretty, and great fun, which indeed she was. He told her so, and danced with her again and again, until Lord Merlin, quite as much put out as Uncle Matthew by what was happening, firmly and very early took his party home.

"See you at the meet tomorrow," said Tony, winding a white silk scarf round his neck.

Linda was silent and preoccupied for the rest of the evening.

"You're not to go hunting, Linda," said Aunt Sadie the next day, when Linda came downstairs in her riding-habit, "it's too rude, you must stay and look after your guests. You can't leave them like that."

"Darling, darling Mummie," said Linda, "the meet's at Cock's Barn, and you know how one can't resist. And Flora hasn't been out for a week, she'll go mad. Be a love and take them to see the Roman villa or something, and I swear to come back early. And they've got Fanny and Louisa after all."

It was this unlucky hunt that clinched matters as far as Linda was concerned. The first person she saw at the meet was Tony, on a splendid chestnut horse. Linda herself was always beautifully mounted, Uncle Matthew was proud of her horsemanship, and had given her two pretty, lively little horses. They found at once, and there was a short sharp run, during which Linda and Tony, both in a somewhat showing-off mood, rode side by side over the stone walls. Presently, on a village green, they checked. One or two hounds put up a hare, which lost its head, jumped into a duckpond, and began to swim about in a hopeless sort of way. Linda's eyes filled with tears.

"Oh, the poor hare!"

Tony got off his horse, and plunged into the pond. He rescued the hare, waded out again, his fine white breeches covered with green muck, and put it, wet and gasping, into Linda's lap. It was the one romantic gesture of his life.

At the end of the day Linda left hounds to take a short cut home across country. Tony opened a gate for her, took off his hat, and said:

"You are a most beautiful rider, you know. Good night, when I'm back in Oxford I'll ring you up."

When Linda got home she rushed me off to the Hons' cupboard and told me all this. She was in love.

Given Linda's frame of mind during the past two endless years, she was obviously destined to fall in love with the first young man who came along. It could hardly have been otherwise; she need not, however, have married him. This was made inevitable by the behaviour of Uncle Matthew. Most unfortunately Lord Merlin, the one person who might perhaps have been able to make Linda see that Tony was not all she thought him, went to Rome the week after the ball, and remained abroad for a year.

Tony went back to Oxford when he left Merlinford, and Linda sat about waiting, waiting, waiting for the telephone bell. Patience again. If this comes out he is thinking of me now this very minute—if this comes out he'll ring up tomorrow—if this comes out he'll be at the meet. But Tony hunted with the Bicester, and never appeared on our side of the country. Three weeks passed, and Linda began to feel in despair. Then one evening, after dinner, the telephone bell rang; by a lucky chance Uncle Matthew had gone down to the stables to see Josh about a horse that had colic, the business-room was empty, and Linda answered the telephone herself. It was Tony. Her heart was choking her, she could scarcely speak.

"Hullo, is that Linda? It's Tony Kroesig here. Will you come to lunch next Thursday?"

"Oh! But I should never be allowed to."

"Oh, rot," very impatiently, "several other girls are coming down from London—bring your cousin if you like."

"All right, that will be lovely."

"See you then—about one—7 King Edward Street, I

expect you know the rooms. Altringham had them when he was up."

Linda came away from the telephone trembling, and whispered to me to come quick to the Hons' cupboard. We were absolutely forbidden to see young men at any hour unchaperoned, and other girls did not count as chaperons. We knew quite well, though such a remote eventuality had never even been mooted at Alconleigh, that we would not be allowed to have luncheon with a young man in his lodgings with any chaperon at all, short of Aunt Sadie herself. The Alconleigh standards of chaperonage were medieval; they did not vary in the slightest degree from those applied to Uncle Matthew's sister, and to Aunt Sadie in youth. The principle was that one never saw any young man alone, under any circumstances, until one was engaged to him. The only people who could be counted on to enforce this rule were one's mother or one's aunts, therefore one must not be allowed beyond the reach of their ever-watchful eyes. The argument, often put forward by Linda, that young men were not very likely to propose to girls they hardly knew, was brushed aside as nonsense. Uncle Matthew had proposed, had he not? to Aunt Sadie, the very first time he ever saw her, by the cage of a two-headed nightingale at an Exhibition at the White City. "They respect you all the more." It never seemed to dawn upon the Alconleighs that respect is not an attitude of mind indulged in by modern young men, who look for other qualities in their wives than respectability. Aunt Emily, under the enlightened influence of Davey, was far more reasonable, but, of course, when staying with the Radletts, I had to obey the same rules.

In the Hons' cupboard we talked and talked. There was

no question in our minds but that we must go, not to do so would be death for Linda, she would never get over it. But how to escape? There was only one way that we could devise, and it was full of risk. A very dull girl of exactly our age called Lavender Davis lived with her very dull parents about five miles away, and once in a blue moon, Linda, complaining vociferously, was sent over to luncheon with them, driving herself in Aunt Sadie's little car. We must pretend that we were going to do that, hoping that Aunt Sadie would not see Mrs. Davis, that pillar of the Women's Institute, for months and months, hoping also that Perkins, the chauffeur, would not remark on the fact that we had driven sixty miles and not ten.

As we were going upstairs to bed, Linda said to Aunt Sadie, in what she hoped was an offhand voice, but one which seemed to me vibrant with guilt:

"That was Lavender ringing up. She wants Fanny and me to lunch there on Thursday."

"Oh, duck," said Aunt Sadie, "you can't have my car, I'm afraid."

Linda became very white, and leant against the wall.

"Oh, please, Mummy, oh please do let me, I do so terribly want to go."

"To the Davises," said Aunt Sadie in astonishment, "but darling, last time you said you'd never go again as long as you lived—great haunches of cod you said, don't you remember? Anyhow, I'm sure they'll have you another day, you know."

"Oh, Mummy, you don't understand. The whole point is, a man is coming who brought up a baby badger, and I do so want to meet him."

It was known to be one of Linda's greatest ambitions, to bring up a baby badger.

"Yes, I see. Well, couldn't you ride over?"

"Staggers and ringworm," said Linda, her large blue eyes slowly filling with tears.

"What did you say, darling?"

"In their stables—staggers and ringworm. You wouldn't want me to expose poor Flora to that."

"Are you sure? Their horses always look so wonderful."

"Ask Josh."

"Well, I'll see. Perhaps I can borrow Fa's Morris, and, if not, perhaps Perkins can take me in the Daimler. It's a meeting I must go to, though."

"Oh, you are kind, you are kind. Oh, do try. I do so long for a badger."

"If we go to London for the season you'll be far too busy to think of a badger. Good night then, ducks."

"We must get hold of some powder."

"And rouge."

These commodities were utterly forbidden by Uncle Matthew, who liked to see female complexions in a state of nature, and often pronounced that paint was for whores and not for his daughters.

"I once read in a book that you can use geranium juice for rouge."

"Geraniums aren't out at this time of year, silly."

"We can blue our eyelids out of Jassy's paint-box."

"And sleep in curlers."

"I'll get the verbena soap out of Mummy's bathroom. If we let it melt in the bath, and soak for hours in it, we shall smell delicious."

"I thought you loathed Lavender Davis."

"Oh, shut up, Jassy."

"Last time you went you said she was a horrible Counter-Hon, and you would like to bash in her silly face with
the Hons' mallet."

"I never said so. Don't invent lies."

"Why have you got your London suit on for Lavender
Davis?"

"Do go away, Matt."

"Why are you starting already, you'll be hours too
early."

"We're going to see the badger before luncheon."

"How red your face is, Linda. Oh, oh you do look so
funny!"

"If you don't shut up and go away, Jassy, I swear I'll
put your newt back in the pond."

Persecution, however, continued until we were in the
car and out of the garage yard.

"Why don't you bring Lavender back for a nice long
cosy visit?" was Jassy's parting shot.

"Not very honnish of them," said Linda, "do you think
they can possibly have guessed?"

We left our car in the Clarendon yard, and, as we were
very early, having allowed half an hour in case of two
punctures, we made for Elliston & Cavell's ladies-room,
and gazed at ourselves, with a tiny feeling of uncertainty,
in the looking-glasses there. Our cheeks had round scarlet
patches, our lips were the same colour, but only at the
edges, inside it had already worn off, and our eyelids were
blue, all out of Jassy's paint-box. Our noses were white,
Nanny having produced some powder with which, years
ago, she used to dust Robin's bottom. In short, we looked
like a couple of Dutch dolls.

"We must keep our ends up," said Linda, uncertainly.

"Oh, dear," I said, "the thing about me is, I always feel so much happier with my end down."

We gazed and gazed, hoping thus, in some magical way, to make ourselves feel less peculiar. Presently we did a little work with damp handkerchiefs, and toned our faces down a bit. We then sallied forth into the street, looking at ourselves in every shop window that we passed. (I have often noticed that when women look at themselves in every reflection, and take furtive peeps into their hand looking-glasses, it is hardly ever, as is generally supposed, from vanity, but much more often from a feeling that all is not quite as it should be.)

Now that we had actually achieved our objective, we were beginning to feel horribly nervous, not only wicked, guilty and frightened, but also filled with social terrors. I think we would both gladly have got back into the car and made for home.

On the stroke of one o'clock we arrived in Tony's room. He was alone, but evidently a large party was expected, the table, a square one with a coarse white linen cloth, seemed to have a great many places. We refused sherry and cigarettes, and an awkward silence fell.

"Been hunting at all?" he asked Linda.

"Oh, yes, we were out yesterday."

"Good day?"

"Yes, very. We found at once, and had a five-mile point and then——" Linda suddenly remembered that Lord Merlin had once said to her: "Hunt as much as you like, but never talk about it, it's the most boring subject in the world."

"But that's marvellous, a five-mile point. I must come out with the Heythrop again soon, they are doing awfully well this season, I hear. We had a good day yesterday, too."

He embarked on a detailed account of every minute of it, where they found, where they ran to, how his first horse had gone lame, how, luckily, he had then come upon his second horse, and so on. I saw just what Lord Merlin meant. Linda, however, hung upon his words with breathless interest.

At last noises were heard in the street, and he went to the window.

"Good," he said, "here are the others."

The others had come down from London in a huge Daimler, and poured, chattering, into the room. Four pretty girls and a young man. Presently some undergraduates appeared, and completed the party. It was not really very enjoyable from our point of view, they all knew each other too well. They gossiped away, roared with laughter at private jokes, and showed off; still, we felt that this was Life, and would have been quite happy just looking on had it not been for that ghastly feeling of guilt, which was now beginning to give us a pain rather like indigestion. Linda turned quite pale every time the door opened, I think she really felt that Uncle Matthew might appear at any moment, cracking a whip. As soon as we decently could, which was not very soon, because nobody moved from the table until after Tom had struck four, we said good-bye, and fled for home.

The miserable Matt and Jassy were swinging on the garage gate.

"So how was Lavender? Did she roar at your eyelids? Better go and wash before Fa sees you. You have been hours. Was it cod? Did you see the badger?"

Linda burst into tears.

"Leave me alone, you horrible Counter-Hons," she cried, and rushed upstairs to her bedroom.

Love had increased threefold in one short day.

On Saturday the blow fell.

"Linda and Fanny, Fa wants you in the business-room. And sooner you than me by the look of him," said Jassy, meeting us in the drive as we came in from riding. Our hearts plunged into our boots. We looked at each other with apprehension.

"Better get it over," said Linda, and we hurried to the business-room, where we saw at once that the worst had occurred.

Aunt Sadie, looking unhappy, and Uncle Matthew, grinding his teeth, confronted us with our crime. The room was full of blue lightning flashing from his eyes, and Jove's thunder was not more awful than what he now roared at us:

"Do you realize," he said, "that, if you were married women, your husbands could divorce you for doing this?"

Linda began to say no they couldn't. She knew the laws of divorce from having read the whole of the Russell case off newspapers with which the fires in the spare bed-rooms were laid.

"Don't interrupt your father," said Aunt Sadie, with a warning look.

Uncle Matthew, however, did not even notice. He was in the full flood and violence of his storm.

"Now we know you can't be trusted to behave your-selves, we shall have to take certain steps. Fanny can go straight home tomorrow, and I never want you here again, do you understand? Emily will have to control you in future, if she can, but you'll go the same way as your mother, sure as eggs is eggs. As for you, miss, there's no more question of a London season now—we shall have to watch you in future every minute of the day—not very agreeable, to have a child one can't trust—and there would be too many opportunities in London for slipping off. You can stew in your own juice here. And no more hunting this year. You're damned lucky not to be thrashed; most fathers would give you a good hiding, do you hear? Now you can both go to bed, and you're not to speak to each other before Fanny leaves. I'm sending her over in the car tomorrow."

It was months before we knew how they found out. It seemed like magic, but the explanation was simple. Somebody had left a scarf in Tony Kroesig's rooms, and he had rung up to ask whether it belonged to either of us.

CHAPTER 8

As always, Uncle Matthew's bark was worse than his bite, though, while it lasted, it was the most terrible row within living memory at Alconleigh. I was sent back to Aunt Emily the next day, Linda waving and crying out of her bedroom window: "Oh, you *are* lucky, not to be me," (most unlike her, her usual cry being, "Isn't it lovely to be lovely *one*.") and she was stopped from hunting once or twice. Then relaxation began, the thin end of the wedge, and gradually things returned to normal, though it was reckoned in the family that Uncle Matthew had got through a pair of dentures in record time.

Plans for the London season went on being made, and went on including me. I heard afterwards that both Davey and John Fort William took it upon themselves to tell Aunt Sadie and Uncle Matthew (especially Uncle Matthew) that, according to modern ideas, what we had done was absolutely normal, though, of course, they were obliged to own that it was very wrong of us to have told so many and such shameless lies.

We both said we were very sorry, and promised faithfully that we would never act in such an underhand way again, but always ask Aunt Sadie if there was something we specially wanted to do.

"Only then, of course, it will always be no," as Linda said, giving me a hopeless look.

Aunt Sadie took a furnished house for the summer near Belgrave Square. It was a house with so little character that I can remember absolutely nothing about it, except that my bedroom had a view over chimney-pots, and that on hot summer evenings I used to sit and watch the swallows, always in pairs, and wish sentimentally that I too could be a pair with somebody.

We really had great fun, although I don't think it was dancing that we enjoyed so much as the fact of being grown up and in London. At the dances the great bar to enjoyment was what Linda called the chaps. They were terribly dull, all on the lines of the ones Louisa had brought to Alconleigh; Linda, still in her dream of love for Tony, could not distinguish between them, and never even knew their names. I looked about hopefully for a possible life-partner, but, though I honestly tried to see the best in them, nothing remotely approximating my requirements turned up.

Tony was at Oxford for his last term, and did not come to London until quite the end of the season.

We were chaperoned, as was to be expected, with Victorian severity. Aunt Sadie or Uncle Matthew literally never let us out of the sight of one or the other; as Aunt Sadie liked to rest in the afternoon, Uncle Matthew would solemnly take us off to the House of Lords, park us in the Peeresses' Gallery, and take his own forty winks on a back bench opposite. When he was awake in the house, which was not often, he was a perfect nuisance to the Whips, never voting with the same party twice running; nor were the workings of his mind too easy to follow. He voted, for instance, in favour of steel traps, of blood sports and of steeplechasing, but against vivisection and the exporting of old horses to Belgium. No doubt he had his reasons, as Aunt Sadie would remark, with finality, when we commented on this inconsistency. I rather liked those drowsy afternoons in the dark Gothic chamber, fascinated by the mutterings and antics that went on the whole time, and besides, the occasional speech one was able to hear was generally rather interesting. Linda liked it too, she was far away, thinking her own thoughts. Uncle Matthew would wake up at tea-time, conduct us to the Peers' dining-room for tea and buttered buns, and then take us home to rest and dress for the dance.

Saturday to Monday was spent by the Radlett family at Alconleigh, they rolled down in their huge, rather sickmaking Daimler, and by me at Shenley, where Aunt Emily and Davey were always longing to hear every detail of our week.

Clothes were probably our chief preoccupation at this time. Once Linda had been to a few dress shows, and got her eye in, she had all hers made by Mrs. Josh, and, somehow, they had a sort of originality and prettiness that I never achieved, although mine, which were bought at expensive shops, cost about five times as much. This showed, said Davey, who used to come and see us whenever he was in London, that either you get your clothes in Paris or it is a toss-up. Linda had one particularly ravishing ball-dress made of masses of pale grey tulle down to her feet. Most of the dresses were still short that summer, and Linda made a sensation whenever she appeared in her yards of tulle, very much disapproved of by Uncle Matthew, on the grounds that he had known three women burnt to death in tulle ball-dresses.

She was wearing this dress when Tony proposed to her in the Berkeley Square summer-house at six o'clock on a fine July morning. He had been down from Oxford about a fort-night, and it was soon obvious that he had eyes for nobody but her. He went to all the same dances, and, after stumping round with a few other girls, would take Linda to supper, and thereafter spend the evening glued to her side. Aunt Sadie seemed to notice nothing, but to the whole rest of the debutante world the outcome was a foregone conclusion, the only question being when and where Tony would propose.

The ball from which they had emerged (it was in a lovely old house on the east side of Berkeley Square, since demolished) was only just alive, the band sleepily thump-thumped its tunes through the nearly empty rooms; poor Aunt Sadie sat on a little gold chair trying to keep her eyes open and passionately longing for bed, with me beside her, dead tired and very cold, my partners all gone home. It was broad daylight. Linda had been away for hours, nobody seemed to have set eyes on her since supper-time, and Aunt Sadie, though dominated by her fearful sleepiness, was apprehensive, and rather angry. She was beginning to wonder whether Linda had not committed the unforgivable sin, and gone off to a night club.

Suddenly the band perked up and began to play "John Peel" as a prelude to "God Save the King"; Linda, in a grey cloud, was galloping up and down the room with Tony; one look at her face told all. We climbed into a taxi behind Aunt Sadie (she never would keep a chauffeur up at night), we splashed away past the great hoses that were washing the streets, we climbed the stairs to our rooms, without a word being spoken by any of us. A thin oblique sunlight was striking the chimney-pots as

I opened my window. I was too tired to think, I just fell into bed.

We were allowed to be late after dances, though Aunt Sadie was always up and seeing to the household arrangements by nine o'clock. As Linda came sleepily downstairs the next morning, Uncle Matthew shouted furiously at her from the hall:

"That bloody Hun Kroesig has just telephoned, he wanted to speak to you. I told him to get to hell out of it. I don't want you mixed up with any Germans, do you understand?"

"Well, I am mixed up," said Linda, in an offhand, would-be casual voice, "as it happens I'm engaged to him."

At this point Aunt Sadie dashed out of her little morning-room on the ground floor, took Uncle Matthew by the arm, and led him away. Linda locked herself into her bedroom and cried for an hour, while Jassy, Matt, Robin, and I speculated upon future developments in the nursery.

There was a great deal of opposition to the engagement, not only from Uncle Matthew, who was beside himself with disappointment and disgust at Linda's choice, but also quite as much from Sir Leicester Kroesig. He did not want Tony to marry at all until he was well settled in his career in the City, and then he had hoped for an alliance with one of the other big banking families. He despised the landed gentry, whom he regarded as feckless, finished and done with in the modern world, he also knew that the vast, the enviable capital sums which such families undoubtedly still possessed, and of which they made so foolishly little use, were always entailed upon the eldest son, and that very small provision, if any, was made for the dowries of daughters. Sir Leicester and Uncle Matthew met, disliked each other on sight, and were at one in their determination to stop the marriage. Tony was sent off to America, to work in a bank house in New York, and poor Linda, the season now being at an end, was taken home to eat her heart out at Alconleigh.

"Oh, Jassy, darling Jassy, lend me your running-away money to go to New York with."

"No, Linda. I've saved and scraped for five years, ever since I was seven, I simply can't begin all over again now. Besides I shall want it for when I run away myself."

"But, darling, I'll give it you back, Tony will, when we're married."

"I know men," said Jassy, darkly.

She was adamant.

"If only Lord Merlin were here," Linda wailed. "He would help me." But Lord Merlin was still in Rome.

She had 15s. 6d. in the world, and was obliged to content herself with writing immense screeds to Tony every day. She carried about in her pocket a quantity of short, dull letters in an immature handwriting and with a New York postmark.

After a few months Tony came back, and told his father that he could not settle down to business or banking, or think about his future career at all, until the date for his marriage had been fixed. This was quite the proper line to take with Sir Leicester. Anything that interfered with making money must be regulated at once. If Tony, who was a sensible fellow, and had never given his father one moment's anxiety in his life, assured him that he could only be serious about banking after marriage, then married he must be, the sooner the better. Sir Leicester explained at length what he considered the disadvantages of the union. Tony agreed in principle, but said that Linda was young, intelligent, energetic, that he had great influence with her, and did not doubt that she could be made into a tremendous asset. Sir Leicester finally gave his consent.

"It might have been worse," he said, "after all, she is a lady."

Lady Kroesig opened negotiations with Aunt Sadie. As Linda had virtually worked herself into a decline, and was poisoning the lives of all around her by her intense disagreeableness, Aunt Sadie, secretly much relieved by the turn things had taken, persuaded Uncle Matthew that the marriage, though by no means ideal, was inevitable, and that, if he did not wish to alienate for ever his favourite child, he had better put a good face on it.

"I suppose it might have been worse," Uncle Matthew said doubtfully, "at least the fella's not a Roman Catholic."

CHAPTER 9

THE engagement was duly announced in *The Times*. The Kroesigs now invited the Alconleighs to spend a Saturday to Monday at their house near Guildford. Lady Kroesig, in her letter to Aunt Sadie, called it a week-end, and said it would be nice to get to know each other better. Uncle Matthew flew into a furious temper. It was one of his idiosyncrasies that, not only did he never stay in other people's houses (except, very occasionally, with relations), but he regarded it as a positive insult that he should be invited to do so. He despised the expression "week-end," and gave a sarcastic snort at the idea that it would be nice to know the Kroesigs better. When Aunt Sadie had calmed him down a bit, she put forward the suggestion that the Kroesig family, father, mother, daughter Marjorie and Tony, should be asked instead if they would spend Saturday to Monday at Alconleigh. Poor Uncle Matthew, having swallowed the great evil of Linda's engagement, had, to do him justice, resolved to put the best face he could on it, and had no wish to make trouble for her with her future in-laws. He had at heart a great respect for family connections, and once, when Bob and Jassy were slanging a cousin whom the whole family, including Uncle Matthew himself, very much disliked, he had turned upon them, knocked their heads together sharply, and said:

"In the first place he's a relation, and in the second, place he's a clergyman, so shut up."

It had become a classical saying with the Radletts.

So the Kroesigs were duly invited. They accepted, and the date was fixed. Aunt Sadie then got into a panic, and summoned Aunt Emily and Davey. (I was staying at Alconleigh anyhow, for a few weeks' hunting.) Louisa was feeding her second baby in Scotland, but hoped to come south for the wedding later on.

The arrival at Alconleigh of the four Kroesigs could not have been more inauspicious. As the car which had met them at the station was heard humming up the drive, every single light in the whole house fused—Davey had brought a new ultra-violet lamp with him, which had done the trick. The guests had to be led into the hall in pitch darkness, while Logan fumbled about in the pantry for a candle, and Uncle Matthew rushed off to the fuse box. Lady Kroesig and Aunt Sadie chatted politely about this and that, Linda and Tony giggled in the corner, and Sir Leicester hit his gouty foot on the edge of a refectory table, while the voice of an invisible Davey could be heard, apologizing in a high wail, from the top of the staircase. It was really very embarrassing.

At last the lights went up, and the Kroesigs were re-vealed. Sir Leicester was a tall fair man with grey hair, whose undeniable good looks were marred by a sort of silliness in his face; his wife and daughter were two dumpy little fluffy females. Tony evidently took after his father, and Marjorie after her mother. Aunt Sadie, thrown out of her stride by the sudden transformation of what had been mere voices in the dark into flesh and blood, and feeling herself unable to produce more topics of conversation, hurried them upstairs to rest, and dress for

dinner. It was always considered at Alconleigh that the
journey from London was an experience involving great
exhaustion, and people were supposed to be in need of
rest after it.

"What is this lamp?" Uncle Matthew asked Davey,
who was still saying how sorry he was, still clad in the
exiguous dressing-gown which he had put on for his sun-
bath.

"Well, you know how one never can digest anything
in the winter months."

"I can, damn you," said Uncle Matthew. This, ad-
dressed to Davey, could be interpreted as a term of en-
dearment.

"You think you can, but you can't really. Now this
lamp pours its rays into the system, your glands begin
to work, and your food does you good again."

"Well, don't pour any more rays until we have had the
voltage altered. When the house is full of bloody Huns
one wants to be able to see what the hell they're up to."

For dinner, Linda wore a white chintz dress with an
enormous skirt, and a black lace scarf. She looked entirely
ravishing, and it was obvious that Sir Leicester was much
taken with her appearance—Lady Kroesig and Miss Marjorie, in bits of georgette and lace, seemed not to notice it.
Marjorie was an intensely dreary girl, a few years older
than Tony, who had failed so far to marry, and seemed to
have no biological reason for existing.

"Have you read *Brothers*?" Lady Kroesig asked Uncle
Matthew, conversationally, as they settled down to their
soup.

"What's that?"

"The new Ursula Langdok—*Brothers*—it's about two
brothers. You ought to read it."

"My dear Lady Kroesig, I have only read one book in my life, and that is *White Fang*. It's so frightfully good I've never bothered to read another. But Davey here reads books—you've read *Brothers*, Davey, I bet."

"Indeed, I have not," said Davey petulantly.

"I'll lend it to you," said Lady Kroesig, "I have it with me, and I finished it in the train."

"You shouldn't," said Davey, "read in trains, ever. It's madly wearing to the optic nerve centres, it imposes a most fearful strain. May I see the menu, please? I must explain that I'm on a new diet, one meal white, one meal red. It's doing me so much good. Oh, dear, what a pity. Sadie—oh, she's not listening—Logan, could I ask for an egg, very lightly boiled, you know. This is my white meal, and we are having saddle of mutton I see."

"Well, Davey, have your red meal now and your white meal for breakfast," said Uncle Matthew. "I've opened some Mouton Rothschild, and I know how much you like that—I opened it specially for you."

"Oh, it is too bad," said Davey, "because I happen to know that there are kippers for breakfast, and I do so love them. What a ghastly decision. No! it must be an egg now, with a little hock. I could never forgo the kippers, so delicious, so digestible, but, above all, so full of proteins."

"Kippers," said Bob, "are brown."

"Brown counts as red. Surely you can see that."

But when a chocolate cream, in generous supply, but never quite enough when the boys were at home, came round, it was seen to count as white. The Radletts often had cause to observe that you could never entirely rely upon Davey to refuse food, however unwholesome, if it was really delicious.

Aunt Sadie was making heavy weather with Sir Leicester. He was full of boring herbaceous enthusiasms, and took it for granted that she was too.

"What a lot you London people always know about gardens," she said. "You must talk to Davey, he is a great gardener."

"I am not really a London person," said Sir Leicester, reproachfully. "I work in London, but my home is in Surrey."

"I count that," Aunt Sadie said, gently but firmly, "as the same."

The evening seemed endless. The Kroesigs obviously longed for bridge, and did not seem to care so much for racing demon when it was offered as a substitute. Sir Leicester said he had had a tiring week, and really should go to bed early.

"Don't know how you chaps can stand it," said Uncle Matthew, sympathetically. "I was saying to the bank manager at Merlinford only yesterday, it must be the hell of a life fussing about with other blokes' money all day, indoors."

Linda went to ring up Lord Merlin, who had just returned from abroad. Tony followed her, they were gone a long time, and came back looking flushed and rather self-conscious.

The next morning, as we were hanging about in the hall waiting for the kippers, which had already announced themselves with a heavenly smell, two breakfast trays were seen going upstairs, for Sir Leicester and Lady Kroesig.

"No, really, that beats everything, dammit," said Uncle Matthew. "I never heard of a *man* having breakfast in bed before." And he looked wistfully at his entrenching tool.

He was slightly mollified, however, when they came downstairs, just before eleven, all ready to go to church. Uncle Matthew was a great pillar of the church, read the lessons, chose the hymns, and took round the bag, and he liked his household to attend. Alas, the Kroesigs turned out to be blasted idolators, as was proved when they turned sharply to the east during the creed. In short, they were of the company of those who could do no right, and signs of relief echoed through the house when they decided to catch an evening train back to London.

"Tony is Bottom to Linda, isn't he?" I said, sadly.

Davey and I were walking together through Hen's Grove the next day. Davey always knew what you meant, it was one of the nice things about him.

"Bottom," he said sadly. He adored Linda.

"And nothing will wake her up?"

"Not before it's too late, I fear. Poor Linda, she has an intensely romantic character, which is fatal for a woman. Fortunately for them, and for all of us, most women are madly matter of fact, otherwise the world could hardly carry on."

Lord Merlin was braver than the rest of us, and said right out what he thought. Linda went over to see him and asked him.

"Are you pleased about my engagement?" to which he replied:

"No, of course not. Why are you doing it?"

"I'm in love," said Linda proudly.

"What makes you think so?"

"One doesn't think, one knows," she said.

"Fiddlesticks."

"Oh, you evidently don't understand about love, so what's the use of talking to you."

Lord Merlin got very cross, and said that neither did immature little girls understand about love.

"Love," he said, "is for grown-up people, as you will discover one day. You will also discover that it has nothing to do with marriage. I'm all in favour of you marrying soon, in a year or two, but for God's sake, and all of our sakes, don't go and marry a bore like Tony Kroesig."

"If he's such a bore, why did you ask him to stay?"

"I didn't ask him. Baby brought him, because Cecil had 'flu and couldn't come. Besides, I can't guess you'll go and marry every stopgap I have in my house."

"You ought to be more careful. Anyhow, I can't think why you say Tony's a bore, he knows everything."

"Yes, that's exactly it, he does. And what about Sir Leicester? And have you seen Lady Kroesig?"

But the Kroesig family was illuminated for Linda by the great glow of perfection which shone around Tony, and she would hear nothing against them. She parted rather coldly from Lord Merlin, came home, and abused him roundly. As for him, he waited to see what Sir Leicester was giving her for a wedding present. It was a pigskin dressing-case with dark tortoiseshell fittings and her initials on them in gold. Lord Merlin sent her a morocco one double the size, fitted with blonde tortoise-shells, and instead of initials, LINDA in diamonds.

He had embarked upon an elaborate series of Kroesig-teases of which this was to be the first.

The arrangements for the wedding did not go smoothly. There was trouble without end over settlements. Uncle Matthew, whose estate provided a certain sum of money for younger children, to be allocated by him as he thought best, very naturally did not wish to settle anything on Linda, at the expense of the others, in view of the fact that she was marrying the son of a millionaire. Sir Leicester, however, refused to settle a penny unless Uncle Matthew did—he had no great wish to make a settlement in any case, saying that it was against the policy of his family to tie up capital sums. In the end, by sheer persistence, Uncle Matthew got a beggarly amount for Linda. The whole thing worried and upset him very much, and confirmed him, if need be, in his hatred of the Teutonic race.

Tony and his parents wanted a London wedding, Uncle Matthew said he had never heard of anything so common and vulgar in his life. Women were married from their homes; he thought fashionable weddings the height of degradation, and refused to lead one of his daughters up the aisle of St. Margaret's through a crowd of gaping strangers. The Kroesigs explained to Linda that, if she had a country wedding, she would only get half the number of wedding presents, and also that the important, influential people, who would be of use, later, to Tony, would never come down to Gloucestershire in the depth of winter. All these arguments were lost on Linda. Since the days when she was planning to marry the Prince of Wales she had had a mental picture of what her wedding would be like, that is, as much like a wedding in a pantomime as possible, in a large church, with crowds both outside and in, with photographers, arum lilies, tulle, bridesmaids, and an enormous choir singing her favourite tune, "The Lost Chord." So she sided with the Kroesigs against poor Uncle Matthew, and, when fate tipped the scales in their favour by putting out of action the heating in Alconleigh church, Aunt Sadie took a London house, and the wedding was duly celebrated with every circumstance of publicized vulgarity at St. Margaret's.

What with one thing and another, by the time Linda was married, her parents and her parents-in-law were no longer on speaking terms. Uncle Matthew cried without restraint all through the ceremony; Sir Leicester seemed to be beyond tears.

CHAPTER 10

I THINK Linda's marriage was a failure almost from the beginning, but I really never knew much about it. Nobody did. She had married in the face of a good deal of opposition; the opposition proved to have been entirely well founded, and, Linda being what she was, maintained, for as long as possible, a perfect shop-front.

They were married in February, had a hunting honeymoon from a house they took at Melton, and settled down for good in Bryanston Square after Easter. Tony then started work in his father's old bank, and prepared to step into a safe Conservative seat in the House of Commons, an ambition which was very soon realized.

Closer acquaintance with their new in-laws did not make either the Radlett or the Kroesig families change their minds about each other. The Kroesigs thought Linda eccentric, affected, and extravagant. Worst of all, she was supposed not to be useful to Tony in his career. The Radletts considered that Tony was a first-class bore. He had a habit of choosing a subject, and then droning round and round it like an inaccurate bomb-aimer round his target, ever unable to hit; he knew vast quantities of utterly dreary facts, of which he did not hesitate to inform his companions, at great length and in great detail, whether they appeared to be interested or not. He was infinitely serious, he no longer laughed at Linda's jokes, and the high spirits which, when she first knew him, he had seemed to possess, must have been due to youth, drink, and good health. Now that he was grown up and married he put all three resolutely behind him, spending his days in the bank house and his evenings at Westminster, never having any fun or breathing fresh air: his true self emerged, and he was revealed as a pompous, money-grubbing ass, more like his father every day.

He did not succeed in making an asset out of Linda. Poor Linda was incapable of understanding the Kroesig point of view; try as she might (and in the beginning she tried very hard, having an infinite desire to please) it remained mysterious to her. The fact is that, for the first time in her life, she found herself face to face with the bourgeois attitude of mind; and the fate often foreseen for me by Uncle Matthew as a result of my middle-class education had actually befallen her. The outward and visible signs which he so deprecated were all there—the Kroesigs said notepaper, perfume, mirror and mantelpiece, they even invited her to call them Father and Mother, which, in the first flush of love, she did, only to spend the rest of her married life trying to get out of it by addressing them to their faces as "you," and communicating with them by postcard or telegram. Inwardly their spirit was utterly commercial, everything was seen by them in terms of money. It was their barrier, their defence, their hope for the future, their support for the present, it raised them above their fellowmen, and with it they warded off evil. The only mental qualities that they respected were those which produced money in substantial quantities, it was their one criterion of success, it was power and it was glory. To say that a man was poor was to label him a rotter, bad at his job, idle, feckless, immoral. If it was somebody whom they really rather liked, in spite of this can-

'cer, they could add that he had been unlucky. They had taken care to insure against this deadly evil in many ways. That it should not overwhelm them through such cataclysms beyond their control as war or revolution they had placed large sums of money in a dozen different countries; they owned ranches, and estancias, and South African farms, an hotel in Switzerland, a plantation in Malaya, and they possessed many fine diamonds, not sparkling round Linda's lovely neck to be sure, but lying in banks, stone by stone, easily portable.

Linda's upbringing had made all this incomprehensible to her; for money was a subject that was absolutely never mentioned at Alconleigh. Uncle Matthew had no doubt a large income, but it was derived from, tied up in, and a good percentage of it went back into, his land. His land was to him something sacred, and, sacred above that, was England. Should evil befall his country he would stay and share it, or die, never would the notion have entered his head that he might save himself, and leave old England in any sort of lurch. He, his family and his estates were part of her and she was part of him, for ever and ever. Later on, when war appeared to be looming upon the horizon, Tony tried to persuade him to send some money to America.

"What for?" said Uncle Matthew.

"You might be glad to go there yourself, or send the children. It's always a good thing to have——"

"I may be old, but I can still shoot," said Uncle Matthew, furiously, "and I haven't got any children—for the purposes of fighting they are all grown up."

"Victoria——"

"Victoria is thirteen. She would do her duty. I hope, if any bloody foreigners ever got here, that every man, woman and child would go on fighting them until one side or the other was wiped out. Anyhow, I loathe abroad, nothing would induce me to live there, I'd rather live in the gamekeeper's hut in Hen's Grove, and, as for foreigners, they are all the same, and they all make me sick," he said, pointedly, glowering at Tony, who took no notice, but went droning on about how clever he had been in transferring various funds to various places. He had always remained perfectly unaware of Uncle Matthew's dislike for him, and, indeed, such was my uncle's eccentricity of behaviour, that it was not very easy for somebody as thick-skinned as Tony to differentiate between Uncle Matthew's behaviour towards those he loved and those he did not.

On the first birthday she had after her marriage, Sir Leicester gave Linda a cheque for £1,000. Linda was delighted and spent it that very day on a necklace of large half pearls surrounded by rubies, which she had been admiring for some time in a Bond Street shop. The Kroesigs had a small family dinner party for her, Tony was to meet her there, having been kept late at his office. Linda arrived, wearing a very plain white satin dress cut very low, and her necklace, went straight up to Sir Leicester, and said: "Oh, you were kind to give me such a wonderful present—look——"

Sir Leicester was stupefied.

"Did it cost all I sent you?" he said.

"Yes," said Linda. "I thought you would like me to buy one thing with it, and always remember it was you who gave it to me."

"No, dear. That wasn't at all what I intended. £1,000 is what you might call a capital sum, that means something on which you expect a return. You should not just spend it on a trinket which you wear three or four times a year, and which is most unlikely to appreciate in value. (And, by the way, if you buy jewels, let it always be diamonds —rubies and pearls are too easy to copy, they won't keep their price.) But, as I was saying, one hopes for a return. So you could either have asked Tony to invest it for you, or, which is what I really intended, you could have spent it on entertaining important people who would be of use to Tony in his career."

These important people were a continual thorn in poor Linda's side. She was always supposed by the Kroesigs to be a great hindrance to Tony, both in politics and in the City, because, try as she might, she could not disguise how tedious they seemed to her. Like Aunt Sadie, she was apt to retire into a cloud of boredom on the smallest provocation, a vague look would come into her eyes, and her spirit would absent itself. Important people did not like this; they were not accustomed to it; they like to be listened and attended to by the young with concentrated deference when they were so kind as to bestow their company. What with Linda's yawns, and Tony informing them how many harbour-masters there were in the British Isles, important people were inclined to eschew the young Kroesigs. The old Kroesigs deeply deplored this state of affairs, for which they blamed Linda. They saw that she did not take the slightest interest in Tony's work. She tried to at first but it was beyond her; she simply could not understand how somebody who already had plenty of money could go and shut himself away from God's fresh air and blue skies, from the spring, the summer, the autumn, the winter, letting them merge into each other unaware that they were passing, simply in order to make more. She was far too young to be interested in politics, which were anyhow, in those days before Hitler came along to brighten them up, a very esoteric amusement.

"Your father was cross," she said to Tony, as they walked home after dinner. Sir Leicester lived in Hyde Park Gardens, it was a beautiful night, and they walked.

"I don't wonder," said Tony, shortly.

"But look, darling, how pretty it is. Don't you see how one couldn't resist it?"

"You are so affected. Do try and behave like an adult, won't you?"

The autumn after Linda's marriage Aunt Emily took a little house in St. Leonard's Terrace, where she, Davey and I installed ourselves. She had been rather unwell, and Davey thought it would be a good thing to get her away from all her country duties and to make her rest, as no woman ever can at home. His novel, *The Abrasive Tube*, had just appeared, and was having a great success in intellectual circles. It was a psychological and physiological study of a South Polar explorer, snowed up in a hut where he knows he must eventually die, with enough rations to keep him going for a few months. In the end he dies. Davey was fascinated by Polar expeditions; he liked to observe, from a safe distance, how far the body can go when driven upon thoroughly indigestible foodstuffs deficient in vitamins.

"Pemmican," he would say, gleefully, falling upon the delicious food for which Aunt Emily's cook was renowned, "must have been so bad for them."

Aunt Emily, shaken out of the routine of her life at Shenley, took up with old friends again, entertained for us, and enjoyed herself so much that she talked of living half the year in London. As for me, I have never, before or since, been happier. The London season I had with Linda had been the greatest possible fun; it would be untrue and ungrateful to Aunt Sadie to deny that; I had even quite enjoyed the long dark hours we spent in the Peeresses' gallery; but there had been a curious unreality about it all, it was not related, one felt, to life. Now I had my feet firmly planted on the ground. I was allowed to do what I liked, see whom I chose, at any hour, peacefully, naturally, and without breaking rules, and it was wonderful to bring my friends home and have them greeted in a friendly, if somewhat detached manner, by Davey, instead of smuggling them up the back stairs for fear of a raging scene in the hall.

During this happy time I became happily engaged to Alfred Wincham, then a young don at, now Warden of, St. Peter's College, Oxford. With this kindly scholarly man I have been perfectly happy ever since, finding in our home at Oxford that refuge from the storms and puzzles of life which I had always wanted. I say no more about him here; this is Linda's story, not mine.

We saw a great deal of Linda just then; she would come and chat for hours on end. She did not seem to be unhappy, though I felt sure she was already waking from her Titania-trance, but was obviously lonely, as her husband was at his work all day and at the House in the evening. Lord Merlin was abroad, and she had, as yet, no other very intimate friends; she missed the comings and goings, the cheerful bustle and hours of pointless chatter which had made up the family life at Alconleigh. I reminded her how much, when she was there, she had longed to escape, and she agreed, rather doubtfully, that it was wonderful to be on one's own. She was much pleased by my engagement, and liked Alfred.

"He has such a serious, clever look," she said. "What pretty little black babies you'll have, both of you so dark."

He only quite liked her; he suspected that she was a tough nut, and rather, I must own, to my relief, she never exercised over him the spell in which she had entranced Davey and Lord Merlin.

One day, as we were busy with wedding invitations, she came in and announced:

"I am in pig, what d'you think of that?"

"A most hideous expression, Linda dear," said Aunt Emily, "but I suppose we must congratulate you."

"I suppose so," said Linda. She sank into a chair with an enormous sigh. "I feel awfully ill, I must say."

"But think how much good it will do you in the long run," said Davey, enviously, "such a wonderful clear-out."

"I see just what you mean," said Linda. "Oh, we've got such a ghastly evening ahead of us. Some important Americans. It seems Tony wants to do a deal or something, and these Americans will only do the deal if they take a fancy to me. Now can you explain that? I know I shall be sick all over them, and my father-in-law will be so cross. Oh, the horror of important people—you are lucky not to know any."

Linda's child, a girl, was born in May. She was ill for a long time before, and very ill indeed at her confinement. The doctors told her that she must never have another child, as it would almost certainly kill her if she did. This was a blow to the Kroesigs, as bankers, it seems, like kings, require many sons, but Linda did not appear to mind at all. She took no interest whatever in the baby she had got.

I went to see her as soon as I was allowed to. She lay in a bower of blossom and pink roses, and looked like a corpse. I was expecting a baby myself, and naturally took a great interest in Linda's.

"What are you going to call her—where is she, any-way?"

"In Sister's room—it shrieks. Moira, I believe."

"Not Moira, darling, you can't. I never heard such an awful name."

"Tony likes it, he had a sister called Moira who died, and what d'you think I found out (not from him, but from their old nanny)? She died because Marjorie whacked her on the head with a hammer when she was four months old. Do you call that interesting? And then they say we are an uncontrolled family—why even Fa has never actually murdered anybody, or do you count that beater?"

"All the same, I don't see how you can saddle the poor little thing with a name like Moira, it's too unkind."

"Not really, if you think. It'll have to grow up a Moira if the Kroesigs are to like it (people always grow up to their names I've noticed) and they might as well like it because frankly, I don't."

"Linda, how can you be so naughty, and, anyway, you can't possibly tell whether you like her or not, yet," I ventured.

"Oh, yes I can. I can always tell if I like people from the start, and I don't like Moira, that's all. She's a fearful Counter-Hon, wait till you see her."

At this point the Sister came in, and Linda introduced us.

"Oh, you are the cousin I hear so much about," she said. "You'll want to see the baby."

She went away and presently returned carrying a Moses basket full of wails.

"Poor thing," said Linda indifferently. "It's really kinder not to look."

"Don't pay any attention to her," said the Sister. "She pretends to be a wicked woman, but it's all put on."

I did look, and, deep down among the frills and lace, there was the usual horrid sight of a howling orange in a fine black wig.

"Isn't she sweet," said the Sister. "Look at her little hands."

I shuddered slightly, and said:

"Well, I know it's dreadful of me, but I don't much like them as small as that; I'm sure she'll be divine in a year or two."

The wails now entered on a crescendo, and the whole room was filled with hideous noise.

"Poor soul," said Linda. "I think it must have caught sight of itself in a glass. Do take it away, Sister."

Davey now came into the room. He was meeting me there to drive me down to Shenley for the night. The Sister came back and shooed us both off, saying that Linda had had enough. Outside her room, which was in the largest and most expensive nursing home in London, I paused, looking for the lift.

"This way," said Davey, and then, with a slightly self-conscious giggle: "Brought up in the harem, I know my way around. Oh, how are you, Sister Thesiger? How very nice to see you."

"Captain Warbeck—I must tell Matron you are here."

And it was nearly an hour before I could drag Davey out of this home away from home. I hope I am not giving the impression that Davey's whole life was centred round his health. He was fully occupied with his work, writing, and editing a literary review, but his health was his hobby, and, as such, more in evidence during his spare time, the time when I saw most of him. How he enjoyed it! He seemed to regard his body with the affectionate preoccupation of a farmer towards a pig—not a good doer, the small one of the litter, which must somehow be made to be a credit to the farm. He weighed it, sunned it, aired it, exercised it, and gave it special diets, new kinds of patent food and medicine, but all in vain. It never put on so much as a single ounce of weight, it never became a credit to the farm, but, somehow it lived, enjoying good things, enjoying its life, though falling victim to the ills that flesh is heir to, and other imaginary ills as well, through which it was nursed with unfailing care, with concentrated attention, by the good farmer and his wife.

Aunt Emily said at once, when I told her about Linda and poor Moira:

"She's too young. I don't believe very young mothers ever get wrapped up in their babies. It's when women are older that they so adore their children, and maybe it's better for the children to have young unadoring mothers and to lead more detached lives."

"But Linda seems to loathe her."

"That's so like Linda," said Davey. "She has to do things by extremes."

"But she seemed so gloomy. You must say that's not very like her."

"She's been terribly ill," said Aunt Emily. "Sadie was in despair. Twice they thought she would die."

"Don't talk of it," said Davey. "I can't imagine the world without Linda."

CHAPTER 11

LIVING in Oxford, engrossed with my husband and young family, I saw less of Linda during the next few years than at any time in her life. This, however, did not affect the intimacy of our relationship, which remained absolute, and, when we did meet, it was still as though we were seeing each other every day. I stayed with her in London from time to time, and she with me in Oxford, and we corresponded regularly. I may as well say here that the one thing she never discussed with me was the deterioration of her marriage; in any case it would not have been necessary, the whole thing being as plain as relations between married people ever can be. Tony was, quite obviously, not good enough as a lover to make up, even at first, for his shortcomings in other respects, the boredom of his company and the mediocrity of his character. Linda was out of love with him by the time the child was born, and, thereafter, could not care a rap for the one or the other. The young man she had fallen in love with, handsome, gay, intellectual and domineering, melted away upon closer acquaintance, and proved to have been a chimera, never to have existed outside her imagination. Linda did not commit the usual fault of blaming Tony for what was entirely her own mistake, she merely turned from him in absolute indifference. This was made easier by the fact that she saw so little of him.

Lord Merlin now launched a tremendous Kroesig-tease. The Kroesigs were always complaining that Linda never 'went out, would not entertain, unless absolutely forced to, and did not care for society. They told their friends that she was a country girl, entirely sporting, that if you went into her drawing-room she would be found training a retriever with dead rabbits hidden behind the sofa cushions. They pretended that she was an amiable, half-witted, beautiful rustic, incapable of helping poor Tony, who was obliged to battle his way through life alone. There was a grain of truth in all this, the fact being that the Kroesig circle of acquaintances was too ineffably boring; poor Linda, having been unable to make any headway at all in it, had given up the struggle, and retired to the more congenial company of retrievers and dormice.

Lord Merlin, in London for the first time since Linda's marriage, at once introduced her into his world, the world towards which she had always looked, that of smart bohemianism; and here she found her feet, was entirely happy, and had an immediate and great success. She became very gay and went everywhere. There is no more popular unit in London society than a young, beautiful, but perfectly respectable woman who can be asked to dinner without her husband, and Linda was soon well on the way to having her head turned. Photographers and gossip writers dogged her footsteps, and indeed one could not escape the impression, until half an hour of her company put one right again, that she was becoming a bit of a bore. Her house was full of people from morning till night, chatting. Linda, who loved to chat, found many congenial spirits in the carefree, pleasure-seeking London of those days, when unemployment was rife as much among the upper as the lower classes. Young men, pensioned off by their relations, who would sometimes suggest in a perfunctory manner that it might be a good thing if they found some work, but without seriously helping them to do so (and, anyhow, what work was there for such as they?) clustered round Linda like bees round honey, buzz, buzz, buzz, chat, chat, chat. In her bedroom, on her bed, sitting on the stairs outside while she had a bath, in the kitchen while she ordered the food, shopping, walking round the park, cinema, theatre, opera, ballet, dinner, supper, night clubs, parties, dances, all day, all night—endless, endless, chat.

"But what do you suppose they talk about?" Aunt Sadie, disapproving, used to wonder. What, indeed?

Tony went early to his bank, hurrying out of the house with an air of infinite importance, an attaché case in one hand and a sheaf of newspapers under his arm. His departure heralded the swarm of chatterers, almost as if they had been waiting round the street corner to see him leave, and thereafter the house was filled with them. They were very nice, very good-looking, and great fun—their manners were perfect. I never was able, during my short visits, to distinguish them much one from another, but I saw their attraction, the unfailing attraction of vitality and high spirits. By no stretch of the imagination, however, could they have been called "important," and the Kroesigs were beside themselves at this turn of affairs.

Tony did not seem to mind; he had long given up Linda as hopeless from the point of view of his career, and was rather pleased and flattered by the publicity which now launched her as a beauty. "The beautiful wife of a clever young M.P." Besides, he found that they were invited to large parties and balls, to which it suited him very well to go, coming late after the House, and where there were often to be found not only Linda's unimportant friends, with whom she would amuse herself, but also colleagues of his own, and by no means unimportant ones, whom he could buttonhole and bore at the bar. It would have been useless, however, to explain this to the old Kroesigs, who had a deeply rooted distrust of smart society, of dancing, and of any kind of fun, all of which led, in their opinion, to extravagance, without compensating material advantages. Fortunately for Linda, Tony at this time was not on good terms with his father, owing to a conflict of policies in the bank; they did not go to Hyde Park Gardens as much as when they were first married, and visits to Planes, the Kroesig house in Surrey, were, for the time being, off. When they did meet, however, the old Kroesigs made it clear to Linda that she was not proving a satisfactory daughter-in-law. Even Tony's divergence of views was put down to her, and Lady Kroesig told her friends, with a sad shake of the head, that Linda did not bring out the best in him.

Linda now proceeded to fritter away years of her youth, with nothing whatever to show for them. If she had had an intellectual upbringing the place of all this pointless chatter, jokes and parties might have been taken by a serious interest in the arts, or by reading; if she had been happy in her marriage that side of her nature which craved for company could have found its fulfilment by the nursery fender; things being as they were, however, all was frippery and silliness.

Alfred and I once had an argument with Davey about her, during which we said all this. Davey accused us of being prigs, though at heart he must have known that we were right.

"But Linda gives one so much pleasure," he kept saying, "she is like a bunch of flowers. You don't want people like that to bury themselves in serious reading; what would be the good?"

However, even he was forced to admit that her behaviour to poor little Moira was not what it should be. (The child was fat, fair, placid, dull and backward, and Linda still did not like her; the Kroesigs, on the other hand, adored her, and she spent more and more time, with her nanny, at Planes. They loved having her there, but that did not stop them from ceaseless criticism of Linda's behaviour. They now told everybody that she was a silly society butterfly, hard-hearted neglecter of her child.)

Alfred said, almost angrily:

"It's so odd that she doesn't even have love affairs. I don't see what she gets out of her life, it must be dreadfully empty."

Alfred likes people to be filed neatly away under some heading that he can understand; careerist, social climber, virtuous wife and mother, or adulteress.

Linda's social life was completely aimless; she simply collected around her an assortment of cosy people who had the leisure to chat all day; whether they were millionaires or paupers, princes or refugee Rumanians, was a matter of complete indifference to her. In spite of the fact that, except for me and her sisters, nearly all her friends were men, she had such a reputation for virtue that she was currently suspected of being in love with her husband.

"Linda believes in love," said Davey, "she is passionately romantic. At the moment I am sure she is, subconsciously, waiting for an irresistible temptation. Casual affairs would not interest her in the least. One must hope that when it comes it will not prove to be another Bottom."

"I suppose she is really rather like my mother," I said, "and all of hers have been Bottoms."

"Poor Bolter!" said Davey, "but she's happy now, isn't she, with her white hunter?"

Tony soon became, as was to be expected, a perfect mountain of pomposity, more like his father every day. He was full of large, clear-sighted ideas for bettering the condition of the capitalist classes, and made no bones of his hatred and distrust of the workers.

"I hate the lower classes," he said one day, when Linda and I were having tea with him on the terrace of the House of Commons. "Ravening beasts, trying to get my money. Let them try, that's all."

"Oh, shut up, Tony," said Linda, bringing a dormouse out of her pocket, and feeding it with crumbs. "I love them, anyway I was brought up with them. The trouble with you is you don't know the lower classes and you don't belong to the upper classes, you're just a rich foreigner who happens to live here. Nobody ought to be in Parliament who hasn't lived in the country, anyhow part of their life—why, my old Fa knows more what he's talking about, when he does talk in the House, than you do."

"I have lived in the country," said Tony. "Put that dormouse away, people are looking."

He never got cross, he was far too pompous.

"Surrey," said Linda, with infinite contempt.

"Anyhow, last time your Fa made a speech, about the Peeresses in their own right, his only argument for keeping them out of the House was that, if once they got in, they might use the Peers' lavatory."

"Isn't he a love?" said Linda. "It's what they all thought, you know, but he was the only one who dared to say it."

"That's the worst of the House of Lords," said Tony. "These backwoodsmen come along just when they think they will, and bring the whole place into disrepute with a few dotty remarks, which get an enormous amount of publicity and give people the impression that we are governed by a lot of lunatics. These old peers ought to realize that it's their duty to their class to stay at home and keep quiet. The amount of excellent, solid, necessary work done in the House of Lords is quite unknown to the man in the street."

Sir Leicester was expecting soon to become a peer, so this was a subject close to Tony's heart. His general attitude to what he called the man in the street was that he ought constantly to be covered by machine-guns; this having become impossible, owing to the weakness, in the past, of the great Whig families, he must be doped into submission with the fiction that huge reforms, to be engineered by the Conservative party, were always just round the next corner. Like this he could be kept quiet indefinitely, as long as there was no war. War brings people together and opens their eyes, it must be avoided at all costs, and especially war with Germany, where the Kroesigs had financial interests and many relations. (They were originally a Junkers family, and snobbed their Prussian connections as much as the latter looked down on them for being in trade.)

Both Sir Leicester and his son were great admirers of Herr Hitler: Sir Leicester had been to see him during a visit to Germany, and had been taken for a drive in a Mercedes-Benz by Dr. Schacht.

Linda took no interest in politics, but she was instinctively and unreasonably English. She knew that one Englishman was worth a hundred foreigners, whereas Tony thought that one capitalist was worth a hundred workers. Their outlook upon this, as upon most subjects, differed fundamentally.

CHAPTER 12

By a curious irony of fate it was at her father-in-law's house in Surrey that Linda met Christian Talbot. The little Moira, aged six, now lived permanently at Planes; it seemed a good arrangement as it saved Linda, who disliked housekeeping, the trouble of running two establishments, while Moira was given the benefit of country air and food. Linda and Tony were supposed to spend a couple of nights there every week, and Tony generally did so. Linda, in fact, went down for Sunday about once a month.

Planes was a horrible house. It was an overgrown cottage, that is to say, the rooms were large with all the disadvantages of a cottage, low ceilings, small windows with diamond panes, uneven floorboards, and a great deal of naked knotted wood. It was furnished neither in good nor in bad taste, but simply with no attempt at taste at all, and was not even very comfortable. The garden which lay around it would be a lady water-colourist's heaven, herbaceous borders, rockeries and water-gardens were carried to a perfection of vulgarity, and flaunted a riot of huge and hideous flowers, each individual bloom appearing twice as large, three times as brilliant as it ought to have been and if possible of a different colour from that which nature intended. It would be hard to say whether it was more frightful, more like glorious techni-

color, in spring, in summer, or in autumn. Only in the
depth of winter, covered by the kindly snow, did it melt
into the landscape and become tolerable.

One April Saturday morning, in 1937, Linda, with
whom I had been staying in London, took me down
there for the night, as she sometimes did. I think she liked
to have a buffer between herself and the Kroesigs, perhaps especially between herself and Moira. The old
Kroesigs were by way of being very fond of me, and Sir
Leicester sometimes took me for walks and hinted how
much he wished that it had been me, so serious, so well
educated, such a good wife and mother, whom Tony
had married.

We motored down past acres of blossom.

"The great difference," said Linda, "between Surrey
and proper, real country, is that in Surrey, when you see
blossom, you know there will be no fruit. Think of the
Vale of Evesham, and then look at all this pointless pink
stuff—it gives you quite a different feeling. The garden at
Planes will be a riot of sterility, just you wait."

It was. You could hardly see any beautiful, pale, bright,
yellow-green of spring, every tree appeared to be entirely
covered with a waving mass of pink or mauve tissue-
paper. The daffodils were so thick on the ground that
they too obscured the green, they were new varieties of
a terrifying size, either dead white or dark yellow, thick
and fleshy; they did not look at all like the fragile friends
of one's childhood. The whole effect was of a scene for
musical comedy, and it exactly suited Sir Leicester, who,
in the country, gave a surprisingly adequate performance
of the old English squire. Picturesque. Delightful.

He was pottering in the garden as we drove up, in an
old pair of corduroy trousers, so much designed as an

old pair that it seemed improbable that they had ever been new, an old tweed coat on the same lines, secateurs in his hand, a depressed Corgi at his heels, and a mellow smile on his face.

"Here you are," he said, heartily. (One could almost see, as in the strip advertisements, a bubble coming out of his head—thinks—"You are a most unsatisfactory daughter-in-law, but nobody can say it's our fault, we always have a welcome and a kind smile for you.") "Car going well, I hope? Tony and Moira have gone out riding, I thought you might have passed them. Isn't the garden looking grand just now, I can hardly bear to go to London and leave all this beauty with no one to see it. Come for a stroll before lunch—Foster will see to your gear— just ring the front-door bell, Fanny, he may not have heard the car."

He led us off into Madam Butterfly-land.

"I must warn you," he said, "that we have got rather a rough diamond coming to lunch. I don't know if you've ever met old Talbot who lives in the village, the old professor? Well, his son, Christian. He's by way of being rather a Communist, a clever chap gone all wrong, and a journalist on some daily rag. Tony can't bear him, never could as a child, and he's very cross with me for asking him today, but I always think it's as well to see something of these Left-wing fellows. If people like us are nice to them they can be tamed wonderfully."

He said this in the tone of one who might have saved the life of a Communist in the war, and, by this act, turned him, through gratitude, into a true-blue Tory. But in the first world war Sir Leicester had considered that, with his superior brain, he would have been wasted as cannon fodder, and had fixed himself in an office in

Cairo. He neither saved nor took any lives, nor did he risk his own, but built up many valuable business contacts, became a major and got an O.B.E., thus making the best of all worlds.

So Christian came to luncheon, and behaved with the utmost intransigence. He was an extraordinarily handsome young man, tall and fair, in a completely different way from that of Tony, thin and very English-looking. His clothes were outrageous—he wore a really old pair of grey flannel trousers, full of little round moth-holes in the most embarrassing places, no coat, and a flannel shirt, one of the sleeves of which had a tattered tear from wrist to elbow.

"Has your father been writing anything lately?" Lady Kroesig asked, as they sat down to luncheon.

"I suppose so," said Christian, "as it's his profession. I can't say I've asked him, but one assumes he has, just as one assumes that Tony has been banking something lately."

He then planted his elbow, bare through the rent, onto the table between himself and Lady Kroesig and swivelling right round to Linda, who was on his other side, he told her, at length and in immense detail, of a production of *Hamlet* he had seen lately in Moscow. The cultured Kroesigs listened attentively, throwing off occasional comments calculated to show that they knew *Hamlet* well—"I don't think that quite fits in with my idea of Ophelia," or "But Polonius was a very old man," to all of which Christian turned an utterly deaf ear, gobbling his food with one hand, his elbow on the table, his eyes on Linda.

After luncheon he said to Linda:

"Come back and have tea with my father, you'd like

him," and they went off together, leaving the Kroesigs to behave for the rest of the afternoon like a lot of hens who have seen a fox.

Sir Leicester took me to his water-garden, which was full of enormous pink forget-me-nots, and dark-brown irises, and said:

"It is really rather too bad of Linda, little Moira has been so much looking forward to showing her the ponies. That child idolizes her mother."

She didn't, actually, in the least. She was fond of Tony and quite indifferent to Linda, calm and stolid and not given to idolatry, but it was part of the Kroesigs' creed that children should idolize their mothers.

"Do you know Pixie Townsend?" he asked me, suddenly.

"No," I said, which was true, nor did I then know anything about her. "Who is she?"

"She's a very delightful person." He changed the subject.

Linda returned just in time to dress for dinner, looking extremely beautiful. She made me come and chat while she had her bath—Tony was reading to Moira upstairs in the night nursery. Linda was perfectly enchanted with her outing. Christian's father, she said, lived in the smallest house imaginable, an absolute contrast to what Christian called the Kroesighof, because, although absolutely tiny, it had nothing whatever of a cottage about it—it was in the grand manner, and full of books. Every available wall space was covered with books, they lay stacked on tables and chairs and in heaps on the floor. Mr. Talbot was the exact opposite of Sir Leicester, there was nothing picturesque about him, or anything to indicate that he was a learned man, he was brisk and matter-of-fact, and had made some very funny jokes about Davey, whom he knew well.

"He's perfect heaven," Linda kept saying, her eyes shining. What she really meant, as I could see too clearly, was that Christian was perfect heaven. She was dazzled by him. It seemed that he had talked without cease, and his talk consisted of variations upon a single theme—the betterment of the world through political change. Linda, since her marriage, had heard no end of political shop talked by Tony and his friends, but this related politics entirely to personalities and jobs. As the persons all seemed to her infinitely old and dull, and as it was quite immaterial to her whether they got jobs or not, Linda had classed politics as a boring subject, and used to go off into a dream when they were discussed. But Christian's politics did not bore her. As they walked back from his father's house that evening he had taken her for a tour of the world. He showed her Fascism in Italy, Nazism in Germany, civil war in Spain, inadequate Socialism in France, tyranny in Africa, starvation in Asia, reaction in America and Right-wing blight in England. Only the U.S.S.R., Norway and Mexico came in for a modicum of praise.

Linda was a plum ripe for shaking. The tree was now shaken, and down she came. Intelligent and energetic, but with no outlet for her energies, unhappy in her marriage, uninterested in her child, and inwardly oppressed with a sense of futility, she was in the mood either to take up some cause, or to embark upon a love affair. That a cause should now be presented by an attractive young man made both it and him irresistible.

CHAPTER 13

THE poor Alconleighs were now presented with crises in the lives of three of their children almost simultaneously. Linda ran away from Tony, Jassy ran away from home, and Matt ran away from Eton. The Alconleighs were obliged to face the fact, as parents must sooner or later, that their children had broken loose from control and had taken charge of their own lives. Distracted, disapproving, worried to death, there was nothing they could do; they had become mere spectators of a spectacle which did not please them in the least. This was the year when the parents of our contemporaries would console themselves, if things did not go quite as they hoped for their own children, by saying: "Never mind, just think of the poor Alconleighs!"

Linda threw discretion, and what worldly wisdom she may have picked up during her years in London society, to the winds; she became an out-and-out Communist, bored and embarrassed everybody to death by preaching her new-found doctrine, not only at the dinner-table, but also from a soap-box in Hyde Park, and other equally squalid rostra, and finally, to the infinite relief of the Kroesig family, she went off to live with Christian. Tony started proceedings for divorce. This was a great blow to my aunt and uncle. It is true that they had never liked Tony, but they were infinitely old-fashioned in their ideas; marriage, to their way of thinking, was marriage, and adultery was wrong. Aunt Sadie was, in particular, profoundly shocked by the light-hearted way in which Linda had abandoned the little Moira. I think it all reminded her too much of my mother, and that she envisaged Linda's future from now on as a series of uncontrollable bolts.

Linda came to see me in Oxford. She was on her way back to London after having broken the news at Alconleigh. I thought it was really very brave of her to do it in person, and indeed, the first thing she asked for (most unlike her) was a drink. She was quite unnerved.

"Goodness," she said. "I'd forgotten how terrifying Fa can be—even now, when he's got no power over one. It was just like after we lunched with Tony; in the business-room just the same, and he simply roared, and poor Mummy looked miserable, but she was pretty furious too, and you know how sarcastic she can be. Oh, well, that's over. Darling, it's heaven to see you again."

I hadn't seen her since the Sunday at Planes when she met Christian, so I wanted to hear all about her life.

"Well," she said, "I'm living with Christian in his flat, but it's very small, I must say, but perhaps that is just as well, because I'm doing the housework, and I don't seem to be very good at it, but luckily he is."

"He'll need to be," I said.

Linda was notorious in the family for her unhandiness, she could never even tie her own stock, and on hunting days either Uncle Matthew or Josh always had to do it for her. I so well remember her standing in front of a looking-glass in the hall, with Uncle Matthew tying it from behind, both the very picture of concentration, Linda saying: "Oh, now I see. Next time I know I shall be able to manage." As she had never in her life done so much as make her own bed, I could not imagine that Christian's flat could be very tidy or comfortable if it was being run by her.

"You are horrid. But oh how dreadful it is, cooking, I mean. That oven—Christian puts things in and says: 'Now you take it out in about half an hour.' I don't dare tell him how terrified I am, and at the end of half an hour I summon up all my courage and open the oven, and there is that awful hot blast hitting one in the face. I don't wonder people sometimes put their heads in and leave them out of sheer misery. Oh, dear, and I wish you could have seen the Hoover running away with me, it suddenly took the bit between its teeth and made for the lift shaft. How I shrieked—Christian only just rescued me in time. I think housework is far more tiring and frightening than hunting is, no comparison, and yet after hunting we had eggs for tea and were made to rest for hours, but after housework people expect one to go on just as if nothing special had happened." She sighed.

"Christian is very strong," she said, "and very brave. He doesn't like it when I shriek."

She seemed tired I thought and rather worried, and I looked in vain for signs of great happiness or great love.

"So what about Tony—how has he taken it?"

"Oh, he's awfully pleased, actually, because he can now marry his mistress without having a scandal, or being divorced, or upsetting the Conservative Association."

It was so like Linda never to have hinted, even to me, that Tony had a mistress.

"Who is she?" I said.

"Called Pixie Townsend. You know the sort, young face, with white hair dyed blue. She adores Moira, lives near Planes, and takes her out riding every day. She's a terrific Counter-Hon, but I'm only too thankful now that she exists, because I needn't feel in the least bit guilty— they'll all get on so much better without me."

"Married?"

"Oh, yes, and divorced her husband years ago. She's frightfully good at all poor Tony's things, golf and business and Conservatism, just like I wasn't, and Sir Leicester thinks she's perfect. Goodness, they'll be happy."

"Now I want to hear more about Christian, please."

"Well, he's heaven. He's a frightfully serious man, you know, a Communist, and so am I now, and we are surrounded by comrades all day, and they are terrific Hons, and there's an anarchist. The comrades don't like anarchists, isn't it queer? I always thought they were the same thing, but Christian likes this one because he threw a bomb at the King of Spain; you must say it's romantic. He's called Ramon, and he sits about all day and broods over the miners at Oviedo because his brother is one."

"Yes, but, darling, tell about Christian."

"Oh, he's perfect heaven—you must come and stay— or perhaps that wouldn't be very comfortable—come and see us. You can't think what an extraordinary man he is, so detached from other human beings that he hardly notices whether they are there or not. He only cares for ideas."

"I hope he cares for you."

"Well, I think he does, but he is very strange and absent-minded. I must tell you, the evening before I ran away with him (I only moved down to Pimlico in a taxi, but running away sounds romantic) he dined with his brother, so naturally I thought they'd talk about me and discuss the whole thing, so I couldn't resist ringing him up at about midnight and saying: 'Hullo, darling, did you have a nice evening, and what did you talk about?' and he said: 'I can't remember—oh, guerrilla warfare, I think.'"

"Is his brother a Communist too?"

"Oh, no, he's in the Foreign Office. Fearfully grand, looks like a deep-sea monster—you know."

"Oh, that Talbot—yes, I see. I haven't connected them. So now what are your plans?"

"Well, he says he's going to marry me when I'm divorced. I think it's rather silly, I rather agree with Mummy that once is enough, for marriage, but he says I'm the kind of person one marries if one's living with them, and the thing is it would be bliss not to be called Kroesig any more. Anyway, we'll see."

"Then what's your life? I suppose you don't go to parties and things now, do you?"

"Darling, such killing parties, you can't think—he won't let us go to ordinary ones at all. Grandi had a dinner-dance last week, and he rang me up himself and asked me to bring Christian, which I thought was awfully nice of him actually—he always has been nice to me— but Christian got into quite a temper and said if I couldn't see any reason against going I'd better go, but nothing would induce him to. So in the end, of course, neither of us went, and I heard afterwards it was the greatest fun. And we mayn't go to the Ribs or to . . . " and she mentioned several families known as much for their hospitality as for their Right-wing convictions.

"The worst of being a Communist is that the parties you may go to are—well—awfully funny and touching, but not very gay, and they're always in such gloomy places. Next week, for instance, we've got three, some

Czechs at the Sacco and Vanzetti Memorial Hall at Golders Green, Ethiopians at the Paddington Baths, and the Scotsboro boys at some boring old rooms or other. You know."

"The Scotsboro boys," I said. "Are they really still going? They must be getting on."

"Yes, and they've gone downhill socially," said Linda, with a giggle. "I remember a perfectly divine party Brian gave for them—it was the first party Merlin ever took me to so I remember it well, oh, dear, it was fun. But next Thursday won't be the least like that. (Darling, I am being disloyal, but it is such heaven to have a chat after all these months. The comrades are sweet, but they never chat, they make speeches all the time.) But I'm always saying to Christian how much I wish his buddies would either brighten up their parties a bit or else stop giving them, because I don't see the point of sad parties, do you? And Left-wing people are always sad because they mind dreadfully about their causes, and the causes are always going so badly. You see, I bet the Scotsboro boys will be electrocuted in the end, if they don't die of old age first, that is. One does feel so much on their side, but it's no good, people like Sir Leicester always come out on top, so what can one do? However, the comrades don't seem to realize that, and, luckily for them, they don't know Sir Leicester, so they feel they must go on giving these sad parties."

"What do you wear at them?" I asked, with some interest, thinking that Linda, in her expensive-looking clothes, must seem very much out of place at these baths and halls.

"You know, that was a great tease at first, it worried me dreadfully, but I've discovered that, so long as one wears wool or cotton, everything is all right. Silk and satin would be the blunder. But I only ever do wear wool and cotton, so I'm on a good wicket. No jewels, of course, but then I left them behind at Bryanston Square, it's the way I was brought up but I must say it gave me a pang. Christian doesn't know about jewellery—I told him, because I thought he'd be rather pleased I'd given them all up for him, but he only said: 'Well, there's always the Burma Jewel Company.' Oh, dear, he is such a funny man, you must meet him again soon. I must go, darling, it has so cheered me up to see you."

I don't quite know why, but I felt somehow that Linda had been once more deceived in her emotions, that this explorer in the sandy waste had only seen another mirage. The lake was there, the trees were there, the thirsty camels had gone down to have their evening drink; alas, a few steps forward would reveal nothing but dust and desert as before.

A few minutes only after Linda had left me to go back to London, Christian and the comrades, I had another caller. This time it was Lord Merlin. I liked Lord Merlin very much, I admired him, I was predisposed in his favour, but I was by no means on such intimate terms with him as Linda was. To tell the real truth he frightened me. I felt that, in my company, boredom was for him only just round the corner, and that, anyhow, I was merely regarded as pertaining to Linda, not existing on my own except as a dull little don's wife. I was nothing but the confidante in white linen.

"This is a bad business," he said, abruptly, and without preamble, though I had not seen him for several years.

"I'm just back from Rome, and what do I find—Linda and Christian Talbot. It's an extraordinary thing that I can't ever leave England without Linda getting herself mixed up with some thoroughly undesirable character. This is a disaster—how far has it gone? Can nothing be done?"

I told him that he had just missed Linda, and said something about her marriage with Tony having been unhappy. Lord Merlin waved this remark aside—it was a disconcerting gesture and made me feel a fool.

"Naturally she never would have stayed with Tony—nobody expected that. The point is that she's out of the frying-pan into an empty grate. How long has it been going on?"

I said I thought it was partly the Communism that had attracted her.

"Linda has always felt the need of a cause."

"Cause," he said, scornfully. "My dear Fanny, I think you are mixing up cause with effect. No, Christian is an attractive fellow, and I quite see that he would provide a perfect reaction from Tony, but it is a disaster. If she is in love with him he will make her miserable, and, if not, it means she has embarked upon a career like your mother's, and that, for Linda, would be very bad indeed. I don't see a ray of comfort anywhere. No money either, of course, and she needs money, she ought to have it."

He went to the window, and looked across the street at Christ Church gilded by the westerly sun.

"I've known Christian," he said, "from a child—his father is a great friend of mine. Christian is a man who goes through the world attached to nobody—people are nothing in his life. The women who have been in love with him have suffered bitterly because he has not even noticed that they are there. I expect he is hardly aware that Linda has moved in on him—his head is in the clouds and he is always chasing after some new idea."

"This is rather what Linda has just been saying."

"Oh, she's noticed it already? Well, she is not stupid, and, of course, at first it adds to the attraction—when he comes out of the clouds he is irresistible, I quite see that. But how can they ever settle down? Christian has never had a home, or felt the need for one; he wouldn't know what to do with it—it would hamper him. He'll never sit and chat to Linda, or concentrate upon her in any way, and she is a woman who requires, above all things, a great deal of concentration. Really it is too provoking that I should have been away when this happened, I'm sure I could have stopped it. Now, of course, nobody can."

He turned from the window and looked at me so angrily that I felt it had all been my fault—actually I think he was unaware of my presence.

"What are they living on?" he said.

"Very little. Linda has a small allowance from Uncle Matthew, I believe, and I suppose Christian makes something from his journalism. I hear the Kroesigs go about saying that there is one good thing, she is sure to starve."

"Oh, they do, do they?" said Lord Merlin, taking out his notebook, "can I have Linda's address, please, I am on my way to London now."

Alfred came in, as usual unaware of exterior events and buried in some pamphlet he was writing.

"You don't happen to know," he said to Lord Merlin, "what the daily consumption of milk is in Vatican City?"

"No, of course not," said Lord Merlin, angrily. "Ask

Tony Kroesig, he'll be sure to. Well, good-bye, Fanny
I'll have to see what I can do."

What he did was to present Linda with the freehold of
a tiny house far down Cheyne Walk. It was the prettiest
little dolls' house that ever was seen, on that great bend
of the river where Whistler had lived. The rooms were
full of reflections of water and full of south and west sunlight; it had a vine and a Trafalgar balcony. Linda adored
it. The Bryanston Square house, with an easterly outlook,
had been originally dark, cold and pompous. When Linda
had had it done up by some decorating friend, it had
become white, cold, and tomblike. The only thing of
beauty that she had possessed was a picture, a fat tomato-
colored bathing-woman, which had been given her by
Lord Merlin to annoy the Kroesigs. It had annoyed them,
very much. This picture looked wonderful in the Cheyne
Walk house, you could hardly tell where the real water-
reflections ended and the Renoir ones began. The pleasure which Linda derived from her new surroundings,
the relief which she felt at having once and for all got
rid of the Kroesigs, were, I think, laid by her at Christian's door, and seemed to come from him. Thus the dis-
covery that real love and happiness had once more eluded
her was delayed for quite a long time.

CHAPTER 14

THE Alconleighs were shocked and horrified over the whole Linda affair, but they had their other children to think of, and were, just now, making plans for the coming out of Jassy, who was as pretty as a peach. She, they hoped, would make up to them for their disappointment with Linda. It was most unfair, but very typical of them, that Louisa, who had married entirely in accordance with their wishes and had been a faithful wife and most prolific mother, having now some five children, hardly seemed to count any more. They were really rather bored by her.

Jassy went with Aunt Sadie to a few London dances at the end of the season, just after Linda had left Tony. She was thought to be rather delicate, and Aunt Sadie had an idea that it would be better for her to come out properly in the less strenuous autumn season, and, accordingly, in October, took a little house in London into which she prepared to move with a few servants, leaving Uncle Matthew in the country, to kill various birds and animals. Jassy complained very much that the young men she had met so far were dull and hideous, but Aunt Sadie took no notice. She said that all girls thought this at first, until they fell in love.

A few days before they were to have moved to London Jassy ran away. She was to have spent a fortnight with

Louisa in Scotland, had put Louisa off without telling Aunt Sadie, had cashed her savings, and, before anybody even knew that she was missing, had arrived in America. Poor Aunt Sadie received, out of the blue, a cable saying: "On way Hollywood. Don't worry. Jassy."

At first the Alconleighs were completely mystified. Jassy had never shown the smallest interest in stage or cinema, they felt certain she had no wish to become a film star, and yet, why Hollywood? Then it occurred to them that Matt might know something, he and Jassy being the two inseparables of the family, and Aunt Sadie got into the Daimler and rolled over to Eton. Matt was able to explain everything. He told Aunt Sadie that Jassy was in love with a film star called Gary Coon (or Cary Goon, he could not remember which), and that she had written to Hollywood to ask him if he were married, telling Matt that if he proved not to be she was going straight out there to marry him herself. Matt said all this, in his wobbling half grown-up, half little-boy voice, as if it were the most ordinary situation imaginable.

"So I suppose," he ended up, "that she got a letter saying he's not married and just went off. Lucky she had her running-away money. What about some tea, Mum?"

Aunt Sadie, deeply preoccupied as she was, knew the rules of behaviour and what was expected of her, and stayed with Matt while he consumed sausages, lobsters, eggs, bacon, fried sole, banana mess and a chocolate sundae.

As always in times of crisis, the Alconleighs now sent for Davey, and, as always, Davey displayed a perfect competence to deal with the situation. He found out in no time that Cary Goon was a second-rate film actor whom Jassy must have seen when she was in London for the last parties of the summer. He had been in a film then showing called *One Splendid Hour*. Davey got hold of the film, and Lord Merlin put it on in his private cinema for the benefit of the family. It was about pirates, and Cary Goon was not even the hero, he was just a pirate and seemed to have nothing in particular to recommend him; no good looks, talent, or visible charm, though he did display a certain agility shinning up and down ropes. He also killed a man with a weapon not unlike the entrenching tool, and this, we felt, may have awakened some hereditary emotion in Jassy's bosom. The film itself was one of those of which it is very difficult for the ordinary English person, as opposed to the film fan, to make head or tail, and every time Cary Goon appeared the scene had to be played over again for Uncle Matthew, who had come determined that no detail should escape him. He absolutely identified the actor with his part, and kept saying:

"What does the fella want to do that for? Bloody fool, he might know there would be an ambush there. I can't hear a word the fella says—put that bit on again, Merlin."

At the end he said he didn't think much of the cove, he appeared to have no discipline and had been most impertinent to his commanding officer. "Needs a haircut! and I shouldn't wonder if he drinks."

Uncle Matthew said how do you do good-bye quite civilly to Lord Merlin. He really seemed to be mellowing with age and misfortune.

After great consultations it was decided that some member of the family, not Aunt Sadie or Uncle Matthew, would have to go to Hollywood and bring Jassy home. But who? Linda, of course, would have been the obvious person, had she not been under a cloud and, furthermore, engrossed with her own life. But it would be of no use to send one bolter to fetch back another bolter, so somebody else must be found. In the end, after some persuasion ("madly inconvenient just now that I have started this course of inoculations") Davey consented to go with Louisa—the good, the sensible Louisa.

By the time this had been decided, Jassy had arrived in Hollywood, had broadcast her matrimonial intentions to all and sundry, and the whole thing appeared in the newspapers, which devoted pages of space to it, and (it was a silly season with nothing else to occupy their readers) turned it into a sort of serial story. Alconleigh now entered upon a state of siege. Journalists braved Uncle Matthew's stock-whips, his bloodhounds, his terrifying blue flashes, and hung around the village, penetrating even into the house itself in their search for local colour. Their stories were a daily delight. Uncle Matthew was made into something between Heathcliff, Dracula, and the Earl of Dorincourt, Alconleigh a sort of Nightmare Abbey or House of Usher, and Aunt Sadie a character not unlike David Copperfield's mother. Such courage, ingenuity and toughness was displayed by these correspondents that it came as no surprise to any of us when, later on, they did so well in the war. "War report by So-and-So——"

Uncle Matthew would then say:

"Isn't that the damned sewer I found hiding under my bed?"

He greatly enjoyed the whole affair. Here were opponents worthy of him, not jumpy housemaids, and lachrymose governesses with wounded feelings, but tough young men who did not care what methods they used so long as they could get inside his house and produce a story.

He also seemed greatly to enjoy reading about himself in the newspapers and we all began to suspect that Uncle Matthew had a hidden passion for publicity. Aunt Sadie, on the other hand, found the whole thing very distasteful indeed.

It was thought most vital to keep it from the press that Davey and Louisa were leaving on a voyage of rescue, as the sudden surprise of seeing them might prove an important element in influencing Jassy to return. Unfortunately, Davey could not embark on so long and so trying a journey without a medicine chest, specially designed. While this was being made they missed one boat, and, by the time it was ready, the sleuths were on their track—this unlucky medicine chest having played the same part that Marie Antoinette's *nécessaire* did in the escape to Varennes.

Several journalists accompanied them on the crossing, but did not reap much of a reward, as Louisa was prostrated with sea-sickness and Davey spent his whole time closeted with the ship's doctor, who asserted that his trouble was a cramped intestine, which could easily be cured by manipulation, rays, diet, exercises and injections, all of which, or resting after which, occupied every moment of his day.

On their arrival in New York, however, they were nearly torn to pieces, and we were able, in common with the whole of the two great English-speaking nations, to follow their every move. They even appeared on the newsreel, looking worried and hiding their faces behind books.

It proved to have been a useless trip. Two days after

their arrival in Hollywood Jassy became Mrs. Cary Goon. Louisa telegraphed this news home, adding, "Cary is a terrific Hon."

There was one comfort, the marriage killed the story.

"He's a perfect dear," said Davey, on his return. "A little man like a nut. I'm sure Jassy will be madly happy with him."

Aunt Sadie, however, was neither reassured nor consoled. It seemed hard luck to have reared a pretty love of a daughter in order for her to marry a little man like a nut, and live with him thousands of miles away. The house in London was cancelled, and the Alconleighs lapsed into such a state of gloom that the next blow, when it fell, was received with fatalism.

Matt, aged sixteen, ran away from Eton, also in a blaze of newspaper publicity, to the Spanish war. Aunt Sadie minded this very much, but I don't think Uncle Matthew did. The desire to fight seemed to him entirely natural, though, of course, he deplored the fact that Matt was fighting for foreigners. He did not take a particular line against the Spanish reds, they were brave boys and had had the good sense to bump off a lot of idolatrous monks, nuns and priests, a proceeding of which he approved, but it was surely a pity to fight in a second-class war when there would so soon be a first-class one available. It was decided that no steps should be taken to retrieve Matt.

Christmas that year was a very sad one at Alconleigh. The children seemed to be melting away like the ten little Indians. Bob and Louisa, neither of whom had given their parents one moment of disquiet in their lives, John Fort William, as dull as a man could be, Louisa's children, so good, so pretty, but lacking in any sort of originality, could not make up for the absence of Linda, Matt and

Jassy, while Robin and Victoria, full as they were of jokes and fun, were swamped by the general atmosphere, and kept to themselves as much as possible in the Hons' cupboard.

Linda was married in the Caxton Hall as soon as her divorce was through. The wedding was as different from her first as the Left-wing parties were different from the other kind. It was not exactly sad, but dismal, uncheerful, and with no feeling of happiness. Few of Linda's friends, and none of her relations except Davey and me were there; Lord Merlin sent two Aubusson rugs and some orchids but did not turn up himself. The pre-Christian chatters had faded out of Linda's life, discouraged, loudly bewailing the great loss she was in theirs.

Christian arrived late, and hurried in, followed by several comrades.

"I must say he is wonderful-looking," Davey hissed in my ear, "but oh, bother it all!"

There was no wedding breakfast, and, after a few moments of aimless and rather embarrassed hanging about in the street outside the hall, Linda and Christian went off home. Feeling provincial, up in London for the day and determined to see a little life, I made Davey give me luncheon at the Ritz. This had a still further depressing effect on my spirits. My clothes, so nice and suitable for the George, so much admired by the other dons' wives ("My dear, where did you get that lovely tweed?"), were, I now realized, almost bizarre in their dowdiness; it was the floating panels of taffeta all over again. I thought of those dear little black children, three of them now, in their nursery at home, and of dear Alfred in his study, but just for the moment this thought was no consolation. I

passionately longed to have a tiny fur hat, or a tiny ostrich
hat, like the two ladies at the next table. I longed for a
neat black dress, diamond clips and a dark mink coat,
shoes like surgical boots, long crinkly black suède gloves,
and smooth polished hair. When I tried to explain all this
to Davey, he remarked, absentmindedly:

"Oh, but it doesn't matter a bit for you, Fanny, and,
after all, how can you have time to keep yourself well
groomed with so many other, more important things to
think of."

I suppose he thought this would cheer me up.

Soon after her marriage the Alconleighs took Linda
back into the fold. They did not count second weddings
of divorced people, and Victoria had been severely repri-
manded for saying that Linda was engaged to Christian.

"You can't be engaged when you're married."

It was not the fact of the ceremony which had mollified
them, in their eyes Linda would be living from now on in
a state of adultery, but they felt the need of her too
strongly to keep up a quarrel. The thin end of the wedge
(luncheon with Aunt Sadie at Gunters) was inserted, and
soon everything was all right again between them, Linda
went quite often to Alconleigh, though she never took
Christian there, feeling that it would benefit nobody were
she to do so.

Linda and Christian lived in their house in Cheyne
Walk, and, if Linda was not as happy as she had hoped to
be, she exhibited, as usual, a wonderful shop-front. Christian was certainly very fond of her, and, in his way, he
tried to be kind to her, but, as Lord Merlin had prophe-
sied, he was much too detached to make any ordinary
woman happy. He seemed, for weeks on end, hardly to

be aware of her presence; at other times he would wander off and not reappear for days, too much engrossed in whatever he was doing to let her know where he was or when she might expect to see him again. He would eat and sleep where he happened to find himself—on a bench at St. Pancras' station, or just sitting on the doorstep of some empty house. Cheyne Walk was always full of comrades, not chatting to Linda, but making speeches to each other, restlessly rushing about, telephoning, typewriting, drinking, quite often sleeping in their clothes, but without their boots, on Linda's drawing-room sofa.

Money troubles accrued. Christian, though he never appeared to spend any money, had a disconcerting way of scattering it. He had few, but expensive amusements, one of his favourites being to ring up the Nazi leaders in Berlin, and other European politicians, and have long teasing talks with them, costing pounds a minute. "They never can resist a call from London," he would say, nor, unfortunately, could they. At last, greatly to Linda's relief, the telephone was cut off, as the bill could not be paid.

I must say that Alfred and I both liked Christian very much. We are intellectual pinks ourselves, enthusiastic agreers with the *New Statesman*, so that his views, while rather more advanced than ours, had the same foundation of civilized humanity, and he seemed to us a great improvement on Tony. All the same, he was a hopeless husband for Linda. Her craving was for love, personal and particular, centred upon herself; wider love, for the poor, the sad, and the unattractive, had no appeal for her, though she honestly tried to believe that it had. The more I saw of Linda at this time, the more certain I felt that another bolt could not be very far ahead.

Twice a week Linda worked in a Red bookshop. It was run by a huge, perfectly silent comrade, called Boris. Boris liked to get drunk from Thursday afternoon, which was closing day in that district, to Monday morning, so Linda said she would take it over on Friday and Saturday. An extraordinary transformation would then occur. The books and tracts which mouldered there month after month, getting damper and dustier until at last they had to be thrown away, were hurried into the background, and their place taken by Linda's own few but well-loved favourites. Thus for *Whither British Airways?* was substituted *Round the World in Forty Days, Karl Marx, the Formative Years* was replaced by *The Making of a Marchioness*, and *The Giant of the Kremlin* by *Diary of a Nobody*, while *A Challenge to Coal-Owners* made way for *King Solomon's Mines.*

Hardly would Linda have arrived in the morning on her days there, and taken down the shutters, than the slummy little street would fill with motor-cars, headed by Lord Merlin's electric brougham. Lord Merlin did great propaganda for the shop, saying that Linda was the only person who had ever succeeded in finding him *Froggie's Little Brother* and *Le Père Goriot.* The chatters came back in force, delighted to find Linda so easily accessible again, and without Christian, but sometimes there were embarrassing moments when they came face to face with comrades. Then they would buy a book and beat a hasty retreat, all except Lord Merlin, who had never felt disconcerted in his life. He took a perfectly firm line with the comrades.

"How are you today?" he would say with great emphasis, and then glower furiously at them until they left the shop.

All this had an excellent effect upon the financial side of the business. Instead of showing, week by week, an enormous loss, to be refunded from one could guess where, it now became the only Red bookshop in England to make a profit. Boris was greatly praised by his employers, the shop received a medal, which was stuck upon the sign, and the comrades all said that Linda was a good girl and a credit to the Party.

The rest of her time was spent in keeping house for Christian and the comrades, an occupation which entailed trying to induce a series of maids to stay with them, and making sincere, but sadly futile, efforts to take their place when they had left, which they usually did at the end of the first week. The comrades were not very nice or very thoughtful to maids.

"You know, being a Conservative is much more restful," Linda said to me once in a moment of confidence, when she was being unusually frank about her life, "though one must remember that it is bad, not good. But it does take place within certain hours, and then finish, whereas Communism seems to eat up all one's life and energy. And the comrades are such Hons, but sometimes they make me awfully cross, just as Tony used to make one furious when he talked about the workers. I often feel rather the same when they talk about us—you see, just like Tony, they've got it all wrong. I'm all for them stringing up Sir Leicester, but if they started on Aunt Emily and Davey, or even on Fa, I don't think I could stand by and watch. I suppose one is neither fish, flesh, nor good red herring, that's the worst of it."

"But there is a difference," I said, "between Sir Leicester and Uncle Matthew."

"Well, that's what I'm always trying to explain. Sir

Leicester grubs up his money in London, goodness knows how, but Fa gets it from his land, and he puts a great deal back into the land, not only money, but work. Look at all the things he does for no pay—all those boring meetings, County Council, J.P., and so on. And he's a good landlord, he takes trouble. You see, the comrades don't know the country—they didn't know you could get a lovely cottage with a huge garden for 2s. 6d. a week until I told them, and then they hardly believed it. Christian knows, but he says the system is wrong, and I expect it is."

"What exactly does Christian do?" I said.

"Oh, everything you can think of. Just at the moment he's writing a book on famine—goodness! it's sad—and there's a dear little Chinese comrade who comes and tells him what famine is like, you never saw such a fat man in your life."

I laughed.

Linda said, hurriedly and guiltily:

"Well, I may seem to laugh at the comrades, but at least one does know they are doing good not harm, and not living on other people's slavery like Sir Leicester, and really you know I do simply love them, though I sometimes wish they were a little more fond of chatting, and not quite so sad and earnest and down on everybody."

CHAPTER 15

EARLY in 1939, the population of Catalonia streamed over the Pyrenees into the Roussillon, a poor and little-known province of France, which now, in a few days, found itself inhabited by more Spaniards than Frenchmen. Just as the lemmings suddenly pour themselves in mass suicide off the coast of Norway, knowing neither whence they come nor whither bound, so great is the compulsion that hurls them into the Atlantic, thus half a million men, women and children suddenly took flight into the bitter mountain weather, without pausing for thought. It was the greatest movement of population, in the time it took, that had ever hitherto been seen. Over the mountains they found no promised land; the French government, vacillating in its policy, neither turned them back with machine-guns at the frontier, nor welcomed them as brothers-in-arms against Fascism. It drove them like a herd of beasts down to the cruel salty marshes of that coast, enclosed them, like a herd of beasts, behind barbed-wire fences, and forgot all about them.

Christian, who had always, I think, had a half-guilty feeling about not having fought in Spain, immediately rushed off to Perpignan to see what was happening, and what, if anything, could be done. He wrote an endless series of reports, memoranda, articles and private letters about the conditions he had found in the camps, and then settled down to work in an office financed by various English humanitarians with the object of improving the camps, putting refugee families in touch again, and getting as many as possible out of France. This office was run by a young man who had lived many years in Spain called Robert Parker. As soon as it became clear that there would not be, as at first was expected, an outbreak of typhus, Christian sent for Linda to join him in Perpignan.

It so happened that Linda had never before been abroad in her life. Tony had found all his pleasures, hunting, shooting, and golf, in England, and had grudged the extra days out of his holiday which would have been spent in travelling; while it would never have occurred to the Alconleighs to visit the Continent for any other purpose than that of fighting. Uncle Matthew's four years in France and Italy between 1914 and 1918 had given him no great opinion of foreigners.

"Frogs," he would say, "are slightly better than Huns or Wops, but abroad is unutterably bloody and foreigners are fiends."

The bloodiness of abroad, the fiendishness of foreigners, had, in fact, become such a tenet of the Radlett family creed that Linda set forth on her journey with no little trepidation. I went to see her off at Victoria, she was looking intensely English in her long blond mink coat, the *Tatler* under her arm, and Lord Merlin's morocco dressing-case, with a canvas cover, in her hand.

"I hope you have sent your jewels to the bank," I said.

"Oh, darling, don't tease, you know how I haven't got any now. But my money," she said with a self-conscious giggle, "is sewn into my stays. Fa rang up and begged me to, and I must say it did seem quite an idea. Oh, why aren't you coming? I do feel so terrified—think of sleeping in the train, all alone."

"Perhaps you won't be alone," I said. "Foreigners are greatly given, I believe, to rape."

"Yes, that would be nice, so long as they didn't find my stays. Oh, we are off—good-bye, darling, do think of me," she said, and, clenching her suède-covered fist, she shook it out of the window in a Communist salute.

I must explain that I know everything that now happened to Linda, although I did not see her for another year, because afterwards, as will be shown, we spent a long quiet time together, during which she told it all to me, over and over again. It was her way of re-living happiness.

Of course the journey was an enchantment to her. The porters in their blue overalls, the loud, high conversations, of which, although she thought she knew French quite well, she did not understand a single word, the steamy, garlic-smelling heat of the French train, the delicious food, to which she was summoned by a little hurried bell, it was all from another world, like a dream.

She looked out of the window and saw chateaux, lime avenues, ponds and villages exactly like those in the Pink Library of her childhood—she thought she must, at any moment, see Sophie in her white dress and unnaturally small black pumps cutting up goldfish, gorging herself on new bread and cream, or scratching the face of good, uncomplaining Paul. Her very stilted, very English French, got her across Paris and into the train for Perpignan without a hitch. Paris. She looked out of the window at the lighted dusky streets, and thought that never could any town have been so hauntingly beautiful. A strange stray thought came into her head that, one day, she would come back here and be very happy, but she knew that it was not likely, Christian would never want to live in Paris. Happiness and Christian were still linked together in her mind at this time.

At Perpignan she found him in a whirl of business. Funds had been raised, a ship had been chartered, and plans were on foot for sending six thousand Spaniards out of the camps to Mexico. This entailed an enormous amount of staff work, as families (no Spaniard would think of moving without his entire family) had to be re-united from camps all over the place, assembled in a camp in Perpignan, and taken by train to the port of Cette, whence they finally embarked. The work was greatly complicated by the fact that Spanish husbands and wives do not share a surname. Christian explained all this to Linda almost before she was out of the train; he gave her an absent-minded peck on the forehead and rushed her to his office, hardly giving her time to deposit her luggage at an hotel on the way and scouting the idea that she might like a bath. He did not ask how she was or whether she had had a good journey—Christian always assumed that people were all right unless they told him to the contrary, when, except in the case of destitute, coloured, oppressed, leprous, or otherwise unattractive strangers, he would take absolutely no notice. He was really only interested in mass wretchedness, and never much cared for individual cases, however genuine their misery, while the idea that it is possible to have three square meals a day and a roof and yet be unhappy or unwell, seemed to him intolerable nonsense.

The office was a large shed with a yard round it. This yard was permanently full of refugees with mountains of luggage and quantities of children, dogs, donkeys, goats, and other appurtenances, who had just struggled over the mountains in their flight from Fascism, and were hoping that the English would be able to prevent them being put into camps. In certain cases they could be lent money, or given railway tickets enabling them to join relations in France and French Morocco, but the vast majority waited hours for an interview, only to be told that there was no hope for them. They would then, with great and heart-breaking politeness, apologize for having been a nuisance and withdraw. Spaniards have a highly developed sense of human dignity.

Linda was now introduced to Robert Parker and to Randolph Pine, a young writer who, having led a more or less playboy existence in the South of France, had gone to fight in Spain, and was now working in Perpignan from a certain feeling of responsibility towards those who had once been fellow soldiers. They seemed pleased that Linda had arrived, and were most friendly and welcoming, saying that it was nice to see a new face.

"You must give me some work to do," said Linda.

"Yes, now what can we think of for you?" said Robert. "There's masses of work, never fear, it's just a question of finding the right kind. Can you speak Spanish?"

"No."

"Oh, well, you'll soon pick it up."

"I'm quite sure I shan't," said Linda doubtfully.

"What do you know about welfare work?"

"Oh, dear, how hopeless I seem to be. Nothing, I'm afraid."

"Lavender will find her a job," said Christian, who had settled down at his table and was flapping over a card index.

"Lavender?"

"A girl called Lavender Davis."

"No! I know her quite well, she used to live near us in the country. In fact she was one of my bridesmaids."

"That's it," said Robert, "she said she knew you, I'd forgotten. She's wonderful, she really works with the Quakers in the camps, but she helps us a great deal too. There's absolutely nothing she doesn't know about calories and babies' nappies, and expectant mummies, and so on, and she's the hardest worker I've ever come across."

"I'll tell you," said Randolph Pine, "what you can do. There's a job simply waiting for you, and that is to arrange the accommodation on this ship that's going off next week."

"Oh, yes, of course," said Robert, "the very thing. She can have this table and start at once."

"Now look," said Randolph. "I'll show you. (What delicious scent you have, Après l'Ondée? I thought so.) Now here is a map of the ship—see—best cabins, not such good cabins, lousy cabins, and battened down under the hatches. And here is a list of the families who are going. All you have to do is to allocate each family its cabin—when you have decided which they are to have, you put the number of the cabin against the family—here—you see? And the number of the family on the cabin here, like that. Quite easy, but it takes time, and must be done so that when they arrive on the boat they will know exactly where to go with their things."

"But how do I decide who gets the good ones and who is battened? Awfully tricky, isn't it?"

"Not really. The point is it's a strictly democratic ship run on republican principles, class doesn't enter into it. I should give decent cabins to families where there are small children or babies. Apart from that do it any way you like. Take a pin if you like. The only thing that matters is that it should be done, otherwise there'll be a wild scramble for the best places when they get on board."

Linda looked at the list of families. It took the form of a card index, the head of each family having a card on which was written the number and names of his dependents.

"It doesn't give their ages," said Linda. "How am I to know if there are young babies?"

"That's a point," said Robert. "How is she to?"

"Quite easy," said Christian. "With Spaniards you can always tell. Before the war they were called either after saints or after episodes in the sex life of the Virgin—Annunciata, Asuncion, Purificacion, Concepcion, Consalacion, etc. Since the Civil War they are all called Carlos after Charlie Marx, Federico after Freddie Engels or Estalina (very popular until the Russians let them down with a wallop), or else nice slogans like Solidaridad-Obreara, Libertad, and so on. Then you know the children are under three. Couldn't be simpler, really."

Lavender Davis now appeared. She was indeed the same Lavender, dowdy, healthy and plain, wearing an English country tweed and brogues. Her short brown hair curled over her head, and she had no make-up. She greeted Linda with enthusiasm, indeed, it had always been a fiction in the Davis family that Lavender and Linda were each other's greatest friends. Linda was delighted to see her, as one always is delighted to see a familiar face, abroad.

"Come on," said Randolph, "now we're all here let's go and have a drink at the Palmarium."

For the next weeks, until her private life began to occupy Linda's attention, she lived in an atmosphere of alternate fascination and horror. She grew to love Perpignan, a strange little old town, so different from anything she had ever known, with its river and broad quays, its network of narrow streets, its huge wild-looking plane trees, and all around it the bleak vine-growing country of the Roussillon bursting into summery green under her very eyes. Spring came late, but when it came it was hand-in-hand with summer, and almost at once everything was baking and warm, and in the villages the people danced every night on concrete dancing floors under the plane trees. At week-ends the English, unable to eradicate such a national habit, shut up the office and made for Collioure on the coast, where they bathed and sunbathed and went for Pyrenean picnics.

But all this had nothing to do with the reason for their presence in these charming surroundings—the camps. Linda went to the camps nearly every day, and they filled her soul with despair. As she could not help very much in the office owing to her lack of Spanish, nor with the children, since she knew nothing about calories, she was employed as a driver, and was always on the road in a Ford van full of supplies, or of refugees, or just taking messages to and from the camps. Often she had to sit and wait for hours on end while a certain man was found and his case dealt with; she would quickly be surrounded by a perfect concourse of men talking to her in their heavy guttural French. By this time the camps were quite decently organized; there were rows of orderly, though depressing huts, and the men were getting regular meals, which, if not very appetizing, did at least keep body and soul together. But the sight of these thousands of human beings, young and healthy, herded behind wire away from their womenfolk, with nothing on earth to do day after dismal day, was a recurring torture to Linda. She began to think that Uncle Matthew had been right—that abroad, where such things could happen, was indeed unutterably bloody, and that foreigners, who could inflict them upon each other, must be fiends.

One day as she sat in her van, the centre, as usual, of a crowd of Spaniards, a voice said:

"Linda, what on earth are you doing here?"

And it was Matt.

He looked ten years older than when she had last seen him, grown up, in fact, and extremely handsome, his Radlett eyes infinitely blue in a dark-brown face.

"I've seen you several times," he said, "and I thought you had been sent to fetch me away so I made off, but then I found out you are married to that Christian fellow. Was he the one you ran away from Tony with?"

"Yes," said Linda. "I'd no idea, Matt. I thought you'd have been sure to go back to England."

"Well, no," said Matt. "I'm an officer you see—must stay with the boys."

"Does Mummy know you're all right?"

"Yes, I told her—at least if Christian posted a letter I gave him."

"I don't suppose so—he's never been known to post a letter in his life. He is funny, he might have told me."

"He didn't know—I sent it under cover to a friend of mine to forward. Didn't want any of the English to find out I was here, or they would start trying to get me home. I know."

"Christian wouldn't," said Linda. "He's all for people doing what they want to in life. You're very thin, Matt, is there anything you'd like?"

"Yes," said Matt, "some cigarettes and a couple of thrillers."

After this Linda saw him most days. She told Christian, who merely grunted and said: "He'll have to be got out before the world war begins. I'll see to that," and she wrote and told her parents. The result was a parcel of clothes from Aunt Sadie, which Matt refused to accept, and a packing-case full of vitamin pills from Davey, which Linda did not even dare to show him. He was cheerful and full of jokes and high spirits, but then there is a difference, as Christian said, between staying in a place because you are obliged to, and staying there because you think it right. But in any case, with the Radlett family, cheerfulness was never far below the surface.

The only other cheerful prospect was the ship. It was only going to rescue from hell a few thousand of the refugees, a mere fraction of the total amount, but, at any rate, they would be rescued, and taken to a better world, with happy and useful future prospects.

When she was not driving the van Linda worked hard over the cabin arrangements, and finally got the whole thing fixed and finished in time for the embarkation.

All the English except Linda went to Cette for the great day, taking with them two M.P.s and a duchess, who had helped the enterprise in London and had come out to see the fruit of their work. Linda went over by bus to Argelès to see Matt.

"How odd the Spanish upper classes must be," she said, "they don't raise a finger to help their own people, but leave it all to strangers like us."

"You don't know Fascists," Matt said, gloomily.

"I was thinking yesterday when I was taking the Duchess round Barcarès—yes, but why an English duchess, aren't there any Spanish ones, and, come to that, why is it nothing but English working in Perpignan? I knew several Spaniards in London, why don't they come and help a bit? They'd be awfully useful. I suppose they speak Spanish."

"Fa was quite right about foreigners being fiends," said Matt, "upper-class ones are, at least. All these boys are terrific Hons, I must say."

"Well, I can't see the English leaving each other in the lurch like this, even if they did belong to different parties. I think it's shameful."

Christian and Robert came back from Cette in a cheerful mood. The arrangements had gone like clockwork, and a baby which had been born during the first half-hour on the ship was named Embarcacion. It was the kind of joke Christian very much enjoyed. Robert said to Linda:

"Did you work on any special plan when you were arranging the cabins, or how did you do it?"

"Why? Wasn't it all right?"

"Perfect. Everybody had a place, and made for it. But I just wondered what you went by when you allocated the good cabins, that's all."

"Well, I simply," said Linda, "gave the best cabins to the people who had *Labrador* on their card, because I used to have one when I was little and he was such a terrific—so sweet, you know."

"Ah," said Robert, gravely, "all is now explained. *Labrador* in Spanish happens to mean labourer. So you see under your scheme (excellent by the way, most democratic) the farm hands all found themselves in luxury while the intellectuals were battened. That'll teach them not to be so clever. You did very well, Linda, we were all most grateful."

"He was such a sweet Labrador," said Linda dreamily,

"I wish you could have seen him. I do miss not having pets."

"Can't think why you don't make an offer for the leech," said Robert.

One of the features of Perpignan was a leech in a bottle in the window of a chemist's shop, with a typewritten notice saying: "IF THE LEECH GOES UP IN THE BOTTLE, THE WEATHER WILL BE FAIR. IF THE LEECH GOES DOWN—STORMY."

"It might be nice," said Linda, "but I can't somehow imagine her getting very fond of one—too busy fussing about the weather all day, up and down, up and down—no time for human relationships."

CHAPTER 16

LINDA never could remember afterwards whether she had really minded when she discovered that Christian was in love with Lavender Davis, and, if so, how much. She could not at all remember her emotions at that time. Certainly wounded pride must have played a part, though perhaps less so with Linda than it would have with many women, as she did not suffer from much inferiority feeling. She must have seen that the past two years, her running away from Tony, all now went for nothing—but was she stricken at the heart, was she still in love with Christian, did she suffer the ordinary pangs of jealousy? I think not.

All the same, it was not a flattering choice. Lavender had seemed, for years and years, stretching back into childhood, to epitomize everything that the Radletts considered most unromantic: a keen girl guide, hockey player, tree climber, head girl at her school, rider astride. She had never lived in a dream of love; the sentiment was, quite obviously, far removed from her thoughts, although Louisa and Linda, unable to imagine that anybody could exist without some tiny spark of it, used to invent romances for Lavender—the games mistress at her school or Dr. Simpson of Merlinford (of whom Louisa had made up one of her nonsense rhymes—"He's doctor and king's proctor too, and she's in love with him but he's in love with you"). Since those days she had trained as a nurse and as a welfare worker, had taken a course of law and political economy, and, indeed, might have done it all, Linda saw only too well, with the express intention of fitting herself to be a mate for Christian. The result was that in their present surroundings, with her calm assured confidence in her own ability, she easily outshone poor Linda. There was no competition, it was a walk-over.

Linda did not discover their love in any vulgar way—surprising a kiss, or finding them in bed together. It was all far more subtle, more dangerous than that, being quite simply borne in upon her week after week that they found perfect happiness in each other, and that Christian depended entirely on Lavender for comfort and encouragement in his work. As this work now absorbed him heart and soul, as he thought of nothing else and never relaxed for a moment, dependence upon Lavender involved the absolute exclusion of Linda. She felt uncertain what to do. She could not have it out with Christian; there was nothing tangible to have out, and, in any case, such a proceeding would have been absolutely foreign to Linda's character. She dreaded scenes and rows more than anything else in the world, and she had no illusions about what Christian thought of her. She felt that he really rather despised her for having left Tony and her child so easily, and that, in his opinion, she took a silly, light-hearted and superficial view of life. He liked serious, educated women, especially those who had made a study of welfare, especially Lavender. She had no desire to hear all this said. On the other hand she began to think that it would be as well for her to get away from Perpignan herself before Christian and Lavender went off together, as it seemed to her most probable that they would, wander-

ing off hand in hand to search for and relieve other forms
of human misery. Already she felt embarrassed when she
was with Robert and Randolph, who were obviously very
sorry for her and were always making little manœuvres to
prevent her noticing that Christian was spending every
minute of the day with Lavender.

One afternoon, looking idly out of the window of her
hotel bedroom, she saw them walking up the Quai Sadi
Carnot together, completely absorbed, utterly contented
in each other's company, radiating happiness. Linda was
seized by an impulse and acted on it. She packed her
things, wrote a hasty letter to Christian saying that she
was leaving him for good, as she realized that their marriage had been a failure. She asked him to look after Matt.
She then burnt her boats by adding a postscript (a fatal
feminine practice), "I think you had much better marry
Lavender." She bundled herself and her luggage into a
taxi and took the night train for Paris.

The journey this time was horrible. She was, after all,
very fond of Christian, and as soon as the train had left
the station, she began to ask herself whether she had not
in fact behaved stupidly and badly. He probably had a
passing fancy for Lavender, based on common interests,
which would fade away as soon as he got back to London.
Possibly it was not even that, but simply that he was
obliged, for his work, to be with Lavender all the time.
His absentminded treatment of Linda was, after all, nothing new, it had begun almost as soon as he had got her
under his roof. She began to feel that she had done wrong
to write that letter.

She had her return ticket, but very little money indeed,
just enough, she reckoned, for dinner on the train and
some food the next day. Linda always had to translate

French money into pounds, shillings and pence before she knew where she was with it. She seemed to have about 18s. 6d. with her, so there could be no question of a sleeper. She had never before sat up all night in a train, and the experience appalled her; it was like some dreadful feverish illness, when the painful hours drag by, each one longer than a week. Her thoughts brought her no comfort. She had torn up her life of the past two years, all that she had tried to put into her relationship with Christian, and thrown it away like so much waste-paper. If this was to be the outcome why had she ever left Tony, her real husband for better or for worse, and her child? That was where her duty had lain, and well she knew it. She thought of my mother and shuddered. Could it be that she, Linda, was from now on doomed to a life that she utterly despised, that of a bolter?

And in London what would she find? A little empty, dusty house. Perhaps, she thought, Christian would pursue her, come and insist that she belonged to him. But in her heart she knew that he would not, and that she did not, and that this was the end. Christian believed too sincerely that people must be allowed to do as they wish in life, without interference. He was fond of Linda, she knew, but disappointed in her, she also knew; he would not himself have made the first move to separate, but would not much regret the fact that she had done so. Soon he would have some new scheme in his head, some new plan for suffering mortals, any mortals, anywhere, so long as there were enough of them and their misery was great. Then he would forget Linda, and possibly also Lavender, as if they had never been. Christian was not in passionate quest of love, he had other interests, other aims, and it mattered very little to him what woman happened to be in his life at a given moment. But in his nature, she knew, there was a certain ruthlessness. She felt that he would not forgive what she had done, or try to persuade her to go back on it, nor, indeed, was there any reason why he should do so.

It could not be said, thought Linda, as the train pursued its way through the blackness, that her life so far had been a marked success. She had found neither great love nor great happiness, and she had not inspired them in others. Parting with her would have been no death blow to either of her husbands, on the contrary, they would both have turned with relief to a much-preferred mistress, who was more suited to them in every way. Whatever quality it is that can hold indefinitely the love and affection of a man she plainly did not possess, and now she was doomed to the lonely, hunted life of a beautiful but unattached woman. Where now was love that would last to the grave and far beyond? What had she done with her youth? Tears for her lost hopes and ideals, tears of self-pity in fact, began to pour down her cheeks. The three fat Frenchmen who shared the carriage with her were in a snoring sleep, she wept alone.

Sad and tired as Linda was, she could not but perceive the beauty of Paris that summer morning as she drove across it to the Gare du Nord. Paris in the early morning has a cheerful, bustling aspect, a promise of delicious things to come, a positive smell of coffee and croissants, quite peculiar to itself.

The people welcome a new day as if they were certain of liking it, the shopkeepers pull up their blinds serene in the expectation of good trade, the workers go happily to their work, the people who have sat up all night in

night-clubs go happily to their rest, the orchestra of
motor-car horns, of clanking trams, of whistling police-
men tunes up for the daily symphony, and everywhere
is joy. This joy, this life, this beauty did but underline
poor Linda's fatigue and sadness, she felt it but was not of
it. She turned her thoughts to old familiar London, she
longed above all for her own bed, feeling as does a
wounded beast when it crawls home to its lair. She only
wanted to sleep undisturbed in her own bedroom.

But when she presented her return ticket at the Gare
du Nord she was told, furiously, loudly and unsympa-
thetically, that it had expired.

"See, Madame—May 29th. Today's the 30th, isn't it?
So—!" Tremendous shruggings.

Linda was paralysed with horror. Her 18s. 6d. was by
now down to 6s. 3d. hardly enough for a meal. She knew
nobody in Paris, she had absolutely no idea what she
ought to do, she was too tired and too hungry to think
clearly. She stood like a statue of despair. Her porter,
tired of waiting beside a statue of despair, deposited the
luggage at its feet and went grumbling off. Linda sank
onto her suitcase and began to cry; nothing so dreadful
had ever happened to her before. She cried bitterly,
she sould not stop. People passed to and fro as if weeping
ladies were the most ordinary phenomenon at the Gare
du Nord. "Fiends! fiends!" she sobbed. Why had she
not listened to her father, why had she ever come to this
bloody abroad? Who would help her? In London there
was a society, she knew, which looked after ladies
stranded at railway stations; here, more likely, there
would be one for shipping them off to South America.
At any moment now somebody, some genial-looking old

woman might come up and give her an injection, after which she would disappear for ever.

She became aware that somebody was standing beside her, not an old lady, but a short, stocky, very dark Frenchman in a black Homburg hat. He was laughing. Linda took no notice, but went on crying. The more she cried the more he laughed. Her tears were tears of rage now, no longer of self-pity.

At last she said, in a voice which was meant to be angrily impressive, but which squeaked and shook through her handkerchief:

"Leave me alone."

For answer he took her hand and pulled her to her feet.

"Hello, hello," he said.

"Will you please leave me alone?" said Linda, rather more doubtfully, here at least was a human being who showed signs of taking some interest in her. Then she thought of South America.

"I should like to point out that I am not," she said, "a white slave. I am the daughter of a very important British nobleman."

The Frenchman gave a great bellow of laughter.

"One does not," he said in the nearly perfect English of somebody who has spoken it from a child, "have to be Sherlock Holmes to guess that."

Linda was rather annoyed. An Englishwoman abroad may be proud of her nationality and her virtue without wishing them to jump so conclusively to the eye.

"French ladies," he went on, "covered with the outward signs of wealth never sit crying on their suitcases at the Gare du Nord in the very early morning, while white slaves always have protectors, and it is only too clear that you are unprotected just now."

This sounded all right, and Linda was mollified.

"Now," he said, "I invite you to luncheon with me, but first you must have a bath and rest and a cold compress on your face."

He picked up her luggage and walked to a taxi.

"Get in, please."

Linda got in. She was far from certain that this was not the road to Buenos Aires, but something made her do as he said. Her powers of resistance were at an end, and she really saw no alternative.

"Hotel Montalembert," he told the taxi man. "Rue du Bac. I apologize, madame, for not taking you to the Ritz, but I have a feeling for the Hotel Montalembert just now, that it will suit your mood this morning."

Linda sat upright in her corner of the taxi, looking, she hoped, very prim. As she could not think of anything pertinent to say she remained silent. Her companion hummed a little tune, and seemed vastly amused. When they arrived at the hotel, he took a room for her, told the liftman to show her to it, told the *concierge* to send her up a *café complet*, kissed her hand, and said:

"Good-bye for the present—I will fetch you a little before one o'clock and we will go out to luncheon."

Linda had her bath and breakfast and got into bed. When the telephone bell rang she was so sound asleep that it was a struggle to wake up.

"A gentleman is waiting for you, Madame."

"Say I will be right down," said Linda, but it took her quite half an hour to get ready.

CHAPTER 17

"AH! You keep me waiting," he said, kissing her hand, or at least making a gesture of raising her hand towards his lips and then dropping it rather suddenly. "That is a very good sign."

"Sign of what?" said Linda. He had a two-seater outside the hotel and she got into it. She was feeling more like herself again.

"Oh, of this and that," he said, letting in the clutch, "a good augury for our affair, that it will be happy and last long."

Linda became intensely stiff, English and embarrassed, and said, self-consciously:

"We are not having an affair."

"My name is Fabrice—may one ask yours?"

"Linda."

"Linda. What a pretty name! With me, it usually lasts five years."

He drove to a restaurant where they were shown, with some deference, to a table in a red plush corner. He ordered the luncheon and the wine in rapid French, the sort of French that Linda frankly could not follow, then, putting his hands on his knees, he turned to her and said:

"Now tell me, madame."

"Tell you what?"

"Well, but of course, the story. Who was it that left you to cry on that suitcase?"

"He didn't. I left him. It was my second husband and I have left him for ever because he has fallen in love with another woman—a welfare worker, not that you'd know what that is, because I'm sure they don't exist in France. It just makes it worse, that's all."

"What a very curious reason for leaving one's second husband. Surely with your experience of husbands you must have noticed that falling in love with other women is one of the things they do? However, it's an ill wind, and I don't complain. But why the suitcase? Why didn't you put yourself in the train and go back to Monsieur the important lord, your father?"

"That's what I was doing until they told me that my return ticket had expired. I only had 6s. 3d., and I don't know anybody in Paris, and I was awfully tired, so I cried."

"The second husband—why not borrow some money from him? Or had you left a note on his pillow—women never can resist these little essays in literature, and they do make it rather embarrassing to go back, I know."

"Well, anyhow he's in Perpignan, so I couldn't have."

"Ah, you come from Perpignan. And what were you doing there, in the name of heaven?"

"In the name of heaven we were trying to stop you frogs from teasing the poor Epagnards," said Linda with some spirit.

"E-spa-gnols! So we are teasing them, are we?"

"Not so badly now—terribly at the beginning."

"What were we supposed to do with them? We never invited them to come, you know."

"You drove them into camps in that cruel wind, and gave them no shelter for weeks. Hundreds died."

"It is quite a job to provide shelter, at a moment's

notice, for half a million people. We did what we could —we fed them—the fact is that most of them are still alive."

"Still herded in camps."

"My dear Linda, you could hardly expect us to turn them loose on the countryside with no money—what would be the result? Do use your common sense."

"You should mobilize them to fight in the war against Fascism that's coming any day now."

"Talk about what you know and you won't get so angry. We haven't enough equipment for our own soldiers in the war against Germany that's coming—not any day, but after the harvest, probably in August. Now go on telling me about your husbands. It's so very much more interesting."

"Only two. My first was a Conservative, and my second is a Communist."

"Just as I guessed, your first is rich, your second is poor. I could see you once had a rich husband, the dressing-case and the fur coat, though it is a hideous colour, and no doubt, as far as one could see, with it bundled over your arm, a hideous shape. Still, mink usually betokens a rich husband somewhere. Then this dreadful linen suit you are wearing has ready-made written all over it."

"You are rude, it's a very pretty suit."

"And last year's. Jackets are getting longer you will find. I'll get you some clothes—if you were well dressed you would be quite good-looking, though it's true your eyes are small. Blue, a good colour, but small."

"In England," said Linda, "I am considered a beauty."

"Well, you have points."

So this silly conversation went on and on, but it was only froth on the surface. Linda was feeling, what she had never so far felt for any man, an overwhelming physical attraction. It made her quite giddy, it terrified her. She could see that Fabrice was perfectly certain of the outcome, so was she perfectly certain, and that was what frightened her. How could one, how could she, Linda, with the horror and contempt she had always felt for casual affairs, allow herself to be picked up by any stray foreigner, and, having seen him only for an hour, long and long to be in bed with him? He was not even good-looking, he was exactly like dozens of other dark men in Homburgs that can be seen in the streets of any French town. But there was something about the way he looked at her which seemed to be depriving her of all balance. She was profoundly shocked, and, at the same time, intensely excited.

After luncheon they strolled out of the restaurant into brilliant sunshine.

"Come and see my flat," said Fabrice.

"I would rather see Paris," said Linda.

"Do you know Paris well?"

"I've never been here before in my life."

Fabrice was really startled.

"Never been here before?" he could not believe it. "What a pleasure for me, to show it all to you. There is so much to show, it will take weeks."

"Unfortunately," said Linda, "I leave for England to-morrow."

"Yes, of course. Then we must see it all this afternoon."

They drove slowly round a few streets and squares, and then went for a stroll in the Bois. Linda could not believe that she had only just arrived there, that this was still the very day which she had seen unfolding itself, so full of promise, through her mist of morning tears.

"How fortunate you are to live in such a town," she said to Fabrice. "It would be impossible to be very unhappy here."

"Not impossible," he said. "One's emotions are intensified in Paris—one can be more happy and also more unhappy here than in any other place. But it is always a positive source of joy to live here, and there is nobody so miserable as a Parisian in exile from his town. The rest of the world seems unbearably cold and bleak to us, hardly worth living in." He spoke with great feeling.

After tea, which they had out of doors in the Bois, he drove slowly back into Paris. He stopped the car outside an old house in the Rue Bonaparte, and said, again:

"Come and see my flat."

"No, no," said Linda. "The time has now come for me to point out that I am *une femme sérieuse.*"

Fabrice gave his great bellow of laughter.

"Oh," he said, shaking helplessly, "how funny you are. What a phrase, *femme sérieuse*, where did you find it? And if so serious, how do you explain the second husband?"

"Yes, I admit that I did wrong, very wrong indeed, and made a great mistake. But that is no reason for losing control, for sliding down the hill altogether, for being picked up by strange gentlemen at the Gare du Nord and then immediately going with them to see their flat. And please, if you will be so kind as to lend me some money, I want to catch the London train tomorrow morning."

"Of course, by all means," said Fabrice.

He thrust a roll of banknotes into her hand, and drove her to the Hotel Montalembert. He seemed quite unmoved by her speech, and announced he would come back at eight o'clock to take her out to dinner.

Linda's bedroom was full of roses, it reminded her of when Moira was born.

"Really," she thought with a giggle, "this is a very penny-novelettish seduction, how can I be taken in by it?"

But she was filled with a strange, wild, unfamiliar happiness, and knew that this was love. Twice in her life she had mistaken something else for it; it was like seeing somebody in the street who you think is a friend, you whistle and wave and run after him, and it is not only not the friend, but not even very like him. A few minutes later the real friend appears in view, and then you can't imagine how you ever mistook that other person for him. Linda was now looking upon the authentic face of love, and she knew it, but it frightened her. That it should come so casually, so much by a series of accidents, was frightening. She tried to remember how she had felt when she had first loved her two husbands. There must have been strong and impelling emotion; in both cases she had disrupted her own life, upset her parents and friends remorselessly, in order to marry them, but she could not recall it. Only she knew that never before, not even in dreams, and she was a great dreamer of love, had she felt anything remotely like this. She told herself, over and over again, that tomorrow she must go back to London, but she had no intention of going back, and she knew it.

Fabrice took her out to dinner and then to a night club, where they did not dance, but chatted endlessly. She told him about Uncle Matthew, Aunt Sadie and Louisa and Jassy and Matt, and he could not hear enough, and egged her on to excesses of exaggeration about her family and all their various idiosyncrasies.

"And Jassy—and Matt—go on, tell me."

And she recounted, for hours.

In the taxi on their way home she refused again to go back with him or to let him come into the hotel with her. He did not insist, he did not try to hold her hand, or touch her at all. He merely said:

"You are putting up a magnificent fight, madame, and I offer you my heartfelt felicitations."

Outside the hotel she gave him her hand to say good night. He took it in both of his and really kissed it.

"Till tomorrow," he said, and got back into the taxi.

"*Allô—allô.*"

"Hullo."

"Good morning. Are you having your breakfast?"

"Yes."

"I thought I heard a coffee-cup clattering. It is good?"

"It's so delicious that I have to keep stopping, for fear of finishing it too quickly. Are you having yours?"

"Had it. I must tell you that I like very long conversations in the morning, and I shall expect you to tell me some stories."

"Like Scheherazade?"

"Yes, just like. And you're not to get that note in your voice of 'now I'm going to ring off,' as English people always do."

"What English people do you know?"

"I know some. I was at school in England, and at Oxford."

"No! When?"

"1920."

"When I was nine. Fancy, perhaps I saw you in the street—we used to do all our shopping in Oxford."

"Elliston & Cavell?"

"Oh, yes, and Webber's."

There was a silence.

"Go on," he said.

"Go on, what?"

"I mean don't ring off. Go on telling."

"I shan't ring off. As a matter of fact I adore chatting. It's my favourite thing, and I expect you will want to ring off ages before I do."

They had a long and very silly conversation, and, at the end of it, Fabrice said:

"Now get up, and in an hour I will fetch you and we will go to Versailles."

At Versailles, which was an enchantment to Linda, she was reminded of a story she had once read about two English ladies who had seen the ghost of Marie Antoinette sitting in her garden at the Little Trianon. Fabrice found this intensely boring, and said so.

"Stories," he said, "are only of interest when they are true, or when you have made them up specially to amuse me. Ghost stories, made up by some dim old English virgins, are neither true nor interesting. So no more ghost stories, please, Madame."

"All right," said Linda, crossly. "I'm doing my best to please—you tell me a story."

"Yes, I will—and this story is true. My grandmother was very beautiful and had many lovers all her life, even when she was quite old. A short time before she died she was in Venice with my mother, her daughter, and one day, floating up some canal in their gondola, they saw a little palazzo of pink marble, very exquisite. They stopped the gondola to look at it, and my mother said: 'I don't believe anybody lives there, what about trying to see the inside?'

"So they rang the bell, and an old servant came and said that nobody had lived there for many, many years, and he would show it to them if they liked. So they went in and upstairs to the *salone*, which had three windows looking over the canal and was decorated with fifteenth-century plaster work, white on a pale blue background. It was a perfect room. My grandmother seemed strangely moved, and stood for a long time in silence. At last she said to my mother:

"'If, in the third drawer of that bureau there is a filigree box containing a small gold key on a black velvet ribbon, this house belongs to me.'

"And my mother looked, and there was, and it did. One of my grandmother's lovers had given it to her years and years before, when she was quite young, and she had forgotten all about it."

"Goodness," said Linda, "what fascinating lives you foreigners do lead."

"And it belongs to me now."

He put his hand up to Linda's forehead and stroked back a strand of hair which was loose:

"And I would take you there tomorrow if——"

"If what?"

"One must wait here now, you see, for the war."

"Oh, I keep forgetting the war," said Linda.

"Yes, let's forget it. How badly your hair is done, my dear."

"If you don't like my clothes and don't like my hair and think my eyes are so small, I don't know what you see in me."

"Nevertheless I admit there is something," said Fabrice.

Again they dined together.

Linda said: "Haven't you any other engagements?"

"Yes, of course. I have cancelled them."

"Who are your friends?"

"Society people. And yours?"

"When I was married to Tony, that is, my first husband, I used to go out in society, it was my life. In those days I loved it. But then Christian didn't approve of it, he stopped me going to parties and frightened away my friends, whom he considered frivolous and idiotic, and we saw nothing but serious people trying to put the world right. I used to laugh at them, and rather long for my other friends, but now I don't know. Since I was at Perpignan perhaps I have become more serious myself."

"Everybody is getting more serious, that's the way things are going. But, whatever one may be in politics, right, left, Fascist, Communist, society people are the only possible ones for friends. You see, they have made a fine art of personal relationships and of all that pertains to them—manners, clothes, beautiful houses, good food, everything that makes life agreeable. It would be silly not to take advantage of that. Friendship is something to be built up carefully, by people with leisure, it is an art, nature does not enter into it. You should never despise social life—that of high society—I mean, it can be a very satisfying one, entirely artificial of course, but absorbing. Apart from the life of the intellect and the contemplative religious life, which few people are qualified to enjoy, what else is there to distinguish man from the animals but his social life? And who understands it so well and who can make it so smooth and so amusing as society people? But one cannot have it at the same time as a love affair, one must be whole-hearted to enjoy it, so I have cancelled all my engagements."

"What a pity," said Linda, "because I'm going back to London tomorrow morning."

"Ah yes, I had forgotten. What a pity."

"*Allô—allô.*"

"Hullo."

"Were you asleep?"

"Yes, of course. What's the time?"

"About two. Shall I come round and see you?"

"Do you mean now?"

"Yes."

"I must say it would be very nice, but the only thing is, what would the night porter think?"

"My dear, how English you are. Well, I shall tell you— he will be in no doubt whatsoever."

"No, I suppose not."

"But I don't imagine he's under any illusion as it is. After all, I come here for you three times every day— you've seen nobody else, and French people are quite quick at noticing these things, you know."

"Yes—I see——"

"All right then—I'll be over directly."

The next day Fabrice installed her in a flat, he said it was more convenient. He said, "When I was young I liked to be very romantic and run all kinds of risks. I used to hide in wardrobes, be brought into the house in a trunk, disguise myself as a footman, and climb in at windows. How I used to climb! I remember once, half-way up a creeper there was a wasps' nest—oh the agony —I wore a Kestos *soutien-gorge* for a week afterwards.

But now I prefer to be comfortable, to follow a certain routine, and have my own key."

Indeed, Linda thought, nobody could be less romantic and more practical than Fabrice, no nonsense about him. A little nonsense, she thought, would have been rather nice.

It was a beautiful flat, large and sunny, and decorated in the most expensive kind of modern taste. It faced south and west over the Bois de Boulogne, and was on a level with the tree-tops. Tree-tops and sky made up the view. The enormous windows worked like windows of a motor-car, the whole of the glass disappearing into the wall. This was a great joy to Linda, who loved the open air and loved to sunbathe for hours with no clothes on, until she was hot and brown and sleepy and happy. Belonging to the flat, belonging, it was evident, to Fabrice, was a charming elderly housekeeper called Germaine. She was assisted by various other elderly women who came and went in a bewildering succession. She was obviously most efficient, she had all Linda's things out of her suitcase, ironed and folded away, in a moment, and then went off to the kitchen, where she began to prepare dinner. Linda could not help wondering how many other people Fabrice had kept in this flat; however, as she was unlikely to find out, and, indeed, had no wish to know, she put the thought from her. There was no trace of any former occupant, not so much as a scribbled telephone number or the mark of a lipstick anywhere to be seen; the flat might have been done up yesterday.

In her bath, before dinner, Linda thought rather wistfully of Aunt Sadie. She, Linda, was now a kept woman and an adulteress, and Aunt Sadie, she knew, wouldn't like that. She hadn't liked it when Linda had committed adultery with Christian, but he, at least, was English, and Linda had been properly introduced to him and knew his surname. Also, Christian had all along intended to marry her. But how much less would Aunt Sadie like her daughter to pick up an unknown, nameless foreigner and go off to live with him in luxury. It was a long step from lunching in Oxford to this, though Uncle Matthew would, no doubt, have considered it a step down the same road if he knew her situation, and he would disown her for ever, throw her out into the snow, shoot Fabrice, or take any other violent action which might occur to him. Then something would happen to make him laugh, and all would be well again. Aunt Sadie was a different matter. She would not say very much, but she would brood over it and take it to heart, and wonder if there had not been something wrong about her method of bringing up Linda which had led to this; Linda most profoundly hoped that she would never find out.

In the middle of this reverie the telephone bell rang. Germaine answered it, tapped on the bathroom door, and said:

"The duke will be a bit late, madame."

"All right—thank you," said Linda.

At dinner she said:

"Could one know your name?"

"Oh," said Fabrice. "Haven't you discovered that? What an extraordinary lack of curiosity. My name is Sauveterre. In short, *madame*, I am happy to tell you that I am a very rich duke, a most agreeable thing to be, even in these days."

"How lovely for you. And, while we are on the subject of your private life, are you married?"

"No."

"Why not?"

"My fiancée died."

"Oh, how sad—what was she like?"

"Very pretty."

"Prettier than me?"

"Much prettier. Very correct."

"More correct than me?"

"You—you are mad, madame, not correct at all. And she was kind—really kind."

For the first time since she knew him, Fabrice had become infinitely sentimental, and Linda was suddenly shaken by the pangs of a terrible jealousy, so terrible that she felt quite faint. If she had not already recognized the fact, she would have known now, for certain and always, that this was to be the great love of her life.

"Five years," she said, "is quite a long time when it's all in front of you."

But Fabrice was still thinking of the fiancée.

"She died much more than five years ago—fifteen years in the autumn. I always go and put late roses on her grave, those little tight roses with very dark green leaves that never open properly—they remind me of her. God, how sad it was."

"And what was her name?" said Linda.

"Louise. The only daughter of the last Duke de Rancé. I often go and see her mother, who is still alive, a remarkable old woman. She was brought up in England at the court of the Empress Eugénie, and Rancé married her in spite of that, for love. You can imagine how strange everybody found it."

A deep melancholy settled on them both. Linda saw too clearly that she could not hope to compete with a fiancée who was not only prettier and more correct than she was, but also dead. It seemed most unfair. Had she remained alive her prettiness would surely, after fifteen years of marriage, have faded away, her correctness have become a bore; dead, she was embalmed for ever in her youth, her beauty, and her *gentillesse*.

After dinner, however, Linda was restored to happiness. Being made love to by Fabrice was an intoxication, quite different from anything she had hitherto experienced.

("I was forced to the conclusion," she said, when telling me about this time, "that neither Tony nor Christian had an inkling of what we used to call the facts of life. But I suppose all Englishmen are hopeless as lovers."

"Not all," I said, "the trouble with most of them is that their minds are not on it, and it happens to require a very great deal of application. Alfred," I told her, "is wonderful."

"Oh, good," she said, but she sounded unconvinced I thought.)

They sat until late looking out of the open window. It was a hot evening, and, when the sun had gone, a green light lingered behind the black bunches of the trees until complete darkness fell.

"Do you always laugh when you make love?" said Fabrice.

"I hadn't thought about it, but I suppose I do. I generally laugh when I'm happy and cry when I'm not, I am a simple character, you know. Do you find it odd?"

"Very disconcerting at first, I must say."

"But why—don't most women laugh?"

"Indeed, they do not. More often they cry."

"How extraordinary—don't they enjoy it?"

"It has nothing to do with enjoyment. If they are young they call on their mothers, if they are religious they call on the Virgin to forgive them. But I have never known one who laughed except you. But I suppose it's to be expected; you're mad."

Linda was fascinated.

"What else do they do?"

"What they all do, except you, is to say; 'How you must despise me.'"

"But why should you despise them?"

"Oh, really, my dear, one does, that's all."

"Well, I call that most unfair. First you seduce them, then you despise them, poor things. What a monster you are."

"They like it. They like grovelling about and saying 'What have I done. Good heavens, Fabrice, what must you think of me? Oh, I am ashamed.' It's all part of the thing to them. But you, you seem unaware of your shame, you just roar with laughter. It is very strange. And not unpleasant, I must admit."

"Then what about the fiancée," said Linda, "didn't you despise her?"

"Of course not. She was a virtuous woman."

"Do you mean to say you never went to bed with her."

"Never. Never would such a thing have crossed my mind in a thousand thousand years."

"Goodness," said Linda. "In England we always do."

"My dear, the animal side of the English is well known. The English are a drunken and an incontinent race, it is well known."

"They don't know it. They think it's foreigners who are all those things."

"French women are the most virtuous in the world," said Fabrice, in the tones of exaggerated pride with which Frenchmen always talk about their women.

"Oh, dear," said Linda, sadly. "I was so virtuous once. I wonder what happened to me. I went wrong when I married my first husband, but how was I to know? I thought he was a god and that I should love him for ever. Then I went wrong again when I ran away with Christian, but I thought I loved him, and I did too, much more than Tony, but he never really loved me, and very soon I bored him, I wasn't serious enough, I suppose. Anyhow, if I hadn't done these things, I shouldn't have ended up on a suitcase at the Gare du Nord and I would never have met you, so, really, I'm glad. And in my next life, wherever I happen to be born, I must remember to fly to the boulevards as soon as I'm of marriageable age, and find a husband there."

"How nice," said Fabrice, "and, as a matter of fact, French marriages are generally very very happy you know. My father and mother had a cloudless life together, they loved each other so much that they hardly went out in society at all. My mother still lives in a sort of afterglow of happiness from it. What a good woman she is!"

"I must tell you," Linda went on, "that my mother and one of my aunts, one of my sisters and my cousin, are virtuous women, so virtue is not unknown in my family. And anyway, Fabrice, what about your grandmother?"

"Yes," said Fabrice, with a sigh. "I admit that she was a great sinner. But she was also a very great lady, and she died fully redeemed by the rites of the Church."

CHAPTER 18

THEIR life now began to acquire a routine. Fabrice dined with her every night in the flat—he never took her out to a restaurant again—and stayed with her until seven o'clock the following morning. "I hate sleeping alone," he said. At seven he would get up, dress, and go home, in time to be in his bed at eight o'clock, when his breakfast was brought in. He would have his breakfast, read the newspapers, and at nine, ring up Linda and talk nonsense for half an hour, as though he had not seen her for days.

"Go on," he would say, if she showed any signs of flagging. "Go on, tell me some more."

During the day she hardly ever saw him. He always lunched with his mother, who had the first-floor flat in the house where he lived on the ground floor. Sometimes he took Linda sightseeing in the afternoon, but generally he did not appear until about half-past seven, soon after which they dined.

Linda occupied her days buying clothes, which she paid for with great wads of banknotes given her by Fabrice.

"Might as well be hanged for a sheep as a lamb," she thought. "And as he despises me anyway it can't make very much difference."

Fabrice was delighted. He took an intense interest in her clothes, looked them up and down, made her parade round her drawing-room in them, forced her to take them

181

back to the shops for alterations which seemed to her quite unnecessary, but which proved in the end to have made all the difference. Linda had never before fully realized the superiority of French clothes to English. In London she had been considered exceptionally well dressed, when she was married to Tony; she now realized that never could she have had, by French standards, the smallest pretensions to *chic*. The things she had with her seemed to her so appallingly dowdy, so skimpy and miserable and without line, that she went to the Galeries Lafayette and bought herself a ready-made dress there before she dared to venture into the big houses. When she did finally emerge from them with a few clothes, Fabrice advised her to get a great many more. Her taste, he said, was not at all bad, for an Englishwoman, though he doubted whether she would really become *élégante* in the true sense of the word.

"Only by trial and error," he said, "can you find out your type, can you see where you are going. So keep on, my dear, work at it. You're not doing at all badly."

The weather now became hot and sultry, holiday, seaside weather. But this was 1939, and men's thoughts were not of relaxation, but of death, not of bathing-suits but of uniforms, not of dance music but of trumpets, while beaches for the next few years were to be battle and not pleasure grounds. Fabrice said every day how much he longed to take Linda to the Rivièra, to Venice and to his beautiful chateau in the Dauphiné. But he was a reservist, and would be called up any day now. Linda did not mind staying in Paris at all. She could sunbathe in her flat as much as she wanted to. She felt no particular apprehensions about the coming war, she was essentially a person who lived in the present.

"I couldn't sunbathe naked like this anywhere else," she said, "and it's the only holiday thing I enjoy. I don't like swimming, or tennis, or dancing, or gambling, so you see I'm just as well off here sunbathing and shopping, two perfect occupations for the day, and you, my darling love, at night. I should think I'm the happiest woman in the world."

One boiling hot afternoon in July she arrived home wearing a new and particularly ravishing straw hat. It was large and simple, with a wreath of flowers and two blue bows. Her right arm was full of roses and carnations, and in her left hand was a striped bandbox, containing another exquisite hat. She let herself in with her latchkey, and stumped, on the high cork soles of her sandals, to the drawing-room.

The green venetian blinds were down, and the room was full of warm shadows, two of which suddenly re-solved themselves into a thin man and a not so thin man—Davey and Lord Merlin.

"Good heavens," said Linda, and she flopped down onto a sofa, scattering the roses at her feet.

"Well," said Davey, "you do look pretty."

Linda felt really frightened, like a child caught out in some misdeed, like a child whose new toy is going to be taken away. She looked from one to the other. Lord Mer-lin was wearing black spectacles.

"Are you in disguise?" said Linda.

"No, what do you mean? Oh, the spectacles—I have to wear them when I go abroad, I have such kind eyes you see, beggars and things cluster round and annoy me."

He took them off and blinked.

"What have you come for?"

"You don't seem very pleased to see us," said Davey. "We came, actually, to see if you were all right. As it's only too obvious that you are, we may as well go away again."

"How did you find out? Do Mummy and Fa know?" she added, faintly.

"No, absolutely nothing. They think you're still with Christian. We haven't come in the spirit of two Victorian uncles, my dear Linda, if that's what you're thinking. I happened to see a man I know who had been to Perpignan, and he mentioned that Christian was living with Lavender Davis——"

"Oh good," said Linda.

"What? And that you had left six weeks ago. I went round to Cheyne Walk and there you obviously weren't, and then Mer and I got faintly worried to think of you wandering about the Continent, so ill suited (we thought, how wrong we were) to look after yourself, and at the same time madly curious to know your whereabouts and present circumstances, so we put in motion a little discreet detective work, which revealed your whereabouts—your circumstances are now as clear as daylight, and I, for one, feel most relieved."

"You gave us a fright," said Lord Merlin, crossly. "Another time, when you are putting on this Cléo de Mérode act, you might send a postcard. For one thing, it is a great pleasure to see you in the part, I wouldn't have missed it for worlds. I hadn't realized, Linda, that you were such a beautiful woman."

Davey was laughing quietly to himself.

"Oh, goodness, how funny it all is—so wonderfully old-fashioned. The shopping! The parcels! The flowers! So tremendously Victorian. People have been delivering cardboard boxes every five minutes since we arrived. What an interest you are in one's life, Linda dear. Have you told him he must give you up and marry a pure young girl yet?"

Linda said disarmingly: "Don't tease, Dave. I'm *so* happy you can't think."

"Yes, you look happy I must say. Oh, this flat is such a joke."

"I was just thinking," said Lord Merlin, "that, however much taste may change, it always follows a stereotyped plan. Frenchmen used to keep their mistresses in *appartements*, each exactly like the other, in which the dominant note, you might say, was lace and velvet. The walls, the bed, the dressing-table, the very bath itself were hung with lace, and everything else was velvet. Nowadays for lace you substitute glass, and everything else is satin. I bet you've got a glass bed, Linda?"

"Yes—but——"

"And a glass dressing-table, and bathroom, and I wouldn't be surprised if your bath were made of glass, with goldfish swimming about in the sides of it. Goldfish are a prevailing motif all down the ages."

"You've looked," said Linda sulkily. "Very clever."

"Oh, what heaven," said Davey. "So it's true! He hasn't looked, I swear, but you see it's not beyond the bounds of human ingenuity to guess."

"But there are some things here," said Lord Merlin, "which do raise the level, all the same. A Gauguin, those two Matisses (chintzy, but accomplished) and this Savonnerie carpet. Your protector must be very rich."

"He is," said Linda.

"Then, Linda dear, could one ask for a cup of tea?"

She rang the bell, and soon Davey was falling upon

éclairs and *mille feuilles* with all the abandon of a school-boy.

"I shall pay for this," he said, with a devil-may-care smile, "but never mind, one's not in Paris every day."

Lord Merlin wandered round with his tea-cup. He picked up a book which Fabrice had given Linda the day before, of romantic nineteenth-century poetry.

"Is this what you're reading now?" he said. " *'Dieu, que le son du cor est triste au fond des bois.'* I had a friend, when I lived in Paris, who had a boa constrictor as a pet, and this boa constrictor got itself inside a French horn. My friend rang me up in a fearful state, saying: *'Dieu, que le son du boa est triste au fond du cor.'* I've never forgotten it."

"What time does your lover generally arrive?" said Davey, taking out his watch.

"Not till about seven. Do stay and see him, he's such a terrific Hon."

"No, thank you, not for the world."

"Who is he?" said Lord Merlin.

"He's called the Duke of Sauveterre."

A look of great surprise, mingled with horrified amusement, passed between Davey and Lord Merlin.

"Fabrice de Sauveterre?"

"Yes. Do you know him?"

"Darling Linda, one always forgets, under that look of great sophistication, what a little provincial you really are. Of course we know him, and all about him, and, what's more, so does everyone except you."

"Well, don't you think he's a terrific Hon?"

"Fabrice," said Lord Merlin with emphasis, "is undoubtedly one of the wickedest men in Europe, as far as women are concerned. But I must admit that he's an extremely agreeable companion."

"Do you remember in Venice," said Davey, "one used to see him at work in that gondola, one after another, bowling them over like rabbits, poor dears?"

"Please remember," said Linda, "that you are eating his tea at this moment."

"Yes, indeed, and so delicious. Another *éclair*, please, Linda. That summer," he went on, "when he made off with Ciano's girl friend, what a fuss there was, I never shall forget, and then, a week later, he dumped her in Cannes and went to Salzburg with Martha Birmingham, and poor old Claud shot at him four times, and always missed him."

"Fabrice has a charmed life," said Lord Merlin. "I suppose he has been shot at more than anybody, and, as far as I know, he's never had a scratch."

Linda was unmoved by these revelations, which had been forestalled by Fabrice himself. Anyhow, no woman really minds hearing of the past affairs of her lover, it is the future alone that has the power to terrify.

"Come on, Mer," said Davey. "Time the little lady got herself into a *négligée*. Goodness, what a scene there'll be when he smells Mer's cigar, there'll be a *crime passionel*, I shouldn't wonder. Good-bye, Linda darling, we're off to dine with our intellectual friends, you know, shall you be lunching with us at the Ritz tomorrow? About one, then. Good-bye—give our love to Fabrice."

When Fabrice came in he sniffed about, and asked whose cigar. Linda explained.

"They say they know you."

"Surely—Merlin, such a nice chap, and poor Warbeck,

always so ill. I knew them in Venice. What did they think of all this?"

"Well, they roared at the flat."

"Yes, I can imagine. It is quite unsuitable for you, this flat, but it's convenient, and with the war coming——"

"Oh, but I love it, I wouldn't like anything else half so much. Wasn't it clever of them, though, to find me?"

"Do you mean to say you never told anybody where you were?"

"I really didn't think of it—the days go by, you know —one simply doesn't remember these things."

"And it was six weeks before they thought of looking for you? As a family you seem to me strangely disorganized."

Linda suddenly threw herself into his arms, and said, with great passion:

"Never, never let me go back to them."

"My darling—but you love them. Mummy and Fa, Matt and Robin and Victoria and Fanny. What is all this?"

"I never want to leave you again as long as I live."

"Aha! But you know you will probably have to, soon. The war is going to begin, you know."

"Why can't I stay here? I could work—I could become a nurse—well, perhaps not a nurse, actually, but something."

"If you promise to do what I tell you, you may stay here for a time. At the beginning we shall sit and look at the Germans across the Maginot Line, then I shall be a great deal in Paris, between Paris and the front, but mostly here. At that time I shall want you here. Then somebody, we or the Germans, but I am very much afraid the Germans, will pour across the line, and a war of movement will begin. I shall have notice of that stage, and what you must promise me is that the very minute I tell you to leave for London you will leave, even if you can see no reason for doing so. I should be hampered beyond words in my duties if you were still here. So will you solemnly promise, now?"

"All right," said Linda. "Solemnly. I don't believe anything so dreadful could happen to me, but I promise to do as you say. Now will you promise that you will come to London as soon as it's all over and find me again? Promise?"

"Yes," said Fabrice. "I will do that."

Luncheon with Davey and Lord Merlin was a gloomy meal. Preoccupation reigned. The two men had stayed up late and merrily with their literary friends, and showed every sign of having done so. Davey was beginning to be aware of the cruel pangs of dyspepsia, Lord Merlin was suffering badly from an ordinary straightforward hangover, and, when he removed his spectacles, his eyes were seen to be not kind at all. But Linda was far the most wretched of the three, she was, in fact, perfectly distracted by having overheard two French ladies in the foyer talking about Fabrice. She had arrived, as, from old habits of punctuality drummed into her by Uncle Matthew she always did, rather early. Fabrice had never taken her to the Ritz, she thought it delightful, she knew she was looking quite as pretty, and nearly as well dressed, as anybody there, and settled herself happily to await the others. Suddenly she heard, with that pang which the heart receives when the loved one's name is mentioned by strangers:

"And have you seen Fabrice at all?"

"Well, I have, because I quite often see him at Mme. de Sauveterre's, but he never goes out anywhere, as you know."

"Then what about Jacqueline?"

"Still in England. He is utterly lost without her, poor Fabrice, he is like a dog looking for its master. He sits sadly at home, never goes to parties, never goes to the club, sees nobody. His mother is really worried about him."

"Who would ever have expected Fabrice to be so faithful. How long is it?"

"Five years, I believe. A wonderfully happy *ménage*."

"Surely Jacqueline will come back soon."

"Not until the old aunt has died. It seems she changes her will incessantly, and Jacqueline feels she must be there all the time—after all, she has her husband and children to consider."

"Rather hard on Fabrice?"

"What else could one expect? His mother says he rings her up every morning and talks for an hour——"

It was at this point that Davey and Lord Merlin, looking tired and cross, arrived, and took Linda off to luncheon with them. She was longing to stay and hear more of this torturing conversation, but, eschewing cocktails with a shudder, they hurried her off to the dining-room, where they were only fairly nice to her, and frankly disagreeable to each other.

She thought the meal would never come to an end, and, when at last it did, she threw herself into a taxi and drove to Fabrice's house. She must find out about Jacqueline, she must know his intentions. When Jacqueline returned would that be the moment for her, Linda, to leave as she had promised? War of movement indeed!

The servant said that M. le Duc had just gone out with Madame la Duchesse, but that he would be back in about an hour. Linda said she would wait, and he showed her into Fabrice's sitting-room. She took off her hat, and wandered restlessly about. She had been here several times before, with Fabrice, and it had seemed, after her brilliantly sunny flat, a little dismal. Now that she was alone in it she began to be aware of the extreme beauty of the room, a grave and solemn beauty which penetrated her. It was very high, rectangular in shape, with grey boiseries and cherry-coloured brocade curtains. It looked into a courtyard and never could get a ray of sunshine, that was not the plan. This was a civilized interior, it had nothing to do with out of doors. Every object in it was perfect. The furniture had the severe lines and excellent proportions of 1780, there was a portrait by Lancret of a lady with a parrot on her wrist, a bust of the same lady by Bouchardon, a carpet like the one in Linda's flat, but larger and grander, with a huge coat of arms in the middle. A high carved bookcase contained nothing but French classics bound in contemporary morocco, with the Sauveterre crest, and, open on a map table, lay a copy of Redouté's roses.

Linda began to feel much more calm, but, at the same time, very sad. She saw that this room indicated a side of Fabrice's character which she had hardly been allowed to apprehend, and which had its roots in old civilized French grandeur. It was the essential Fabrice, something in which she could never have a share—she would always be outside in her sunny modern flat, kept away from all this, kept rigidly away even if their liaison were to go on for ever. The origins of the Radlett family were lost in the mists of antiquity, but the origins of Fabrice's family were not lost at all, there they were, each generation clutching at the next. The English, she thought, throw off their ancestors. It is the great strength of our aristocracy, but Fabrice has his round his neck, and he will never get away from them.

She began to realize that here were her competitors, her enemies, and that Jacqueline was nothing in comparison. Here, and in the grave of Louise. To come here and make a scene about a rival mistress would be utterly meaningless, she would be one unreality complaining about another. Fabrice would be annoyed, as men always are annoyed on these occasions, and she would get no satisfaction. She could hear his voice, dry and sarcastic:

"Ah! You amaze me, madame."

Better go, better ignore the whole affair. Her only hope was to keep things on their present footing, to keep the happiness which she was enjoying day by day, hour by hour, and not to think about the future at all. It held nothing for her, leave it alone. Besides, everybody's future was in jeopardy now the war was coming, this war which she always forgot about.

She was reminded of it, however, when, that evening, Fabrice appeared in uniform.

"Another month I should think," he said. "As soon as they have got the harvest in."

"If it depended on the English," said Linda, "they would wait until after the Christmas shopping. Oh, Fabrice, it won't last very long, will it?"

"It will be very disagreeable while it does last," said Fabrice. "Did you come to my flat today?"

"Yes, after lunching with those two old cross-patches I suddenly felt I wanted to see you very much."

"How nice!" He looked at her quizzically, as though something had occurred to him, "But why didn't you wait?"

"Your ancestors frightened me off."

"Oh, they did? But you have ancestors yourself I believe, *madame*?"

"Yes, but they don't hang about in the same way as yours do."

"You should have waited," said Fabrice, "it is always a very great pleasure to see you, both for me and for my ancestors. It cheers us all up."

Germaine now came into the room with huge armfuls of flowers and a note from Lord Merlin, saying:

"Here are some coals for Newcastle. We are tottering home by the ferry-boat. Do you think I shall get Davey back alive? I enclose something which might, one day, be useful."

It was a note for 20,000 francs.

"I must say," said Linda, "considering what cruel eyes he has, he does think of everything."

She felt sentimental after the occurrences of the day.

"Tell me, Fabrice," she said, "what did you think the first moment you ever saw me?"

"If you really want to know, I thought: 'Why, she looks like the little Bosquet girl.'"

"Who is that?"

"There are two Bosquet sisters, the elder, who is a beauty, and a little one who looks like you."

"Thanks so much," said Linda, "I would prefer to look like the other one."

Fabrice laughed. "Then, I said to myself, how funny, how old-fashioned all this seems——"

When the war, which had for so long been pending, did actually break out some six weeks later, Linda was strangely unmoved by the fact. She was enveloped in the present, in her own detached and futureless life, which, anyhow, seemed so precarious, so much from one hour to another: exterior events hardly impinged on her consciousness. When she thought about the war it seemed to her almost a relief that it had actually begun, in so far as a beginning is the first step towards an end. That it had only begun in name and not in fact did not occur to her. Of course, had Fabrice been taken away by it her attitude would have been very different, but his job, an intelligence one, kept him mostly in Paris, and, indeed, she now saw rather more of him than formerly, as he moved into her flat, shutting up his own and sending his mother to the country. He would appear and disappear at all sorts of odd moments of the night and day, and, as the sight of him was a constant joy to Linda, as she could imagine no greater happiness than she always felt when the empty space in front of her eyes became filled by his form, these sudden apparitions kept her in a state of happy suspense and their relationship at fever point.

Since Davey's visit Linda had been getting letters from her family. He had given Aunt Sadie her address and told her that Linda was doing war work in Paris, providing comforts for the French army, he said vaguely, and with some degree of truth. Aunt Sadie was pleased about this, she thought it very good of Linda to work so hard (all night sometimes, Davey said), and was glad to hear that she earned her keep. Voluntary work was often unsatisfactory and expensive. Uncle Matthew thought it a pity to work for foreigners, and deplored the fact that his children were so fond of crossing oceans, but he also was very

much in favour of war work. He was himself utterly disgusted that the War Office were not able to offer him the
opportunity of repeating his exploit with the entrenching
tool, or, indeed, any job at all, and he went about like a
bear with a sore head, full of unsatisfied desire to fight for
his King and country.

I wrote to Linda and told her about Christian, who was
back in London, had left the Communist party and had
joined up. Lavender had also returned: she was now an
A.T.S.

Christian did not show the slightest curiosity about
what had happened to Linda, he did not seem to want to
divorce her or to marry Lavender, he had thrown himself
heart and soul into army life and thought of nothing but
the war.

Before leaving Perpignan he had extricated Matt, who,
after a good deal of persuasion, had consented to leave his
Spanish comrades in order to join the battle against Fascism on another front. He went into Uncle Matthew's old
regiment, and was said to bore his brother officers in the
mess very much by arguing that they were training the
men all wrong, and that, during the battle of the Ebro,
things had been done thus and thus. In the end his colonel,
who was rather brighter in the head than some of the
others hit upon the obvious reply, which was, "Well anyway, your side lost!" This shut Matt up on tactics, but got
him going on statistics—"30,000 Germans and Italians,
500 German 'planes," and so forth—which were almost
equally dull and boring.

Linda heard no more about Jacqueline, and the wretchedness into which she had been thrown by those few
chance words overheard at the Ritz was gradually forgotten. She reminded herself that nobody ever really knew

the state of a man's heart, not even, perhaps specially not, his mother, and that in love it is actions that count. Fabrice had no time now for two women, he spent every spare moment with her and that in itself reassured her. Besides, just as her marriages with Tony and Christian had been necessary in order to lead up to her meeting with Fabrice, so this affair had led up to his meeting with her: undoubtedly he must have been seeing Jacqueline off at the Gare du Nord when he found Linda crying on her suitcase. Putting herself in Jacqueline's shoes, she realized how much preferable it was to be in her own: in any case it was not Jacqueline who was her dangerous rival, but that dim, virtuous figure from the past, Louise. Whenever Fabrice showed signs of becoming a little less practical, a little more nonsensical and romantic, it was of his fiancée that he would speak, dwelling with a gentle sadness upon her beauty, her noble birth, her vast estates and her religious mania. Linda once suggested that, had the fiancée lived to become a wife, she might not have been a very happy one.

"All that climbing," she said, "in at other people's bedroom windows, might it not have upset her?"

Fabrice looked intensely shocked and reproachful and said that there never would have been any climbing, that, where marriage was concerned, he had the very highest ideals, and that his whole life would have been devoted to making Louise happy. Linda felt herself rebuked, but was not entirely convinced.

All this time Linda watched the tree-tops from her window. They had changed, since she had been in the flat, from bright green against a bright blue sky, to dark green against a lavender sky, to yellow against a cerulean sky, until now they were black skeletons against a sky of moleskin, and it was Christmas Day. The windows could no longer be opened until they disappeared, but, whenever the sun did come out, it shone into her rooms, and the flat was always as warm as toast. On this Christmas morning Fabrice arrived, quite unexpectedly, before she was up, his arms full of parcels, and soon the floor of her bedroom was covered with waves of tissue paper through which, like wrecks and monsters half submerged beneath a shallow sea, appeared fur coats, hats, real mimosa, artificial flowers, feathers, scent, gloves, stockings, underclothes and a bulldog puppy.

Linda had spent Lord Merlin's 20,000 francs on a tiny Renoir for Fabrice: six inches of seascape, a little patch of brilliant blue, which she thought would look just right in his room in the Rue Bonaparte. Fabrice was the most difficult person to buy presents for, he possessed a larger assortment of jewels, knick-knacks and rare objects of all kinds than anybody she had ever known. He was delighted with the Renoir, nothing, he said, could have pleased him more, and Linda felt that he really meant it.

"Oh, such a cold day," he said. "I've just been to church."

"Fabrice, how can you go to church when there's me?"

"Well, why not?"

"You're a Roman Catholic, aren't you?"

"Of course I am. What do you suppose? Do you think I look like a Calvinist?"

"But then aren't you living in mortal sin? So what about when you confess?"

"One doesn't go into detail," said Fabrice, carelessly, "and, in any case, these little sins of the body are quite unimportant."

Linda would have liked to think that she was more in

Fabrice's life than a little sin of the body, but she was used to coming up against these closed doors in her relationship with him, and had learnt to be philosophical about it and thankful for the happiness that she did receive.

"In England," she said, "people are always renouncing each other on account of being Roman Catholics. It's sometimes very sad for them. A lot of English books are about this, you know."

"The English are madmen, I have always said it. You almost sound as if you want to be given up. What has happened since Saturday? Not tired of your war work, I hope?"

"No, no, Fabrice. I just wondered, that's all."

"But you look so sad, *ma chérie*, what is it?"

"I was thinking of Christmas Day at home. I always feel sentimental at Christmas."

"If what I said might happen does happen and I have to send you back to England, shall you go home to your father?"

"Oh, no," said Linda, "anyway, it won't happen. All the English papers say we are killing Germany with our blockade."

"Blockade," said Fabrice, impatiently. "What nonsense! Let me tell you, *madame*, they don't give a damn about your blockade. So where would you go?"

"To my own house in Chelsea, and wait for you to come."

"It might be months, or years."

"I shall wait," she said.

The skeleton tree-tops began to fill out, they acquired a pinkish tinge, which gradually changed to golden-green. The sky was often blue, and, on some days, Linda could once more open her windows and lie naked in the sun, whose rays by now had a certain strength. She always loved the spring, she loved the sudden changes of temperature, the dips backward into winter and forward into summer, and, this year, living in beautiful Paris, her perceptions heightened by great emotion, she was profoundly affected by it. There was now a curious feeling in the air, very different from and much more nervous than that which had been current before Christmas, and the town was full of rumours. Linda often thought of the expression "*fin de siècle*." There was a certain analogy, she thought, between the state of mind which it denoted and that prevailing now, only now it was more like "*fin de vie*." It was as though everybody around her, and she herself, were living out the last few days of their lives, but this curious feeling did not disturb her, she was possessed by a calm and happy fatalism. She occupied the hours of waiting between Fabrice's visits by lying in the sun, when there was any, and playing with her puppy. On Fabrice's advice she even began to order some new clothes for the summer. He seemed to regard the acquisition of clothes as one of the chief duties of woman, to be pursued through war and revolution, through sickness, and up to death. It was as one who might say, "whatever happens the fields must be tilled, the cattle tended, life must go on." He was so essentially urban that to him the slow roll of the seasons was marked by the spring tailored suits, the summer prints, the autumn *ensembles*, and the winter furs of his mistress.

On a beautiful windy blue and white day in April the blow fell. Fabrice, whom Linda had not seen for nearly a week, arrived from the front looking grave and worried, and told her that she must go back to England at once.

"I've got a place for you in the aeroplane," he said, "for this afternoon. You must pack a small suitcase, and the rest of your things must go after you by train. Germaine will see to them. I have to go to the Ministère de la Guerre, I'll be back as soon as possible, and anyhow in time to take you to Le Bourget. Come on," he added, "just time for a little war work." He was in his most practical and least romantic mood.

When he returned he looked more preoccupied than ever. Linda was waiting for him, her box was packed, she was wearing the blue suit in which he had first seen her, and had her old mink coat over her arm.

"Well," said Fabrice, who always at once noticed what she had on, "what is this? A fancy-dress party?"

"Fabrice, you must understand that I can't take away the things you have given me. I loved having them while I was here, and while they gave you pleasure seeing me in them, but, after all, I have some pride. After all, I wasn't brought up in a bordello."

"*Ma chère*, try not to be so middle-class, it doesn't suit you at all. There's no time for you to change—wait, though——" He went into her bedroom, and came out again with a long sable coat, one of his Christmas presents. He took her mink coat, rolled it up, threw it into the waste-paper basket, and put the other over her arm in its place.

"Germaine will send your things after you," he said. "Come now, we must go."

Linda said good-bye to Germaine, picked up the bull-dog puppy, and followed Fabrice into the lift, out into the street. She did not fully understand that she was leaving that happy life behind her for ever.

CHAPTER 19

A T FIRST, back in Cheyne Walk, she still did not understand. The world was grey and cold certainly, the sun had gone behind a cloud, but only for a time: it would come out again, she would soon once more be enveloped in that heat and light which had left her in so warm a glow, there was still much blue in the sky, this little cloud would pass. Then, as sometimes happens, the cloud, which had seemed at first such a little one, grew and grew, until it became a thick grey blanket smothering the horizon. The bad news began, the terrible days, the unforgettable weeks. A great horror of steel was rolling over France, was rolling towards England, swallowing on its way the puny beings who tried to stop it, swallowing Fabrice, Germaine, the flat, and the past months of Linda's life, swallowing Alfred, Bob, Matt, and little Robin, coming to swallow us all. London people cried openly in the buses, in the streets, for the English army which was lost.

Then, suddenly one day, the English army turned up again. There was a feeling of such intense relief, it was as if the war were over and won. Alfred and Bob and Matt and little Robin all reappeared, and, as a lot of French soldiers also arrived, Linda had a wild hope that Fabrice might be with them. She sat all day by the telephone, and when it rang and it was not Fabrice she was furious with the unlucky telephoner—I know, because it happened to me. She was so furious that I dropped the receiver and went straight round to Cheyne Walk.

I found her unpacking a huge trunk, which had just arrived from France. I had never seen her looking so beautiful. It made me gasp, and I remembered how Davey had said, when he got back from Paris, that at last Linda was fulfilling the promise of her childhood, and had become a beauty.

"How do you imagine this got here?" she said, between tears and laughter. "What an extraordinary war. The Southern Railway people brought it just now and I signed for it, all as though nothing peculiar were happening—I don't understand a word of it. What are you doing in London, darling?"

She seemed unaware of the fact that half an hour ago she had spoken to me, and indeed bitten my head off, on the telephone.

"I'm with Alfred. He's got to get a lot of new equipment and see all sorts of people. I believe he's going abroad again very soon."

"Awfully good of him," said Linda, "when he needn't have joined up at all, I imagine. What does he say about Dunkirk?"

"He says it was like something out of the *Boy's Own*—he seems to have had a most fascinating time."

"They all did, the boys were here yesterday and you never heard anything like their stories. Of course they never quite realized how desperate it all was until they got to the coast. Oh, isn't it wonderful to have them back? If only—if only one knew what had happened to one's French buddies——" She looked at me under her eyelashes, and I thought she was going to tell me about her life, but, if so, she changed her mind and went on unpacking.

"I shall have to put these winter things back in their boxes really," she said. "I simply haven't any cupboards that will hold them all, but it's something to do, and I like to see them again."

"You should shake them," I said, "and put them in the sun. They may be damp."

"Darling, you are wonderful, you always know."

"Where did you get that puppy?" I said enviously. I had wanted a bulldog for years, but Alfred never would let me have one because of the snoring.

"Brought him back with me. He's the nicest puppy I ever had, so anxious to oblige, you can't think."

"What about quarantine then?"

"Under my coat," said Linda, laconically. "You should have heard him grunting and snuffling, it shook the whole place, I was terrified, but he was so good. He never budged. And talking of puppies, those ghastly Kroesigs are sending Moira to America, isn't it typical of them? I've made a great thing with Tony about seeing her before she goes, after all I am her mother."

"That's what I can't ever understand about you, Linda."

"What?"

"How you could have been so dreadful to Moira."

"Dull," said Linda. "Uninteresting."

"I know, but the point is that children are like puppies, and if you never see puppies, if you give them to the groom or the gamekeeper to bring up, look how dull and uninteresting they always are. Children are just the same

—you must give them much more than their life if they are to be any good. Poor Little Moira—all you gave her was that awful name."

"Oh, Fanny, I do know. To tell you the truth I believe it was always in the back of my mind that, sooner or later, I should have to run away from Tony, and I didn't want to get too fond of Moira, or make her too fond of me. She might have become an anchor, and I simply didn't dare let myself be anchored to the Kroesigs."

"Poor Linda."

"Oh, don't pity me. I've had eleven months of perfect and unalloyed happiness, very few people can say that, in the course of long long lives, I imagine."

I imagined so too. Alfred and I are happy, as happy as married people can be. We are in love, we are intellectually and physically suited in every possible way, we rejoice in each other's company, we have no money troubles and three delightful children. And yet, when I consider my life, day by day, hour by hour, it seems to be composed of a series of pinpricks. Nannies, cooks, the endless drudgery of housekeeping, the nerve-racking noise and boring repetitive conversation of small children (boring in the sense that it bores into one's very brain), their absolute incapacity to amuse themselves, their sudden and terrifying illnesses, Alfred's not infrequent bouts of moodiness, his invariable complaints at meals about the pudding, the way he will always use my tooth-paste and will always squeeze the tube in the middle. These are the components of marriage, the wholemeal bread of life, rough, ordinary, but sustaining; Linda had been feeding upon honey-dew, and that is an incomparable diet.

The old woman who had opened the door to me came

in and said was that everything, because, if so, she would be going home.

"Everything," said Linda. "Mrs. Hunt," she said to me, when she had gone. "A terrific Hon—she comes daily."

"Why don't you go to Alconleigh?" I said, "or to Shenley? Aunt Emily and Davey would love to have you, and I'm going there with the children as soon as Alfred is off again."

"I'd like to come for a visit some time, when I know a little more what is happening, but at the moment I must stop here. Give them my love though. I've got such masses to tell you, Fanny, what we really need is hours and hours in the Hons' cupboard."

After a good deal of hesitation Tony Kroesig and his wife, Pixie, allowed Moira to go and see her mother before leaving England. She arrived at Cheyne Walk in Tony's car, still driven by a chauffeur in uniform not the King's. She was a plain, stodgy, shy little girl, with no echo of the Radletts about her; not to put too fine a point on it she was a real little Gretchen.

"What a sweet puppy," she said, awkwardly, when Linda had kissed her. She was clearly very much embarrassed.

"What's his name?"

"Plon-plon."

"Oh. Is that a French name?"

"Yes, it is. He's a French dog, you see."

"Daddy says the French are terrible."

"I expect he does."

"He says they have let us down, and what can we expect if we have anything to do with such people."

"Yes, he would."

"Daddy thinks we ought to fight with the Germans and not against them."

"M'm. But Daddy doesn't seem to be fighting very much with anybody, or against anybody, or at all, as far as I can see. Now, Moira, before you go I have got two things for you, one is a present and the other is a little talk. The talk is very dull, so we'll get that over first, shall we?"

"Yes," said Moira, apathetically. She lugged the puppy onto the sofa beside her.

"I want you to know," said Linda, "and to remember, please, Moira (stop playing with the puppy a minute and listen carefully to what I am saying) that I don't at all approve of you running away like this, I think it most dreadfully wrong. When you have a country which has given you as much as England has given all of us, you ought to stick to it, and not go wandering off as soon as it looks like being in trouble."

"But it's not my fault," said Moira, her forehead puckering. "I'm only a child and Pixie is taking me. I have to do what I'm told, don't I?"

"Yes, of course, I know that's true. But you'd much rather stay, wouldn't you?" said Linda, hopefully.

"Oh no, I don't think so. There might be air-raids."

At this Linda gave up. Children might or might not enjoy air-raids actually in progress, but a child who was not thrilled by the idea of them was incomprehensible to her, and she could not imagine having conceived such a being. Useless to waste any more time and breath on this unnatural little girl. She sighed and said:

"Now wait a moment and I'll get your present."

She had in her pocket, in a velvet box, a coral hand

holding a diamond arrow, which Fabrice had given her, but she could not bear to waste anything so pretty on this besotted little coward. She went to her bedroom and found a sports wristwatch, one of her wedding presents when she had married Tony and which she had never worn, and gave this to Moira, who seemed quite pleased by it, and left the house as politely and unenthusiastically as she had arrived.

Linda rang me up at Shenley and told me about this interview.

"I'm in such a temper," she said, "I must talk to somebody. To think I ruined nine months of my life in order to have that. What do your children think about air-raids, Fanny?"

"I must say they simply long for them, and I am sorry to say they also long for the Germans to arrive. They spend the whole day making booby-traps for them in the orchard."

"Well that's a relief anyhow—I thought perhaps it was the generation. Actually of course, it's not Moira's fault, it's all that bloody Pixie—I can see the form only too clearly, can't you? Pixie is frightened to death and she has found out that going to America is like the children's concert, you can only make it if you have a child in tow. So she's using Moira—well, it does serve one right for doing wrong." Linda was evidently very much put out. "And I hear Tony is going too, some Parliamentary mission or something. All I can say is what a set."

All through those terrible months of May, June and July, Linda waited for a sign from Fabrice, but no sign came. She did not doubt that he was still alive, it was not in Linda's nature to imagine that anyone might be dead. She knew that thousands of Frenchmen were in German hands, but felt certain that, had Fabrice been taken prisoner (a thing which she did not at all approve of, incidentally, taking the old-fashioned view that, unless in exceptional circumstances, it is a disgrace), he would undoubtedly manage to escape. She would hear from him before long, and, meanwhile, there was nothing to be done, she must simply wait. All the same, as the days went by with no news, and as all the news there was from France was bad, she did become exceedingly restless. She was really more concerned with his attitude than with his safety—his attitude towards events and his attitude towards her. She felt sure that he would never be associated with the armistice, she felt sure that he would want to communicate with her, but she had no proof, and, in moments of great loneliness and depression, she allowed herself to lose faith. She realized how little she really knew of Fabrice, he had seldom talked seriously to her, their relationship having been primarily physical while their conversations and chats had all been based on jokes.

They had laughed and made love and laughed again, and the months had slipped by with no time for anything but laughter and love. Enough to satisfy her, but what about him? Now that life had become so serious, and, for a Frenchman, so tragic, would he not have forgotten that meal of whipped cream as something so utterly unimportant that it might never have existed? She began to think, more and more, to tell herself over and over again, to force herself to realize, that it was probably all finished, that Fabrice might never be anything for her now but a memory.

At the same time the few people she saw never failed when talking, everybody talked then, about France to emphasize that the French "one knew," the families who were "*bien*," were all behaving very badly, convinced Pétainists. Fabrice was not one of them, she thought, she felt, but she wished she knew, she longed for evidence.

In fact, she alternated between hope and despair, but as the months went by without a word, a word that she was sure he could have sent if he had really wanted to, despair began to prevail.

Then, on a sunny Sunday morning in August, very early, her telephone bell rang. She woke up with a start, aware that it had been ringing already for several moments, and she knew with absolute certainty that this was Fabrice.

"Are you Flaxman 2815?"

"Yes."

"I've got a call for you. You're through."

"*Allô—allô?*"

"Fabrice?"

"*Oui.*"

"Oh! Fabrice—I've been waiting for you for so long."

"How nice! Then I may come right away?"

"Oh, wait—yes, you can come at once, but don't go for a minute, go on talking, I want to hear the sound of your voice."

"No, no, I have a taxi outside, I shall be with you in five minutes. There's too much one can't do on the telephone, my dear, so look——" Click.

She lay back, and all was light and warmth. Life, she thought, is sometimes sad and often dull, but there are currants in the cake and here is one of them. The early morning sun shone past her window onto the river, her ceiling danced with water-reflections. The Sunday silence was broken by two swans winging slowly upstream, and then by the chugging of a little barge, while she waited for that other sound, a sound more intimately connected with the urban love affair than any except the telephone bell, that of a stopping taxicab. Sun, silence, and happiness. Presently she heard it in the street, slowly, slower, it stopped, the flag went up with a ring, the door slammed, voices, clinking coins, footsteps. She rushed downstairs.

Hours later Linda made some coffee.

"So lucky," she said, "that it happens to be Sunday, and Mrs. Hunt isn't here. What would she have thought?"

"Just about the same as the night porter at the Hotel Montalembert, I expect," said Fabrice.

"Why did you come, Fabrice? To join General de Gaulle?"

"No, that was not necessary, because I have joined him already. I was with him in Bordeaux. My work has to be in France, but we have ways of communicating when we want to. I shall go and see him, of course, he expects me at midday, but actually I came on a private mission."

He looked at her for a long time.

"I came to tell you that I love you," he said, at last.

Linda felt giddy.

"You never said that to me in Paris."

"No."

"You always seemed so practical."

"Yes, I suppose so. I had said it so often and often before in my life, I had been so romantic with so many women, that when I felt this to be different I really could not bring out all those stale old phrases again, I couldn't utter them. I never said I loved you, I never tutoyé'd you, on purpose. Because from the first moment I knew that this was as real as all the others were false, it was like recognizing somebody—there, I can't explain."

"But that is exactly how I felt too," said Linda, "don't try to explain, you needn't, I know."

"Then, when you had gone, I felt I had to tell you, and it became an obsession with me to tell you. All those dreadful weeks were made more dreadful because I was being prevented from telling you."

"How ever did you get here?"

"One moves about," said Fabrice, vaguely. "I must leave again tomorrow morning, very early, and I shan't come back until the war is over, but you'll wait for me, Linda, and nothing matters so much now that you know. I was tormented, I couldn't concentrate on anything, I was becoming useless in my work. In future I may have much to bear, but I shan't have to bear you going away without knowing what a great great love I have for you."

"Oh, Fabrice, I feel—well, I suppose religious people sometimes feel like this."

She put her head on his shoulder, and they sat for a long time in silence.

When he had paid his visit to Carlton Gardens they lunched at the Ritz. It was full of people Linda knew, all very smart, very gay, and talking with the greatest flippancy about the imminent arrival of the Germans. Had it not been for the fact that all the young men there had fought bravely in Flanders, and would, no doubt, soon be fighting bravely again, and this time with more experience, on other fields of battle, the general tone might have been considered shocking. Even Fabrice looked grave, and said they did not seem to realize——

Davey and Lord Merlin appeared. Their eyebrows went up when they saw Fabrice.

"Poor Merlin has the wrong kind," Davey said to Linda.

"The wrong kind of what?"

"Pill to take when the Germans come. He's just got the sort you give to dogs."

Davey brought out a jewelled box containing two pills, one white and one black.

"You take the white one first and then the black one —he really must go to my doctor."

"I think one should let the Germans do the killing," said Linda. "Make them add to their own crimes and use up a bullet. Why should one smooth their path in any way? Besides, I back myself to do in at least two before they get me."

"Oh, you're so tough, Linda, but I'm afraid it wouldn't be a bullet for me, they would torture me, look at the things I've said about them in the *Gazette*."

"No worse than you've said about all of us," Lord Merlin remarked.

Davey was known to be a most savage reviewer, a perfect butcher, never sparing even his dearest friends. He wrote under several pseudonyms, which in no way disguised his unmistakable style, his cruellest essays appearing over the name Little Nell.

"Are you here for long, Sauveterre?"

"No, not for long."

Linda and Fabrice went in to luncheon. They talked of this and that, mostly jokes. Fabrice told her scandalous stories about some of the other lunchers known to him of old, with a wealth of unlikely detail. He spoke only once about France, only to say that the struggle must be carried on, everything would be all right in the end. Linda thought how different it would have been with Tony or Christian. Tony would have held forth about his experiences and made boring arrangements for his own future, Christian would have launched a monologue on world conditions subsequent to the recent fall of France, its probable repercussions in Araby and far Cashmere, the inadequacy of Pétain to deal with such a wealth of displaced persons, the steps that he, Christian, would have taken had he found himself in his, the Marshal's, shoes. Both would have spoken to her exactly, in every respect, as if she had been some chap in their club. Fabrice talked to her, at her, and for only her, it was absolutely personal talk, scattered with jokes and allusions private to them both. She had a feeling that he would not allow himself to be serious, that if he did he would have to embark on tragedy, and that he wanted her to carry away a happy memory of his visit. But he also gave an impression of boundless optimism and faith, very cheering at that dark time.

Early the next morning, another beautiful, hot, sunny morning, Linda lay back on her pillows and watched Fabrice while he dressed, as she had so often watched him in Paris. He made a certain kind of face when he was pulling his tie into a knot, she had quite forgotten it in the months between, and it brought back their Paris life to her suddenly and vividly.

"Fabrice," she said. "Do you think we shall ever live together again?"

"But of course we shall, for years and years and years, until I am ninety. I have a very faithful nature."

"You weren't very faithful to Jacqueline."

"Aha—so you know about Jacqueline, do you? She

was so lovely, poor thing—lovely, elegant, but aggravating, my God! Anyway, I was immensely faithful to her and it lasted five years, it always does with me (either five days or five years). But as I love you ten times more than the others that brings it to when I am ninety, and, by then, it will have become such a habit with me——"

"And how soon shall I see you again?"

"I'll be back and forth." He went to the window. "I thought I heard a car—oh yes, it is turning round. There, I must go. *Au revoir, madame.*"

He kissed her hand politely, almost absentmindedly, it was as if he had already gone, and walked quickly from the room. Linda went to the open window and leaned out. He was getting into a large motor-car with two French soldiers on the box and a Free French flag waving from the bonnet. As it moved away he looked up.

"Back and forth—back and forth——" cried Linda with a brilliant smile. Then she got back into bed and cried very much. She felt utterly in despair at this second parting.

CHAPTER 20

THE air-raids on London now began. Early in September, just as I had moved there with my family, a bomb fell in the garden of Aunt Emily's little house in Kent. It was a small bomb compared with what one saw later, and none of us were hurt, but the house was more or less wrecked. Aunt Emily, Davey, my children and I, then took refuge at Alconleigh, where Aunt Sadie welcomed us with open arms, begging us to make it our home for the war. Louisa had already arrived there with her children, John Fort William had gone back to his regiment and their Scotch home had been taken over by the Navy.

"The more the merrier," said Aunt Sadie. "I should like to fill the house, and, besides, it's better for rations. Nice, too, for your children to be brought up all together, just like old times. With the boys away and Victoria in the Wrens Matthew and I would be a very dreary old couple here all alone."

The big rooms at Alconleigh were filled with the contents of some science museum and no evacuees had been billeted there, I think it was felt that nobody who had not been brought up to such rigours could stand the cold of that house.

Soon the party received a very unexpected addition. I was upstairs in the nursery bathroom doing some washing for Nanny, measuring out the soap-flakes with wartime parsimony and wishing that the water at Alconleigh were not so dreadfully hard, when Louisa burst in.

"You'll never guess," she said, "in a thousand thousand years who has arrived."

"Hitler," I said, stupidly.

"Your mother, Auntie Bolter. She just walked up the drive and walked in."

"Alone?"

"No, with a man."

"The Major?"

"He doesn't look like a major. He's got a musical instrument with him and he's very dirty. Come on, Fanny, leave those to soak——"

And so it was. My mother sat in the hall drinking a whisky-and-soda and recounting in her birdlike voice with what incredible adventures she had escaped from the Riviera. The major with whom she had been living for some years, always having greatly preferred the Germans to the French, had remained behind to collaborate, and the man who now accompanied my mother was a ruffianly looking Spaniard called Juan, whom she had picked up during her travels, and without whom, she said, she could never have got away from a ghastly prison camp in Spain. She spoke of him exactly as though he were not there at all, which produced rather a curious effect, and indeed seemed most embarrassing until we realized that Juan understood no word of any language except Spanish. He sat staring blankly into space, clutching a guitar and gulping down great draughts of whisky. Their relationship was only too obvious, Juan was undoubtedly (nobody doubted for a moment, not even Aunt Sadie), the Bolter's lover, but they were quite

incapable of verbal exchange, my mother being no lin
guist.

Presently Uncle Matthew appeared, and the Bolter
told her adventures all over again to him. He said he was
delighted to see her, and hoped she would stay as long
as she liked, he then turned his blue eyes upon Juan in a
most terrifying and uncompromising stare. Aunt Sadie
led him off to the business-room, whispering, and we
heard him say:

"All right then, but only for a few days."

One person who was off his head with joy at the
sight of her was dear old Josh.

"We must get her ladyship up onto a horse," he said,
hissing with pleasure.

My mother had not been her ladyship since three
husbands, (four, if one were to include the Major), but
Josh took no account of this, she would always be her
ladyship to him. He found a horse, not worthy of her, in
his eyes, but not an absolute dud either, and had her out
cub-hunting within a week of her arrival.

As for me it was the first time in my life that I had
really found myself face to face with my mother. When
a small child I had been obsessed by her and the few
appearances she had made had absolutely dazzled me,
though, as I have said, I never had any wish to emulate
her career. Davey and Aunt Emily had been very clever
in their approach to her, they, and especially Davey, had
gradually and gently and without in any way hurting
my feelings, turned her into a sort of joke. Since I was
grown up I had seen her a few times, and had taken
Alfred to visit her on our honeymoon, but the fact that,
in spite of our intimate relationship, we had no past life
in common put a great strain upon us and these meetings

were not a success. At Alconleigh, in contact with her morning, noon and night, I studied her with the greatest curiosity; apart from anything else she was, after all, the grandmother of my children. I couldn't help rather liking her. Though she was silliness personified there was something engaging about her frankness and high spirits and endless good nature. The children adored her, Louisa's as well as mine, and she soon became an extra unofficial nurserymaid, and was very useful to us in that capacity.

She was curiously dated in her manner, and seemed still to be living in the 1920's. It was as though, at the age of thirty-five, having refused to grow any older, she had pickled herself, both mentally and physically, ignoring the fact that the world was changing and that she was withering fast. She had a short canary-coloured shingle (windswept) and wore trousers with the air of one still flouting the conventions, ignorant that every suburban shopgirl was doing the same. Her conversation, her point of view, the very slang she used, all belonged to the late 'twenties, that period now deader than the dodo. She was intensely unpractical, foolish, and apparently fragile, and yet she must have been quite a tough little person really, to have walked over the Pyrenees, to have escaped from a Spanish camp, and to have arrived at Alconleigh looking as if she had stepped out of the chorus of *No, No, Nanette*.

Some confusion was caused in the household at first by the fact that none of us could remember whether she had, in the end, actually married the Major (a married man himself and father of six) or not, and, in consequence, nobody knew whether her name was now Mrs. Rawl or Mrs. Plugge. Rawl had been a white hunter, the only husband she had ever lost respectably through death, having shot him by accident in the head during a safari. The question of names was soon solved, however, by her ration book, which proclaimed her to be Mrs. Plugge.

"This Gewan," said Uncle Matthew, when they had been at Alconleigh a week or so, "what's going to be done about him?"

"Well, Matthew dulling," she larded her phrases with the word darling, and that is how she pronounced it. "Hoo-arn saved my life, you know, over and over again, and I can't very well tear him up and throw him away, now can I, my sweet?"

"I can't keep a lot of dagoes here, you know." Uncle Matthew said this in the same voice with which he used to tell Linda that she couldn't have any more pets, or if she did they must be kept in the stables. "You'll have to make some other arrangements for him, Bolter, I'm afraid."

"Oh, dulling, keep him a little longer, please, just a few more days, Matthew dulling," she sounded just like Linda, pleading for some smelly old dog, "and then I promise I'll find some place for him and tiny me to go to. You can't think what a lousy time we had together, I must stick to him now, I really must."

"Well, another week if you like, but it's not to be the thin end of the wedge, Bolter, and after that he must go. You can stay as long as you want to, of course, but I do draw the line at Gewan."

Louisa said to me, her eyes as big as saucers: "He rushes into her room before tea and lives with her." Louisa always describes the act of love as living with. "Before tea, Fanny, can you imagine it?"

"Sadie, dear," said Davey. "I am going to do an unpardonable thing. It is for the general good, for your own good too, but it is unpardonable. If you feel you can't forgive me when I've said my say, Emily and I will have to leave, that's all."

"Davey," said Aunt Sadie in astonishment, "what can be coming?"

"The food, Sadie, it's the food. I know how difficult it is for you in wartime, but we are all, in turns, being poisoned. I was sick for hours last night, the day before Emily had diarrhea, Fanny has that great spot on her nose, and I'm sure the children aren't putting on the weight they should. The fact is, dear, that if Mrs. Beecher were a Borgia she could hardly be more successful—all that sausage mince is poison, Sadie. I wouldn't complain if it were merely nasty, or insufficient, or too starchy, one expects that in the war, but actual poison does, I feel, call for comment. Look at the menus this week—— Monday, poison pie; Tuesday, poison burger steak; Wednesday, Cornish poison——"

Aunt Sadie looked intensely worried.

"Oh, dear, yes, she is an awful cook, I know, but Davey, what can one do? The meat ration only lasts about two meals, and there are fourteen meals in a week, you must remember. If she minces it up with a little sausage meat—poison meat (I do so agree with you really)—it goes much further, you see."

"But in the country surely one can supplement the ration with game and farm produce? Yes, I know the home farm is let, but surely you could keep a pig and some hens? And what about game? There always used to be such a lot here."

"The trouble is Matthew thinks they'll be needing all their ammunition for the Germans, and he refuses to waste a single shot on hares or partridges. Then you see

Mrs. Beecher (oh, what a dreadful woman she is, though of course, we are lucky to have her) is the kind of cook who is quite good at a cut off the joint and two veg., but she simply hasn't an idea of how to make up delicious foreign oddments out of little bits of nothing at all. But you are quite, absolutely right, Davey, it's not wholesome. I really will make an effort to see what can be done."

"You always used to be such a wonderful housekeeper, Sadie dear, it used to do one so much good, coming here. I remember one Christmas I put on four and a half ounces. But now I am losing steadily, my wretched frame is hardly more than a skeleton and I fear that, if I were to catch anything, I might peter out altogether. I take every precaution against that, everything is drenched in T.C.P., I gargle at least six times a day, but I can't disguise from you that my resistance is very low, very."

Aunt Sadie said: "It's quite easy to be a wonderful housekeeper when there is a first-rate cook, two kitchen-maids, a scullerymaid, and when you can get all the food you want. I'm afraid I am dreadfully stupid at managing on rations, but I really will try and take a pull. I'm very glad indeed that you mentioned it, Davey, it was absolutely right of you, and of course, I don't mind at all."

But no real improvement resulted. Mrs. Beecher said "yes, yes" to all suggestions, and continued to send up Hamburger steaks, Cornish pasty and shepherd pie, which continued to be full of poison sausage. It was very nasty and very unwholesome, and, for once, we all felt that Davey had not gone a bit too far. Meals were no pleasure to anybody and a positive ordeal to Davey, who sat, a pinched expression on his face, refusing food and resorting more and more often to the vitamin pills with which his place at the table was surrounded—too many by far even for his collection of jewelled boxes—a little forest of bottles, Vitamin A, vitamin B, vitamins A and C, vitamins B₃ and D, one tablet equals two pounds of summer butter—ten times the strength of a gallon of cod-liver oil—for the blood—for the brain—for muscle—for energy—anti this and protection against that—all but one bore a pretty legend.

"And what's in this, Davey?"

"Oh, that's what the panzer troops have before going into action."

Davey gave a series of little sniffs. This usually denoted that his nose was about to bleed, pints of valuable red and white corpuscles so assiduously filled with vitamins would be wasted, his resistance still further lowered.

Aunt Emily and I looked up in some anxiety from the rissoles we were sadly pushing round our plates.

"Bolter," he said, severely, "you've been at my Mary Chess again."

"Oh, Davey dulling, such a tiny droppie."

"A tiny drop doesn't stink out the whole room. I'm sure you have been pouring it into the bath with the stopper out. It is a shame. That bottle is my quota for a month, it is too bad of you, Bolter."

"Dulling, I swear I'll get you some more—I've got to go to London next week, to have my wiggie washed, and I'll bring back a bottle, I swear."

"And I very much hope you'll take Gewan with you and leave him there," growled Uncle Matthew. "Because I won't have him in this house much longer, you know. I've warned you, Bolter."

Uncle Matthew was busy from morning to night with his Home Guard. He was happy and interested and in a particularly mellow mood, for it looked as if his favourite hobby, that of clocking Germans, might be available again at any moment. So he only noticed Juan from time to time, and, whereas in the old days he would have had him out of the house in the twinkling of an eye, Juan had now been an inmate of Alconleigh for nearly a month. However, it was beginning to be obvious that my uncle had no intention of putting up with his presence for ever and things were clearly coming to a head where Juan was concerned. As for the Spaniard himself, I never saw a man so wretched. He wandered about miserably, with nothing whatever to do all day, unable to talk to anybody, while at mealtimes the disgust on his face fully equalled that of Davey. He hadn't even the spirit to play his guitar.

"Davey, you must talk to him," said Aunt Sadie.

My mother had gone to London to have her hair dyed, and a family council was gathered in her absence to decide upon the fate of Juan.

"We obviously can't turn him out to starve, as the Bolter says he saved her life, and, anyhow, one has human feelings."

"Not towards Dagoes," said Uncle Matthew, grinding his dentures.

"But what we can do is to get him a job, only first we must find out what his profession is. Now, Davey, you're good at languages, and you're so clever, I'm sure if you had a look at the Spanish dictionary in the library you could just manage to ask him what he used to do before the war. Do try, Davey."

"Yes, darling, do," said Aunt Emily. "The poor fellow looks too miserable for words at present, I expect he'd love to have some work."

Uncle Matthew snorted.

"Just give me the Spanish dictionary," he muttered. "I'll soon find the word for 'get out.' "

"I'll try," said Davey, "but I can guess what it will be I'm afraid. G for gigolo."

"Or something equally useless, like M for matador or H for hidalgo," said Louisa.

"Yes. Then what?"

"Then B for be off," said Uncle Matthew, "and the Bolter will have to support him, but not anywhere near me, I beg. It must be made perfectly clear to both of them that I can't stand the sight of the sewer lounging about here any longer."

When Davey takes on a job he does it thoroughly. He shut himself up for several hours with the Spanish dictionary, and wrote down a great many words and phrases on a piece of paper. Then he beckoned Juan into Uncle Matthew's business-room and shut the door.

They were only there a short time, and, when they emerged, both were wreathed in happy smiles.

"You've sacked him, I hope?" Uncle Matthew said, suspiciously.

"No, indeed, I've not sacked him," said Davey, "on the contrary, I've engaged him. My dears, you'll never guess, it's too absolutely glamorous for words, Juan is a cook, he was the cook, I gather, of some cardinal before the Civil War. You don't mind I hope, Sadie. I look upon this as an absolute lifeline—Spanish food, so delicious, so unconstipating, so digestible, so full of glorious garlic. Oh, the joy, no more poison-burger—how soon can we get rid of Mrs. Beecher?"

Davey's enthusiasm was fully justified, and Juan in the kitchen was the very greatest possible success. He was more than a first-class cook, he had an extraordinary talent for organization, and soon, I suspect, became king of the local black market. There was no nonsense about foreign dishes made out of little bits of nothing at all; succulent birds, beasts, and crustaceans appeared at every meal, the vegetables ran with extravagant sauces, the puddings were obviously based upon real ice-cream.

"Juan is wonderful," Aunt Sadie would remark in her vague manner, "at making the rations go round. When I think of Mrs. Beecher—really, Davey, you were so clever."

One day she said: "I hope the food isn't too rich for you now, Davey?"

"Oh no," said Davey. "I never mind rich food, it's poor food that does one such an infinity of harm."

Juan also pickled and bottled and preserved from morning till night, until the store cupboard, which he had found bare except for a few tins of soup, began to look like a pre-war grocer's shop. Davey called it Aladdin's Cave, or Aladdin for short, and spent a lot of his time there, gloating. Months of tasty vitamins stood there in neat rows, a barrier between him and that starvation which had seemed, under Mrs. Beecher's régime, only just round the corner.

Juan himself was now a very different fellow from the dirty and disgruntled refugee who had sat about so miserably. He was clean, he wore a white coat and hat, he seemed to have grown in stature, and he soon acquired a manner of great authority in his kitchen. Even Uncle Matthew acknowledged the change.

"If I were the Bolter," he suggested, "I should marry him."

"Knowing the Bolter," said Davey, "I've no doubt at all that she will."

Early in November I had to go to London for the day, on business for Alfred, who was now in the Middle East, and to see my doctor. I went by the eight o'clock train, and, having heard nothing of Linda for some weeks, I took a taxi and drove straight to Cheyne Walk. There had been a heavy raid the night before, and I passed through streets which glistened with broken glass. Many fires still smouldered, and fire engines, ambulances, and rescue men hurried to and fro, streets were blocked, and several times we had to drive quite a long way round. There seemed to be a great deal of excitement in the air. Little groups of people were gathered outside shops and houses, as if to compare notes; my taxi-driver talked incessantly to me over his shoulder. He had been up all night, he said, helping the rescue workers. He described what he had found.

"It was a spongy mass of red," he said, ghoulishly, "covered with feathers."

"Feathers?" I said, horrified.

"Yes. A feather bed, you see. It was still breathing, so I takes it to the hospital, but they says that's no good to us, take it to the mortuary. So I sews it in a sack and takes it to the mortuary."

"Goodness," I said.

"Oh, that's nothing to what I have seen."

Linda's nice daily woman, Mrs. Hunt, opened the door to me at Cheyne Walk.

"She's very poorly, ma'am, can't you take her back to the country with you? It's not right for her to be here, in her condition. I hate to see her like this."

Linda was in her bathroom, being sick. When she came out she said:

"Don't think it's the raid that's upset me. I like them. I'm in the family way, that's what it is."

"Darling, I thought you weren't supposed to have another baby."

"Oh, doctors! They don't know anything, they are such fearful idiots. Of course I can, and I'm simply longing for it, this baby won't be the least bit like Moira, you'll see."

"I'm going to have one too."

"No—how lovely—when?"

"About the end of May."

"Oh, just the same as me."

"And Louisa, in March."

"Haven't we been busy? I do call that nice, they can all be Hons together."

"Now, Linda, why don't you come back with me to Alconleigh? Whatever is the sense of stopping here in all this? It can't be good for you or the baby."

"I like it," said Linda. "It's my home, and I like to be in it. And besides, somebody might turn up, just for a few hours you know, and want to see me, and he knows where to find me here."

"You'll be killed," I said, "and then he won't know where to find you."

"Darling Fanny, don't be so silly. There are seven million people living in London, do you really imagine they are all killed every night? Nobody is killed in air-raids, there is a great deal of noise and a great deal of mess, but people really don't seem to get killed much."

"Don't—don't——" I said. "Touch wood. Apart from being killed or not it doesn't suit you. You look awful, Linda."

"Not so bad when I'm made up. I'm so fearfully sick, that's the trouble, but it's nothing to do with the raids, and that part will soon be over now and I shall be quite all right again."

"Well, think about it," I said, "it's very nice at Alconleigh, wonderful food——"

"Yes, so I hear. Merlin came to see me, and his stories of caramelized carrots swimming in cream made my mouth water. He said he was preparing to throw morality to the winds and bribe this Juan to go to Merlinford, but he found out it would mean having the Bolter too and he couldn't quite face that."

"I must go," I said uncertainly. "I don't like to leave you, darling, I do wish you'd come back with me."

"Perhaps I will later on, we'll see."

I went down to the kitchen and found Mrs. Hunt. I gave her some money in case of emergency, and the Alconleigh telephone number, and begged her to ring me up if she thought there was anything I could do.

"She won't budge," I said. "I've done all I can to make her, but it doesn't seem to be any good, she's as obstinate as a donkey."

"I know, ma'am. She won't even leave the house for a breath of air, sits by that telephone day in day out playing cards with herself. It ain't hardly right she should sleep here all alone in my opinion, either, but you can't get her to listen to sense. Last night, ma'am, whew! it was terrible, walloping down all night, and those wretched guns never got a single one, whatever they may tell you in the papers. It's my opinion they must have got women on those guns, and, if so, no wonder. Women!"

A week later Mrs. Hunt rang me up at Alconleigh.

Linda's house had received a direct hit and they were still digging for her.

Aunt Sadie had gone on an early bus to Cheltenham to do some shopping, Uncle Matthew was nowhere to be found, so Davey and I simply took his car, full of Home Guard petrol, and drove to London, hell for leather. The little house was an absolute ruin, but Linda and her bulldog were unhurt, they had just been got out and put to bed in the house of a neighbour. Linda was flushed and excited, and couldn't stop talking.

"You see," she said. "What did I tell you, Fanny, about air-raids not killing people. Here we are, right as rain. My bed simply went through the floor, Plon-plon and I went on it, most comfortable."

Presently a doctor arrived and gave her a sedative. He told us she would probably go to sleep and that when she woke up we could drive her down to Alconleigh. I telephoned to Aunt Sadie and told her to have a room ready.

The rest of the day was spent by Davey in salvaging what he could of Linda's things. Her house and furniture, her beautiful Renoir, and everything in her bedroom was completely wrecked, but he was able to rescue a few oddments from the splintered, twisted remains of her cupboards, and in the basement he found, untouched, the two trunks full of clothes which Fabrice had sent after her from Paris. He came out looking like a miller, covered with white dust from head to foot, and Mrs. Hunt took us round to her own little house and gave us some food.

"I suppose Linda may miscarry," I said to Davey, "and I'm sure it's to be hoped she will. It's most dangerous for her to have this child—my doctor is horrified."

However, she did not, in fact she said that the experience had done her a great deal of good, and had quite stopped her from feeling sick. She demurred again at leaving London, but without much conviction. I pointed out that if anybody was looking for her and found the Cheyne Walk house a total wreck they would be certain at once to get into touch with Alconleigh. She saw that this was so, and agreed to come with us.

CHAPTER 21

WINTER now set in with its usual severity on those Cotswold uplands. The air was sharp and bracing, like cold water; most agreeable if one only goes out for short brisk walks or rides, and if there is a warm house to go back to. But the central-heating apparatus at Alconleigh had never been really satisfactory and I suppose that by now the pipes, through old age, had become thoroughly furred up—in any case they were hardly more than tepid. On coming into the hall from the bitter outside air one did feel a momentary glow of warmth; this soon lessened, and gradually, as circulation died down, one's body became pervaded by a cruel numbness. The men on the estate, the old ones that is, who were not in the army, had no time to chop up logs for the fires; they were occupied from morning till night, under the leadership of Uncle Matthew, in drilling, constructing barricades and blockhouses, and otherwise preparing to make themselves a nuisance to the German army before ending up as cannon-fodder.

"I reckon," Uncle Matthew would say proudly, "that we shall be able to stop them for two hours—possibly three—before we are all killed. Not bad for such a little place."

We made our children go out and collect wood, Davey became an assiduous and surprisingly efficient woodman (he had refused to join the Home Guard, he said he always fought better out of uniform), but, somehow, they only produced enough to keep the nursery fire going, and the one in the brown sitting-room, if it was lit after tea, and, as the wood was pretty wet, this only really got warm just when it was time to tear oneself away and go up the freezing stairs to bed. After dinner the two arm-chairs on each side of the fire were always occupied by Davey and my mother. Davey pointed out that it would be more trouble for everybody in the end if he got one of his chills; the Bolter just dumped herself down. The rest of us sat in a semicircle well beyond the limits of any real warmth, and looked longingly at the little flickering yellow flames, which often subsided into sulky smoke. Linda had an evening coat, a sort of robe from head to foot, of white fox lined with white ermine. She wrapped herself in this for dinner, and suffered less than we others did. In the daytime she either wore her sable coat and a pair of black velvet boots lined with sable to match, or lay on the sofa tucked up in an enormous mink bedspread lined with white velvet quilting.

"It used to make me so laugh when Fabrice said he was getting me all these things because they would be useful in the war, the war would be fearfully cold he always said, but I see now how right he was."

Linda's possessions filled the other females in the house with a sort of furious admiration.

"It does seem rather unfair," Louisa said to me one afternoon when we were pushing our two youngest children out in their prams together. We were both dressed in stiff Scotch tweeds, so different from supple flattering French ones, in woollen stockings, brogues, and jerseys, knitted by ourselves, of shades carefully chosen to "go with" though not "to match" our coats and skirts. "Linda goes off and has this glorious time in Paris, and comes back covered with rich furs, while you and I—what do we get for sticking all our lives to the same dreary old husbands? Three-quarter-length shorn lamb."

"Alfred isn't a dreary old husband," I said loyally. But of course I knew exactly what she meant.

Aunt Sadie thought Linda's clothes too pretty.

"What lovely taste, darling," she would say when another ravishing garment was brought out. "Did that come from Paris too? It's really wonderful what you can get there, on no money, if you're clever."

At this my mother would give tremendous winks in the direction of anybody whose eye she might happen to catch, including Linda herself. Linda's face would then become absolutely stony. She could not bear my mother; she felt that, before she met Fabrice, she had been heading down the same road herself, and she was appalled to see what lay at the end of it. My mother started off by trying a "let's face it, dear, we are nothing but two fallen women" method of approach to Linda, which was most unsuccessful. Linda became not only stiff and cold, but positively rude to the poor Bolter, who, unable to see what she could have done to offend, was at first very much hurt. Then she began to be on her dignity, and said it was great nonsense for Linda to go on like this; in fact, considering she was nothing but a high-class tart, it was most pretentious and hypocritical of her. I tried to explain Linda's intensely romantic attitude towards Fabrice and the months she had spent with him, but the Bolter's own feelings had been dulled by time, and she either could not or would not understand.

"It was Sauveterre she was living with, wasn't it?" my

mother said to me, soon after Linda arrived at Alconleigh.

"How do you know?"

"Everybody knew on the Riviera. One always knew about Sauveterre somehow. And it was rather a thing, because he seemed to have settled down for life with that boring Lamballe woman; then she had to go to England on business and clever little Linda nabbed him. A very good cop for her, dulling, but I don't see why she has to be so high-hat about it. Sadie doesn't know, I quite realize that, and of course wild horses wouldn't make me tell her, I'm not that kind of a girl, but I do think, when we're all together, Linda might be a tiny bit more jolly."

The Alconleighs still believed that Linda was the devoted wife of Christian, who was now in Cairo, and, of course, it had never occurred to them for a moment that the child might not be his. They had quite forgiven her for leaving Tony, though they thought themselves distinctly broad-minded for having done so. They would ask her from time to time what Christian was doing, not because they were interested, but so that Linda shouldn't feel out of it when Louisa and I talked about our husbands. She would then be obliged to invent bits of news out of imaginary letters from Christian.

"He doesn't like his Brigadier very much," or,

"He says Cairo is great fun, but one can have enough of it."

In point of fact Linda never got any letters at all. She had not seen her English friends now for so long, they were scattered in the war to the ends of the earth, and, though they might not have forgotten about Linda, she was no longer in their lives. But, of course, there was only one thing she wanted, a letter, a line even, from Fabrice. Just after Christmas it came. It was forwarded in a typewritten envelope from Carlton Gardens with General de Gaulle's stamp on it. Linda, when she saw it lying on the hall table, became perfectly white. She seized it and rushed up to her bedroom.

About an hour later she came to find me.

"Oh, darling," she said, her eyes full of tears. "I've been all this time and I can't read one word. Isn't it torture? Could you have a look?"

She gave me a sheet of the thinnest paper I ever saw, on which were scratched, apparently with a rusty pin, a series of perfectly incomprehensible hieroglyphics. I could not make out one single word either, it seemed to bear no relation to handwriting, the marks in no way resembled letters.

"What can I do?" said poor Linda. "Oh, Fanny."

"Let's ask Davey," I said.

She hesitated a little over this, but feeling that it would be better, however intimate the message, to share it with Davey than not to have it at all, she finally agreed.

Davey said she was quite right to ask him.

"I am very good at French handwriting."

"Only you wouldn't laugh at it?" Linda said, in a breathless voice like a child.

"No, Linda, I don't regard it as a laughing matter any longer," Davey replied, looking with love and anxiety at her face, which had become very drawn of late. But when he had studied the paper for some time, he too was obliged to confess himself absolutely stumped by it.

"I've seen a lot of difficult French writings in my life," he said, "and this beats them all."

In the end Linda had to give up. She went about with the piece of paper, like a talisman, in her pocket, but never knew what Fabrice had written to her on it. It was cruelly tantalizing. She wrote to him at Carlton Gardens, but this letter came back with a note regretting that it could not be forwarded.

"Never mind," she said. "One day the telephone bell will ring again and he'll be there."

Louisa and I were busy from morning to night. We now had one Nanny (mine) among eight children. Fortunately they were not at home all the time. Louisa's two eldest were at a private school, and two of hers and two of mine went for lessons to a convent Lord Merlin had most providentially found for us at Merlinford. Louisa got a little petrol for this, and she or I or Davey drove them there in Aunt Sadie's car every day. It can be imagined what Uncle Matthew thought of this arrangement. He ground his teeth, flashed his eyes, and always referred to the poor good nuns as "those damned parachutists." He was absolutely convinced that whatever time they could spare from making machine-gun nests for other nuns, who would presently descend from the skies, like birds, to occupy the nests, was given to the seduction of the souls of his grandchildren and great-nieces.

"They get a prize you know for anybody they can catch—of course you can see they are men, you've only got to look at their boots."

Every Sunday he watched the children like a lynx for genuflections, making the sign of the Cross, and other Papist antics, or even for undue interest in the service, and when none of these symptoms was to be observed he was hardly reassured.

"These Romans are so damned artful."

He thought it most subversive of Lord Merlin to harbour such an establishment on his property, but only really what one might expect of a man who brought Germans to one's ball and was known to admire foreign music. Uncle Matthew had most conveniently forgotten all about "Une voce poco fa," and now played, from morning to night, a record called "The Turkish Patrol," which started piano, became forte, and ended up pianissimo.

"You see," he would say, "they come out of a wood, and then you can hear them go back into the wood. Don't know why it's called Turkish, you can't imagine Turks playing a tune like that, and of course there aren't any woods in Turkey. It's just the name, that's all."

I think it reminded him of his Home Guard, who were always going into woods and coming out of them again, poor dears, often covering themselves with branches as when Birnam Wood came to Dunsinane.

So we worked hard, mending and making and washing, doing any chores for Nanny rather than actually look after the children ourselves. I have seen too many children brought up without Nannies to think this at all desirable. In Oxford, the wives of progressive dons did it often as a matter of principle; they would gradually become morons themselves, while the children looked like slum children and behaved like barbarians.

As well as looking after the clothes of our existing families we also had to make for the babies we were expecting, though they did inherit a good deal from brothers and sisters. Linda, who naturally had no store of baby clothes, did nothing of all this. She arranged one of the slatted shelves in the Hons' cupboard as a sort of bunk, with pillows and quilts from spare bedrooms, and here, wrapped in her mink bedspread, she would lie all day with Plon-plon beside her, reading fairy stories. The Hons' cupboard, as of old, was the warmest, the one really warm place in the house. Whenever I could I brought my sewing and sat with her there, and then she would put down the blue or the green fairy book, Anderson or Grimm, and tell me at length about Fabrice and her happy life with him in Paris. Louisa sometimes joined us there, and then Linda would break off and we would talk about John Fort William and the children. But Louisa was a restless busy creature, not much of a chatter, and, besides, she was irritated to see how Linda did absolutely nothing, day after day.

"Whatever is the baby going to wear, poor thing," she would say crossly to me, "and who is going to look after it, Fanny? It's quite plain already that you and I will have to, and really, you know, we've got enough to do as it is. And another thing, Linda lies there covered in sables or whatever they are, but she's got no money at all, she's a pauper—I don't believe she realizes that in the least. And what is Christian going to say when he hears about the baby, after all, legally his, he'll have to bring a suit to illegitimize it, and then there'll be such a scandal. None of these things seems to have occurred to Linda. She ought to be beside herself with worry, instead of which she is behaving like the wife of a millionaire in peacetime. I've no patience with her."

All the same, Louisa was a good soul. In the end it was she who went to London and bought a layette for the baby. Linda sold Tony's engagement ring, at a horribly low price, to pay for it.

"Do you never think about your husbands?" I asked her one day, after she had been talking for hours about Fabrice.

"Well, funnily enough, I do quite often think of Tony.

Christian, you see, was such an interlude, he hardly counts in my life at all, because, for one thing, our marriage lasted a very short time, and then it was quite overshadowed by what came after. I don't know, I find these things hard to remember, but I think that my feelings for him were only really intense for a few weeks, just at the very beginning. He's a noble character, a man you can respect, I don't blame myself for marrying him, but he has no talent for love.

"But Tony was my husband for so long, more than a quarter of my life, if you come to think of it. He certainly made an impression. And I see now that the thing going wrong was hardly his fault, poor Tony, I don't believe it would have gone right with anybody (unless I had happened to meet Fabrice) because in those days I was so extremely nasty. The really important thing, if a marriage is to go well, without much love, is very very great niceness—*gentillesse*—and wonderful good manners. I was never *gentille* with Tony, and often I was hardly polite to him, and, very soon after our honeymoon, I became exceedingly disagreeable. I'm ashamed now to think what I was like. And poor old Tony was so good-natured, he never snapped back, he put up with it all for years and then just ambled off to Pixie. I can't blame him. It was my fault from beginning to end."

"Well, he wasn't very nice really, darling, you shouldn't worry yourself about it too much, and look how he's behaving now."

"Oh, he's the weakest character in the world, it's Pixie and his parents who made him do that. If he'd still been married to me he would have been a Guards officer by now, I bet you."

One thing Linda never thought about, I'm quite sure,

was the future. Some day the telephone bell would ring and it would be Fabrice, and that was as far as she got. Whether he would marry her, and what would happen about the child, were questions which not only did not preoccupy her, but which never seemed to enter her head. Her mind was entirely on the past.

"It's rather sad," she said one day, "to belong, as we do, to a lost generation. I'm sure in history the two wars will count as one war and that we shall be squashed out of it altogether, and people will forget that we ever existed. We might just as well never have lived at all, I do think it's a shame."

"It may become a sort of literary curiosity," Davey said. He sometimes crept, shivering, into the Hons' cupboard to get up a little circulation before he went back to his writing. "People will be interested in it for all the wrong reasons, and collect Lalique dressing-table sets and shagreen boxes and cocktail cabinets lined with looking-glass and find them very amusing. Oh good," he said, peering out of the window, "that wonderful Juan is bringing in another pheasant."

(Juan had an invaluable talent, he was expert with a catapult. He spent all his odd moments—how he had odd moments was a mystery, but he had—creeping about the woods or down by the river armed with this weapon. As he was an infallible shot, and moreover, held back by no sporting inhibitions, that a pheasant or a hare should be sitting or a swan the property of the King being immaterial to Juan, the results of these sallies were excellent from the point of view of larder and stock-pot. When Davey really wanted to relish his food to the full he would recite, half to himself, a sort of little grace, which began: "Remember Mrs. Beecher's tinned tomato soup."

The unfortunate Craven was, of course, tortured by these goings on, which he regarded as little better than poaching. But his nose, poor man, was kept well to the grindstone by Uncle Matthew, and, when he was not on sentry-go, or fastening the trunks of trees to bicycle-wheels across the lanes to make barricades against tanks, he was on parade. Uncle Matthew was a byword in the county for the smartness of his parades. Juan, as an alien, was luckily excluded from these activities, and was able to devote all his time to making us comfortable and happy, in which he very notably succeeded.)

"I don't want to be a literary curiosity," said Linda. "I should like to have been a living part of a really great generation. I think it's too dismal to have been born in 1911."

"Never mind, Linda, you will be a wonderful old lady."

"You will be a wonderful old gentleman, Davey," said Linda.

"Oh, me? I fear I shall never make old bones," replied Davey, in accents of the greatest satisfaction.

And, indeed, there was a quality of agelessness about him. Although he was quite twenty years older than we and only about five years younger than Aunt Emily, he had always seemed much nearer to our generation than to hers, nor had he altered in any respect since the day when he had stood by the hall fire looking unlike a captain and unlike a husband.

"Come on, dears, tea, and I happen to know that Juan has made a layer-cake, so let's go down before the Bolter gets it all."

Davey carried on a great meal-time feud with the Bolter. Her table manners had always been casual, but certain of her habits, such as eating jam with a spoon which

she put back into the jam-pot, and stubbing out her cigarette in the sugar-basin, drove poor Davey, who was very
ration-conscious, to a frenzy of irritation, and he would
speak sharply to her, like a governess to a maddening
child.

He might have spared himself the trouble. The Bolter
took absolutely no notice whatever, and went on spoiling
food with insouciance.

"Dulling," she would say, "whatever does it matter, my
perfectly divine Hoo-arn has got plenty more up his tiny
sleeve, I promise you."

At this time there was a particularly alarming invasion
scare. The arrival of the Germans, with full paraphernalia
of airborne troops dressed as priests, ballet dancers, or
what you will, was expected from one day to the next.
Some unkind person put it about that they would all be
the doubles of Mrs. Davis, in W.V.S. uniform. She had
such a knack of being in several places at once that it already seemed as if there were a dozen Mrs. Davises para-
chuting about the countryside. Uncle Matthew took the
invasion very seriously indeed, and one day he gathered
us all together, in the business-room and told us in detail
the part that we were expected to play.

"You women, with the children, must go to the cellar
while the battle is on," he said, "there is an excellent tap,
and I have provisioned you with bully-beef for a week.
Yes, you may be there several days, I warn you."

"Nanny won't like that," Louisa began, but was quelled
by a furious look.

"While we are on the subject of Nanny," Uncle Matthew said, "I warn you, there's to be no question of cluttering up the roads with your prams, mind, no evacuation

under any circumstances at all. Now, there is one very important job to be done, and that I am entrusting to you, Davey. You won't mind it I know, old boy, if I say that you are a very poor shot—as you know, we are short of ammunition, and what there is must, under no circumstances, be wasted—every bullet must tell. So I don't intend to give you a gun, at first, anyhow. But I've got a fuse and a charge of dynamite (I will show you, in a moment,) and I shall want you to blow up the store-cupboard for me."

"Blow up Aladdin," said Davey. He turned quite pale. "Matthew, you must be mad."

"I would let Gewan do it, but the fact is, though I rather like old Gewan now, I don't altogether trust the fella. Once a foreigner always a foreigner in my opinion. Now I must explain to you why I regard this as a most vital part of the operations. When Josh and Craven and I and all the rest of us have been killed there is only one way in which you civilians can help, and that is by becoming a charge on the German army. You must make it their business to feed you—never fear, they'll do so, they don't want typhus along their lines of communication— but you must see that it's as difficult as possible for them. Now that store cupboard would keep you going for weeks, I've just had a look at it; why, it would feed the entire village. All wrong. Make them bring in the food and muck up their transport, that's what we want, to be a perfect nuisance to them. It's all you'll be able to do, by then, just be a nuisance, so the store cupboard will have to go, and Davey must blow it up."

Davey opened his mouth to make another observation, but Uncle Matthew was in a very frightening mood and he thought better of it.

"Very well, dear Matthew," he said, sadly, "you must show me what to do."

But as soon as Uncle Matthew's back was turned he gave utterance to loud complaints.

"No, really, it is too bad of Matthew to insist on blowing up Aladdin," he said. "It's all right for him, he'll be dead, but he really should consider us a little more."

"But I thought you were going to take those black and white pills," said Linda.

"Emily doesn't like the idea, and I had decided only to take them if I were arrested, but now I don't know. Matthew says the German army will have to feed us, but he must know as well as I do that if they feed us at all, which is extremely problematical, it will be on nothing but starch—it will be Mrs. Beecher again, only worse, and I can't digest starch especially in the winter months. It is such a shame. Horrid old Matthew, he's so thoughtless."

"Well, but Davey," said Linda, "how about us? We're all in the same boat, but we don't grumble."

"Nanny will," said Louisa with a sniff, which plainly said, "and I wish to associate myself with Nanny."

"Nanny! She lives in a world of her own," said Linda. "But we're all supposed to know why we're fighting, and, speaking for myself, I think Fa is absolutely right. And if I think that, in my condition——"

"Oh, you'll be looked after," said Davey, bitterly, "pregnant women always are. They'll send you vitamins and things from America, you'll see. But nobody will bother about me, and I am so delicate, it simply won't do for me to be fed by the German army, and I shall never be able to make them understand about my inside. I know Germans."

"You always said nobody understood as much about your inside as Dr. Meyerstein."

"Use your common sense, Linda. Are they likely to drop Dr. Meyerstein over Alconleigh? You know perfectly well he's been in a camp for years. No, I must make up my mind to a lingering death—not a very pleasant prospect, I must say."

Linda took Uncle Matthew aside after that, and made him show her how to blow up Aladdin.

"Davey's spirit is not so frightfully willing," she said, "and his flesh is definitely weak."

There was a certain coldness between Linda and Davey for a little while after this, each thought the other had been quite unreasonable. It did not last, however. They were much too fond of each other (in fact, I am sure that Davey really loved Linda most in the world) and, as Aunt Sadie said, "Who knows, perhaps the necessity for these dreadful decisions will not arise."

So the winter slowly passed. The spring came with extraordinary beauty, as always at Alconleigh, with a brilliance of colouring, a richness of life, that one had forgotten to expect during the cold grey winter months. All the animals were giving birth, there were young creatures everywhere, and we now waited with longing and impatience for our babies to be born. The days, the very hours, dragged slowly by, and Linda began to say "better than that" when asked the time.

"What's the time, darling?"

"Guess."

"Half-past twelve?"

"Better than that, a quarter to one."

We three pregnant women had all become enormous, we dragged ourselves about the house like great figures of fertility, heaving tremendous sighs, and feeling the heat of the first warm days with exaggerated discomfort.

Useless to her now were Linda's beautiful Paris clothes, she was down to the level of Louisa and me in a cotton smock, maternity skirt and sandals. She abandoned the Hons' cupboard, and spent her days, when it was fine weather, sitting by the edge of the wood, while Plon-plon, who had become an enthusiastic, though unsuccessful, rabbiter, plunged panting to and fro in the green mists of the undergrowth.

"If anything happens to me, darling, you will look after Plon-plon," she said. "He has been such a comfort to me all this time."

But she spoke idly, as one who knows, in fact, that she will live for ever, and she mentioned neither Fabrice nor the child, as surely she would have done had she been touched by any premonition.

Louisa's baby, Angus, was born at the beginning of April. It was her sixth child and third boy, and we envied her from the bottom of our hearts for having got it over.

On the 28th May both our babies were born—both boys. The doctors who said that Linda ought never to have another child were not such idiots after all. It killed her. She died, I think, completely happy, and without having suffered very much, but for us at Alconleigh, for her father and mother, brothers and sisters, for Davey and for Lord Merlin a light went out, a great deal of joy that never could be replaced.

At about the same time as Linda's death Fabrice was caught by the Gestapo and subsequently shot. He was a hero of the Resistance, and his name has become a legend in France.

I have adopted the little Fabrice, with the consent of Christian, his legal father. He has black eyes, the same shape as Linda's blue ones, and is a most beautiful and enchanting child. I love him quite as much as, and perhaps more than, I do my own.

The Bolter came to see me while I was still in the Oxford nursing home where my baby had been born and where Linda had died.

"Poor Linda," she said, with feeling, "poor little thing. But Fanny, don't you think perhaps it's just as well? The lives of women like Linda and me are not so much fun when one begins to grow older."

I didn't want to hurt my mother's feelings by protesting that Linda was not that sort of woman.

"But I think she would have been happy with Fabrice," I said. "He was the great love of her life, you know."

"Oh, dulling," said my mother, sadly. "One always thinks that. Every, every time."

Love in a Cold Climate

To Lord Berners

PART I

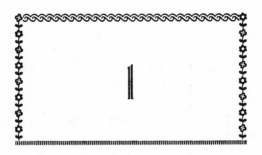

I AM obliged to begin this story with a brief account of the Hampton family, because it is necessary to emphasise the fact once and for all that the Hamptons were very grand as well as very rich. A short session with Burke or with Debrett would be quite enough to make this clear, but these large volumes are not always available, while the books on the subject by Lord Montdore's brother-in-law, Boy Dougdale, are all out of print. His great talent for snobbishness and small talent for literature have produced three detailed studies of his wife's forebears, but they can only be read now by asking a bookseller to get them at second hand. (The bookseller will put an advertisement in his trade paper, *The Clique*: "H. Dougdale, any by." He will be snowed under with copies at about a shilling each and will then proudly inform his customer that he has "managed to find what you want," implying hours of careful search on barrows, dirt cheap, at 30/– the three.) *Georgiana Lady Montdore and Her Circle, The Magnificent Montdores* and *Old Chronicles of Hampton,* I have them beside me as I write, and see that the opening paragraph of the first is:

"Two ladies, one dark, one fair, both young and lovely, were driving briskly towards the little village of Kensington on a fine May morning. They were Georgiana, Countess of Montdore and her great friend Walburga, Duchess of Paddington, and they made a delightfully animated picture as they discussed the burning question of the hour—should one or should one not subscribe to a parting present for poor dear Princess Lieven?"

This book is dedicated, by gracious permission, to Her Royal Highness, the Grand Duchess Peter of Russia, and has eight full-page illustrations.

It must be said that when this trilogy first came out it had quite a vogue with the lending-library public.

"The family of Hampton is ancient in the West of England, indeed Fuller, in his *Worthies* mentions it as being of stupendous antiquity."

Burke makes it out just a shade more ancient than does Debrett, but both plunge back into the mists of mediaeval times from which they drag forth ancestors with P. G. Wodehouse names, Ugs and Berts and Threds, and Walter Scott fates. "His Lordship was attainted—beheaded—convicted—proscribed—exiled—dragged from prison by a furious mob—slain at the Battle of Crécy—went down in the White Ship—perished during the third crusade—killed in a duel." There were very few natural deaths to record in the early misty days. Both Burke and Debrett linger with obvious enjoyment over so genuine an object as this family, unspoilt by the ambiguities of female line and deed poll. Nor could any of those horrid books, which came out in the nineteenth century, devoted to research and aiming to denigrate the nobility, make the object seem less genuine. Tall, golden-haired barons, born in wedlock and all looking very much alike, succeeded each other at Hampton, on lands which had never been bought or sold, generation after generation until, in 1770, the Lord Hampton of the day brought back, from a visit to Versailles, a French bride, a Mademoiselle de Montdore. Their son had brown eyes, a dark skin and presumably, for it is powdered in all the pictures of him, black hair. This blackness did not persist in the family. He married a golden-haired heiress from Derbyshire, and the Hamptons reverted to their blue-and-gold looks, for which they are famous to this day. The son of the Frenchwoman was rather clever and very worldly; he dabbled in politics and wrote a book of aphorisms, but his chief claim to fame was his great and lifelong friendship with the Regent, which procured him, among other favours, an earldom. His mother's family having all perished during the Terror in France, he took her name as his title. Enormously rich, he spent enormously; he had a taste for French objects of art and acquired, during the years which followed the Revolution, a splendid collection of such things, including many pieces from the royal establishments, and others which had been looted out of the Hotel de Montdore in the rue de Varenne. To make a suitable setting for this collection, he then proceeded to pull down at Hampton the large plain house that Adam had built for his grandfather and to drag over to England stone by stone (as modern American millionaires are supposed to do) a Gothic French chateau. This he assembled round a splendid tower of his own designing, covered the walls of the rooms with French panelling and silks and set it in a formal landscape which he also designed and planted himself. It was all very grand and very mad, and in the between-wars period of which I write, very much out of fashion. "I suppose it is beautiful," people used to say, "but frankly I don't admire it."

This Lord Montdore also built Montdore House in Park Lane and a castle on a crag in Aberdeenshire. He was really much the most interesting and original character the family produced, but no member of it deviated from a tradition of authority. A solid, worthy, powerful Hampton can be found on every page of English history, his influence enormous in the West of England and his counsels not unheeded in London.

The tradition was carried on by the father of my friend, Polly Hampton. If an Englishman could be descended from the gods it would be he, so much the very type of English nobleman that those who believed in aristocratic government would always begin by pointing to him as a justification of their argument. It was generally felt, indeed, that if there were more people like him the country would not be in its present mess, even Socialists conceding his excellence, which they could afford to do since there was only one of him and he was getting on. A scholar, a Christian, a gentleman, finest shot in the British Isles, best-looking Viceroy we ever sent to India, a popular landlord, a pillar of the Conservative Party, a wonderful old man, in short, who nothing common ever did or mean. My cousin Linda

and I, two irreverent little girls whose opinion makes
no odds, used to think that he was a wonderful old
fraud, and it seemed to us that in that house it was
Lady Montdore who really counted. Now Lady Montdore was forever doing common things and mean, and
she was intensely unpopular, quite as much disliked as
her husband was loved, so that anything he might do
that was considered not quite worthy of him, or which
did not quite fit in with his reputation, was immediately
laid at her door. "Of course she made him do it." On
the other hand, I have often wondered whether without her to bully him and push him forward and plot
and intrigue for him and "make him do it," whether, in
fact, without the help of those very attributes which
caused her to be so much disliked, her thick skin and
ambition and boundless driving energy, he would ever
have done anything at all noteworthy in the world.

This is not a popular theory. I am told that by the
time I really knew him, after they got back from India,
he was already tired out and had given up the struggle,
and that when he was in his prime he had not only controlled the destinies of men but also the vulgarities of
his wife. I wonder. There was an ineffectiveness about
Lord Montdore which had nothing to do with age; he
was certainly beautiful to look at, but it was an empty
beauty, like that of a woman who has no sex appeal; he
looked wonderful and old, but it seemed to me that, in
spite of the fact that he still went regularly to the House
of Lords, attended the Privy Council, sat on many com-
mittees, and often appeared in the Birthday Honours,
he might just as well have been made of cardboard.

Lady Montdore, however, was flesh and blood all
right. She was born a Miss Perrotte, the handsome

daughter of a country squire of small means and no particular note, so that her marriage to Lord Montdore was a far better one than she could reasonably have been expected to make. As time went on, when her worldly greed and snobbishness, her terrible relentless rudeness had become proverbial and formed the subject of many a legendary tale, people were inclined to suppose that her origins must have been low or transatlantic, but, in fact, she was perfectly well born and had been decently brought up, what used to be called "a lady," so that there were no mitigating circumstances, and she ought to have known better.

No doubt her rampant vulgarity must have become more evident and less controlled with the years. In any case, her husband never seemed aware of it and the marriage was a success. Lady Montdore soon embarked him upon a public career, the fruits of which he was able to enjoy without much hard work, since she made it her business to see that he was surrounded by a host of efficient underlings, and though he pretended to despise the social life which gave meaning to her existence, he put up with it very gracefully, exercising a natural talent for agreeable conversation and accepting as his due the fact that people thought him wonderful.

"Isn't Lord Montdore wonderful? Sonia, of course, is past a joke, but he is so brilliant, such a dear, I do love him."

The people who benefited by their hospitality were fond of pretending that it was solely on his account that they ever went to the house at all, but this was great nonsense because the lively quality, the fun of Lady Montdore's parties had nothing whatever to do with him, and, hateful as she may have been in many ways, she excelled as a hostess.

In short, they were happy together and singularly well suited. But for years they suffered one serious vexation in their married life: they had no children. Lord Montdore minded this because he naturally wanted an heir, as well as for more sentimental reasons. Lady Montdore minded passionately. Not only did she also want an heir, but she disliked any form of failure, could not bear to be thwarted and was eager for an object on which she could concentrate such energy as was not absorbed by society and her husband's career. They had been married nearly twenty years, and quite given up all idea of having a child when Lady Montdore began to feel less well than usual. She took no notice, went on with her usual occupations and it was only two months before it was born that she realized she was going to have a baby. She was clever enough to avoid the ridicule which often attaches to such a situation by pretending to have kept the secret on purpose, so that instead of roaring with laughter, everybody said, "Isn't Sonia absolutely phenomenal?"

I know all this because my uncle Davey Warbeck has told me. Having himself for many years suffered (or enjoyed) most of the distempers in the medical dictionary, he is very well up in nursing-home gossip.

The fact that the child, when it was born, turned out to be a daughter, never seems to have troubled the Montdores at all. It is possible that, as Lady Montdore was under forty when she was born, they did not at first envisage her as an only child and by the time they realized that they would never have another, they loved her so much that the idea of her being in any way different, a different person, a boy, had become unthinkable. Naturally they would have liked to have had a boy, but only if it could have been as well as, and not instead of, Polly. She was their treasure, the very hub of their universe.

Polly Hampton had beauty, and this beauty was her outstanding characteristic. She was one of those people you cannot think of except in regard to their looks which, in her case, were unvarying, independent of clothes, of age, of circumstances and even of health. When ill or tired, she merely looked fragile, but never yellow, withered or diminished; she was born beautiful and never, at any time when I knew her, went off or became less beautiful, but on the contrary her looks always steadily improved. The beauty of Polly and the importance of her family are essential elements of this story. But, whereas the Hamptons can be studied in various books of reference, it is not much use turning to old *Tatlers* and seeing Polly as Lenare, as Dorothy Wilding saw her. The bones, of course, are there; hideous hats, old-fashioned poses cannot conceal them; the bones and the shape of her face are always perfection. But beauty is more, after all, than bones, for, while bones belong to death and endure after decay, beauty is a living thing; it is, in fact, skin deep, blue shadows on a white skin, hair falling like golden feathers on a white smooth forehead, embodied in the movement, in the smile and, above all, in the regard of a beautiful woman. Polly's regard was a blue flash, the bluest and most sudden thing I ever saw, so curiously unrelated to the act of seeing that it was almost impossible to believe that those opaque blue stones observed, assimilated, or did anything except confer a benefit upon the object of their direction.

No wonder her parents loved her. Even Lady Montdore, who would have been a terrible mother to an ugly girl, or to an eccentric, wayward boy, had no difficulty in being perfect to a child who must, it seemed, do her great credit in the world and crown her ambitions; literally, perhaps, crown. Polly was certainly destined for an exceptional marriage—was Lady Montdore not envisaging something very grand indeed when she gave her the name Leopoldina? Had this not a royal, a vaguely Coburg flavour which might one day be most suitable? Was she dreaming of an altar, an Archbishop, a voice saying, "I, Albert Christian George Andrew Patrick David take thee Leopoldina"? It was not an impossible dream. On the other hand, nothing could be more wholesome and unpretentious than "Polly."

My cousin Linda Radlett and I used to be borrowed from a very early age to play with Polly, for, as so often happens with the parents of only children, the Montdores were always much preoccupied with her possible loneliness. I know that my own adopted mother, Aunt Emily, had the same feeling about me and would do anything rather than keep me alone with her during the holidays. Hampton Park is not far from Linda's home, Alconleigh, and she and Polly, being more or less of an age, seemed destined to become each other's greatest friends. For some reason, however, they never really took to each other much, while Lady Montdore disliked Linda, and as soon as she was able to converse at all pronounced her conversation "unsuitable." I can see Linda now, at luncheon in the big dining room at

Hampton (that dining room in which I have, at various
times in my life been so terrified, that its very smell, a
bouquet left by a hundred years of rich food, rich wine,
rich cigars and rich women, is still to me as the smell of
blood is to an animal), I can hear her loud singsong
Radlett voice, "Did you ever have worms, Polly? I did.
You can't imagine how fidgetty they are. Then, oh, the
heaven of it, Doctor Simpson came and wormed me.
Well, you know how Doc Simp has always been the love
of my life—so you do see . . ."

This was too much for Lady Montdore and Linda was
never asked to stay again. But I went for a week or so
almost every holiday, packed off there on my way to or
from Alconleigh, as children are, without ever being
asked if I enjoyed it or wanted to go. My father was related to Lord Montdore through his mother. I was a
well-behaved child, and I think Lady Montdore quite
liked me; anyhow, she must have considered me "suitable," a word which figured prominently in her vo-
cabulary, because at one moment there was a question
of my going to live there during the term, to do lessons
with Polly. When I was thirteen, however, they went
off to govern India, after which Hampton and its owners
became a dim, though always alarming, memory to me.

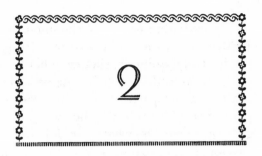

BY THE time the Montdores and Polly returned from India, I was grown-up and had already had a season in London. Linda's mother, my Aunt Sadie (Lady Alconleigh), had taken Linda and me out together, that is to say, we went to a series of debutante dances where the people we met were all as young and as shy as we were ourselves, and the whole thing smelt strongly of bread and butter; it was quite unlike the real world, and almost as little of a preparation for it as childrens' parties are. When the summer ended Linda became engaged to be married, and I went back to my home in Kent, to another aunt and uncle, Aunt Emily and Uncle Davey, who had relieved my own divorced parents of the boredom and the burden of bringing up a child.

I was finding it dull at home, as young girls do, when, for the first time, they have neither lessons nor parties to occupy their minds, and then one day into this dullness fell an invitation to stay at Hampton in October. Aunt Emily came out to find me—I was sitting in the garden —with Lady Montdore's letter in her hand.

"Lady Montdore says it will be rather a grown-up affair, but she particularly wants you as company for Polly. She says there will be two young men for you girls, of course. Oh, what a pity it happens to be Davey's day for getting drunk. I long to tell him, he'll be so much interested."

There was nothing for it, however, but to wait. Davey had quite passed out and his stertorous breathing could be heard all over the house. Davey's lapses into insobriety had no vice about them; they were purely therapeutic. The fact is he was following a new regime for perfect health, much in vogue at that time, he assured us, on the Continent.

"The aim is to warm up your glands with a series of jolts. The worst thing in the world for the body is to settle down and lead a quiet little life of regular habits; if you do that it soon resigns itself to old age and death. Shock your glands, force them to react, startle them back into youth, keep them on tiptoe so that they never know what to expect next, and they have to keep young and healthy to deal with all the surprises."

Accordingly, he ate in turns like Ghandi and like Henry VIII, went for ten-mile walks or lay in bed all day, shivered in a cold bath or sweated in a hot one. Nothing in moderation. "It is also very important to get drunk every now and then." Davey, however, was too much of a one for regular habits to be irregular otherwise than regularly, so he always got drunk at the full moon. Having once been under the influence of Rudolph Steiner, he was still very conscious of the waxing and waning of the moon and had, I believe, a vague idea that the waxing and waning of the capacity of his stomach coincided with its periods.

Uncle Davey was my one contact with the world, not the world of bread-and-butter misses, but the great wicked world itself. Both my aunts had renounced it at an early age so that, for them, its existence had no reality, while their sister, my mother, had long since disappeared from view into its maw. Davey, however, had a modified liking for it, and often made little bachelor excursions into it from which he would return with a bag of interesting anecdotes. I could hardly wait to have a chat with him about this new development in my life.

"Are you sure he's too drunk, Aunt Emily?"

"Quite sure, dear. We must leave it until to-morrow."

Meanwhile she wrote (she always answered letters by return of post) and accepted. But the next day when Davey re-appeared looking perfectly green and with an appalling headache ("Oh, but that's splendid, don't you see, such a challenge to the metabolism, I've just spoken to Dr. England and he is most satisfied with my reaction"), he was rather doubtful whether she had been right to do so.

"My darling Emily, the child will die of terror, that's all," he said. He was examining Lady Montdore's letter. I knew quite well that what he said was true. I had known it in my heart ever since Aunt Emily had read me the letter, but nevertheless I was determined to go; the idea had a glittering fascination for me.

"I'm not a child any longer, Davey," I said.

"Grown-up people have died of terror at Hampton before now," he replied. "Two young men for Fanny and Polly, indeed! Two old lovers of two of the old ladies there, if I know anything about it. What a look, Emily! If you intend to launch this poor child in high society you must send her away armed with knowledge of the facts of life, you know. But I really don't understand what your policy is. First of all, you take care that she should only meet the most utterly innocuous people, keep her nose firmly to Pont Street—quite a point of view, don't think I'm against it for a moment—but then all of a sudden you push her off the rocks into Hampton and expect that she will be able to swim."

"Your metaphors Davey—it's all those spirits," Aunt Emily said, crossly for her.

"Never mind the spirits and let me tell poor Fanny the form. First of all, dear, I must explain that it's no good counting on these alleged young men to amuse you, because they won't have any time to spare for little girls, that's quite certain. On the other hand, who is sure to be there is the Lecherous Lecturer, and, as you are probably still just within his age group, there's no saying what fun and games you may not have with him."

"Oh, Davey," I said, "you are dreadful."

The Lecherous Lecturer was Boy Dougdale. The Radlett children had given him this name after he had once lectured at Aunt Sadie's Women's Institute. The lecture, it seemed, (I was not there at the time) had been very dull, but the things the lecturer did afterwards to Linda and Jassy were not dull at all.

"You know what secluded lives we lead," Jassy had told me when next I was at Alconleigh. "Naturally it's not very difficult to arouse our interest. For example, do you remember that dear old man who came and lectured on the Toll Gates of England and Wales? It was rather tedious, but we liked it—he's coming again, Green Lanes this time. . . . Well, the Lecherous Lecturer's lecture was duchesses and, of course, one always prefers people to gates. But the fascinating thing was after the lecture he gave us a foretaste of sex. Think what a thrill! He took Linda up onto the roof and did all sorts of blissful things to her; at least she could easily see how they would be blissful with anybody except the Lecturer. And I got some great sexy pinches as he passed the nursery landing when he was on his way down to dine. Do admit, Fanny."

Of course my Aunt Sadie had no inkling of all this, she would have been perfectly horrified. Both she and Uncle Matthew always had very much disliked Mr. Dougdale, and, when speaking of the lecture, she said it was exactly what she would have expected, snobbish, dreary and out of place with a village audience, but she had such difficulty filling up the Women's Institute programme month after month in such a remote district that when he had himself written and suggested coming she had thought, "Oh, well. . . !" No doubt she supposed that her children called him the Lecherous Lecturer for alliterative rather than factual reasons, and, indeed, with the Radletts you never could tell. Why, for instance, would Victoria bellow like a bull and half kill Jassy whenever Jassy said, in a certain tone of voice, pointing her finger with a certain look, "Fancy?" I think they hardly knew why, themselves.

When I got home I told Davey about the Lecturer, and he had roared with laughter but said I was not to breathe a word to Aunt Emily or there would be an appalling row and the one who would really suffer would be Lady Patricia Dougdale, Boy's wife.

"She has enough to put up with as it is," he said, "and besides, what would be the good? Those Radletts are clearly heading for one bad end after another, except that for them nothing ever will be the end. Poor dear Sadie just doesn't realize what she has hatched out, luckily for her."

All this happened a year or two before the time of which I am writing and the name of Lecturer for Boy Dougdale had passed into the family language so that none of us children ever called him anything else, and even the grown-ups had come to accept it, though Aunt Sadie, as a matter of form, made an occasional vague protest. It seemed to suit him perfectly.

"Don't listen to Davey," Aunt Emily said. "He's in a very naughty mood. Another time we'll wait for the waning moon to tell him these things. He's only really sensible when he's fasting, I've noticed. Now we shall have to think about your clothes, Fanny. Sonia's parties are always so dreadfully smart. I suppose they'll be sure to change for tea? Perhaps if we dyed your Ascot dress a nice dark shade of red that would do? It's a good thing we've got nearly a month."

Nearly a month was indeed a comforting thought. Although I was bent on going to this house party, the very idea of it made me shake in my shoes with fright, not so much as the result of Davey's teasing as because ancient memories of Hampton now began to revive in force, memories of my childhood visits there and of how little, really, I had enjoyed them. Downstairs had been so utterly terrifying. It might be supposed that nothing could frighten somebody accustomed, as I was, to a downstairs inhabited by my uncle Matthew Alconleigh. But that rumbustious ogre, that eater of little girls was by no means confined to one part of his house. He raged and roared about the whole of it, and indeed the safest place to be in, as far as he was concerned, was downstairs in Aunt Sadie's drawing room, since she alone had any control over him. The terror at Hampton was of a different quality, icy and dispassionate, and it reigned downstairs. You were forced down into it after tea, frilled up, washed and curled, when quite little, or in a tidy frock when older, into the Long Gallery where there would seem to be dozens of grown-ups, all, usually, playing bridge. The worst of bridge is that out of every four people playing it, one is always at liberty to roam about and say kind words to little girls.

Still, on the whole, there was not much attention to spare from the cards and we could sit on the long white fur of the polar bear in front of the fireplace, looking at a picture book propped against its head, or just chatting to each other until welcome bedtime. It quite often happened, however, that Lord Montdore, or Boy Dougdale, if he was there, would give up playing in order to amuse us. Lord Montdore would read aloud from Hans Andersen or Lewis Carroll and there was something about the way he read that made me squirm with secret embarrassment; Polly used to lie with her head on the bear's head, not listening, I believe, to a single word. It was far worse when Boy Dougdale organized hide and seek or sardines, two games of which he was extremely fond, and which he played in what Linda and I considered a stchoopid way. The word stupid, pronounced like that, had a meaning of its own in our language when we (the Radletts and I) were little; it was not until after the Lecturer's lecture that we realized its full implication and that Boy Dougdale had not been stupid so much as lecherous.

When bridge was in progress, we would at least be spared the attention of Lady Montdore, who, even when dummy, had eyes for nothing but the cards; but if by chance there should not be a four staying in the house she would make us play racing demon, a game which has always given me an inferiority feeling because I do pant along so slowly.

"Hurry up, Fanny—we're all waiting for that seven, you know, don't be so moony, dear."

She always won at demon by hundreds, never missing a trick. She never missed a detail of one's appearance, either—the shabby old pair of indoor shoes, the stockings that did not quite match each other, the tidy frock too short and too tight, grown out of, in fact—it was all chalked up on the score.

That was downstairs. Upstairs was all right, perfectly safe, anyhow, from intrusion, the nursery being occupied by nurses, the schoolroom by governesses and neither being subject to visits from the Montdores who, when they wished to see Polly, sent for her to go to them. But it was rather dull, not nearly as much fun as staying at Alconleigh. No Hons' cupboard (the Hons was the Radlett secret society and the Hons' cupboard its headquarters), no talking bawdy, no sallies into the woods to hide the steel traps or to unstop an earth, no nests of baby bats being fed with fountain-pen fillers in secret from the grown-ups, who had absurd ideas about bats, that they were covered with vermin, or got into your hair. Polly was a withdrawn, formal little girl, who went through her day with the sense of ritual, the poise, the absolute submission to etiquette of a Spanish Infanta. You had to love her, she was so beautiful and so friendly, but it was impossible to feel very intimate with her.

She was the exact opposite of the Radletts, who always "told" everything. Polly "told" nothing, and if there were anything to tell it was all bottled up inside her. When Lord Montdore once read us the story of the Snow Queen (I could hardly listen, he put in so much expression) I remember thinking that it must be about Polly and that she surely had a glass splinter in her heart. For what did she love? That was the great puzzle to me. My cousins and I poured out love, we lavished it to right and to left, on each other, on the grown-ups, on a variety of animals and, above all, on the characters (often historical or even fictional) with whom we were *in* love. There was no reticence, and we all knew everything there was to know about each other's feelings for every other creature, whether real or imaginary. Then there were the shrieks. Shrieks of laughter and happiness and high spirits which always resounded through Alconleigh, except on the rare occasions when there were floods. It was shrieks or floods in that house, usually shrieks. But Polly did not pour or lavish or shriek, and I never saw her in tears. She was always the same, always charming, sweet and docile, polite, interested in what one said, rather amused by one's jokes, but all without exuberance, without superlatives, and certainly without any confidences.

Nearly a month then to this visit about which my feelings were so uncertain. All of a sudden, not only not nearly a month but now, to-day, now this minute, and I found myself being whirled through the suburbs of Oxford in a large black Daimler. One mercy, I was alone, and there was a long drive, some twenty miles, in front of me. I knew the road well from my hunting days in that neighbourhood. Perhaps it would go on nearly for ever. Lady Montdore's writing paper was headed Hampton Place, Oxford, station Twyfold. But Twyfold, with the change and hour's wait at Oxford which it involved, was only inflicted upon such people as were never likely to be in a position to get their own back on Lady Montdore, anybody for whom she had the slightest regard being met at Oxford. "Always be civil to the girls, you never know who they may marry," is an aphorism which has saved many an English spinster from being treated like an Indian widow.

So I fidgetted in my corner, looking out at the deep intense blue dusk of autumn, profoundly wishing that I could be safe back at home or going to Alconleigh or, indeed, anywhere rather than to Hampton. Well-known landmarks kept looming up; it got darker and darker but I could just see the Merlinford road, branching off with a big sign post, and then in a moment, or so it seemed, we were turning in at lodge gates. Horrors! I had arrived.

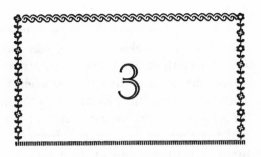

3

A S C R U N C H of gravel, the car gently stopped and exactly as it did so the front door opened, casting a panel of light at my feet. Once inside, the butler took charge of me, removed my nutria coat (a coming-out present from Davey) led me through the hall, under the great steep Gothic double staircase up which rushed a hundred steps, halfway to heaven, meeting at a marble group which represented the sorrows of Niobe, through the octagonal ante-chamber, through the green drawing room and the red drawing room into the Long Gallery where, without asking it, he pronounced my name, very loud and clear, and then abandoned me.

The Long Gallery was, as I always remember it being, full of people. There were perhaps twenty or thirty on this occasion, a few very old ones, contemporaries of Lady Montdore, sitting stiffly round a tea table by the fire, while further down the room, glasses instead of cups in their hands, the rest of the party stood watching games of backgammon. Younger than Lady Montdore, they still seemed elderly to me, being about the age of my own mother. They were chattering like starlings in a tree, did not stop their chatter when I came in, when Lady Montdore introduced me to them, merely broke off what they were saying, stared at me for a moment and went straight on again. However, when she pronounced my name, one of them said,

"Not the Bolter's daughter?"

I was quite accustomed to hearing my mother referred to as the Bolter, indeed nobody, not even her own sisters, ever called her anything else, so, when Lady Montdore paused with a disapproving look at the speaker, I piped up, "Yes."

It then seemed as though all the starlings rose in the air and settled on a different tree, and that tree was me.

"The Bolter's girl?"

"Don't be funny—how could the Bolter have a grown-up daughter?"

"Veronica, do come here a minute, do you know who this is? She's the Bolter's daughter, that's all."

"Come and have your tea, Fanny," said Lady Montdore. She led me to the tea table and the starlings went on with their chatter about my mother in eggy-peggy, a language I happened to know quite well.

"Eggis sheggee reggeally, peggoor sweggeet! I couldn't be more interested, naturally, when you come to think of it, considering that the very first person the Bolter ever bolted with, was my hubsand—wasn't it, Chad? Tiny me got you next, didn't I, my angel, but not until she had bolted away from you again."

"I don't believe it. The Bolter can't be more than

thirty-six. I know she can't, we used to go to Miss Vacani together, and you used to come, too, Roly—couldn't remember it better—poker and tongs on the floor for the sword dance and Roly in his tiny kilt. What do you say, darling—can she be more than thirty-six?"

"That's right. Do the sum, birdbrain. She married at eighteen, eighteen and eighteen are thirty-six. Correct —no?"

"Well, steady on though, how about the nine months?"

"Not nine, darling, nothing like nine, don't you remember how bogus it all was and how shamingly huge her bouquet had to be, poor sweet? It was the whole point."

"Careful, Veronica. Really, Veronica always goes too far. Come on, let's finish the game. . . ."

I had half an ear on this rivetting conversation, and half on what Lady Montdore was saying. Having given me a characteristic and well-remembered look, up and down, a look which told me what I knew too well, that my tweed skirt bulged behind and why had I no gloves? (why, indeed, left them in the motor no doubt and how would I ever have the courage to ask for them?), said in a most friendly way that I had changed more in five years than Polly had, but that Polly was now much taller than I. How was Aunt Emily? And Davey?

"You'll have your tea?" she said.

That was where her charm lay. She would suddenly be nice just when it seemed that she was about to go for you tooth and nail; it was the charm of a purring puma. She now sent one of the men off to look for Polly.

"Playing billiards with Boy, I think," and poured me out a cup of tea.

"And here," she said, to the company in general, "is Montdore."

She always called her husband Montdore to those she regarded as her equals, but to borderline cases such as the estate agent or Dr. Simpson he was Lord Montdore, if not His Lordship. I never heard her refer to him as "my husband." It was all part of the attitude to life that made her so generally un-beloved, a determination to show people what she considered to be their proper place and keep them in it.

The chatter did not continue while Lord Montdore, radiating wonderful oldness, came into the room. It stopped dead, and those who were not already standing up, respectfully did so. He shook hands all round, a suitable word for each in turn.

"And this is my friend Fanny? Quite grown-up now, and do you remember that last time I saw you, we were weeping together over the 'Little Match Girl?' "

Perfectly untrue, I thought. Nothing about human beings ever had the power to move me as a child. *Black Beauty* now. . . !

He turned to the fire, holding his thin white hands which shook a little to the blaze, while Lady Montdore poured out his tea. There was a long silence in the room. Presently he took a scone, buttered it, put it in his saucer, and turning to another old man said, "I've been wanting to ask you."

They sat down together, talking in low voices, and by degrees the starling chatter broke loose again.

I was beginning to see that there was no occasion to feel alarmed in this company, because, as far as my fellow guests were concerned, I was clearly endowed

with protective colouring, their momentary initial interest in me having subsided, I might just as well not
have been there at all, and could keep happily to myself
and observe their antics. The various house parties for
people of my own age that I had been to during the past
year had really been much more unnerving, because
there I knew that I was expected to play a part, to
sing for my supper by being, if possible, amusing. But
here, a child once more among all these old people, it
was my place to be seen and not heard. Looking round
the room, I wondered vaguely which were the young
men Lady Montdore had mentioned as being specially
invited for Polly and me. They could not yet have arrived, as certainly none of these were the least bit young,
all well over thirty, I should have said, and probably
all married, though it was impossible to guess which of
the couples were husbands and wives, because they all
spoke to each other as if they all were, in voices and
with endearments which, in the case of my aunts, could
only have meant that it was their own husbands they
were addressing.

"Have the Sauveterres not arrived yet, Sonia?" said
Lord Montdore coming up for another cup of tea.

There was a movement among the women. They
turned their heads like dogs who think they hear somebody unwrapping a piece of chocolate.

"Sauveterres? Do you mean Fabrice? Don't tell me
Fabrice is married? I couldn't be more amazed."

"No, no, of course not. He's bringing his mother to
stay. She's an old flame of Montdore's—I've never seen
her, and Montdore hasn't for quite forty years. Of course,
we've always known Fabrice, and he came to us in

India; he's such fun, a delightful creature. He was very much taken up with the little Ranee of Rawalpur; in fact, they do say her last baby . . ."

"Sonia. . . !" said Lord Montdore, quite sharply for him. She took absolutely no notice.

"Dreadful old man the Rajah, I only hope it was. Poor creatures, it's one baby after another; you can't help feeling sorry for them, like little birds, you know. I used to go and visit the ones who were kept in purdah and of course they simply worshipped me, it was really touching."

Lady Patricia Dougdale was announced. I had seen the Dougdales from time to time while the Montdores were abroad because they were neighbours at Alconleigh and although my Uncle Matthew by no means encouraged neighbours it was beyond even his powers to suppress them altogether and prevent them from turning up at the meets, the local point to points, on Oxford platform for the 9.10 and Paddington for the 4.45, or at the Merlinford market. Besides, the Dougdales had brought house parties to Alconleigh for Aunt Sadie's dances when Louisa and Linda came out and had given Louisa, for a wedding present, an antique pin cushion, curiously heavy because full of lead. The romantic Louisa, making sure it was curiously heavy because full of gold, "Somebody's savings, don't you see?" had ripped it open with her nail scissors, only to find the lead, with the result that none of her wedding presents could be shown, for fear of hurting Lady Patricia's feelings.

Lady Patricia was a perfect example of beauty that is but skin deep. She had once had the same face as Polly, but the fair hair had now gone white and the white skin yellow, so that she looked like a classical statue that has been out in the weather, with a layer of snow on its head, the features smudged and smeared by damp. Aunt Sadie said that she and Boy had been considered the handsomest couple in London, but of course that must have been years ago; they were old now, fifty or something, and life would soon be over for them. Lady Patricia's life had been full of sadness and suffering, sadness in her marriage and suffering in her liver. (Of course I am now quoting Davey.) She had been passionately in love with Boy, who was younger than she, for some years before he had married her, which he was supposed to have done because he could not resist the relationship with his esteemed Hampton family. The great sorrow of his life was childlessness, since he had set his heart on a quiverful of little half-Hamptons, and people said that the disappointment had almost unhinged him for a while, but that his niece, Polly, was now beginning to take the place of a daughter, he was so extremely devoted to her.

"Where is Boy?" Lady Patricia said when she had greeted, in the usual English way of greeting, the people who were near the fire, sending a wave of her gloves or half a smile to the ones who were further off. She wore a felt hat, sensible tweeds, silk stockings and beautifully polished calf shoes.

"I do wish they'd come," said Lady Montdore. "I want him to help me with the table. He's playing billiards with Polly. I've sent word once, by Rory—oh, here they are."

Polly kissed her aunt and kissed me. She looked round the room to see if anybody else had arrived to whom she had not yet said, "How do you do?" (she and her parents, as a result, no doubt, of the various official positions Lord Montdore had held, were rather formal in their manners) and then turned back again to me.

"Fanny," she said, "have you been here long? Nobody told me."

She stood there, rather taller now than me, embodied once more instead of a mere nebulous memory of my childhood, and all the complicated feelings that we have for the beings who matter in our lives, came rushing back to me. My feelings for the Lecturer came rushing back, too, uncomplicated.

"Ha!" he was saying, "here, at last, is my lady wife." He gave me the creeps, with his crinkly black hair going grey now and his perky, jaunty figure. He was shorter than his wife and tried to make up for this by having very thick soles to his shoes. He always looked horribly pleased with himself; the corners of his mouth turned up when his face was in repose, and if he was at all put out they turned up even more in a maddening smile.

Polly's blue look was now upon me. I suppose she also was rediscovering a person only half-remembered, quite the same person really, a curly little black girl, Aunt Sadie used to say, like a little pony which at any moment might toss its shaggy mane and gallop off. Half an hour ago, I would gladly have galloped but now I felt happily inclined to stay where I was.

As we went upstairs together, Polly put her arm round my waist saying, with obvious sincerity, "It's too lovely to see you again. The things I've got to ask you! When I was in India I used to think and think about you. Do you remember how we both had black velvet dresses with red sashes for coming down after tea and how Linda had worms? It does seem another life, so long ago. What is Linda's fiancé like?"

"Very good-looking," I said. "Very hearty. They don't care for him much at Alconleigh, any of them."

"Oh, how sad. Still, if Linda does . . . Fancy, though, Louisa married and Linda engaged already! Of course before India we were all babies really, and now we are of marriageable age, it makes a difference, doesn't it?" She sighed deeply.

"I suppose you came out in India?" I said. Polly, I knew, was a little older than I was.

"Well, yes, I did, I've been out two years, actually. It was all very dull, this coming out seems a great, great bore. Do you enjoy it, Fanny?"

I had never thought about whether I enjoyed it or not and found it difficult to answer her question. Girls have to come out, I knew. It is a stage in their existence, just as the public school is for boys, which must be passed before life, real life, could begin. Dances are supposed to be delightful. They cost a lot of money and it is most good of the grown-ups to give them, most good, too, of Aunt Sadie to have taken me to so many. But at these dances, although I quite enjoyed going to them, I always had the uncomfortable feeling that I missed something; it was like going to a play in a foreign language. Each time I used to hope that I should see the point, but I never did, though the people round me were all so evidently seeing it. Linda, for instance, had seen it clearly but then she had been successfully pursuing love.

"What I do enjoy," I said, truthfully, "is the dressing up."

"Oh, so do I! Do you think about dresses and hats all the time, even in church? I do, too. Heavenly tweed, Fanny, I noticed it at once."

"Only it's bagging," I said.

"They always bag, except on very smart little thin women, like Veronica. Are you pleased to be back in this room? It's the one you used to have, do you remember?"

Of course I remembered. It always had my name in full "The Honble Frances Logan" written in a careful copperplate on a card on the door, even when I was so small that I came with my nanny, and this had greatly impressed and pleased me as a child.

"Is this what you're going to wear to-night?" Polly went up to the huge red four-poster where my dress was laid out.

"How lovely—green velvet and silver. I call that a dream, so soft and delicious, too." She rubbed a fold of the skirt against her cheek. "Mine's silver lamé. It smells like a bird cage when it gets hot, but I do love it. Aren't you thankful evening skirts are long again? But I want to hear more about what coming out is like in England."

"Dances," I said, "girls' luncheon parties, tennis, if you can, dinner parties to go to, plays, Ascot, being presented. Oh, I don't know, I expect you can just about imagine."

"And all going on like the people downstairs?"

"Chattering all the time? Well, but the downstairs people are old, Polly, coming out is with people of one's own age, you see."

"They don't think they're old a bit," she said, laughing.

"Well," I said, "all the same, they are."

"I don't see them as so old myself, but I expect that's because they seem young beside Mummy and Daddy. Just think of it, Fanny, your mother wasn't born when

Mummy married, and Mrs. Warbeck was only just old enough to be her bridesmaid. Mummy was saying so before you came. No, but what I really want to know about coming out here is, what about love? Are they all always having love affairs the whole time? Is it their one and only topic of conversation?"

I was obliged to admit that this was the case.

"Oh, bother. I felt sure, really, you would say that. It was so in India, of course, but I thought perhaps in a cold climate. . . ! Anyway, don't tell Mummy if she asks you. Pretend that English debutantes don't bother about love. She is in a perfect fit because I never fall in love with people; she teases me about it all the time. But it isn't any good, because if you don't you don't. I should have thought, at my age, it's natural not to."

I looked at her in surprise, it seemed to me highly unnatural, though I could well understand not wanting to talk about such things to the grown-ups, and specially not to Lady Montdore if she happened to be one's mother. But a new idea struck me.

"In India," I said, "could you have fallen in love?" Polly laughed.

"Fanny darling, what do you mean? Of course I could have. Why not? I just didn't happen to, you see."

"White people?"

"White or black," she said, teasingly.

"Fall in love with blacks?" What would Uncle Matthew say?

"People do, like anything. You don't understand about Rajahs, I see, but some of them are awfully attractive. I had a friend there who nearly died of love for one. And I'll tell you something, Fanny. I honestly believe Mamma would rather I fell in love with an Indian than not at all. Of course there would have been a fearful row, and I should have been sent straight home, but even so she would have thought it quite a good thing. What she minds so much is the not at all. I bet you anything she's only asked this Frenchman to stay because she thinks no woman can resist him. They could think of nothing else in Delhi. I wasn't there at the time, I was in the hills with Boy and Auntie Patsy. We did a heavenly, heavenly trip. I must tell you about it, but not now."

"But would your mother like you to marry a Frenchman?" I said. At this time love and marriage were inextricably knotted in my mind.

"Oh, not marry, good gracious, no. She'd just like me to have a little weakness for him, to show that I'm capable of it. She wants to see if I'm like other women. Well, she'll see. There's the dressing bell—I'll call for you when I'm ready. I don't live up here any more, I've got a new room over the porch. Heaps of time, Fanny, quite an hour."

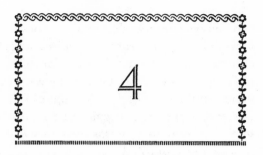

4

MY BEDROOM was in the tower, where Polly's nurseries had been when she was small. Whereas all the other rooms at Hampton were classical in feeling, the tower rooms were exaggeratedly Gothic, the Gothic of fairy-story illustrations. In this one the bed, the cupboards and the fireplace had pinnacles; the wallpaper was a design of scrolls and the windows were casements. An extensive work of modernisation had taken place all over the house while the family was in India, and looking round I saw that in one of the cupboards there was now a tiled bathroom.

In the old days I used to sally forth, sponge in hand, to the nursery bathroom which was down a terrifying, twisting staircase, and I could still remember how cold it used to be outside, in the passages, though there was always a blazing fire in my room. But now the central heating had been brought up to date and the temperature everywhere was that of a hot-house. The fire which flickered away beneath the spires and towers of the chimney-piece was merely there for show, and no longer to be lighted at 7 A.M., before one was awake, by a little maid scuffling about like a mouse. The age of luxury was ended and that of comfort had begun. Being conservative by nature, I was glad to see that the decoration of the room had not been changed at all, though the lighting was very much improved. There was a new quilt on the bed, the mahogany dressing table had acquired a muslin petticoat and a triple looking-glass, and the whole room and bathroom were close carpeted. Otherwise everything was exactly as I remembered it, including two large yellow pictures which could be seen from the bed, Caravaggio's "The Gamesters" and "A Courtesan" by Raphael.

I dressed for dinner, passionately wishing that Polly and I could have spent the evening together upstairs, supping off a tray, as we used to do, in the schoolroom. I was dreading this grown-up dinner ahead of me because I knew that once I found myself in the dining room, seated between two of the old gentlemen downstairs, it would no longer be possible to remain a silent spectator. I should be obliged to try and think of things to say. It had been drummed into me all my life, especially by Davey, that silence at meal times is antisocial.

"So long as you chatter, Fanny, it's of no consequence what you say. Better recite out of the A.B.C. than sit like a deaf mute. Think of your poor hostess—it simply isn't fair on her."

In the dining room, between the man called Rory and the man called Roly, I found things even worse than I had expected. The protective colouring, which had worked so well in the drawing room, was now going on and off like a deficient electric light. I was visible, one of my neighbours would begin a conversation with me and seem quite interested in what I was telling him when, without any warning at all, I would become invisible and Rory and Roly were both shouting across the table at the lady called Veronica, while I was left in mid-air with some sad little remark. It then became too obvious that they had not heard a single word I had been saying but had all along been entranced by the infinitely more fascinating conversation of this Veronica lady. All right then, invisible, which really I much preferred, able to eat happily away in silence. But no, not at all, unaccountably visible again.

"Is Lord Alconleigh your uncle then? Isn't he quite barmy? Doesn't he hunt people with bloodhounds by full moon?"

I was still enough of a child to accept the grown-ups of my own family without a question and to suppose that each in their own way was more or less perfect, and it gave me a shock to hear this stranger refer to my uncle as quite barmy.

"Oh, but we love it," I began. "You can't imagine what fun . . ." No good, even as I spoke I became invisible.

"No, no, Veronica, the whole point was he bought the microscope to look at his own . . .",

"Well, I dare you to say the word at dinner, that's all," said Veronica. "Even if you know how to pronounce it, which I doubt, it's too shame-making, not a dinner thing at all. . . ." And so they went on backwards and forwards.

"I couldn't think Veronica much funnier, could you?"

The two ends of the table were quieter. At one, Lady Montdore was talking to the Duc de Sauveterre, who was politely listening to what she said, but whose brilliant, good-humoured little black eyes were nevertheless slightly roving, and, at the other, Lord Montdore and the Lecturer were having a lovely time showing off their faultless French by talking in it across the old Duchesse de Sauveterre to each other. I was near enough to listen to what they were saying, which I did during my periods of invisibility and, though it may not have been as witty as the conversation round Veronica, it had the merit of being, to me, more comprehensible. It was all on these lines:

Montdore: *"Alors, le Duc du Maine était le fils de qui?"*

Boy: *"Mais, dîtes donc, mon vieux, de Louis XIV."*

Montdore: *"Bien entendu, mais sa mère?"*

Boy: *"La Montespan."*

At this point, the Duchess, who had been munching away in silence and not apparently listening to them said, in a loud and very disapproving voice, *"Madame* de Montespan."

Boy: *"Oui—oui—oui, parfaitement, Madame la Duchesse."* (In an English aside to his brother-in-law, "The Marquise de Montespan was an aristocrat, you know. They never forget it.")

"Elle avait deux fils d'ailleurs, le Duc du Maine et le Comte de Toulouse, et Louis XIV les avait tous deux légitimés. Et sa fille a épousé le Régent. Tout cela est exacte, n'est-ce pas, Madame la Duchesse?"

But the old lady for whose benefit this linguistic performance was presumably being staged was totally uninterested in it. She was eating as hard as she could, only pausing in order to ask the footman for more bread. When directly appealed to, she said, "I suppose so."

"It's all in St. Simon," said the Lecturer. "I've been reading him again and so must you Montdore. Simply fascinating." Boy was versed in all the court memoirs that had ever been written, thus acquiring a reputation for great historical knowledge.

"You may not like Boy, but he does know a lot about history, there's nothing he can't tell you."

All depending on what you wanted to find out. The Empress Eugénie's flight from the Tuileries, yes, the Tolpuddle Martyr's martyrdom, no. Boy's historical knowledge was a sublimation of snobbery.

Lady Montdore now turned to her other neighbour, and everybody else followed suit. I got Rory instead of Roly, which was no change as both by now were entirely absorbed in what was going on on the other side of the table, and the Lecturer was left to struggle alone with the Duchess. I heard him say, *"Dans le temps j'étais très lié avec le Duc de Souppes, qu'est-ce qu'il est devenu, Madame la Duchesse?"*

"How, you are a friend to that poor Souppes?" she said. "He is such an annoying boy." Her accent was very strange, a mixture of French and Cockney.

"Il habite toujours ce ravissant hôtel dans la rue du Bac?"

"I suppose so."

"Et la vieille duchesse est toujours en vie?"

But his neighbour was now quite given over to eating and he never got another word out of her. At the end of each course she craned to see what was coming next; when plates were given round after the pudding she touched hers and I heard her say approvingly to herself, *"Encore une assiette chaude, très-très bien."* She was loving her food.

I was loving mine, too, especially now that the protective colouring was in perfect order again, and indeed continued to work for the rest of the evening with hardly another breakdown. I thought what a pity it was that Davey could not be here for one of his overeating days. He always complained that Aunt Emily never really provided him with enough different dishes on these occasions to give his metabolism a proper shock.

"I don't believe you understand the least bit what I need," he would say, crossly for him. "I've got to be giddy, exhausted from overeating, if it's to do me any good. That feeling you have after a meal in a Paris restaurant is what we've got to aim at, when you're too full to do anything but lie on your bed like a cobra, for hours and hours, too full even to sleep. Now there must be a great many different courses to coax my appetite— second helpings don't count; I must have them anyway, a great many different courses of really rich food, Emily dear. Naturally, if you'd rather, I'll give up the cure, but it seems a pity, just when it's doing me so much good. If it's the house books you're thinking of, you must remember there are my starvation days. You never seem to take them into account at all."

But Aunt Emily said the starvation days made absolutely no difference to the house books and that he might call it starvation but anybody else would call it four square meals.

Some two dozen metabolisms round this table were

getting a jolly good jolt, I thought, as the meal went on and on. Soup, fish, pheasant, beefsteak, asparagus, pudding, savoury, fruit. Hampton food, Aunt Sadie used to call it, and indeed it had a character of its own which can best be described by saying that it was like mountains of the very most delicious imaginable nursery food, plain and wholesome, made of the best materials, each thing tasting strongly of itself. But, like everything else at Hampton, it was exaggerated. Just as Lady Montdore was a little bit too much like a Countess, Lord Montdore too much like an elder statesman, the servants too perfect and too deferential, the beds too soft and the linen too fine, the motor cars too new and too shiny and everything too much in apple-pie order, so the very peaches there were too peach-like. I used to think, when I was a child, that all this excellence made Hampton seem unreal compared with the only other houses I knew, Alconleigh and Aunt Emily's little house. It was like a noble establishment in a book or a play, not like somebody's home, and in the same way the Montdores, and even Polly, never quite seemed to be real flesh-and-blood people.

By the time I was embarked on a too peach-like peach, I had lost all sense of fear, if not of decorum, and was lolling about as I would not have dared to at the beginning of dinner, boldly looking to right and to left. It was not the wine. I had only had one glass of claret and all my other glasses were full (the butler having paid no attention to my shakes of the head) and untouched. It was the food; I was reeling drunk on food. I saw just what Davey meant about a cobra, everything was stretched to its capacity and I really felt as if I had swallowed a goat. I knew that my face was scarlet, and looking round I saw that so were all the other faces, except Polly's.

Polly, between just such a pair as Rory and Roly, had not made the least effort to be agreeable to them, though they had taken a good deal more trouble with her than my neighbours had with me. Nor was she enjoying her food. She picked at it with a fork, leaving most of it on her plate, and seemed to be completely in the clouds, her blank stare shining, like the ray from a blue lamp, in the direction of Boy, but not as though she saw him really or was listening to his terribly adequate French. Lady Montdore gave her a dissatisfied look from time to time, but she noticed nothing. Her thoughts were evidently far away from her mother's dinner table, and after awhile her neighbours gave up the struggle of getting yes and no out of her, and, in chorus with mine, began to shout back chat at the lady called Veronica.

This Veronica was small and thin and sparkling. Her bright gold hair lay on her head like a cap, perfectly smooth, with a few flat curls above her forehead. She had a high bony nose, rather protruding pale-blue eyes and not much chin. She looked decadent, I thought, my drunkenness putting that clever grown-up word into my mind no doubt, but all the same it was no good denying that she was very, very pretty and that her clothes, her jewels, her make-up and her whole appearance were the perfection of smartness. She was evidently considered to be a great wit and as soon as the party began to warm up after a chilly start it revolved entirely round her. She bandied repartee with the various Rorys and Rolys, the other women of her age-group merely giggling away at the jokes but taking no active part in them, as though they realized it would be useless to try and steal any of her limelight, while the even older people at the two ends of the table kept up a steady flow of grave talk, occasionally throwing an indulgent glance at Veronica.

Now that I had become brave, I asked one of my neighbours to tell me her name, but he was so much surprised at my not knowing it that he quite forgot to answer my question.

"Veronica?" he said, stupefied. "But surely you know Veronica?"

It was as though I had never heard of Vesuvius. Afterwards I discovered that her name was Mrs. Chaddesley Corbett, and it seemed strange to me that Lady Montdore, whom I had so often been told was a snob, should have only a Mrs., not even an Hon. Mrs., to stay and treat her almost with deference. This shows how innocent, socially, I must have been in those days, since every schoolboy (every Etonian, that is) knew all about Mrs. Chaddesley Corbett. She was to the other smart women of her day as the star is to the chorus, and had invented a type of looks, as well as a way of talking, walking and behaving, which was slavishly copied by the fashionable set in England for at least ten years. No doubt the reason why I had never heard her name before was that she was such miles, in smartness, above the bread-and-butter world of my acquaintance.

It was terribly late when at last Lady Montdore got up to leave the table. My aunts never allowed such long sitting in the dining room because of the washing up and keeping the servants from going to bed, but that sort of thing simply was not considered at Hampton, nor did Lady Montdore turn to her husband, as Aunt Sadie always did, with an imploring look and a "Not too long, darling," as she went, leaving the men to their port, their brandy, their cigars and their traditional dirty stories which could hardly be any dirtier, it seemed to me, than Veronica's conversation had become during the last half hour or so.

Back in the Long Gallery some of the women went upstairs to "powder their noses." Lady Montdore was scornful.

"I go in the morning," she said, "and that is that. I don't have to be let out like a dog at intervals."

If Lady Montdore had really hoped that Sauveterre would exercise his charm on Polly, she was in for a disappointment. As soon as the men came out of the dining room, where they had remained for quite an hour ("This English habit," I heard him say, "is terrible"), he was surrounded by Veronica and her chorus and never given a chance to speak to anybody else. They all seemed to be old friends of his, called him Fabrice and had a thousand questions to ask about mutual acquaintances in Paris, fashionable foreign ladies with such unfashionable English names as Norah, Cora, Jennie, Daisy, May and Nellie.

"Are all Frenchwomen called after English housemaids?" Lady Montdore said, rather crossly, as she resigned herself to a chat with the old Duchess, the group round Sauveterre having clearly settled down for good. He seemed to be enjoying himself, consumed, one would say, by some secret joke, his twinkling eyes resting with amusement rather than desire, on each plucked and painted face in turn, while in turn, and with almost too obvious an insincerity they asked about their darling Nellies and Daisys. Meanwhile, the husbands of these various ladies, frankly relieved, as Englishmen always are, by a respite from feminine company, were gambling at the other end of the long room, playing, no doubt, for much higher stakes than they would have been allowed to by their wives and with a solid, heavy masculine concentration on the game itself, undisturbed by any of the distractions of sex. Lady Patricia went off to bed; Boy Dougdale began by inserting himself into the group round Sauveterre but finding that nobody there took the slightest notice of him, Sauveterre not even answering when he asked about the Duc de Souppes, beyond saying evasively, "I see poor Nina de Souppes sometimes," he gave up, a hurt, smiling look on his face, and came and sat with Polly and me and showed us how to play backgammon. He held our hands as we shook the dice, rubbed our knees with his, generally behaving I thought, in a stchoopid and lecherous way. Lord Montdore and the other very old man went off to play billiards; he was said to be the finest billiards player in the British Isles.

Meanwhile poor Lady Montdore was being subjected to a tremendous interrogation by the Duchess, who had relapsed, through a spirit of contradiction perhaps, into her native tongue. Lady Montdore's French was adequate, but by no means so horribly wonderful as that of her husband and brother-in-law, and she was soon in difficulties over questions of weights and measures; how many hectares in the park at Hampton, how many metres high was the tower, what it would cost, in francs, to take a house boat for Henley, how many kilometers they were from Sheffield? She was obliged to appeal the whole time to Boy, who never failed her, of course, but the Duchess was not really very much interested in the answers, she was too busy cooking up the next question. They poured out in a relentless torrent, giving Lady Montdore no opportunity whatever to escape to the bridge table as she was longing to do. What sort of electric-light machine was there at Hampton, what was the average weight of a Scotch stag, how long had Lord and Lady Montdore been married (*"Tiens!"*) how was the bath water heated, how many hounds in a pack of fox hounds, where was the Royal Family now? Lady Montdore was undergoing the sensation, novel to her, of being a rabbit with a snake. At last she could bear it no more and broke up the party, taking the women off to bed very much earlier than was usual, at Hampton.

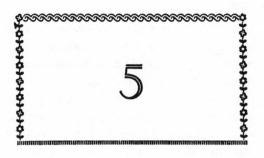

5

AS THIS was the first time I had ever stayed away in such a large grand grown-up house party, I was rather uncertain what would happen, in the morning, about breakfast, so before we said good night I asked Polly.

"Oh," she said vaguely, "nine-ish, you know," and I took that to mean, as it meant at home, between five and fifteen minutes past nine. In the morning I was woken up at eight by a housemaid, who brought me tea with slices of paper-thin bread and butter, asked me, "Are these your gloves, miss, they were found in the car?" and then, after running me a bath, whisked away every other garment within sight, to add them no doubt to the collection she had already made of yesterday's tweed suit, jersey, shoes, stockings and underclothes. I foresaw that soon I should be appearing downstairs in my gloves and nothing else.

By nine o'clock I was bathed and dressed and quite

ready for some food. Curiously enough, the immense dinner of the night before, which ought to have lasted me a week, seemed to have made me hungrier than usual. I waited a few minutes after the stable clock struck nine, so as not to be the first, and then ventured downstairs, but was greatly disconcerted in the dining room to find the table still in its green baize, the door into the pantry wide open and the menservants, in striped waistcoats and shirt sleeves, engaged upon jobs which had nothing to do with an approaching meal, such as sorting out letters and folding up the morning papers. They looked at me, or so I imagined, with surprise and hostility. I found them even more frightening than my fellow guests and was about to go back to my bedroom as quickly as I could when a voice behind me said, "But it's terrible, looking at this empty table."

It was the Duc de Sauveterre. My protective colouring was off, it seemed, by morning light. In fact he spoke as if we were old friends. I was very much surprised, more so when he shook my hand, and most of all when he said, "I also long for my porridge, but we can't stay here. It's too sad. Shall we go for a walk while it comes?"

The next thing I knew I was walking beside him, very fast, running almost to keep up, in one of the great lime avenues of the park. He talked all the time, as fast as he walked.

"Season of mists," he said, "and mellow fruitfulness. Am I not brilliant to know that? But this morning you can hardly see the mellow fruitfulness for the mists."

And indeed there was a thin fog all round us, out of which loomed great yellow trees. The grass was soaking wet and my indoor shoes were already leaking.

"I do love," he went on, "getting up with the lark and going for a walk before breakfast."

"Do you always?" I said.

Some people did, I knew.

"Never, never, never. But this morning I told my man to put a call through to Paris, thinking it would take quite an hour, but it came through at once, so now I am at a loose end with time on my hands. Do I not know wonderful English?"

This ringing up of Paris seemed to me a most dashing extravagance. Aunt Sadie and Aunt Emily only made trunk calls in times of crisis, and even then they generally rang off in the middle of a sentence when the three-minute signal went. Davey, it is true, spoke to his doctor in London most days, but that was only from Kent, and in any case Davey's health could really be said to constitute a perpetual crisis. But Paris, abroad!

"Is somebody ill?" I ventured.

"Not exactly ill, but she bores herself, poor thing. I quite understand it. Paris must be terrible without me. I don't know how she can bear it. I do pity her, really."

"Who?" I said, curiosity overcoming my shyness, and indeed it would be difficult to feel shy for long with this extraordinary man.

"My fiancée," he said, carelessly.

Alas! Something had told me this would be the reply, my heart sank and I said, dimly, "Oh! How exciting! You are engaged?"

He gave me a sidelong whimsical look.

"Oh, yes," he said, "engaged!"

"And are you going to be married soon?"

But why, I wondered had he come away alone, without her? If I had such a fascinating fiancé I would follow him everywhere, I knew, like a faithful spaniel.

"I don't imagine it will be very soon," he said gaily. "You know what it is with the Vatican. Time is nothing to them—a thousand ages, in their sight are as an evening gone. Do I not know a lot of English poetry?"

"If you call it poetry. It's a hymn, really. But what has your marriage got to do with the Vatican? Isn't that in Rome?"

"It is. There is such a thing as the Church of Rome, my dear young lady, which I belong to, and this Church must annul the marriage of my affianced—do you say affianced?"

"You could. It's rather affected."

"My inamorata, my Dulcinea (brilliant?) must annul her marriage before she is at liberty to marry me."

"Goodness! Is she married already?"

"Yes, yes, of course. There are very few unmarried ladies going about, you know. It's not a state that lasts very long with pretty women."

"My aunt Emily doesn't approve of people getting engaged when they are married. My mother is always doing it and it makes Aunt Emily very cross."

"You must tell your dear Aunt Emily that in many ways it is rather convenient. But all the same, she is quite right. I have been a fiancé too often and for too long and now it is time I was married."

"Do you want to be?"

"I am not so sure. Going out to dinner every night with the same person, this must be terrible."

"You might stay in?"

"To break the habit of a life time is rather terrible, too. The fact is, I am so accustomed now to the engaged state that it's hard to imagine anything different."

"But have you been engaged to other people before this one?"

"Many, many times," he admitted.

"So what happened to them all?"

"Various unmentionable fates."

"For instance, what happened to the last one before this?"

"Let me see. Ah, yes—the last one before this did something I couldn't approve of, so I stopped loving her."

"But can you stop loving people because they do things you don't approve of?"

"Yes, I can."

"What a lucky talent," I said. "I'm sure I couldn't."

We had come to the end of the avenue and before us lay a field of stubble. The sun's rays were now beginning to pour down and dissolve the blue mist, turning the trees, the stubble and a group of ricks into objects of gold. I thought how lucky I was to be enjoying such a beautiful moment with so exactly the right person and that this was something I should remember all my life. The Duke interrupted these sentimental reflections, saying:

"Behold how brightly breaks the morning
    Though bleak our lot our hearts are warm. . . .
Am I not a perfect mine of quotations? Tell me, who is Veronica's lover now?"

I was once more obliged to confess that I had not known Veronica before, and I knew nothing of her life. He seemed less astounded by this news than Roly had been, but looked at me reflectively, saying, "You are very young. You have something of your mother. At first I thought not, but now I see there is something."

"And who do you think Mrs. Chaddesley Corbett's lover is?" I said. I was more interested in her than in my mother at the moment, and, besides, all this talk about lovers intoxicated me. One knew of course that they existed, because of the Duke of Monmouth, and so on, but so near, under the very same roof as oneself, that was indeed exciting.

"It doesn't make a pin of difference," he said, "who it is. She lives, as all those sort of women do, in one little tiny group or set, and sooner or later everybody in that set becomes the lover of everybody else, so that when they change their lovers it is more like a cabinet reshuffle than a new government. Always chosen out of the same old lot, you see."

"Is it like that in France?" I said.

"With society people? Just the same all over the world, though in France I should say there is less re-shuffling on the whole than in England; the ministers stay longer in their posts."

"Why?"

"Why? Frenchwomen generally keep their lovers if they want to because they know that there is one in-fallible way of doing so."

"No!" I said. "Oh, do tell."

I was more fascinated by this conversation every minute.

"It's very simple. You must give way to them in every respect."

"Goodness!" I said, thinking hard.

"Now, you see, these English *femmes du monde*, these Veronicas and Sheilas and Brendas and your mother, too, though nobody could say she stays in one little set —if she had done that she would not be so déclassée—

they follow quite a different plan. They are proud and
distant, out when the telephone bell rings, not free to
dine, unless you ask them a week before; in short, *elles
cherchent à se faire valoir,* and it never, never succeeds.
Even Englishmen, who are used to it, don't like it, after
a bit. Of course no Frenchman would put up with it
for a day. So they go on reshuffling."

"They're very nasty ladies, aren't they?" I said, having
formed that opinion the night before.

"Not at all, poor things. They are *les femmes du
monde, voilà tout,* I love them, so easy to get on with.
Not nasty at all. And I love *la mère* Montdore. How
amusing she is, with her snobbishness. I am very much
for snobs, they are always so charming to me."

"And Lord Montdore—and Polly?"

"Lord Montdore is a terrible old hypocrite, very English, very nice, but Polly now . . . ! There is something
I don't quite understand about Polly. Perhaps she does
not have a properly organized sex life, yes, I expect it is
that. She seems so dreamy. I must see what I can do for
her—only there's not much time." He looked at his
watch.

I said primly that very few well-brought-up English
girls of nineteen have a properly organized sex life.
Mine was not organized at all, I knew, but I did not
seem to be so specially dreamy.

"But what a beauty, even in that terrible dress. When
she has had a little love she may become one of the
beauties of our age. It's not certain; it never is with
Englishwomen. She may cram a felt hat on her head
and become a Lady Patricia Dougdale. Everything depends on the lover. So this Boy Dougdale, what about
him?"

"Stupid," I said, meaning, really, "stchoopid."

"But you are impossible, my dear. Nasty ladies, stupid men—you really must try and like people more or you'll never get on in this world."

"How d'you mean, get on?"

"Well, get all those things like husbands and fiancés, and get on with them. They are what really matter in a woman's life, you know."

"And children?" I said.

He roared with laughter. "Yes, yes, of course, children. Husbands first, then children, then fiancés, then more children. . . . Then you have to live near the Parc Monceau because of the nannies. It's a whole programme having children, I can tell you, especially if you happen to prefer the Left Bank, as I do."

I did not understand one word of all this.

"Are you going to be a Bolter," he said, "like your mother?"

"No, no," I said. "A tremendous sticker."

"Really? I'm not quite sure."

Soon, too soon for my liking, we found ourselves back at the house.

"Porridge," said the Duke, again looking at his watch.

The front door opened upon a scene of great confusion. Most of the house party, some in tweeds and some in dressing gowns, were assembled in the hall, as were various outdoor and indoor servants, while a village policeman, who, in the excitement of the moment had brought his bicycle in with him, was conferring with Lord Montdore. High above our heads, leaning over the balustrade in front of Niobe, Lady Montdore, in a mauve satin wrap, was shouting at her husband:

"Tell him we must have Scotland Yard down at once, Montdore. If he won't send for them I shall ring up the Home Secretary myself. Most fortunately I have the number of his private line. In fact, I think I'd better go and do it now."

"No, no, my dear, please not. An Inspector is on his way, I tell you."

"Yes, I daresay, but how do we know it's the very best Inspector? I think I'd better get on to my friend. I think he'd be hurt with me if I didn't, the dear thing. Always so anxious to do what he can."

I was rather surprised to hear Lady Montdore speak so affectionately of a member of the Labour Government, this not being the attitude of other grown-ups, in my experience, but when I came to know her better I realized that power was a positive virtue in her eyes and that she automatically liked those who were invested with it.

My companion, with that look of concentration which comes over French faces when a meal is in the offing, did not wait to hear any of this. He made a bee line for the dining room, but although I was also very hungry indeed after my walk, curiosity got the better of me and I stayed to find out what it all meant. It seemed that there had been a burglary during the night and that nearly everybody in the house, except Lord and Lady Montdore, had been roundly robbed of jewels, loose cash, furs and anything portable of the kind that happened to be lying about. What made it particularly annoying for the victims was that they had all been woken up by somebody prowling in their rooms, but had all immediately concluded that it must be Sauveterre, pursuing his well-known hobby, so that the husbands had merely turned over with a grunt, saying, "Sorry, old chap, it's only me, I should try next door," while the wives had lain quite still in a happy trance of desire, murmuring such words of encouragement as they knew in French. Or so, at least, they were saying about each other, and, when I passed the telephone box on my way upstairs to change my wet shoes, I could hear Mrs. Chaddesley Corbett's birdlike twitters piping her version of the story to the outside world. Perhaps the cabinet changes were becoming a little bit of a bore, after all, and these ladies did rather long, at heart, for a new policy.

The general feeling was now very much against Sauveterre, whose fault the whole thing clearly was. It became positively inflamed when he was known to have had a good night's rest, to have got up at eight to telephone to his mistress in Paris and then to have gone for a walk with that little girl. ("Not the Bolter's child for nothing," I heard somebody say bitterly.) The climax was reached when he was seen to be putting away a huge breakfast of porridge and cream, kedgeree, eggs, cold ham and slice upon slice of toast covered with Cooper's Oxford. Very un-French, not at all in keeping with his reputation, unsuitable behaviour too, in view of the well-known frailty of his fellow guests. Britannia felt herself slighted by this foreigner. Away with him! And away he went, immediately after breakfast, driving hell for leather to Newhaven to catch the boat for Dieppe.

"Castle life," explained his mother, who placidly remained on until Monday, "always annoys Fabrice and makes him so nervous, poor boy."

I never saw Sauveterre again and it was to be many years before I even heard his name, but in the end I found myself adopting his little boy, so small is the world, so strange is fate.

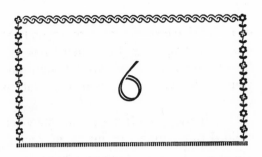

6

THE rest of that day was rather disorganized. The men finally went off shooting, very late, while the women stayed at home to be interviewed by various Inspectors on the subject of their lost possessions. Of course the burglary made a wonderful topic of conversation and indeed nobody spoke of anything else.

"I couldn't care less about the diamond brooch. After all, it's well insured and now I shall be able to have clips instead which will be far and away smarter. Veronica's clips always make me miserable, every time I see her, and, besides, that brooch used to remind me of my bogus old mother-in-law too much. But I couldn't think it more hateful of them to have taken my fur tippet. Burglars never seem to realize one might feel the cold. How would they like it if I took away their wife's shawl?"

"Oh, I know. I'm in a terrible do about my bracelet

of lucky charms—no value to anybody else—it really is too too sick-making. Just when I had managed to get a bit of hangman's rope, Mrs. Thompson too, did I tell you? Roly will never win the National now, poor sweet."

"With me it's Mummy's little locket she had as a child. I can't think why my ass of a maid had to go and put it in. She never does as a rule."

These brassy ladies became quite human as they mourned their lost trinkets, and now that the men were out of the house they suddenly seemed very much nicer. I am speaking of the Veronica chorus, for Mrs. Chaddesley Corbett herself, in common with Lady Montdore and Lady Patricia, was always exactly the same, whatever the company.

At tea time the village policeman reappeared with his bicycle, having wiped the eye of all the grand detectives who had come from London in their shiny cars. He produced a perfect jumble-sale heap of objects which had been discarded by the burglars under a haystack and nearly all the little treasures were retrieved, with high cries of joy, by their owners. As the only things which now remained missing were jewels of considerable value, and as these were felt to be the business of the Insurance Companies, the party continued in a much more cheerful atmosphere. There was, however, a distinctly noticeable current of anti-French feeling. The Norahs and Nellies would have had a pretty poor reception if any of them had turned up just then, and Boy, if it was possible for him to have enough of a Duchess, must have been having enough of this one, since all but he fled from the machine-gun fire of questions, and he was obliged to spend the next two days practically alone with her.

I was hanging about, as one does at house parties, waiting for the next meal; it was not yet quite time to dress for dinner on Sunday evening. One of the pleasures of staying at Hampton was that the huge Louis XV map table in the middle of the Long Gallery was always covered with every imaginable weekly newspaper neatly laid out in rows and rearranged two or three times a day by a footman whose sole occupation this appeared to be.

I seldom saw the *Tatler* and *Sketch,* as my aunts would have thought it a perfectly unwarranted extravagance to subscribe to such papers, and I was greedily gulping down back numbers when Lady Montdore called to me from a sofa where, ever since tea, she had been deep in talk with Mrs. Chaddesley Corbett. I had been throwing an occasional glance in their direction, wondering what it could all be about and wishing I could be a fly on the wall to hear them, thinking also that it would hardly be possible for two women to look more different. Mrs. Chaddesley Corbett, her bony little silken legs crossed and uncovered to above the knee, perched rather than sat on the edge of the sofa. She wore a plain beige kasha dress, which must certainly have been made in Paris, and certainly designed for the Anglo-Saxon market, and smoked cigarette after cigarette with a great play of long thin white fingers, flashing with rings and painted nails. She did not keep still for one moment, though she was talking with great earnestness and concentration.

Lady Montdore sat well back on the sofa, both her feet on the ground. She seemed planted there, immovable and solid, not actually fat, but solid through and through. Smartness, even if she had sought after it, would hardly be attainable by her in a world where it was personified by the other and had become almost as much a question of build, of quick and nervous movement as of actual clothes. Her hair was shingled, but it was grey and fluffy, by no means a smooth cap, her eyebrows grew at will, and when she remembered to use lipstick and powder they were any colour and slapped on anyhow, so that her face, compared with that of Mrs. Chaddesley Corbett was as a hayfield is to a lawn, her whole head looking twice as large as the polished little head beside her. All the same she was not disagreeable to look at. There was a healthiness and liveliness about her face which lent it a certain attraction. Of course she seemed to me, then, very old. She was, in fact, about fifty-eight.

"Come over here, Fanny."

I was almost too much surprised to be alarmed by this summons and hurried over, wondering what it could all be about.

"Sit there," she said, pointing to a needlework chair, "and talk to us. Are you in love?"

I felt myself becoming scarlet in the face. How could they have guessed my secret? Of course I had been in love for two days now, ever since my morning walk with the Duc de Sauveterre. Passionately, but, as indeed I realized, hopelessly in love. In fact the very thing that Lady Montdore had intended for Polly had befallen me.

"There you are, Sonia," said Mrs. Chaddesley Corbett triumphantly, tapping a cigarette with nervous violence against her jewelled case and lighting it with a gold lighter, her pale blue eyes never meanwhile leaving my face. "What did I tell you? Of course she is, poor sweet, just look at that blush, it must be something quite new and horribly bogus. I know, it's my dear old husband. Confess, now! I couldn't mind less, actually."

I did not like to say that I still, after a whole week-end, had no idea at all which of the many husbands present hers might be, but stammered out as quick as I could, "Oh, no, no, not anybody's husband, I prom-ise." Only a fiancé, and such a detached one at that.

They both laughed.

"All right," said Mrs. Chaddesley Corbett, "we're not going to worm. What we really want to know, to settle a bet, is, have you always fancied somebody ever since you can remember? Answer truthfully, please."

I was obliged to admit that this was the case. From a tiny child, ever since I could remember, in fact, some delicious image had been enshrined in my heart, last thought at night, first thought in the morning. Fred Terry as Sir Percy Blakeney, Lord Byron, Rudolph Val-entino, Henry V, Gerald du Maurier, blissful Mrs. Ash-ton at my school, Steerforth, Napoleon, the guard on the 4.45, image had succeeded image. Latterly it had been that of a pale, pompous young man in the Foreign Office who had once, during my season in London, asked me for a dance, had seemed to me the very flower of cosmopolitan civilization, and had remained the pivot of existence until wiped from my memory by Sauve-terre. For that is what always happened to these images. Time and hateful absence blurred them, faded them but never quite obliterated them until some lovely new broom image came and swept them away.

"There you are, you see," Mrs. Chaddesley Corbett turned triumphantly to Lady Montdore. "From kiddie car to hearse, darling, I couldn't know it better. After all, what would there be to think about when one's alone, otherwise?"

What, indeed? This Veronica had hit the nail on the head. Lady Montdore did not look convinced. She, I felt sure, had never harboured romantic yearnings and had plenty to think about when she was alone, which, anyhow, was hardly ever.

"But who is there for her to be in love with, and, if she is, surely I should know it," she said.

I guessed that they were talking about Polly and this was confirmed by Mrs. Chaddesley Corbett saying, "No, darling, you wouldn't, you're her mother. When I remember poor Mummy and her ideas on the subject of my ginks . . ."

"Now, Fanny, tell us what you think. Is Polly in love?"

"Well, she says she's not, but . . ."

"But you don't think it's possible not to be fancying someone? Nor do I."

I wondered. Polly and I had had a long chat the night before, sprawling on my bed in our dressing gowns, and I had felt almost certain then that she was keeping something back which she would half have liked to tell me.

"I suppose it might depend on your nature?" I said, doubtfully.

"Anyhow," said Lady Montdore, "there's one thing only too certain. She takes no notice of the young men I provide for her and they take no notice of her. They worship me, of course, but what is the good of that?"

Mrs. Chaddesley Corbett caught my eye, and I thought she gave me half a wink. I liked her more every minute. Lady Montdore went on:

"Bored and boring. I can't say I'm looking forward to bringing her out in London very much if she goes on like this. She used to be such a sweet easy child, but her whole character seems to have changed, now she is grown-up. I can't understand it."

"Oh, she's bound to fall for some nice chap in London, darling," said Mrs. Chaddesley Corbett. "I wouldn't worry too much, if I were you. Whoever she's in love with now, if she is in love, which Fanny and I know she must be, is probably a kind of dream and she only needs to see some flesh and blood people for her to forget about it. It so often happens, with girls."

"Yes, my dear, that's all very well, but she was out for two years in India, you know. There were some very attractive men there, polo, and so on; not suitable, of course. I was only too thankful she didn't fall in love with any of them, but she could have, it would not have been unnatural at all. Why, poor Delia's girl fell in love with a Rajah, you know."

"I couldn't blame her less," said Mrs. Chaddesley Corbett. "Rajahs must be perfect heaven—all those diamonds."

"Oh, no, my dear—any Englishwoman has better stones than they do. I never saw anything to compare with mine when I was there. But this Rajah was rather attractive, I must say, though of course Polly didn't see it; she never does. Oh, dear, oh, dear! Now, if only we were a French family, they seem to arrange things so very much better. To begin with, Polly would inherit all this, instead of those stupid people in Nova Scotia—

so unsuitable—can you imagine Colonials living here?
—and, to go on with, we should find a husband for her
ourselves, after which he and she would live partly at
his place with his parents and partly here with us. Think
how sensible that is. The old French tart was telling me
the whole system last night."

Lady Montdore was famous for picking up words she
did not quite understand and giving them a meaning of
her own. She clearly took the word tart to mean old
girl, trout, body. Mrs. Chaddesley Corbett was delighted. She gave a happy little squeak and rushed upstairs, saying that she must go and dress for dinner.
When I came up ten minutes later she was still telling
the news through bathroom doors.

After this, Lady Montdore set out to win my heart,
and, of course, succeeded. It was not very difficult. I
was young and frightened, she was old and grand and
frightening, and it only required a very little charm, an
occasional hint of mutual understanding, a smile, a
movement of sympathy to make me think I really loved
her. The fact is that she had charm, and since charm
allied to riches and position is almost irresistible, it so
happened that her many haters were usually people
who had never met her, or people she had purposely
snubbed or ignored. Those whom she made efforts to
please, while forced to admit that she was indefensible,
were very much inclined to say ". . . but all the same
she has been very nice to me and I can't help liking
her." She herself, of course, never doubted for one
moment that she was worshipped, and by every section
of society.

Before I left Hampton on Monday morning Polly

took me up to her mother's bedroom to say good-bye. Some of the guests had left the night before, the others were leaving now, all rolling away in their huge rich motor cars, and the house was like a big school breaking up for the holidays. The bedroom doors we passed were open, revealing litters of tissue paper and unmade beds, servants struggling with suitcases and guests struggling into their coats. Everybody seemed to be in a struggling hurry all of a sudden.

Lady Montdore's room—I remembered it of old— was enormous, more like a ballroom than a bedroom, and was done up in the taste of her own young days when she was a bride. The walls were panelled in pink silk covered with white lace, the huge wicker-work bed on a dais had curtains of pink shot silk, there was a lot of white furniture with fat pink satin upholstery outlined in ribbon roses. Silver flower vases stood on all the tables, and photographs in silver frames, mostly of royal personages, with inscriptions cordial in inverse ratio to the actual importance of the personage, reigning monarchs having contented themselves with merely a Christian name, an R, and perhaps a date, while ex-kings and queens, archduchesses and grand dukes had scattered Dearest and Darling Sonia and Loving all over their trains and uniform trousers.

In the middle of all this silver and satin and silk, Lady Montdore cut rather a comic figure drinking strong tea in bed among masses of lace pillows, her coarse grey hair frizzed out, and wearing what appeared to be a man's striped flannel pyjama top under a feathered wrap. The striped pyjamas were not the only incongruous touch in the room. On her lacy dressing table with its big, solid silver looking-glass and among her silver and enamel brushes, bottles and boxes with their diamond cypher, were a black Mason Pearson hair brush and a pot of Pond's cold cream, while dumped down in the middle of the royalties were a rusty nail file, a broken comb and a bit of cotton wool. While we were talking, Lady Montdore's maid came in and with much clicking of her tongue was about to remove all these objects when Lady Montdore told her to leave them, as she had not finished.

Her quilt was covered with newspapers and opened letters and she held the *Times* neatly folded back at the Court Circular, probably the only part of it she ever looked at, since news, she used to say, can always be gleaned, and far more accurately too, from those who make it. I think she felt it comfortable, rather like reading prayers, to begin the day with their Majesties having attended Divine Service at Sandringham and Mabell Countess of Airlie having succeeded the Lady Elizabeth Motion as Lady in Waiting to the Queen. It indicated that the globe was still revolving in accordance with the laws of nature.

"Good morning, Fanny dear," she said. "This will interest you, I suppose."

She handed me the *Times* and I saw that Linda's engagement to Anthony Kroesig was announced at last.

"Poor Alconleighs," she went on, in tones of deep satisfaction. "No wonder they don't like it! What a silly girl! Well, she always has been, in my opinion. No place. Rich, of course, but banker's money; it comes and it goes and however much of it there may be it's not like marrying all this."

"All this" was a favourite expression of Lady Montdore's. It did not mean all this beauty, this strange and fairy-like house set in the middle of four great avenues rushing up four artificial slopes, the ordered spaces of trees and grass and sky seen from its windows, or the aesthetic joy given by the treasures it contained, for she was not gifted with the sense of beauty and if she admired anything at all it was rather what might be described as stockbroker's picturesque. She had made herself a little garden round a Cotswold well-head, rustic, with heather and rambler roses, and to this she would often retire in order to sketch the sunset. "So beautiful it makes me want to cry." She had all the sentimentality of her generation, and this sentimentality, growing like a green moss over her spirit, helped to conceal its texture of stone, if not from others, at any rate from herself. She was convinced that she was a woman of profound sensibility.

"All this," on her lips, meant position allied to such solid assets as acres, coal mines, real estate, jewels, silver, pictures, incunables, and other possessions of the sort. Lord Montdore owned an almost incredible number of such things, fortunately.

"Not that I ever expected poor little Linda to make a suitable marriage," she went on. "Sadie is a wonderful woman, of course, and I'm devoted to her, but I'm afraid she hasn't the very smallest idea how to bring up girls."

Nevertheless, no sooner did Aunt Sadie's girls show their noses outside the schoolroom than they were snapped up and married, albeit unsuitably, and perhaps this fact was rankling a little with Lady Montdore whose mind appeared to be so much on the subject.

The relations between Hampton and Alconleigh were as follows: Lady Montdore had an irritated fondness for Aunt Sadie, whom she half admired for an integrity which she could not but recognize and half blamed for an unworldliness which she considered out of place in somebody of her position; she could not endure Uncle Matthew and thought him mad. Uncle Matthew, for his part, revered Lord Montdore who was perhaps the only person in the world whom he looked up to, and loathed Lady Montdore to such a degree that he used to say he longed to strangle her. Now that Lord Montdore was back from India, Uncle Matthew continually saw him at the House of Lords, and on the various county organizations which they both attended, and he would come home and quote his most banal remark as if it were the utterance of a prophet. "Montdore tells me . . . Montdore says . . ." And that was that—useless to question it; what Lord Montdore believed on any subject was final in the eyes of my uncle.

"Wonderful fella, Montdore. What I can't imagine is how we ever got on without him in this country all those years. Terribly wasted among the blackamoors when he's the kind of fella we need so badly, here."

He even broke his rule about never visiting other people's houses in favour of Hampton. "If Montdore asks us I think we ought to go."

"It's Sonia who asks us," Aunt Sadie would correct him, mischievously.

"The old she-wolf. I shall never know what can have come over Montdore to make him marry her. I suppose he didn't realize at the time how utterly poisonously bloody she is."

"Darling—darling . . . !"

"Utterly bloody. But if Montdore asks us I think we should go."

As for Aunt Sadie, she was always so vague, so much in the clouds, that it was never easy to know what she really thought of people, but I believe that though she rather enjoyed the company of Lady Montdore in small doses, she did not share my uncle's feelings about Lord Montdore, for when she spoke of him there was always a note of disparagement in her voice.   •

"Something silly about his look," she used to say, though never in front of Uncle Matthew, for it would have hurt his feelings dreadfully.

"So that's Louisa and poor Linda accounted for," Lady Montdore went on. "Now you must be the next one, Fanny."

"Oh, no," I said. "Nobody will ever marry me." And indeed I could not imagine anybody wanting to. I seemed to myself so much less fascinating than the other girls I knew, and I despised my looks, hating my round pink cheeks and rough curly black hair which never could be made to frame my face in silken cords, however much I wetted and brushed it, but would insist on growing the wrong way, upwards, like heather.

"Nonsense. And don't you go marrying just anybody, for love," she said. "Remember that love cannot last; it never, never does; but if you marry all this it's for your life. One day, don't forget, you'll be middle-aged and think what that must be like for a woman who can't have, say, a pair of diamond earrings. A woman of my age needs diamonds near her face, to give a sparkle. Then at meal times, sitting with all the unimportant people for ever and ever. And no car. Not a very nice prospect, you know. Of course," she added as an afterthought, "I was lucky, I had love as well as all this. But it doesn't often happen and when the moment comes for you to choose, just remember what I say. I suppose Fanny ought to go now and catch her train— and when you've seen her off, will you find Boy, please, and send him up here to me, Polly? I want to think over the dinner party for next week with him. Good-bye then, Fanny—let's see a lot of you now we're back."

On the way downstairs we ran into Boy.

"Mummy wants to see you," Polly said, gravely posing her blue look upon him. He put his hand to her shoulder and massaged it with his thumb.

"Yes," he said, "about this dinner party, I suppose. Are you coming to it, old girl?"

"Oh, I expect so," she said. "I'm out now, you see."

"Can't say I'm looking forward to it very much. Your mother's ideas on *placement* get vaguer and vaguer. Really, the table last night, the *duchesse* is still in a temper about it! Sonia really shouldn't have people at all if she can't treat them properly."

A phrase I had often heard on the lips of my Aunt Emily, with reference to animals.

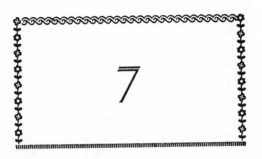

7

BACK at home I was naturally unable to talk of anything but my visit. Davey was much amused and said he had never known me so chatty.

"But my dear child," he said, "weren't you petrified? Sauveterre and the Chaddesley Corbetts . . . ! Even worse than I had expected."

"Well, yes, at first I thought I'd die. But nobody took any notice of me, really, except Mrs. Chaddesley Corbett and Lady Montdore. . . ."

"Oh! And what notice did they take, may I ask?"

"Well, Mrs. Chaddesley Corbett said Mummy bolted first of all with Mr. Chaddesley Corbett."

"So she did," said Davey. "That boring old Chad, I'd quite forgotten. You don't mean to say Veronica told you so? I wouldn't have thought it possible, even of her."

"No, she said it to somebody else—eggy-peggy."

"I see. Well, then what about Sonia?"

"Oh, she was sweet to me."

"She was, was she? This is indeed sinister news."

"What is sinister news?" said Aunt Emily, coming in with her dogs. "It's simply glorious out, I can't imagine why you two are stuffing in here on this heavenly day."

"We're gossiping about the party you so unwisely allowed Fanny to go to. And I was saying that if Sonia has really taken a fancy to our little one, which it seems she has, we must look out for trouble, that's all."

"What trouble?" I said.

"Sonia's terribly fond of juggling with people's lives. I never shall forget when she made me go to her doctor. . . . I can only say he very nearly killed me. It's not her fault if I'm here today. She's entirely unscrupulous. She gets a hold over people much too easily, with her charm and her prestige, and then forces her own values on them."

"Not on Fanny," Aunt Emily said, with confidence. "Look at that chin."

"You always say look at Fanny's chin, but I never can see any other signs of her being strong-minded. Any of the Radletts can make her do whatever they like."

"You'll see," said Aunt Emily. "Siegfried is quite all right again, by the way. He's had a lovely walkiee."

"Oh, good," said Davey. "Olive oil's the thing."

They both looked affectionately at the Pekingese, Siegfried.

But I wanted to get some more interesting gossip out of Davey about the Hamptons. I said coaxingly, "Go on, Dave, do go on telling about Lady Montdore. What was she like when she was young?"

"Exactly the same as she is now."

I sighed. "No, but I mean what did she look like?"

"I tell you, just the same," said Davey. "I've known her ever since I was a little tiny boy and she hasn't changed one scrap."

"Oh, Davey . . ." I began. But I left it at that. It's no good, I thought, you always come up against this blank wall with old people, they always say about each other that they have never looked any different, and how can it be true? Anyway, if it is true they must have been a horrid generation, all withered or blowsy, and grey at the age of eighteen, knobbly hands, bags under the chin, eyes set in a little map of wrinkles, I thought crossly, adding up all these things on the faces of Davey and Aunt Emily as they sat there, smugly thinking that they had always looked exactly the same. Quite useless to discuss questions of age with old people, they have such peculiar ideas on the subject. "Not really old at all, only seventy," you hear them saying, or "Quite young, younger than me, not much more than forty." At eighteen this seems great nonsense, though now, at the more advanced age which I have reached, I am beginning to understand what it all meant, because Davey and Aunt Emily, in their turn, seem to me to look as they have looked ever since I knew them first, when I was a little child, between twenty and thirty years ago.

"Who else was there?" asked Davey, "the Dougdales?"

"Oh, yes. Isn't the Lecturer stchoopid?"

Davey laughed. "And lecherous?" he said.

"No, I must say not actually lecherous, not with me."

"Well, of course he couldn't be with Sonia there, he wouldn't dare. He's been her young man for years, you know."

"Don't tell me!" I said, fascinated. That was the heaven of Davey, he knew everything about everybody, quite unlike my aunts, who, though they had no special objection to our knowing gossip, now that we were grown-up, had always forgotten it themselves, being totally uninterested in the doings of people outside their own family. "Davey—how could she?"

"Well, Boy is very good-looking," said Davey. "I should say, rather, how could he? But, as a matter of fact, I think it's a love-affair of pure convenience, it suits them both perfectly. Boy knows the Gotha by heart, and all that kind of thing. He's like a wonderful extra butler, and Sonia, on her side, gives him an interest in life. I quite see it."

One comfort, I thought, such elderly folk couldn't do anything, but again I kept it to myself because I knew that nothing makes people crosser than being considered too old for love, and Davey and the Lecturer were exactly the same age; they had been at Eton together. Lady Montdore, of course, was even older.

"Let's hear about Polly," said Aunt Emily, "and then I really must insist on you going out of doors before tea. Is she a real beauty, just as we were always being told by Sonia that she would be?"

"Of course she is," said Davey, "doesn't Sonia always get her own way?"

"So beautiful, you can't imagine," I said. "And so nice, the nicest person I ever met."

"Fanny is such a hero-worshipper," said Aunt Emily, amused.

"I expect it's true though, anyway about the beauty," said Davey. "Because, quite apart from Sonia always getting what she wants, Hamptons do have such marvellous looks, and, after all, the old girl herself is very handsome. In fact, I see that she would improve the strain by giving a little solidity—Montdore looks too much like a collie dog."

"And who is this wonderful girl to marry?" said Aunt Emily. "That will be the next problem for Sonia. I can't see who will ever be good enough for her?"

"Merely a question of strawberry leaves," said Davey, "as I imagine she's probably too big for the Prince of Wales, he likes such tiny little women. You know, I can't help thinking that now Montdore is getting older he must feel it dreadfully that he can't leave Hampton to her. I had a long talk about it the other day with Boy in the London Library. Of course, Polly will be very rich—enormously rich, because he can leave her everything else—but they all love Hampton so much, I think it's very sad for them."

"Can he leave Polly the pictures at Montdore House? Surely they must be entailed on the heir?" said Aunt Emily.

"There are wonderful pictures at Hampton," I butted in. "A Raphael and a Caravaggio in my bedroom alone." They both laughed at me, hurting my feelings, rather.

"Oh, my darling child, country-house bedroom pictures! But the ones in London are a world-famous collection, and I believe they can all go to Polly. The young man from Nova Scotia simply gets Hampton and everything in it, but that is an Aladdin's Cave, you know, the furniture, the silver, the library—treasures beyond value. Boy was saying they really ought to get him over and show him something of civilization before he becomes too transatlantic."

"I forget how old he is," said Aunt Emily.

"I know," I said. "He's six years older than I, about twenty-four now. And he's called Cedric, like Lord Fauntleroy. Linda and I used to look him up when we were little to see if he would do for us."

"You would. How typical," said Aunt Emily. "But I should have thought he might really do for Polly—settle everything."

"It would be too much unlike life," said Davey. "Oh, bother, talking to Fanny has made me forget my three o'clock pill."

"Take it now," said Aunt Emily, "and then go out, please, both of you."

From this time on I saw a great deal of Polly. I went to Alconleigh, as I did every year, for some hunting, and from there I often went over to spend a night or two at Hampton. There were no more big house parties but a continual flow of people and, in fact, the Mont-dores and Polly never seemed to have a meal by them-selves. Boy Dougdale came over nearly every day from his own house at Silkin which was only about ten miles away. He quite often went home to dress for dinner and came back again to spend the evening, since Lady Patricia, it seemed, was not at all well, and liked to go to bed early. Boy never seemed to me quite like a real human being, and I think the reason for this was that he was always acting some part. Boy, the Don Juan, alternated with Boy, the Squire of Silkin and Boy, the Cultivated Cosmopolitan. In none of these parts was he quite convincing. Don Juan only made headway with very unsophisticated women, except in the case of

Lady Montdore, and she, whatever their relationship may have been in the past, was treating him by now more as a private secretary than as a lover. The squire played cricket with the village youths and lectured the village women, but never seemed like a real squire for all his efforts, and the cultivated cosmopolitan gave himself away every time he put brush to canvas or pen to paper.

When he was with Lady Montdore they occupied much of their time painting, water-colour sketches out of doors in the summer and large set pieces in oils, using a north bedroom as a studio in the winter. They covered acres of canvas and were such great admirers of their own and each other's work that the opinion of the outside world meant but little to them. Their pictures were always framed and hung about their two houses, the best ones in rooms and the others in passages.

By the evening Lady Montdore was ready for some relaxation.

"I like to work hard all day," she would say, "and then have agreeable company and perhaps a game of cards in the evening."

There were always guests for dinner, an Oxford don or two, with whom Lord Montdore could show off about Livy, Plotinus and the Claudian family, Lord Merlin, who was a great favourite of Lady Montdore and who published her sayings far and wide, and the more important county neighbours strictly in turns. They seldom sat down fewer than ten people. It was very different from Alconleigh.

I enjoyed these visits to Hampton. Lady Montdore terrified me less and charmed me more, Lord Montdore remained perfectly agreeable and colourless, Boy continued to give me the creeps and Polly became my best-friend-next-to-Linda.

Presently Aunt Sadie suggested that I might like to bring Polly back with me to Alconleigh, which I duly did. It was not a very good time for a visit there since everybody's nerves were upset by Linda's engagement, but Polly did not seem to notice the atmosphere and no doubt her presence restrained Uncle Matthew from giving vent to the full violence of his feelings while she was there. Indeed, she said to me as we drove back to Hampton together after the visit that she envied the Radlett children their upbringing in such a quiet, affectionate household, a remark which could only have been made by somebody who had inhabited the best spare room, out of range of Uncle Matthew's early morning gramophone concerts, and who had never happened to see that violent man in one of his tempers. Even so, I thought it strange, coming from Polly, because if anybody had been surrounded by affection all her life it was she; I did not yet fully understand how difficult the relations were beginning to be between her and her mother.

8

P O L L Y and I were bridesmaids at Linda's wedding in February, and when it was over I motored down to Hampton with Polly and Lady Montdore to spend a few days there. I was grateful to Polly for suggesting this, as I remembered too well the horrible feeling of anti-climax there had been after Louisa's wedding, which would certainly be ten times multiplied after Linda's. Indeed, with Linda married, the first stage of my life no less than of hers was finished and I felt myself to be left in a horrid vacuum, with childhood over but married life not yet beginning.

As soon as Linda and Anthony had gone away, Lady Montdore sent for her car and we all three huddled onto the back seat. Polly and I were still in our bridesmaid's dresses (sweet pea tints, in chiffon) but well wrapped up in fur coats and each with a Shetland rug wound round our legs, like children going to a dancing class.

The chauffeur spread a great bearskin over all of us and put a foot warmer under our silver kid shoes. It was not really cold, but shivery, pouring and pouring with rain as it had been all day, getting dark now. The inside of the motor car was like a dry little box, and as we splashed down the long wet shiny roads, with the rain beating against the windows, there was a specially delicious cosiness about being in this little box and knowing that so much light and warmth and solid comfort lay ahead.

"I love being so dry in here," as Lady Montdore put it, "and seeing all those poor people so wet."

She had done the journey twice that day, having driven up from Hampton in the morning, whereas Polly had gone up the day before with her father for a last fitting of her bridesmaid's dress and in order to go to a dinner-dance.

First of all we talked about the wedding. Lady Montdore was wonderful when it came to picking over an occasion of that sort. With her gimlet eye nothing escaped her, nor did any charitable inhibitions tone down her comments on what she had observed.

"How extraordinary Lady Kroesig looked, poor woman! I suppose somebody must have told her that the bridegroom's mother should have a bit of everything in her hat—for luck, perhaps. Fur, feathers, flowers and a scrap of lace—it was all there and a diamond brooch on top to finish it off nicely. Rose diamonds—I had a good look. It's a funny thing that these people who are supposed to be so rich never seem to have a decent jewel to put on. I've often noticed it. And did you see what mangy little things they gave poor Linda? A cheque—yes, that's all very well, but for how much, I wonder. Cultured pearls, at least I imagine so, or they would have been worth quite £10,000, and a hideous little bracelet. No tiara, no necklace—what will the poor child wear at Court? Linen, which we didn't see, all that modern silver and a horrible house in one of those squares by the Marble Arch. Hardly worth being called by that nasty German name, I should say. And Davey tells me there's no proper settlement. Really, Matthew Alconleigh isn't fit to have children if that's all he can do for them. Still, I'm bound to say he looked very handsome coming up the aisle, and Linda looked her very best too, really lovely."

I think she was feeling quite affectionately towards Linda for having removed herself betimes from competition, for, although not a great beauty like Polly, she was certainly far more popular with young men.

"Sadie, too, looked so nice, very young and handsome, and the little things so puddy." She pronounced the word pretty like that.

"Did you see our desert service, Fanny? Oh, did she? I'm glad. She could change it, as it came from Goods, but perhaps she won't want to. I was quite amused, weren't you, to see the difference between our side of the church and the Kroesig side. Bankers don't seem to be much to look at—so extraordinarily unsuitable having to know them at all, poor things, let alone marry them. But those sort of people have got megalomania nowadays, one can't get away from them. Did you notice the Kroesig sister? Oh, yes, of course, she was walking with you, Fanny. They'll have a job to get her off!"

"She's training to be a vet," I said.

"First sensible thing I've heard about any of them. No point in cluttering up the ballrooms with girls who look like that; it's simply not fair on anybody. Now, Polly, I want to hear exactly what you did, yesterday."

"Oh, nothing very much."

"Don't be so tiresome. You got to London at about twelve, I suppose?"

"Yes, we did," said Polly in a resigned voice. She would have to account for every minute of the day, she knew. Quicker to tell of her own accord than to have it pumped out of her. She began to fidget with her bridesmaid's wreath of silver leaves. "Wait a moment," she said. "I must take this off, it's giving me a headache."

It was twisted into her hair with wire. She tugged and pulled at it until finally she got it off and flung it down on the floor.

"Ow," she said, "that did hurt. Well, yes, then, let me think. We arrived, Daddy went straight to his appointment and I had an early luncheon at home."

"By yourself?"

"No, Boy was there. He'd looked in to return some books, and Bullitt said there was plenty of food so I made him stay."

"Well then, go on. After luncheon?"

"Hair."

"Washed and set?"

"Yes, naturally."

"You'd never think it. We really must find you a better hairdresser. No use asking Fanny, I'm afraid, her hair always looks like a mop."

Lady Montdore was becoming cross and like a cross child was seeking to hurt anybody within reach.

"It was quite all right until I had to put that wreath on it. Well then, tea with Daddy at the House, rest after tea, dinner you know about, and bed," she finished in one breath. "Is that all?"

She and her mother seemed to be thoroughly on each other's nerves, or perhaps it was having pulled her hair with the wreath that made her so snappy. She flashed a perfectly vicious look across me at Lady Montdore. It was suddenly illuminated by the headlights of a passing motor. Lady Montdore neither saw it nor, apparently, noticed the edge in her voice and went on, "No, certainly not. You haven't told me about the party yet. Who sat next you at dinner?"

"Oh, Mummy, I can't remember their names."

"You never seem to remember anybody's name. It is too stupid. How can I invite your friends to the house if I don't know who they are?"

"But they're not my friends. They were the most dreadful, dreadful bores you can possibly imagine. I couldn't think of one thing to say to them."

Lady Montdore sighed deeply. "Then after dinner you danced?"

"Yes. Danced, and sat out and ate disgusting ices."

"I'm sure the ices were delicious. Sylvia Waterman always does things beautifully. I suppose there was champagne?"

"I hate champagne."

"And who took you home?"

"Lady Somebody. It was out of her way because she lives in Chelsea."

"How extraordinary," said Lady Montdore, rather cheered up by the idea that some poor ladies have to live in Chelsea. "Now who could she possibly have been?"

The Dougdales had also been at the wedding and were to dine at Hampton on their way home; they were there when we arrived, not having, like us, waited to see Linda go away. Polly went straight upstairs. She looked tired and sent a message by her maid to say that she would have her dinner in bed. The Dougdales, Lady Montdore and I dined, without changing, in the little morning room where they always had meals if there were fewer than eight people. This room was perhaps the most perfect thing at Hampton. It had been brought bodily from France and was entirely panelled in wood carved in a fine and elaborate pattern, painted blue and white; three china cupboards matched three French windows and contained a Sèvres dinner service made for Marie Antoinette; over cupboards, windows and doorways were decorative paintings by Boucher, framed in the panelling.

The talk, at dinner, was of the ball which Lady Montdore intended to give for Polly at Montdore House during the London season.

"May day, I think," she said.

"That's good," said Boy. "It must either be the first or the last ball of the summer, if people are to remember it."

"Oh, not the last, on any account. I should have to invite all the girls whose dances Polly had been to, and nothing is so fatal to a ball as too many girls."

"But if you don't ask them," said Lady Patricia, "will they ask her?"

"Oh, yes," said Lady Montdore shortly. "They'll be dying to have her. I can pay them back in other ways. But, anyhow, I don't propose to take her about in the debutante world very much (all those awful parties,

S.W. something). I don't see the point of it. She would become quite worn out and meet a lot of thoroughly unsuitable young men. I'm planning to let her go to not more than two dances a week, carefully chosen. Quite enough for a girl who's not very strong. I thought later on, if you'll help me, Boy, we could make a list of women to give dinners for my ball. Of course it must be perfectly understood that they are to ask the people I tell them to. Can't have them paying off their own friends and relations on me."

After dinner we sat in the Long Gallery. Boy settled down to his petit point while we three women sat with idle hands. He had a talent for needlework, had hemstitched some of the sheets for the Queen's doll's house and had covered many chairs at Silkin and at Hampton.

He was now engaged upon a fire screen for the Long Gallery, which he had designed himself in a sprawling Jacobean pattern. The theme of it was supposed to be flowers from Lady Montdore's garden, but the flowers looked more like horrid huge insects. Being young and deeply prejudiced, it never occurred to me to admire this work. I merely thought how too dreadful it was to see a man sewing and how hideous he looked, his grizzled head bent over the canvas into which he was deftly stitching various shades of khaki. He had the same sort of thick hair as mine and I knew that the waves in it, the little careless curls (boyish) must have been carefully wetted and pinched in before dinner.

Lady Montdore had sent for paper and a pencil in order to write down the names of dinner hostesses. "We'll put down all the possible ones and then weed," she said. But she soon gave up this occupation in order to complain about Polly, and though I had already heard her on the subject when she had been talking with Mrs. Chaddesley Corbett, the tone of her voice was now much sharper and more aggrieved.

"One does everything for these girls," she said. "Everything. You wouldn't believe it, perhaps, but I assure you I spend quite half my day making plans for Polly—appointments, clothes, parties, and so on. I haven't a minute to see my own friends, I've hardly had a game of cards for months, I've quite given up my painting—in the middle of that nude girl from Oxford, too—in fact, I devote myself entirely to the child. I keep the London house going simply for her convenience. I hate London in the winter as you know and Montdore would be quite happy in two rooms without a cook (all that cold food at the club), but I've got a huge staff there eating their heads off entirely on her account. You'd think she'd be grateful at least, wouldn't you? Not at all. Sulky and disagreeable, I can hardly get a word out of her."

The Dougdales said nothing. He was sorting out wools with great concentration, and Lady Patricia lay back, her eyes closed, suffering as she had suffered for so long, in silence. She was looking more than ever like some garden statue, her skin and her beige London dress exactly the same colour, while her poor face was lined with pain and sadness, the very expression of antique tragedy.

Lady Montdore went on with her piece, talking exactly as if I were not there.

"I take endless trouble so that she can go and stay in nice houses, but she never seems to enjoy herself a bit, she comes home full of complaints and the only ones she ever wants to go back to are Alconleigh and

Emily Warbeck. Both pure waste of time! Alconleigh is a mad-house. . . . Of course, I love Sadie, everybody does, I think she's wonderful, poor dear, and it's not her fault if she has all those eccentric children. . . . She must have done what she can, but they are their father over again and no more need be said. Then I like the child to be with Fanny, and one has known Emily and Davey all one's life—Emily was our bridesmaid and Davey was an elf in the very first pageant I ever organized—but the fact remains Polly never meets anybody there and if she never meets people how can she marry them?"

"Is there so much hurry for her to marry?" said Lady Patricia.

"Well, you know she'll be twenty in May. She can't go on like this for ever. If she doesn't marry what will she do, with no interests in life, no occupation? She doesn't care for sketching or riding or society, she hardly has a friend in the world. . . . Oh, can you tell me how Montdore and I came to have a child like that? When I think of myself at her age! I remember so well Mr. Asquith saying he had never met anybody with such a genius for improvisation. . . ."

"Yes, you were wonderful," said Lady Patricia with a little smile. "But, after all, she may be slower at developing than you were and, as you say, she's not twenty yet. Surely it's rather nice to have her at home for another year or two?"

"The fact is," replied her sister-in-law, "girls are not nice. It's a perfectly horrid age. When they are children, so sweet and pretty, you think how delightful it will be to have their company later on, but what company is Polly to Montdore or to me? She moons about, always half-cross and half-tired and takes no interest in any mortal thing, and what she needs is a husband. Once she is married we shall be on excellent terms again. I've so often seen it happen. I was talking to Sadie the other day, and she agreed. She says she has had a most difficult time lately with Linda. Louisa, of course, was never any trouble. She had a nicer character and then she married straight out of the schoolroom. One thing you can say about the Radletts, no delay in marrying them off, though they might not be the sort of marriages one would like for one's own child. A banker and a dilapidated Scotch peer . . . Still, there it is—they are married. What can be the matter with Polly? So beautiful and no B.A. at all."

"S.A.," said Lady Patricia faintly, "or B.O."

"When we were young none of that existed, thank goodness. S.A. and B.O., perfect rubbish and bosh— one was a beauty or a *jolie-laide,* and that was that. All the same, now they have been invented I suppose it is better if the girls have them. Their partners seem to like it, and Polly hasn't a vestige, you can see that. But how differently," she said with a sigh, "how differently life turns out from what we expect! Ever since she was born, you know, I've worried and fussed over that child, and thought of the awful things that might happen to her—that Montdore might die before she was settled and we should have no proper home, that her looks would go (too beautiful at fourteen, I feared) or that she would have an accident and spend the rest of her days in a spinal chair—all sorts of things. I used to wake in the night and imagine them, but the one thing that never even crossed my mind was that she might end up an old maid."

There was a rising note of aggrieved hysteria in her voice.

"Come now, Sonia," said Lady Patricia rather sharply, "the poor girl is still in her teens. Do wait at least until she has had a London season before you call her an old maid. She'll find somebody she likes there soon enough, you can be quite sure."

"I only wish I could think it, but I have a strong feeling she won't, and that, what's more, they won't like her," said Lady Montdore. "She has no come-hither in her eye. Oh, it is really too bad. She leaves the light on in her bathroom night after night too, I see it shining out. . . ."

Lady Montdore was very mean about such small things as electric light.

AS HER mother had predicted, summer came and went without any change in Polly's circumstances. The London season duly opened with a ball at Montdore House which cost £2000, or so Lady Montdore told everybody, and was certainly very brilliant. Polly wore a white-satin dress with pink roses at the bosom and a pink lining to the sash (touches of pink, as the *Tatler* said) chosen in Paris for her by Mrs. Chaddesley Corbett and brought over in the bag by some South American diplomat, a friend of Lady Montdore's, to save duty, a proceeding of which Lord Montdore knew nothing and which would have perfectly horrified him had he known. Enhanced by this dress, and by a little make-up, Polly's beauty was greatly remarked upon, especially by those of a former generation, who were all saying that since Lady Helen Vincent, since Lily Langtry, since the Wyndham sisters (according to taste), nothing so perfect had been seen in London. Her own contemporaries, however, were not so greatly excited by her. They admitted her beauty but said that she was dull, too large. What they really admired were the little skinny goggling copies of Mrs. Chaddesley Corbett which abounded that season. The many dislikers of Lady Montdore said that she kept Polly too much in the background, and this was not fair because, although it is true to say that Lady Montdore automatically filled the foreground of any picture in which she figured, she was only too anxious to push Polly in front of her, like a hostage, and it was not her fault if she was forever slipping back again.

On the occasion of this ball many of the royalties in Lady Montdore's bedroom had stepped from their silver frames and come to life, dustier and less glamorous, poor dears, when seen in all their dimensions; the huge reception rooms at Montdore House were scattered with them and the words Sir or Ma'am could be heard on every hand. The Ma'ams were really quite pathetic—you would almost say hungry-looking—so old, in such sad and crumpled clothes, while there were some blue-chinned Sirs of dreadfully foreign aspect. I particularly remember one of them because I was told that he was wanted by the police in France and not much wanted anywhere else, especially not, it seemed, in his native land where his cousin, the King, was daily expecting the crown to be blown off his head by a puff of east wind. This Prince smelt strongly, but not deliciously, of camellias and had a *fond de teint* of brilliant sunburn.

"I only ask him for the sake of dear old Princess Irene," Lady Montdore would explain, if people raised their eyebrows at seeing him in such a very respectable house. "I never shall forget what an angel she was to Montdore and me when we were touring the Balkans (one doesn't forget these things). I know people do say he's a daisy, whatever that may be, but if you listen to what everybody says about everybody, you'll end by never having anybody, and, besides, half these rumours are put about by anarchists, I'm positive."

Lady Montdore loved anybody royal. It was a genuine emotion, quite disinterested, since she loved them as much in exile as in power, and the act of curtseying was the consummation of this love. Her curtseys, owing to the solid quality of her frame, did not recall the graceful movement of wheat before the wind. She scrambled down like a camel, rising again backside foremost, like a cow, a strange performance, painful, it might be supposed, to the performer, the expression on whose face, however, belied this thought. Her knees cracked like revolver shots but her smile was heavenly.

I was the only unmarried woman to be asked to dine at Montdore House before the dance. There was a dinner party of forty people with a very grand Sir and Ma'am indeed, on account of whom everybody was punctual to the minute, so that all the guests arrived simultaneously and the large crowd in Park Lane was rewarded by good long stares into the queuing motor cars. Mine was the only cab.

Upstairs a long wait ensued, without cocktails, and even the most brassy people, even Mrs. Chaddesley Corbett, began to twitter with nerves, as though they were being subjected to an intolerable strain; they stood about piping stupidities in their fashionable voices. At last the butler came up to Lord Montdore and murmured something, upon which he and Lady Montdore went down into the hall to receive their guests, while the rest of us, directed by Boy, formed ourselves into a semi-circle. Very slowly Lady Montdore led this tremendous Sir and Ma'am round the semi-circle, making presentations in the tone of voice, low, reverent but distinct which my aunts used for responses in church. Then, arm through exalted arm, the four of them moved off, still in slow motion, through the double doors into the dining room, leaving the rest of us to sort ourselves out and follow. It all went like clockwork.

Soon after dinner, which took a long time and was Hampton food at its climax, crest and top, people began to arrive for the ball. Lady Montdore in gold lamé, and many diamonds, including her famous pink-diamond tiara, Lord Montdore, genial, noble, his long thin legs in silk stockings and knee breeches, the Garter round one of them, its ribbon across his shirt front and a dozen miniatures dangling on his chest, and Polly, in her white dress and her beauty, stood shaking hands at the top of the stairs for quite an hour, and a very pretty sight it was to see the people streaming past them. Lady Montdore, true to her word, had invited very few girls and even fewer mammas. The guests were therefore neither too young nor too old to decorate but were all in their glittering prime.

Nobody asked me to dance. Just as no girls had been invited to the ball so also were there very few young men, except such as were firmly attached to the young married set, but I was quite happy looking on, and since there was not a soul I knew to see me no shame

attached to my situation. All the same I was delighted
when the Alconleighs, with Louisa and Linda and their
husbands, Aunt Emily and Davey, who had all been
dining together, appeared, as they always did at parties,
nice and early. I became assimilated into their cheerful
group and we took up a position, whence we could
have a good view of the proceedings, in the picture
gallery. This opened into the ballroom on one hand
and the supper room on the other. There was a great
deal of coming and going and at the same time never
any crowd, so that we could see the dresses and jewels
to their best advantage. Behind us hung a Coreggio St.
Sebastian with the habitual Buchmanite expression on
his face.

"Awful tripe," said Uncle Matthew. "Fella wouldn't
be grinning, he'd be dead with all those arrows in
him."

On the opposite wall was the Montdore Botticelli
which Uncle Matthew said he wouldn't give 7/6 for,
and when Davey showed him a Leonardo drawing he
said his fingers only itched for an india rubber.

"I saw a picture once," he said, "of shire horses in
the snow. There was nothing else, just a bit of broken-
down fence and three horses. It was dangerous good—
Army and Navy Stores. If I'd been a rich man I'd have
bought that—I mean you could see how cold those poor
brutes must have felt. If all this rubbish is supposed to
be valuable, that must be worth a fortune."

Uncle Matthew, who absolutely never went out in
the evening, let alone to balls, would not hear of refusing an invitation to Montdore House, though Aunt
Sadie, who knew how it tormented him to be kept
awake after dinner, and how his poor eyes would turn

back to front with sleepiness had said, "Really, darling, as we are between daughters, two married, and two not yet out, there's no occasion whatever for us to go, if you'd rather not. Sonia would understand perfectly—and be quite glad of our room, I daresay."

But Uncle Matthew had gloomily replied, "If Montdore asks us to his ball it is because he wants to see us there. I think we ought to go."

Accordingly, with many groans, he had squeezed himself into the knee breeches of his youth, now so perilously tight that he hardly dared sit down, but stood like a stork beside Aunt Sadie's chair, and Aunt Sadie had got all her diamonds out of the bank and lent some to Linda and some to Aunt Emily and even so had quite a nice lot left for herself, and here they were chatting away happily enough with their relations and with various county figures who came and went, and even Uncle Matthew seemed quite amused by it all until a dreadful fate befell him—he was made to take the German Ambassadress to supper. It happened like this. Lord Montdore, at Uncle Matthew's very elbow, suddenly exclaimed in horror, "Good heavens, the German Ambassadress is sitting there quite alone."

"Serve her right," said Uncle Matthew. It would have been more prudent to have held his tongue. Lord Montdore heard him speak, without taking in the meaning of his words, turned sharply round, saw who it was, seized him by the arm and said,

"My dear Matthew, just the very man—Baroness von Rumplemayer, may I present my neighbour, Lord Alconleigh? Supper is quite ready in the music room—you know the way, Matthew."

It was a measure of Lord Montdore's influence over

Uncle Matthew that my uncle did not then and there turn tail and bolt for home. No other living person could have persuaded him to stay and shake hands with a Hun, let alone take it on his arm and feed it. He went off, throwing a mournful backward glance at his wife.

Lady Patricia now came and sat by Aunt Sadie, and they chatted, in rather a desultory way, about local affairs. Aunt Sadie, unlike her husband, really enjoyed going out so long as it was not too often, she did not have to stay up too late, and she was allowed to look on peacefully without feeling obliged to make any conversational effort. Strangers bored and fatigued her. She only liked the company of those people with whom she had day-to-day interests in common, such as country neighbours or members of her own family, and even with them she was generally rather absentminded. But on this occasion it was Lady Patricia who seemed half in the clouds, saying yes and no to Aunt Sadie, and what a monstrous thing it was to let the Skilton village idiot out again, specially now it was known what a fast runner he was, since he had won the asylum 100 yards.

"And he's always chasing people," Aunt Sadie said indignantly.

But Lady Patricia's mind was not on the idiot. She was thinking, I am sure, of parties in those very rooms when she was young, and how much she had worshipped the Lecturer, and what agony it had been when he had danced and flirted, she knew, with other people, and how perhaps it was almost sadder for her that now she could care about nothing any more but the condition of her liver.

I knew from Davey ("Oh, the luck," as Linda used to say, "that Dave is such an old gossip, poor simple us

if it weren't for him!") that Lady Patricia had loved
Boy for several years before he had finally proposed to
her, and had indeed quite lost hope. And then how
short-lived was her happiness, barely six months before
she had found him in bed with a kitchen maid.

"Boy never went out for big stuff," I once heard Mrs.
Chaddesley Corbett say. "He only liked bowling over
the rabbits, and now, of course, he's a joke."

It must be hateful, being married to a joke.

Presently she said to Aunt Sadie, "When was the first
ball you ever came to here?"

"It must have been the year I came out, in 1906. I
well remember the excitement of actually seeing King
Edward in the flesh and hearing his loud foreign
laugh."

"Twenty-four years ago, fancy," said Lady Patricia.
"Just before Boy and I were married. Do you remember
how, in the war, people used to say we should never see
this sort of thing again, and yet, look, only look at the
jewels."

Presently, as Lady Montdore came into sight, she
said,

"You know, Sonia really is phenomenal. I'm sure
she's better looking and better dressed now than she
has ever been in her life."

One of those middle-aged remarks I used to find
incomprehensible. It did not seem to me that Lady
Montdore could be described either as good-looking
or as well-dressed; she was old and that was that. On
the other hand, nobody could deny that on occasions
of this sort she was impressive, almost literally covered
with great big diamonds, tiara, necklace, earrings, a
huge Maltese cross on her bosom, bracelets from wrist

to elbow over her suede gloves and brooches wherever there was possible room for them. Dressed up in these tremendous jewels, surrounded by the exterior signs of "all this," her whole demeanor irradiated with the superiority she so deeply felt in herself, she appeared in her own house as a bull-fighter in his bull-ring, or an idol in its ark, the reason for and the very center of the spectacle.

Uncle Matthew, having made his escape from the Ambassadress with a deep bow, expressive of deep disgust, now came back to the family party.

"Old cannibal," he said. "She kept asking for more *Fleisch*. Can't have swallowed her dinner more than an hour ago—I pretended not to hear—wouldn't pander to the old ogress—after all who won the war? And what for, I should like to know? Wonderful public-spirited of Montdore to put up with all this foreign trash in his house—I'm blowed if I would. I ask you to look at that sewer!" He glared in the direction of a blue-chinned Sir who was heading for the supper room with Polly on his arm.

"Come now, Matthew," said Davey, "the Serbs were our allies, you know."

"Allies!" said Uncle Matthew, grinding his teeth. The word was as a red rag to a bull and naughty Davey knew this and was waving the rag for fun.

"So that's a Serb, is it? Well, just what one would expect. Needs a shave. Hogs, one and all. Of course Montdore only asks them for the sake of the country. I do admire that fella, he thinks of nothing but his duty—what an example to everybody!"

A gleam of amusement crossed Lady Patricia's sad face. She was not without a sense of humour and was one of the few people Uncle Matthew liked, though he could not bring himself to be polite to Boy and gazed furiously into space every time he passed our little colony, which he did quite often, squiring royal old ladies to the supper room. Of his many offences in the eyes of Uncle Matthew, the chief was that, having been A.D.C. to a general in the war, he was once discovered by my uncle sketching a château behind the lines. There must clearly be something wrong about a man who could waste his time sketching, or, indeed, undertake the duties of an A.D.C. at all when he might be slaughtering foreigners all day.

"Nothing but a blasted lady's maid," Uncle Matthew would say whenever Boy's name was mentioned. "I can't stick the sewer. Boy, indeed! Dougdale! What does it all mean? There used to be some perfectly respectable people called Blood at Silkin in the Old Lord's time. Major and Mrs. Blood."

The Old Lord was Lord Montdore's father. Jassy once said, opening enormous eyes, "He *must* have been old," upon which Aunt Sadie had remarked that people do not remain the same age all their lives, and he had no doubt been young in his time, just as one day, though she might not expect it, Jassy herself would become old.

It was not very logical of Uncle Matthew so exaggeratedly to despise Boy's military record, and was just another example of how those he liked could do no wrong and those he disliked no right, because Lord Montdore, his great hero, had never in his life heard the cheerful sound of musketry or been near a battle; he would have been rather elderly to have taken the field in the Great War, it is true, but his early years had vainly offered many a jolly fight, chances to hack away at native flesh, not to speak of Dutch flesh in that Boer war which had provided Uncle Matthew with such radiant memories, having given him his first experience of bivouac and battle.

"Four days in a bullock waggon," he used to tell us, "a hole as big as your fist in my stomach, and maggoty! Happiest time of my life. The only thing was, one got rather tired of the taste of mutton after a bit, no beef in that campaign, you know."

But Lord Montdore was a law unto himself and had even got away with the famous Montdore Letter to the *Morning Post* which suggested that the war had gone on long enough and might be brought to an end, several months before the cowardly capitulation of the Hun had made this boring adjournment necessary. Uncle Matthew found it difficult to condone such spoiling of sport but did so by saying that Lord Montdore must have had some good reason for writing it which nobody else knew anything about.

My thoughts were now concentrated upon the entrance to the ballroom door where I had suddenly perceived the back of somebody's head. So he had come, after all. The fact that I never thought he would (such a serious character) had in no way mitigated my disappointment that he had not; now, here he was. I must explain that the image of Sauveterre, having reigned in my hopeless heart for several months had recently been ousted and replaced by something more serious, with more reality and promise.

The back of a head, seen at a ball, can have a most agitating effect upon a young girl, so different from the backs of other heads that it might be surrounded by a halo. There is the question, will he turn round, will he see her, and, if so, will he merely give a polite good-evening or invite her to dance? Oh, how I wished I could have been whirling gaily round in the arms of some fascinator instead of sitting with my aunts and uncles, too obviously a wall-flower. Not that it mattered. There were a few moments of horrible suspense before the head turned round, but when it did he saw me, came straight over, said good evening more than politely and danced me away. He thought he would never get here, it was a question of borrowed, but mislaid, knee breeches. Then he danced with Aunt Emily, again with me, and with Louisa, having engaged me to have supper after that.

"Who is that brute?" said Uncle Matthew, grinding his teeth as my young man went off with Louisa. "Why does he keep coming over here?"

"He's called Alfred Wincham," I said. "Shall I introduce him to you?"

"For pity's sake, Fanny!"

"What an old Pasha you are," said Davey. And, indeed, Uncle Matthew would clearly have preferred to keep all his female relations in a condition if not of virginity at any rate of exaggerated chastity and could never bear them to be approached by strange men.

When not dancing I went back and sat with my relations. I felt calmer now, having had two dances and the promise of supper and was quite happy to fill in the time by listening to my elders as they conversed.

Presently Aunt Sadie and Aunt Emily went off to have supper together. They always liked to do this at parties. Davey moved up to sit next Lady Patricia and Uncle Matthew stood by Davey's chair, sleeping on his feet as horses can, patiently waiting to be led back to his stable.

"It's this new man, Meyerstein," Davey was saying. "You simply must go to him Patricia. He does it all by salt elimination. You skip in order to sweat out all the salt in your organism and eat saltless meals, of course. Too disgusting. But it does break down the crystals."

"Do you mean skip with a skipping rope?"

"Yes, hundreds of times. You count. I can do three hundred at a go, as well as some fancy steps, now."

"But isn't it horribly tiring?"

"Nothing tires Davey—fella's as strong as a bull," said Uncle Matthew, opening one eye.

Davey cast a sad look at his brother-in-law and said that of course it was, desperately tiring, but well worth it for the results.

Polly was dancing now with her uncle, Boy. She did not look radiant and happy as such a spoilt darling should at her coming-out ball, but tired and pinched about the mouth, nor was she chattering away like the other women.

"I shouldn't care for one of my girls to look like that," Aunt Sadie said. "You'd think she had something on her mind."

And my new friend Mr. Wincham said, as we danced round before going to supper, "Of course she's a beauty. I quite see that she is, but she doesn't attract me, with that sulky expression. I'm sure she's very dull."

I began to deny that she was either sulky or dull when he said Fanny to me, the first time he ever had, and followed this up with a lot of things which I wanted to listen to very carefully so that I could think them over later on, when I was alone.

Mrs. Chaddesley Corbett shouted at me, from the

arms of the Prince of Wales, "Hullo, my sweet! What news of the Bolter? Are you still in love?"

"What's all this?" said my partner. "Who is that woman? Who is the Bolter? And is it true that you are in love?"

"Mrs. Chaddesley Corbett," I said. I felt that the time was not yet ripe to begin explaining about the Bolter.

"And how about love?"

"Nothing," I said, rather pink. "Just a joke."

"Good. I should like you to be on the verge of love but not yet quite in it. That's a very nice state of mind, while it lasts."

But of course I had already dived over that verge and was swimming away in a blue sea of illusion towards, I supposed, the islands of the blest, but really towards domesticity, maternity and the usual lot of womankind.

A holy hush now fell upon the crowd as the Royals prepared to go home, the very grand Royals, serene in the knowledge that they would find the traditional cold roast chicken by their beds, not the pathetic Ma'ams and sinister Sirs who were stuffing away in the supper room as if they were far from sure they would ever see so much food again, nor the gay young Royals who were going to dance until morning with little neat women of the Chaddesley Corbett sort.

"How late they have stayed! What a triumph for Sonia!" I heard Boy saying to his wife.

The dancers divided like the Red Sea, forming a lane of bowing and curtsying subjects, down which Lord and Lady Montdore conducted their guests.

"Sweet of you to say so, Ma'am. Yes, at the next Court. Oh, how kind of you!"

The Montdores came back into the picture gallery,

beaming happily and saying, to nobody in particular, "So simple, so easy, pleased with any little thing one can do for them, such wonderful manners, such a memory. Astounding how much they know about India, the Maharajah was amazed."

They spoke as though these Princes are so remote from life as we know it that the smallest sign of human-ity, the mere fact even that they communicated by means of speech was worth noting and proclaiming.

The rest of the evening was spent by me in a happy trance, and I remember no more about the party, as such. I know that I was taken back to the Goring Hotel, where we were all staying, at five o'clock on a fine May morning by Mr. Wincham, who had clearly shown me, by then, that he was not at all averse to my company.

10

SO POLLY was now "out" in London society and played her part during the rest of the season, as she had at the ball, with a good enough grace, the performance only lacking vitality and temperament to make it perfect. She did all the things her mother arranged, went to the parties, wore the clothes and made the friends that Lady Montdore thought suitable for her, and never branched out on her own or gave any possible cause for complaint. She certainly did nothing to create an atmosphere of fun, but Lady Montdore was perhaps too much employed herself in that very direction to notice that Polly, though good and acquiescent, never for one moment entered into the spirit of the many entertainments they went to. Lady Montdore enjoyed it all prodigiously, appeared to be satisfied with Polly, and was delighted with the publicity that, as the most important and most beautiful debutante of the year, she was receiving. She was really too busy, in too much of a whirl of society while the season was going on to wonder whether Polly was being a success or not. When it was over, they went to Goodwood, Cowes, and Scotland, where, no doubt, among the mists and heather, she had time to take stock of the situation. They vanished from my life for many weeks.

By the time I saw them again, in the autumn, their relationship was back to what it had been before and they were clearly very much on each other's nerves. I was now living in London myself, Aunt Emily having taken a little house in St. Leonard's Terrace for the winter. It was a happy time in my life as presently I became engaged to Alfred Wincham, the same young man whose back view had so much disturbed me at the Montdore ball. During the weeks that preceded my engagement I saw a great deal of Polly.

She would telephone in the morning, "What are you up to, Fanny?"

"Aching," I would reply, meaning aching with boredom, a malaise from which girls, before national service came to relieve them, were apt to suffer considerably.

"Oh, good. So can I bend you to my will? You can't think how dull, but if you are aching anyway? Well, then, I've got to try on that blue velvet hat at Madame Rita, and go and fetch the gloves from Debenhams—they said they would have them to-day. Yes, but the worst is to come—I couldn't possibly bend you to have luncheon with my Aunt Edna at Hampton Court and afterwards to sit and chat while I have my hair done? No, forget I said anything so awful—anyway we'll see. I'll be round for you in half an hour."

I was quite pliable. I had nothing whatever to do and very much enjoyed bouncing round London in the big Daimler and watching Polly who, although such a simple character in many ways, was very conscious of being a beauty, as she went about the business which that demands. Although society, at present, had no charm for Polly, she was very much interested in her own appearance, and would never, I think, have given up bothering about it as Lady Patricia had.

So we went to Madame Rita, and I tried on all the hats in the shop while Polly had her fitting, and wondered why it was that hats never seemed to suit me, something to do with my heather-like hair, perhaps, and then we drove down to Hampton Court where Polly's old great-aunt, the widow of a general, sat all day dealing out cards to herself as she waited for eternity.

"And yet I don't believe she aches, you know," said Polly.

"I've noticed," I said, "that married ladies, and even widows, never do seem to ache. There is something about marriage that seems to stop it for good. I wonder why?"

Polly did not answer. The very mention of the word marriage always shut her up like a clam, it was a thing that had to be remembered in her company.

The afternoon before my engagement was to be announced in the *Times*, Aunt Emily sent me round to Montdore House to tell them the news. It is not at all my nature to be one of those who "drop in." I like to be invited by people to their houses at a given time, so that when I arrive they are expecting me and have made their dispositions accordingly, but I saw Aunt Emily's point when she said that, after all Lady Montdore's kindness to me, and considering that Polly was such a very great friend, I could hardly allow them to become aware of my engagement by reading it casually, in the newspaper.

So round I went, trembling rather. Bullitt, the butler, always frightened me into a fit. He was like Frankenstein's monster and one had to follow his jerky footsteps as though through some huge museum before arriving at the little green room, the only room in the house which did not seem as if it had been cleared ready for a reception, and in which they always sat. To-day, however, the front door was opened by a footman of more human aspect, and, furthermore, he told me the good news that Her Ladyship had not yet come in, but Lady Polly was there alone, so off we trudged and presently discovered her amid the usual five-o'clock paraphernalia of silver kettle on flame, silver tea pot, Crown Derby cups and plates, and enough sugary food to stock a pastrycook's shop. She was sitting on the arm of a chair reading the *Tatler*.

"Heavenly *Tatler* day," she said. "It really does help with the aching. I'm in and Linda's in, but not you this week. Faithful of you to come. I was just wishing somebody nice would—now we can have our tea."

I was uncertain how she would take my engagement. I had, in fact, never spoken to her of Alfred since I had begged her to get him asked to the ball. She always seemed so much against young men, or any talk of love. But when I told her the news she was enthusiastic and only reproached me with having been so secretive.

"I remember you made me ask him to the ball," she said. "But then you never mentioned him again, once."

"I didn't dare to talk about it," I said, "in case—well —it really was of too much importance."

"Oh, I do understand that. I'm so glad you were longing for it before he asked you. I never believe in the other sort, the ones who have to make up their minds, you know. How lucky you are! Oh, fancy being able to marry the person you love. You don't know your luck." Her eyes were full of tears, I saw. "Go on," she said. "Tell everything."

I was rather surprised at this show of feeling, so unusual with Polly, but in my selfish state of great new happiness did not pause to consider what it might mean, besides, I was, of course, longing to tell.

"He was terribly nice to me at your ball. I hadn't a bit expected that he would come to London for it because, for one thing, knee breeches. I knew how he wouldn't have any, and then he's so busy always and hates parties, so you can imagine when I saw him I was all excited. Then he asked me to dance, but he danced with old Louisa too and even Aunt Emily, so I thought oh, well, he doesn't know anybody else, it must be that. So then he took me to supper and said he liked my dress and he hoped I'd go and see him at Oxford, and then he said something which showed he'd remembered a conversation we had had before. You know how encouraging that always is. After that he asked me to Oxford, twice—once he had a luncheon party and once he was alone—but in the holidays he went to Greece. Oxford holidays are terribly long, you know. Not even a postcard, so I thought it was all off. Well, on Thursday I went to Oxford again and this time he proposed to me and look . . ." I said, showing a pretty old ring, a garnet set in diamonds.

"Don't say he had it on him like in *The Making of a Marchioness*," said Polly.

"Just like, except that it's not a ruby."

"Quite the size of a pigeon's egg, though. You are lucky."

Lady Montdore now appeared. She bustled in, still wearing her outdoor clothes and seemed unusually mellow.

"Ah! The girls!" she said. "Talking balls, I suppose, as usual! Going to the Gravesend's tonight, Fanny? Give me some tea, I'm quite dead, such an afternoon with the Grand Duchess, I've just dropped her at Kensington Palace. You'd never believe that woman was nearly eighty. She could run us all off our feet, you know, and such a dear, so human, one doesn't mind what one says to her. We went to Woollands to get some woollens— she does feel the cold. Misses the double windows, so she tells me."

It must have been rather sad for Lady Montdore (though with her talent for ignoring disagreeable subjects she probably never even realized the fact) that friendship with royal personages only ever began for her when their days of glory were finished. Tsarskoe Selo, the Quirinal, Kotrocheny Palace, Miramar, Laecken and the island of Corfu knew her not, unless among an enormous crowd in the state apartments. If she went to a foreign capital with her husband she would, of course, be invited to official receptions, while foreign rulers who came to London would attend her big parties, but there was no intimacy. These potentates may not have had the sense to keep their power, but they were evidently not too stupid to realize that give Lady Montdore an inch and she would take an ell. As soon as they were exiled, however, they began to see her charm, another kingdom gone always meant a few more royal habitués at Montdore House, and when they were completely down and out, and had got through whatever money they had managed to salt away, she was allowed to act as lady-in-waiting and go with them to Woollands.

Polly handed her a cup of tea and told her my news. The happy afterglow from her royal outing immediately faded and she became intensely disagreeable.

"Engaged?" she said. "Well, I suppose that's very nice. Alfred what did you say? Who is he? What is that name?"

"He's a don, at Oxford."

"Oh, dear, how extraordinary. You don't want to go and live at Oxford, surely? I should think he had better go into politics and buy a place—I suppose he hasn't got one, by the way? No, or he wouldn't be a don, not an English don, at least. In Spain, of course, it's quite different—dons are somebody there, I believe. Let's think—yes, why shouldn't your father give you a place as a wedding present? You're the only child he's ever likely to have. I'll write to him at once—where is he now?"

I said vaguely that I believed in Jamaica, but did not know his address.

"Really, what a family! I'll find out from the Colonial Office and write by bag, that will be safest. Then this

Mr. Thing can settle down and write books. It always gives a man status if he writes a book, Fanny. I advise you to start him off on that immediately."

"I'm afraid I haven't much influence with him," I said, uneasily.

"Oh, well, develop it, dear, quick. No use marrying a man you can't influence. Just look what I've done for Montdore, always seen that he takes an interest, made him accept things (jobs, I mean) and kept him up to the mark, never let him slide back. A wife must always be on the lookout, men are so lazy by nature. For example, Montdore is forever trying to have a little nap in the afternoon, but I won't hear of it. Once you begin that, I tell him, you are old, and people who are old find themselves losing interest, dropping out of things and then they might as well be dead. Montdore's only got me to thank if he's not in the same condition as most of his contemporaries, creeping about the Marlborough Club like dying flies and hardly able to drag themselves as far as the House of Lords. I make Montdore walk down there every day. Now, Fanny dear, the more I think of it the more it seems to me quite ridiculous for you to go marrying a don. What does Emily say?"

"She's awfully pleased."

"Emily and Sadie are hopeless. You must ask my advice about this sort of thing. I'm very glad indeed you came round; we must think how we can get you out of it. Could you ring him up now and say you've changed your mind? I believe it would be kindest in the long run to do it that way."

"Oh, no, I can't."

"Why not dear? It isn't in the paper yet."

"It will be tomorrow."

"That's where I can be so helpful. I'll send for Geoffrey Dawson now and have it stopped."

I was quite terrified. "Please," I said, "oh, please not!"

Polly came to my rescue. "But she wants to marry him, Mummy. She's in love, and look at her pretty ring!"

Lady Montdore looked and was confirmed in her opposition. "That's not a ruby," she said, as if I had been pretending it was. "And, as for love, I should have thought the example of your mother would have taught you something. Where has love landed her? Some ghastly white hunter. Love, indeed! Whoever invented love ought to be shot."

"Dons aren't a bit the same as white hunters," said Polly. "You know how fond Daddy is of them."

"Oh, I daresay they're all right for dinner, if you like that sort of thing. Montdore does have them over sometimes, I know, but that's no reason why they should go marrying people. So unsuitable, megalomania, I call it. No, Fanny, I'm very much distressed."

"Oh, please don't be," I said.

"However, if you say its settled, I suppose there's no more I can do, except to try and help you make a success of it. Montdore can ask the Chief Whip if there's something for you to nurse. That will be best."

It was on the tip of my tongue to say that what I hoped to be nursing before long would be sent by God and not the Chief Whip, but I restrained myself, nor did I dare to tell her that Alfred was not a Tory.

The conversation now turned upon the subject of my trousseau, about which Lady Montdore was quite as bossy, though less embarrassing. I was not feeling much interest in clothes at that time, all my thoughts being of how to decorate and furnish a charming little old house which Alfred had taken me to see after placing the pigeon's egg on my finger and which, by a miracle of good luck, was to be let.

"The important thing, dear," she said, "is to have a really good fur coat, I mean a proper, dark one." To Lady Montdore, fur meant mink. She could imagine no other kind except sable, but that would be specified. "Not only will it make all the rest of your clothes look better than they are but you really needn't bother much about anything else as you need never take it off. Above all, don't go wasting money on underclothes; there is nothing stupider—I always borrow Montdore's myself. Now, for evening a diamond brooch is a great help, so long as it has good big stones. Oh, dear, when I think of the diamonds your father gave that woman, it really is too bad. All the same, he can't have got through everything, he was enormously rich when he succeeded. I must write to him. Now, dear, we're going to be very practical. No time like the present."

She rang for her secretary, and said my father's address must be found out.

"You could ring up the Under-Secretary for Colonies with my compliments, and will you make a note that I will write to Lord Logan tomorrow."

She also told her to make a list of places where linen, underclothes and house furnishings could be obtained at wholesale prices.

"Bring it straight back here for Miss Logan when it is ready."

When the secretary had gone, Lady Montdore turned to Polly and spoke to her exactly as if I had gone too, and they were alone. It was a habit she had, and I always found it very embarrassing as I never quite knew what she expected me to do, whether to interrupt her by saying good-bye or simply to look out of the window and pretend that my thoughts were far away. On this occasion, however, I was clearly expected to wait for the list of addresses, so I had no choice.

"Now, Polly, have you thought of a young man yet for me to ask down on the third?"

"Oh, how about John Coningsby?" said Polly, with an indifference which I could plainly see must be maddening to her mother. Lord Coningsby was her official young man, so to speak. She invited him to everything, and this had greatly pleased Lady Montdore to begin with, since he was rich, handsome, agreeable and an "eldest son," which meant, in Lady Montdore's parlance, the eldest son of a peer (never let Jones or Robinson major think of themselves for one moment as eldest sons). Too soon, however, she saw that he and Polly were excellent friends and would never be anything else, after which she regretfully lost all interest in him.

"Oh, I don't count John," she said.

"How d'you mean you don't count him?"

"He's only a friend. Now I was thinking in Woollands—I often do have good ideas in shops—how would it be to ask Joyce Fleetwood?"

Alas, the days when I, Albert Christian George Andrew Patrick David, was considered to be the only person worthy of taking thee, Leopoldina, must have become indeed remote if Joyce Fleetwood was to be put forward as a substitute. Perhaps it was in Lady Montdore's mind that, since Polly showed no inclination to marry an established, inherited position, the next best thing would be somebody who might achieve one by his own efforts. Joyce Fleetwood was a noisy, self-opinionated young Conservative M.P. who had mastered one or two of the drearier subjects of debate, agriculture, the Empire, and so on, and was always ready to hold forth upon them in the House. He had made up to Lady Montdore and she thought him much cleverer than he really was. His parents were known to her, they had a place in Norfolk.

"Well, Polly?"

"Yes, why not?" said Polly. "It's a shower bath when he talks, but do let's, he's so utterly fascinating, isn't he?"

Lady Montdore now lost her temper and her voice got quite out of control. I sympathised with her, really; it was too obvious that Polly was wilfully provoking her.

"It's perfectly stupid to go on like this."

Polly did not reply. She bent her head sideways and pretended to be deeply absorbed in the headlines, upside down, of the evening paper which lay on a chair by her mother. She might just as well have said out loud, "All right, you horrible vulgar woman, go on, I don't care. You are nothing to me," so plain was her meaning.

"Please, listen when I speak to you, Polly."

Polly continued to squint at the headlines.

"Polly, will you pay attention to what I'm saying?"

"What were you saying? Something about Mr. Fleetwood?"

"Let Mr. Fleetwood be, for the present. I want to know what, exactly, you are planning to do with your life. Do you intend to live at home and go mooning on like this for ever?"

"What else can I do? You haven't exactly trained me for a career, have you?"

"Oh, yes indeed, I have. I've trained you for marriage which, in my opinion (I may be old-fashioned) is by far the best career open to any woman."

"That's all very well, but how can I marry if nobody asks me?"

Of course that was really the sore point with Lady Montdore, nobody asking her. A Polly gay and flirtatious, surrounded by eligible suitors, playing one off against the others, withdrawing, teasing, desired by married men, breaking up her friends' romances, Lady Montdore would have been perfectly happy to watch her playing that game for several years, if need be, so long as it was quite obvious that she would finally choose some suitably important husband and settle down with him. What her mother minded so dreadfully was that this acknowledged beauty should appear to have no attraction whatever for the male sex. The eldest sons had a look, said, "Isn't she lovely?" and went off with some chinless little creature from Cadogan Square. There had been three or four engagements of this sort lately which had upset Lady Montdore very much indeed.

"And why don't they ask you? It's only because you give them no encouragement. Can't you try to be a little jollier, nicer with them, no man cares to make love to a dummy, you know. It's too discouraging."

"Thank you, but I don't want to be made love to."

"Oh, dear, oh, dear! Then what is it you do want?"

"Leave me alone, Mother, please."

"To stay on here, with us, until you are old?"

"Daddy wouldn't mind a bit."

"Oh, yes, he would, make no mistake about that. Not for a year or two perhaps, but in the end he would. Nobody wants their girl to be hanging about forever, a sour old maid, and you'll be the sour kind, that's too obvious already, my dear, wizened up and sour."

I could hardly believe my ears. Could this be Lady Montdore speaking, in such frank and dreadful terms, to Polly, her beautiful paragon, whom she used to love so much that she was even reconciled to her being a daughter and not an heir? It seemed to me terrible. I went cold in my very backbone. There was a long and deeply embarrassing silence, broken by Frankenstein's monster who jerked into the room and said that the King of Portugal was on the telephone. Lady Montdore stumped off and I seized the opportunity to escape.

"I hate her," said Polly, kissing me good-bye. "I hate her and I wish she were dead. Oh, Fanny, the luck of not being brought up by your own mother—you've no idea what a horrible relationship it can be."

"Poor Polly," I said, very much upset. "How sad! But when you were little it wasn't horrible?"

"Always, always horrible. I've always hated her from the bottom of my heart."

I did not believe it.

"She isn't like this the whole time?" I said.

"More and more. Better make a dash for it, love, or you'll be caught again. I'll ring up very soon. . . ."

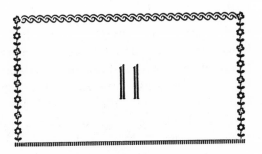

I WAS married at the beginning of the Christmas vacation and when Alfred and I returned from our honeymoon we went to stay at Alconleigh while our little house in Oxford was being got ready. This was an obvious and convenient arrangement as Alfred could go in to Oxford every day for his work, and I was at hand to supervise the decoration of the house, but, although Alconleigh had been a second home to me from my babyhood, it was not without misgivings that I accepted Aunt Sadie's invitation to take my husband there for a long visit, at the very outset of our married life. My Uncle Matthew's likes and dislikes were famous for their violence, for the predomination of the latter over the former, and for the fact that he never made the slightest attempt to conceal them from their object; I could see that he was already prejudiced against poor Alfred. It was an accepted fact in the family that he loathed me, furthermore, he also hated new people, hated men who married his female relations, hated and despised those who did not practise blood sports. I felt there was but little hope for Alfred, especially as, culmination of horror, "the fella reads books."

True, all this had applied to Davey when he had first appeared, engaged to Aunt Emily, but Uncle Matthew had taken an unreasoning fancy to Davey from the very beginning and it was not to be hoped that such a miracle could repeat itself. My fears, however, were not entirely realized. I think Aunt Sadie had probably read the riot act before our arrival. Meanwhile, I had been doing my best with Alfred. I made him have his hair cropped like a guardsman, explained to him that if he must open a book he should do so only in the privacy of his bedroom, and specially urged great punctuality at meal times. Uncle Matthew, as I told him, liked to get us all into the dining room at least five minutes before the meal was ready. "Come on," he would say, "we'll go and sit in." And in the family would sit, clasping hot plates to their bosoms (Aunt Sadie had once done this, absent-mindedly, with a plate of artichoke soup), all eyes upon the pantry door.

I tried to explain these things to Alfred, who listened patiently though uncomprehendingly. I also tried to prepare him for the tremendous impact of my uncle's rages, so that I got the poor man, really quite unnecessarily, into a panic.

"Do let's go to the Mitre," he kept saying.

"It may not be too bad," I replied, doubtfully.

And it was not, in the end, too bad at all. The fact is that Uncle Matthew's tremendous and classical hatred for me, which had begun when I was an infant and which had cast a shadow of fear over all my childhood, had now become more legend than actuality. I was such an habitual member of his household, and he such a conservative, that this hatred, in common with that which he used to nurture against Josh, the groom, and various other old intimates, had not only lost its force but I think had, with the passage of years, actually turned into love; such a lukewarm sentiment as ordinary avuncular affection being, of course, foreign to his experience. Be that as it may, he evidently had no wish to poison the beginning of my married life and made quite touching efforts to bottle up whatever irritation he felt at Alfred's shortcomings, his unmanly incompetence with his motor car, vagueness over time and fatal disposition to spill marmalade at breakfast. The fact that Alfred left for Oxford at nine o'clock, only returning in time for dinner, and that we spent Saturday to Monday of every week in Kent with Aunt Emily made our visit just endurable to Uncle Matthew, and, incidentally to Alfred himself, who did not share my unquestioning adoration for all members of the Radlett family.

The Radlett boys had gone back to their schools, and my cousin Linda, whom I loved best in the world after Alfred, was now living in London and expecting a baby, but, though Alconleigh was never quite the same without her, Jassy and Victoria were at home (none of the Radlett girls went to school) so the house resounded as usual with jingles, and jangles, and idiotic shrieks. There was always some joke being run to death at Alconleigh, and just now it was headlines from the Daily Express which the children had made into a chant and intoned to each other all day.

Jassy: "*Man's* long *agony in* a lift-*shaft*."

Victoria: "Slowly *crushed* to *death* in a *lift*."

Aunt Sadie became very cross about this, said they were really too old to be so heartless, that it wasn't a bit funny, only dull and disgusting and absolutely forbade them to sing it any more. After this they tapped it out to each other, on doors, under the dining-room table, clicking with their tongues or blinking with their eyelids, and all the time in fits of naughty giggles. I could see that Alfred thought them terribly silly and he could hardly contain his indignation when he found out that they did no lessons of any sort.

"Thank heavens for your Aunt Emily," he said. "I really could not have married somebody quite illiterate."

So, of course, I too thanked heavens more than ever for dear Aunt Emily, but at the same time Jassy and Victoria made me laugh so much, and I loved them so much that it was impossible for me to wish them very different from what they were. Hardly had I arrived in the house than I was lugged off to their secret meeting place, the Hons' cupboard, to be asked what IT was like.

"Linda says it's not all it's cracked up to be," said Jassy, "and we don't wonder when we think of Tony."

"But Louisa says, once you get used to it, it's utter utter utter blissikins," said Victoria, "and we do wonder, when we think of John."

"What's wrong with poor Tony and John?"

"Dull and old. Come on then Fanny—tell."

I said I agreed with Louisa but refused to enter into details.

"It is unfair, nobody ever tells. Sadie doesn't even

know, that's quite obvious, and Louisa is an old prig, but we did think we could count on Linda and you. Very well then, we shall go to our marriage beds in ignorance, like Victorian ladies, and in the morning we shall be found stark, staring mad with horror, and live sixty more years in an expensive bin, and then perhaps you'll wish you had been more helpful."

"Weighted down with jewels and Valenciennes costing thousands," said Victoria. "The Lecturer was here last week and he was telling Sadie some very nice sexy stories about that kind of thing. Of course, we weren't meant to hear but you can just guess what happened. Sadie didn't listen and we did."

"I should ask the Lecturer for information," I said. "He'd tell."

"He'd show. No, thank you very much."

Polly came over to see me. She was pale and thinner, had rings under her eyes and seemed quite shut up in herself, though this may have been in contrast with the exuberant Radletts. When she was with Jassy and Victoria, she looked like a swan, swimming in the company of two funny little tumbling ducks. She was very fond of them. She had never got on very well with Linda, for some reason, but she loved everybody else at Alconleigh, especially Aunt Sadie, and was more at her ease with Uncle Matthew than anybody I ever knew, outside his own family circle. He, for his part, bestowed on her some of the deference he felt for Lord Montdore, called her Lady Polly, and smiled every time his eyes fell on her beautiful face.

"Now children," said Aunt Sadie, "leave Fanny and Polly to have a little chat. They don't want you all the time, you know."

"It is unfair—I suppose Fanny's going to *tell* Polly now. Well, back to the medical dictionary and the Bible. I only wish these things didn't look quite so sordid in cold print. What we need is some clean-minded married woman, to explain, but where are we to find her?"

Polly and I had a very desultory little chat, however. I showed her photographs of Alfred and me in the South of France where we had been so that he could meet my poor mother the Bolter, who was living there now with a nasty new husband. Polly said the Dougdales were off there next week, as Lady Patricia was feeling the cold so dreadfully that winter. She told me also that there had been a huge Christmas party at Hampton and that Joyce Fleetwood was in disgrace with her mother for not paying his bridge debts.

"So that's one comfort. We've still got the Grand Duchess, poor old thing. Goodness, she's dull—not that Mummy seems to think so. Veronica Chaddesley Corbett calls her and Mummy Ma'am and Super-Ma'am."

I did not like to ask if Polly and her mother were getting on any better, and Polly volunteered nothing on that subject, but she looked, I thought, very miserable. Presently she said she must go.

"Come over soon and bring Alfred."

But I dreaded the impact of Lady Montdore upon Alfred even more than that of Uncle Matthew, and said he was too busy but I would come alone sometime.

"I hear that she and Sonia are on very bad terms again," Aunt Sadie said when Polly had driven off.

"The hell-hag," said Uncle Matthew. "Drown her, if I were Montdore."

"Or he might cut her to pieces with nail scissors, like that French duke the Lecherous Lecturer was telling you all about, Sadie, when you weren't listening and we were."

"Don't call me Sadie, children, and don't call Mr. Dougdale the Lecherous Lecturer."

"Oh, dear. Well, we always do behind your backs so you see it's bound to slip out sometimes."

Davey arrived. He had come to stay for a week or so for treatment at the Radcliffe Infirmary. Aunt Emily was becoming more and more attached to all her animals and could seldom now be persuaded to leave them, for which, on this occasion, I was thankful, since our Sundays in Kent really were an indispensable refuge to Alfred and me.

"I met Polly in the drive," Davey said. "We stopped and had a word. I think she looks most dreadfully unwell."

"Nonsense," said Aunt Sadie, who believed in no illness except appendicitis. "There's nothing wrong with Polly. She needs a husband, that's all."

"Oh! How like a woman!" said Davey. "Sex, my dear Sadie, is not a sovereign cure for everything, you know. I only wish it were."

"I didn't mean sex at all," said my aunt, very much put out by this interpretation. Indeed, she was what the children called "against" sex, that is to say, it never entered into her calculations. "What I said, and what I meant, was she needs a husband. Girls of her age, living at home, are hardly ever happy and Polly is a specially bad case because she has nothing whatever to do. She doesn't care for hunting, or parties, or anything much that I can see, and she doesn't get on with her mother.

It's true that Sonia teases and lectures her and sets about it all the wrong way. She's a tactless person, but she is perfectly right you know. Polly needs a life of her own, babies, occupations and interests—an establishment, in fact—and for all that she must have a husband."

"Or a lady of Llangollen," said Victoria.

"Time you went to bed, miss, now off you go, both of you."

"Not me, it's not nearly my bedtime yet."

"I said both of you, now begone."

They dragged themselves out of the room as slowly as they dared and went upstairs, stamping out "Man's long agony" on the bare boards of the nursery passage so that nobody in the whole house could fail to hear them.

"Those children read too much," said Aunt Sadie. "But I can't stop them. I honestly believe they'd rather read the label on a medicine bottle than nothing at all."

"Oh, but I love reading the labels of medicine bottles," said Davey. "They're madly enjoyable, you know."

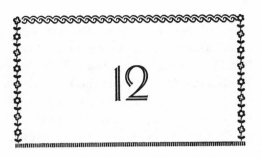

12

THE next morning when I came down to breakfast I found everybody, even the children, looking grave. It seemed that by some mysterious local tom-tom Aunt Sadie had learnt that Lady Patricia Dougdale had died in the night. She had suddenly collapsed, Lord Mont-dore was sent for, but by the time he could arrive she had become unconscious, and an hour later was dead.

"Oh, poor Patricia," Aunt Sadie kept saying, very much upset, while Uncle Matthew, who cried easily, was mopping his eyes as he bent over the hot plate, taking a sausage, or, as he called it, a "banger" with less than his usual enthusiasm.

"I saw her only last week," he said, "at the Clarendon Yard."

"Yes," said Aunt Sadie, "I remember you told me. Poor Patricia, I always liked her so much, though of course all that about being delicate was tiresome."

"Well, now you can see for yourself that she was delicate," said Davey triumphantly. "She's dead. It killed her. Doesn't that show you? I do wish I could make you Radletts understand that there is no such thing as imaginary illness. Nobody who is quite well could possibly be bothered to do all the things that I, for instance, am obliged to, in order to keep my wretched frame on its feet."

The children began to giggle at this, and even Aunt Sadie smiled, because they all knew that so far from it being a bother to Davey it was his all-absorbing occupation and one which he enjoyed beyond words.

"Oh, of course I know you all think it's a great, great joke, and no doubt Jassy and Victoria will scream with laughter when I finally do conk out, but it's not a joke to me, let me tell you, and a liver in that state can't have been much of a joke to poor Patricia, what's more."

"Poor Patricia, and I fear she had a sad life with that boring old Lecturer."

This was so like Aunt Sadie. Having protested for years against the name Lecturer for Boy Dougdale, she was now using it herself. Very soon, no doubt, we should hear her chanting "Man's long agony."

"For some reason that I could never understand, she really loved him."

"Until lately," said Davey. "I think for the past year or two it has been the other way round, and he had begun to depend on her, and then it was too late, she had stopped bothering about him."

"Possibly. Anyway there it is, all very sad. We must send a wreath, darling, at once. What a time of year! It will have to come from Oxford I suppose. . . . Oh, the waste of money!"

"Send a wreath of frog spawn, frog spawn, frog spawn, lovely, lovely frog spawn, it is my favourite thing," sang Jassy.

"If you go on being so silly, children," said Aunt Sadie, who had caught a look of great disapproval on Alfred's face, "I shall be obliged to send you to school, you know."

"But can you afford to?" said Victoria. "You'd have to buy us plimsolls and gym tunics, underclothes in a decent state, and some good strong luggage. I've seen girls going off to school; they are covered with expensive things. Of course, we long for it, pashes for the prefects and rags in the dorm. School has a very sexy side, you know, Sadie. Why, the very word 'mistress,' Sadie, you know . . ."

But Aunt Sadie was not really listening; she was away in her cloud and merely said "Mm, very naughty and silly, and don't call me Sadie."

Aunt Sadie and Davey went off to the funeral together. Uncle Matthew had his Bench that day, and particularly wanted to attend in order to make quite sure that a certain ruffian who was to come up before it should be committed to the Assizes, where, it was very much to be hoped, he would get several years and the cat. One or two of Uncle Matthew's fellow beaks had curious, modern ideas about justice and he was obliged to carry on a strenuous war against them, in which he was greatly assisted by a retired Admiral of the neighbourhood.

So they had to go to the funeral without him, and came back in low spirits.

"It's the dropping off the perches," said Aunt Sadie. "I've always dreaded when that begins. Soon we shall all have gone. . . . Oh, well, never mind."

"Nonsense," Davey said, briskly. "Modern science will keep us alive, and young, too, for many a long day yet. Patricia's insides were a terrible mess. I had a word with Dr. Simpson while you were with Sonia and it's quite obviously a miracle she didn't die years ago. When the children have gone to bed I'll tell you."

"No, thank you," said Aunt Sadie, while the children implored him to go then and there with them to the Hons' cupboard and tell.

"It is unfair, Sadie doesn't want to hear the least bit, and we die to."

"How old was Patricia?" said Aunt Sadie.

"Older than we are," said Davey. "I remember when they married she was supposed to be quite a bit older than Boy."

"And he was looking a hundred in that bitter wind."

"I thought he seemed awfully cut up, poor Boy."

Aunt Sadie, during a little graveside chat with Lady Montdore, had gathered that the death had come as a shock and surprise to all of them, that, although they had known Lady Patricia to be far from well, they had no idea that she was in immediate danger; in fact, she had been greatly looking forward to her trip abroad the following week. Lady Montdore, who resented death, clearly thought it most inconsiderate of her sister-in-law to break up their little circle so suddenly, and Lord Montdore, devoted to his sister, was dreadfully shaken by the midnight drive with a death-bed at the end of it, but, surprisingly enough, the one who had taken it hardest was Polly. It seemed that she had been violently sick on hearing the news, completely prostrated for two days, and was still looking so unwell that her mother had refused to take her to the funeral.

"It seems rather funny," said Aunt Sadie, "in a way. I'd no idea she was so particularly devoted to Patricia, had you, Fanny?"

"Nervous shock," said Davey. "I don't suppose she's ever had a death so near to her before."

"Oh, yes, she has," said Jassy. "Ranger."

"Dogs aren't exactly the same as human beings, my dear Jassy."

But to the Radletts they were exactly the same, except that to them dogs, on the whole, had more reality than people.

"So tell me about the grave," said Victoria.

"Not very much to tell, really," said Aunt Sadie. "Just a grave, you know, lots of flowers and mud."

"They'd lined it with heather," said Davey, "from Craigside. Poor dear, she did love Scotland."

"And where was it?"

"In the graveyard, of course, at Silkin—between the Wellingtonia and the Blood Arms, if you see where I mean. In full view of Boy's bedroom window, incidentally."

Jassy began to talk fast and earnestly.

"You will promise to bury me here, whatever happens, won't you, won't you? There's one exact place I want. I note it every time I go to church—it's next door to that old lady who was nearly a hundred."

"That's not our part of the churchyard—miles away from grandfather."

"No, but it's the bit I want. I once saw a dear little dead baby vole there. Please, please, please, don't forget."

"You'll have married some sewer and gone to live in the Antipodes," said Uncle Matthew who had just come in. "They let that young hog off, said there was no evidence. Evidence be damned, you'd only got to look at his face to see who did it. Afternoon completely wasted. The Admiral and I are going to resign."

"Then bring me back," said Jassy, "pickled. I'll pay, I swear I will. Please, Fa, you must."

"Write it down," said Uncle Matthew, producing a piece of paper and a fountain pen. "If these things don't get written down, they are forgotten. And I'd like a deposit of ten bob, please."

"You can take it out of my birthday present," said Jassy, who was scribbling away with great concentration. "I've made a map like in Treasure Island," she said. "See?"

"Yes, thank you, that's quite clear," said Uncle Matthew. He went to the wall, took his master key from his pocket, opened a safe and put in the piece of paper. Every room at Alconleigh had one of these wall safes, whose contents would have amazed and discomfitted the burglar who managed to open them. Aunt Sadie's jewels, which had some very good stones, were never kept in them, but lay glittering about all over the house and garden, in any place where she might have taken them off and forgotten to put them on again—on the downstairs washbasin, by the flower bed she had been weeding, sent to the laundry pinning up a suspender. Her big party pieces were kept in the bank. Uncle Matthew himself possessed no jewels and despised all men who did. (Boy's signet ring and platinum-and-pearl evening watch chain were great causes for tooth grinding.) His own watch was a large loudly ticking object in gun metal, tested twice a day by Greenwich mean time on a chronometer in the business room, and said to gain three seconds a week, this was attached to his key ring across his mole-skin waistcoat by an ordinary leather bootlace, in which Aunt Sadie often tied knots to remind herself of things.

The safes, nevertheless, were full of treasures, if not of valuables, for Uncle Matthew's treasures were objects of esoteric worth, such as a stone quarried on the estate and said to have imprisoned for two thousand years a living toad; Linda's first shoe; the skeleton of a mouse regurgitated by an owl; a tiny gun for shooting blue-bottles; the hair of all his children made into a bracelet; a silhouette of Aunt Sadie done at a fair; a carved nut; a ship in a bottle; altogether a strange mixture of senti-ment, natural history and little objects which from time to time had taken his fancy.

"Come on, do let's see," said Jassy and Victoria, mak-ing a dash at the door in the wall. There was always great excitement when the safes were opened, as they hardly ever were, and seeing inside was considered a treat.

"Oh! The dear little bit of shrapnel, may I have it?"

"No, you may not. It was once in my groin for a whole week."

"Talk about death," said Davey. "The greatest medi-cal mystery of our times must be the fact that dear Mat-thew is still with us."

"It only shows," said Aunt Sadie, "that nothing really matters the least bit, so why make these fearful efforts to keep alive?"

"Oh, but it's the efforts that one enjoys so much," said Davey, and this time he was speaking the truth.

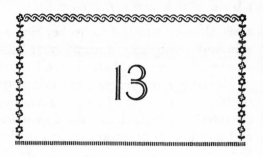

13

I THINK it was about a fortnight after Lady Patricia's funeral that Uncle Matthew stood, after luncheon,
outside his front door, watch in hand, scowling fiercely,
grinding his teeth and awaiting his greatest treat of all
the year, an afternoon's chubb fuddling. The Chubb
Fuddler was supposed to be there at half-past two.

"Twenty-three and a quarter minutes past," Uncle
Matthew was saying furiously, "in precisely six and
three-quarter minutes the damned fella will be late."

If people did not keep their appointments with him
well before the specified time he always counted them
as being late. He would begin to fidget quite half an
hour too soon, and wasted, in this way, as much time as
people do who have no regard for it, besides getting
himself into a thoroughly bad temper.

The famous trout stream that ran through the valley
below Alconleigh was one of Uncle Matthew's most

cherished possessions. He was an excellent dry fly fisher-
man, and was never happier, in and out of the fishing
season, than when messing about the river in waders and
inventing glorious improvements for it. It was the small
boy's dream come true. He built dams, he dug lashers, he
cut the weeds and trimmed the banks, he shot the herons,
he hunted the otters, and he restocked with young trout
every year. But he had trouble with the coarse fish, and
especially the chubb, which not only gobble up the baby
trout, but also their food, and they were a great worry to
him. Then, one day he came upon an advertisement in
Exchange and Mart. "Send for the Chubb Fuddler."

The Radletts always said that their father had never
learnt to read, but in fact he could read quite well, if
really fascinated by his subject, and the proof is that he
found the Chubb Fuddler like this all by himself. He
sat down then and there and sent. It took him some
time, breathing heavily over the writing paper and making, as he always did, several copies of the letter before
finally sealing and stamping it.

"The fella says here to enclose a stamped and ad-
dressed envelope, but I don't think I shall pander to
him. He can take it or leave it."

He took it. He came, he walked along the river bank,
and sowed upon its waters some magic seed, which soon
bore magic fruit for, up to the surface, flapping, swoon-
ing, fainting, choking, thoroughly and undoubtedly
fuddled, came hundreds upon hundreds of chubb. The
entire male population of the village, warned before-
hand and armed with rakes and landing nets fell upon
the fish, several wheelbarrows were filled and the contents taken off to be used as manure for cottage gardens
or chubb pie, according to taste.

Henceforward chubb fuddling became an annual event at Alconleigh, the Fuddler appearing regularly with the snowdrops, and to watch him at his work was a pleasure which never palled. So here we all were, waiting for him, Uncle Matthew pacing up and down outside the front door, the rest of us just inside, on account of the bitter cold, but peering out of the window, while all the men on the estate were gathered in groups down at the river's edge. Nobody, not even Aunt Sadie, wanted to miss a moment of the fuddling except, it seemed, Davey, who had retired to his room saying, "It isn't madly me, you know, and certainly not in this weather."

A motor car was now heard approaching, the scrunch of wheels and a low, rich hoot, and Uncle Matthew, with a last look at his watch, was just putting it back in his pocket, when down the drive came, not at all the Chubb Fuddler's little Standard but the huge black Daimler from Hampton Park containing both Lord and Lady Montdore. This was indeed a sensation! Callers were unknown at Alconleigh. Anybody rash enough to try that experiment would see no sign of Aunt Sadie or the children, who would all be flat on the floor out of sight, though Uncle Matthew, glaring most embarrassingly, would stand at a window, in full view, while they were being told "not at home." The neighbours had long ago given it up as a bad job. Furthermore, the Montdores, who considered themselves King and Queen of the neighbourhood, never called but expected people to go to them, so from every point of view, it seemed most peculiar. I am quite sure that if anybody else had broken in upon the happy anticipation of an afternoon's chubb fuddling, Uncle Matthew would have bellowed at them to "get out of it," possibly even have

hurled a stone at them. When he saw who it was, however, he had one moment of stunned surprise and then
leapt forward to open the door of the motor, like a
squire of olden times leaping to the stirrup of his liege
lord.

The hell-hag, we could all see at once, even through
the window, was in a dreadful state. Her face was blotchy
and swollen as from hours of weeping. She seemed perfectly unaware of Uncle Matthew and did not throw
him either a word or a look as she struggled out of the
car, angrily kicking at the rug round her feet. She then
tottered with the gait of a very old woman, legs all weak
and crooked, towards the house. Aunt Sadie, who had
dashed forward, put an arm round her waist and took
her into the drawing room, giving the door a great "keep
out, children" bang. At the same time, Lord Montdore
and Uncle Matthew disappeared together into my
uncle's business room; Jassy, Victoria and I were left to
goggle at each other with eyes like saucers, struck dumb
by this extraordinary incident. Before we had time to
begin speculating on what it could all mean, the Fuddler
drove up, punctual to the very minute.

"Damned fella," Uncle Matthew said afterwards, "if
he hadn't been so late we should have started by the
time they arrived."

He parked his little tin pot of a motor in line with
the Daimler and bustled, all happy smiles, up to the
front door. At his first visit he had gone modestly up the
back drive, but the success of his magic had so put Uncle
Matthew on his side that he had told him, in future, to
come to the front door, and always gave him a glass of
port before starting work. He would no doubt have
given him Imperial Tokay if he had had any.

Jassy opened the door before the Fuddler had time to ring, and then we all hung about while he drank his port, saying, "Bitter, isn't it?" and not quite knowing what to be at.

"His Lordship's not ill, I hope?" he said, surprised, no doubt, not to have found my uncle champing up and down as usual, his choleric look clearing suddenly into one of hearty welcome as he hurried to slap the Fuddler's back and pour out his wine.

"No, no, we think he'll be here in a moment. He's busy."

"Not so like His Lordship to be late, is it?"

Presently a message came from Uncle Matthew that we were to go down to the river and begin. It seemed too cruel to have the treat without him, but the fuddling had, of course, to be concluded by daylight. So we shivered out of the house, into the temporary shelter of the Fuddler's Standard and out again into the full blast of a north wind which was cutting up the valley. While the Fuddler sprinkled his stuff on the water, we crept back into his car for warmth and began to speculate on the reason for the extraordinary visit now in progress. We were simply dying of curiosity.

"I guess the Government has fallen," said Jassy.

"Why should that make Lady Montdore cry?"

"Well, who would do all her little things for her?"

"There'd soon be another lot for her to fag—Conservatives this time, perhaps. She really likes that better."

"D'you think Polly is dead?"

"No, no, they'd be mourning o'er her lovely corpse, not driving about in motor cars and seeing people."

"Perhaps they've lost all their money and are coming to live with us," said Victoria. This idea cast a regular

gloom, seeming as it did rather a likely explanation. In
those days, when people were so rich and their fortunes
so infinitely secure it was quite usual for them to
think that they were on the verge of losing all their
money, and the Radlett children had always lived under
the shadow of the workhouse, because Uncle Matthew,
though really very comfortably off with about £10,000
a year, gross, had a financial crisis every two or three
years and was quite certain in his own mind that he
would end up on parish relief.

The Fuddler's work was done, his seed was sown and
we got out of the motor with our landing nets. This was
a moment that never failed to thrill. The river banks
were dotted with people all gazing excitedly into the
water, and very soon the poor fish began to squirm
about the surface. I landed a couple of whales and then
a smaller one, and just as I was shaking it out of the net,
a well-known voice behind me, quivering with passion,
said, "Put it back at once, you blasted idiot! Can't you
see it's a greyling, Fanny? Oh, my God, women—incom-
petent—and isn't that my landing net you've got there?
I've been looking for it all over the place."

I gave it up with some relief, ten minutes at the water's
edge was quite enough in that wind. Jassy was saying,
"Look look, they've gone," and there was the Daimler
crossing the bridge, Lord Montdore sitting very upright
in the back seat, bowing a little from side to side, almost
like royalty. They overtook a butcher's van and I saw
him lean forward and give the driver a gracious salute
for having got out of the way. Lady Montdore was
hardly visible, bundled up in her corner. They had
gone, all right.

"Come on, Fanny," said my cousins, downing tools.

"Home, don't you think? Too cold here," they shouted at their father, but he was busy cramming a giant chubb in its death throes into his hare pocket and took no notice.

"And now," said Jassy as we raced up the hill, "for worming it all out of Sadie."

It was not, in fact, necessary to do any worming, Aunt Sadie was bursting with her news. She was more human and natural with her younger children than she had ever been with the elder ones. Her attitude of awe-inspiring vagueness alternating with sudden fits of severity, which had combined with Uncle Matthew's rages to drive Louisa and Linda and the boys underground, so that their real lives were led in the Hons' cupboard, was very much modified with regard to Jassy and Victoria. She was still quite as vague, but never very severe, and far more companionable. She had always been inclined to treat her children as if they were all exactly the same age, and the younger ones were now benefiting from the fact that Louisa and Linda were married women who could be spoken to, and in front of, without reserve.

We found her and Davey in the hall. She was quite pink with interest and, as for Davey, he was looking as much excited as if he had developed some fascinating new symptom.

"Come on," said the children, question marks all over their faces. "Tell."

"You'll never believe it," said Aunt Sadie, addressing herself to me. "Polly Hampton has informed her poor mother that she is going to marry Boy Dougdale. Her uncle, if you please! Did you ever hear such a thing? The wretched Patricia, not cold in her grave . . ."

"Well," said Jassy, aside, "cooling, in this weather . . ."

"Miserable old man!" Aunt Sadie spoke in tones of deep indignation and was clearly a hundred percent on Lady Montdore's side. "You see, Davey, how right Matthew has been about him all these years?"

"Oh, poor Boy, he's not so bad," Davey said, uncomfortably.

"I don't see how you can go on standing up for him after this, Davey."

"But, Sadie," said Victoria, "how can she marry him if he's her uncle?"

"Just exactly what I said. But it seems, with an uncle by marriage that you can. Would you believe that anything so disgustingly dreadful could be allowed?"

"I say," said Jassy. "Come on, Dave."

"Oh, no, dear, thank you. Marry one of you demons? Not for any money!"

"What a law!" said Aunt Sadie. "Whenever was it passed? Why it's the end of all family life, a thing like that."

"Except it's the beginning for Polly."

"Who told Lady Montdore?" Of course I was fascinated. This key-piece of the jig-saw made everything quite clear, and now I could not imagine how I could ever have been so stupid as to have missed it.

"Polly told her," said Aunt Sadie. "It happened like this. They hadn't seen Boy since the funeral because he caught a bad cold at it and stayed indoors. Sonia got an awful cold there too, and still has it, but he had spoken to Sonia every day on the telephone, as he always does. Well, yesterday they both felt a bit better, and he went over to Hampton with the letters he'd had about poor Patricia, from Infantas and things, and they had a good gloat over them, and then a long discussion about what to put on the tombstone. It seems they more or less settled on, 'She shall not grow old as we that are left grow old.' "

"Stupid!" said Jassy. "She had grown old already!"

"Old! A few years older than me," said Davey.

"Well . . . !" said Jassy.

"That's enough, miss. Sonia says he seemed terribly low and unhappy, talking about Patricia and what she'd always been to him, and how empty the house seems without her—just what you'd expect after twenty-three years, or something. Miserable old hypocrite! Well, he was supposed to stay for dinner, without dressing, because of his cold. Sonia and Lord Montdore went upstairs to change, and when Sonia came down again she found Polly, still in her day clothes, sitting on that white rug in front of the fire. She said, 'What are you doing, Polly? It's very late. Go up and dress. Where's Boy, then?' Polly got up and stretched herself and said, 'He's gone home and I've got something to tell you. Boy and I are going to be married!' At first, of course, Sonia didn't believe it, but Polly never jokes, as you know, and she very soon saw she was in deadly earnest and then she was so furious she went sort of mad—how well I can understand that!—and rushed at Polly and boxed her ears, and Polly gave her a great shove into an armchair and went upstairs. I imagine that Sonia was perfectly hysterical by then. Anyway, she rang for her maid who took her up and put her straight to bed. Meanwhile Polly dressed, came down again and calmly spent the evening with her father without saying a single word about it all to him, merely telling him that Sonia had a headache and wouldn't dine. So this morning poor Sonia had to tell him. She said it was terrible, because he so adores Polly. Then she tried to ring up Boy, but the wretched coward has gone away, or pretends to have, leaving no address. Did you ever hear such a story?"

I was speechless with interest. Davey said, "Personally, and speaking as an uncle, the one I feel for over all this is the unhappy Boy."

"Oh, no, Davey, nonsense. Just imagine the Montdores' feelings—while they were trying to argue her out of it this morning she told them she'd been in love with him since before they went to India, when she was a little girl of fourteen."

"Yes, very likely, but how do we know he wanted her to be in love with him? If you ask me, I don't suppose he had the very faintest idea of it."

"Come now, Davey, little girls of fourteen don't fall in love without any encouragement."

"Alas, they do," said Jassy. "Look at me and Mr. Fosdyke. Not one word, not one kindly glance has he ever thrown me and yet he is the light of my life."

Mr. Fosdyke was the local M.F.H.

I asked if Lady Montdore had had an inkling of all this before, knowing really quite well that she had not, as everything always came straight out with her and neither Polly nor Boy would have had one moment's peace.

"Simply no idea at all. It was a complete bolt from the blue. Poor Sonia, we know she has her faults, but I can't think she has deserved this. She said Boy had always been very kind about taking Polly off her hands when they were in London, to the Royal Academy and so on, and Sonia was pleased because the child never seemed to have anybody to amuse her. Polly wasn't a satisfactory girl to bring out, you know. I'm very fond of her myself, I always have been, but you could see that Sonia was having a difficult time in many ways. Oh, poor Sonia, I do feel . . . Now children, will you please go up and wash your fishy hands before tea?"

"This is the very limit. You're obviously going to say things while we're away. What about Fanny's fishy hands then?"

"Fanny's grown-up, she'll wash her hands when she feels like it. Off you go."

When they were safely out of the room, she said, in horror, to Davey and me, "Just imagine, Sonia, who had completely lost control of herself (not that I blame her), sort of hinted to me that Boy had once been her own lover."

"Darling Sadie, you are such an innocent," Davey said, laughing. "It's a famous, famous love affair which everybody except you has known all about for years. I sometimes think your children are right and you don't know the facts of life."

"Well, all I can say is, I'm thankful I don't. How perfectly hateful! Do you think Patricia knew?"

"Of course she did, and she was only too glad of it. Before his affair with Sonia began, Boy used to make Patricia chaperone all the dismal little debutantes that he fancied, and they would sob out broken hearts on her shoulder, and beg her to divorce him. Very last thing he wanted, naturally. She had a lot of trouble with him, you know."

"I remember a kitchen maid," Aunt Sadie said.

"Oh, yes, it was one thing after another before Sonia

took him on, but she had some control over him, and
Patricia's life became much easier and more agreeable,
until her liver got so bad."

"All the same," I said, "we know he still went for
little girls, because look at Linda."

"Did he?" said Aunt Sadie. "I have sometimes wondered. Ugh! What a man! How you can think there's
anything to be said for him, Davey, and how can you
pretend he hadn't the faintest idea Polly was in love
with him? If he made up to Linda, of course he must
have done the same to her."

"Well, Linda's not in love with him, is she? He can't
be expected to guess that because he strokes the hair
of a little girl when she's fourteen she's going to insist
on marrying him when she grows up. Bad luck on a
chap, I call it."

"Davey, you're hopeless! And if I didn't know quite
well that you're only teasing me I should be very cross
with you."

"Poor Sonia," said Davey. "I feel for her, her daughter and her lover at a go. . . . Well, it often happens,
but it can't ever be very agreeable."

"I'm sure it's the daughter she minds," said Aunt
Sadie. "She hardly mentioned Boy. She was moaning
and groaning about Polly, so perfectly beautiful, being
thrown away like that. I should be just the same. I
couldn't bear it for any of mine. . . . That old fellow
they've known all their lives, and it's worse for her,
Polly being the only one."

"And such a treasure, so much the apple of their eye.
Well, the more I see of life the more profoundly thankful I am not to have any children."

"Between two and six they are perfect," said my aunt, rather sadly, I thought. "After that, I must say they are a worry, the funny little things. Then another horror for Sonia is wondering what went on all those years between Polly and Boy. She says last night she couldn't sleep for thinking of times when Polly pretended to have been to the hairdresser and obviously hadn't—that sort of thing—she says it's driving her mad.

"It needn't," I said firmly. "I'm quite sure nothing ever happened. From various things I can remember Polly saying to me I'm quite sure her love for the Lecturer must always have seemed hopeless to her. Polly's very good, you know, and she was very fond of her aunt."

"I daresay you're right, Fanny. Sonia herself said that when she came down and found Polly sitting on the floor she thought at once, 'The girl looks as if she had been making love,' and said she'd never seen her look like that before, flushed, her eyes simply huge and a curl of tousled hair hanging over her forehead. She was absolutely struck by her appearance, and then Polly told her . . ."

I could so well imagine the scene, Polly sitting, it was a very characteristic attitude with her, on the rug, getting up slowly, stretching, and then carelessly and gracefully implanting the cruel banderillas, the first movement of a fight that could only end in death.

"What I guess," I said, "is that he stroked a bit when she was fourteen and she fell in love then without him having any idea of it. Polly always bottles things up, and I don't expect anything more happened between them until the other evening."

"Simply too dreadful," said Aunt Sadie.

"Anyhow, Boy can't have expected to get engaged there and then, or he wouldn't have had all that talk about the Infanta's letter and the gravestone, would he?" said Davey. "I expect what Fanny says is true."

"You've been telling—it is unfair—Fanny's hands are still foully fishy." The children were back, out of breath.

"I do wonder what Uncle Matthew and Lord Mont-dore talked about in the business room," I said. I could not imagine such a tale being unfolded between those two, somehow.

"They topicked," said Aunt Sadie. "I told Matthew afterwards, I've never seen anybody so angry. But I haven't told you yet what it was that Sonia really came about. She's sending Polly here for a week or two."

"No!" we all cried in chorus.

"Oh, the utter fascination!" said Jassy. "But why?"

"Polly wants to come. It was her idea and Sonia can't endure the sight of her for the present, which I can well understand. I must say I hesitated at first, but I am very fond of that little girl, you know. I really love her, and if she stays at home her mother will have driven her into an elopement within a week. If she comes here we might be able to influence her against this horrible marriage—and I don't mean you, children. You'll please try and be tactful for once in your lives."

"I will be," said Jassy, earnestly. "It's dear little Vict you must speak to. There's no tack in her and, person-ally, I think it was a great mistake ever to have told her at all—ow—help—help—Sadie, she's killing me . . . !"

"I mean both of you," said Aunt Sadie, calmly, taking

no notice whatever of the dog-fight in progress. "You can talk about the chubb at dinner. That ought to be a safe subject."

"What?" they said, stopping the fight. "She's not coming today?"

"Yes, she is. After tea."

"Oh, what a thrill. Do you think the Lecturer will have himself carried into the house dressed up as a sack of wood?"

"They shan't meet under my roof," Aunt Sadie said firmly. "I promised Sonia that, but of course I pointed out that I can't control what Polly does elsewhere. I can only leave that to her own sense of what is in good taste, while she is staying with me."

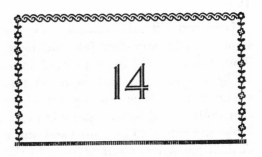

14

POLLY soon made it clear that Aunt Sadie need have no misgivings about her behaviour while at Alconleigh. Her self-possession was complete, the only exterior indication that her life was at a crisis being an aura of happiness, which transformed her whole aspect. Nothing she said or did was at all out of the usual or could have led anybody to suppose that she had recently been involved in scenes of such intensity. And it was obvious that she held no communication of any sort with Boy; she never went near the telephone, she did not sit all day scribbling letters, received very few, and none, so the children informed me, with a Silkin postmark. She hardly ever left the house and then only to get a breath of air with the rest of us, certainly not in order to go for long solitary walks which might end in lovers meetings.

Jassy and Victoria, romantic like all the Radletts, found this incomprehensible and most disappointing. They had expected to be plunged into an atmosphere of light opera and had supposed that the Lecturer would hang, sighing but hopeful, about the precincts, that Polly would hang, sighing but expectant, out of a moonlit window, to be united and put on the first stage of their journey to Gretna Green, by the ingenuity and enterprise of their two young friends.

They lugged a mattress and stocks of food into the Hons' cupboard in case Boy wanted to hide there for a day or two. They had thought of everything, so they informed me, and were busy making a rope ladder. But Polly would not play.

"If you have any letters for the post, Polly, you know what I mean, a letter—we could easily run down to the village with it on our bikes."

"Darling, you are kind, but they'll go just as quickly if I put them on the hall table, won't they?"

"Oh, of course you can do that if you like, but everybody will read the envelope and I just thought . . . Or any messages? There's a telephone in the village post office, rather public, but you could talk in French."

"I don't know French very well. Isn't there a telephone here?"

"Oh, it's a brute, extensions all over the place. Now there's a hollow tree in the park quite big enough for a man to hide in—quite dry and comfy—shall we show you?"

"You must, one day. Too cold to go out to-day, I think."

"You know there's a frightfully nice little temple in

a wood the other side of the river, would you like us to take you there?"

"Do you mean Faulkner's Folly, where they have the meets? But, Jassy, I know it quite well, I've often seen it. Very pretty."

"What I really mean is the key is kept under a stone, and we could show you exactly where, so that you could go inside."

"There's nothing to see inside except cobwebs," I said. "It was never finished, you know."

Jassy made a furious face at me. "Tackless," she muttered.

"Let's go there next summer, darlings," said Polly, "for a picnic. I can't enjoy anything out of doors in this weather my eyes water too much."

The children slouched away, discouraged.

Polly exploded with laughter. "Aren't they too heavenly? But I don't really see the point of making all these great efforts to spend a few minutes with Boy in freezing cold temples, or to write to him about nothing at all, when very soon I shall be with him for the whole rest of my life. Besides, I don't want to annoy Lady Alconleigh when she is being such an angel to have me here."

Aunt Sadie herself, while applauding Polly's attitude, which relieved her of any need to worry, found it most unnatural.

"Isn't it strange?" she said. "You can see by looking at her that she is very happy, but, if it weren't for that, nobody could guess that she was in love. My girls always get so moony, writing reams all day, jumping when the telephone bell rings and so on, but there's none of that with Polly. I was watching her last night when Matthew put '*Che Gelida Manina*' on the gramophone. She didn't look a bit sentimental. Do you remember what an awful time we had with Linda when Tony was in America—never out of floods?"

But Polly had been brought up in a harder school for the emotions than had the Radletts, with a mother determined to find out everything that was in her mind, and to mould her very thoughts to her own wishes. One could only admire the complete success with which she had countered both of these aims. Clearly her character had a steely quality, incomprehensible to my cousins, blown hither and thither as they were upon the winds of sentiment.

I managed to have a few long talks alone with Polly at this time, but it was not very easy. Jassy and Victoria hardly left us for a single minute, so frightened were they of missing something. Furthermore, they were shameless eavesdroppers, while hair-brushing chats at bedtime were ruled out by the fact of my so-recent marriage. Mercifully, the children went riding every day, when an hour or so of peace could be counted on, there was no hunting at this time because of foot-and-mouth disease.

Gradually, the whole thing came out. Polly's reserve, it is true, never really broke down, but every now and then the landscape was illuminated and its character exposed to view by flashes of startling frankness. It all seemed to have been very much as we had thought. For instance, I said to her something about when Boy proposed, and she replied, quite carelessly, "Oh, Boy never proposed to me at all. I don't think he ever would have, being that kind of a person—I mean so wonderfully unselfish and thinking that it matters for me, not being left things in wills and all that rubbish. Besides, he knows Mummy so well and he knew just what a hullabaloo she would make. He couldn't face it for me. No, no, I always realized that I should have to do the proposing, and I did. It wasn't very difficult."

So Davey was right, no doubt, the idea of such a marriage would never have entered the Lecturer's head if it had not been put there by Polly herself. After that it would clearly have been beyond flesh and blood to resist such a prize, greatest beauty and greatest heiress of her generation, potential mother of the children, the little half-Hamptons, he had always longed for. He could never have said no once it all lay at his feet, waiting to be pocketed.

"After all, I've loved him ever since I can remember. Oh, Fanny—isn't being happy wonderful?"

I felt just the same myself and was able to agree with all my heart. But her happiness had a curiously staid quality, and her love seemed less like the usual enchanted rapture of the young girl, newly engaged, than a comfortable love of old establishment, love which does not need to assert itself by continually meeting, corresponding with and talking about its object, but which takes itself, as well as his response, for granted. The doubts and jealousies which can be so painful, and make a hell almost of a budding love affair did not seem to have occurred to Polly, who took the simple view that she and Boy had hitherto been kept apart by one insuperable barrier, and that this barrier having been removed, the path to lifelong bliss lay at their feet.

"What can it matter if we have a few more weeks of

horrid waiting when we are going to live together all the rest of our lives and be buried in the same grave?"

"Fancy being buried in the same grave with the Lecturer," Jassy said, coming into my bedroom before luncheon.

"Jassy, I think it's too awful the way you listen at doors."

"Don't tease, Fan, I intend to be a novelist (child novelist astounds the critics) and I'm studying human nature like mad."

"I really ought to tell Aunt Sadie."

"That's it. Join the reverends, now you are married, just like Louisa. No, but seriously, Fanny, think of sharing a grave with that old Lecturer. Isn't it disgusting? And anyway what about Lady Patricia?"

"Well, she's nice and snug in one all to herself, lined with heather. She's quite all right."

"I think it's shocking."

Meanwhile, Aunt Sadie was doing what she could to influence Polly, but as she was much too shy to speak to her directly on such intimate subjects as sex and marriage, she used an oblique method of letting fall an occasional reflection, hoping that Polly would apply it to her own particular case.

"Always remember, children, that marriage is a very intimate relationship. It's not just sitting and chatting to a person; there are other things, you know."

Boy Dougdale, to her, was physically repulsive, as I think he often was to those women who did not find him irresistible, and she thought that if Polly could be brought to a realization of the physical aspect of marriage she might be put off him for good.

As Jassy very truly observed, however, "Isn't Sadie a

scream? She simply doesn't realize that what put Polly
on the Lecturer's side in the first place must have been
all those dreadful things he did to her, like he once
tried to with Linda and me, and that now what she
really wants most in the world is to roll and roll and
roll about with him in a double bed."

"Yes, poor Sadie, she's not too hot on psychology,"
said Victoria. "Now I should say the only hope of cur-
ing Polly's uncle-fixation is to analyse her. Shall we see
if she'd let us try?"

"Children, I absolutely forbid you to," I said firmly.
"And if you do I promise I'll tell Aunt Sadie about the
eavesdropping, so there."

I knew what dreadful questions they would ask Polly
and that as she was rather prim she would be shocked
and angry. They were very much taken up at this time
with the study and practise of psychoanalysis. They got
hold of a book on the subject ("Elliston's library, would
you believe it?") and several days of peace had ensued
while they read it out to each other in the Hons' cupboard, after which they proceeded to action.

"Come and be analysed," was their parrot cry. "Let
us rid you of the poison that is clogging your mental
processes, by telling you all about yourselves. Now,
suppose we begin with Fa, he's the simplest proposition
in the house."

"What d'you mean, simple?"

"A.B.C. to us. No, no, not your hand, you dear old
thing, we're grown out of palmistry ages ago, this is
science."

"All right, let's hear it."

"Well, so then you're a very straightforward case of
frustration—wanted to be a gamekeeper, were obliged

to be a lord—followed, as is usual, by the development of over-compensation, so that now you're a psycho-neurotic of the obsessive and hysterical type engrafted on to a paranoid and schizoid personality."

"Children, you are not to say these things about your father."

"Scientific truths are nothing to object to, Sadie, and in our experience everybody enjoys learning about themselves. Would you care for us to test your intelligence level with an ink blot, Fa?"

"What's that?"

"We could do it to you all in turn and mark you, if you like. It's quite easy. You show the subject an ordinary blot of ink on white paper and, according to the picture it makes for each individual (you understand what I mean, does it look like a gum boil, or the Himalayas? everybody sees something different), a practised questioner can immediately assess his intelligence level."

"Are you practised questioners?"

"Well, we've practised on each other and all the Joshes and Mrs. Aster. And we've noted the results in our scientific notebook, so come on."

Uncle Matthew gazed at the blot for awhile and then said that it looked to him very much like an ordinary ink blot and reminded him of nothing so much as Stephen's Blue Black.

"It's just as I had feared," said Jassy, "and shows a positively sub-human level—even Baby Josh did better than that. Oh, dear, sub-human, that's bad. . . ."

Jassy had now overstepped the boundary in the perpetual game of Tom Tiddler's Ground that she played with her father. He roared at her in a sudden rage and sent her to bed. She went off chanting, "Paranoid *and* schizoid, paranoid *and* schizoid," which had taken the place of "Man's long agony." She said to me afterwards, "Of course, it's rather grave for all of us because whether you believe in heredity or environment, either way we are boiled, shut up here with this old sub-human of a father."

Davey now decided that it would be only kind to go over and see his old friend Lady Montdore, so he rang her up and was invited to luncheon. He stayed until after tea, and, by good luck, when he got back Polly was lying down in her bedroom, so he was able to tell all.

"She is in a rage," he said. "A rage. Simply frightening. She has taken what the French call a '*coup de vieux*.' She looks a hundred. I wouldn't care to be hated by anyone as much as she hates Boy. After all, you never know. There may be something in Christian Science, and evil thoughts and so on, directed at us with great intensity may affect the body. How she hates him! Just imagine, she has had the tapestry he made for that fire screen cut out quite roughly with a pair of scissors, and the screen is there in front of the fire with a huge hole in it. It gave me quite a shock."

"Poor Sonia, how like her, somehow. And what does she feel about Polly?"

"She mourns her, and she's pretty cross with her too for being so underhand and keeping it a secret all these years. I said, 'You really couldn't expect that she would tell you?' but she didn't agree. She asked me a lot of questions about Polly and her state of mind. I was obliged to say that her state of mind is not revealed to me, but that she is looking twice as pretty as before, if possible, so it can therefore be presumed that she is happy."

"Yes, you can always tell by that, with girls," said Aunt Sadie. "If it weren't for that, I wouldn't have thought she cared a bit, one way or the other. What a strange character she must have, after all."

"Not so strange," said Davey. "Many women are rather enigmatic, very few laugh when they are happy and cry when they are sad to the extent that your children do, my dear Sadie, nor do we all see everything in black and white. Life is oversimplified at Alconleigh. It's part of the charm and I'm not complaining, but you mustn't suppose that all human beings are exactly like Radletts, because it is not so."

"You stayed very late."

"Poor Sonia, she's lonely. She must be, dreadfully, if you come to think of it. We talked about nothing else, too, round and round the subject, every aspect of it. She asked me to go over and see Boy to find out if there's any hope of his giving up the idea and going abroad for a bit. She says Montdore's lawyer has written and told him that the day Polly marries him she will be completely cut out of her father's will and also Montdore will stop Patricia's allowance which he was intending to give Boy for his life. Even so, she fears they will have enough to live on, but it might shake him, I suppose. I didn't promise to go, but I think perhaps I will, all the same."

"Oh, but you must," said Jassy. "There's us to consider."

"Children, do stop interrupting," said Aunt Sadie. "If you can't hold your tongues you will have to leave the room when we are having serious conversations. In fact," she said, becoming strict all of a sudden, just as she used to be when Linda and I were little, "I think you'd better go now. Go on, off with you."

They went. As they reached the door, Jassy said in a loud aside, "This labile and indeterminate attitude to discipline may do permanent damage to our young psychology. I really think Sadie should be more careful."

"Oh, no, Jassy," Victoria said. "After all, it's our complexes that make us so fascinating and unusual."

When they had shut the door, Davey said, rather seriously, "You know, Sadie, you do spoil them."

"Oh, dear," said Aunt Sadie, "I'm afraid so. It comes of having so many children. One can force oneself to be strict for a few years, but after that it becomes too much of an effort. But, Davey, do you honestly imagine it makes the smallest difference when they are grown-up?"

"Probably not to your children, demons one and all. But look how well we brought up Fanny."

"Davey! You were never strict," I said. "Not the least bit. You spoilt me quite completely."

"Yes, now, that's true," said Aunt Sadie. "Fanny was allowed to do all sorts of dreadful things—specially after she came out. Powder her nose, travel alone, go in cabs with young men—didn't she once go to a night club? Fortunately for you she seems to have been born good, though why she should have been, with such parents, is beyond me."

Davey told Polly that he had seen her mother but she merely said, "How was Daddy?"

"In London, House of Lords, something about India. Your mother doesn't look at all well, Polly."

"Temper," said Polly, and left the room.

Davey's next visit was to Silkin. "Frankly, I can't resist it." He bustled off in his little motor car on the chance of finding the Lecturer at home. He still refused to come to the telephone, giving out that he was away for a few weeks, but all other evidence pointed to the fact that he was living in his house, and, indeed, this now proved to be the case.

"Puzzled and lonely and gloomy, poor old Boy, and he's still got an awful cold he can't get rid of. Sonia's evil thoughts, perhaps. He has aged, too. Says he has seen nobody since his engagement to Polly. Of course, he has cut himself off at Silkin, but he seems to think that the people he has run into, at the London Library, and so on, have been avoiding him as if they already knew about it. I expect it's really because he's in mourning—or perhaps they don't want to catch his cold—anyway, he's fearfully sensitive on the subject. Then he didn't say so, but you can see how much he is missing Sonia. Naturally, after seeing her every day all these years. Missing Patricia, too, I expect."

"Did you talk quite openly about Polly?" I asked.

"Oh, quite. He says the whole thing originated with her, wasn't his idea at all."

"Yes, that's true. She told me that herself."

"And if you ask me, it shocks him dreadfully. He can't resist it, of course, but it shocks him and he fully expects to be a social outcast as the result. Now that would have been the card for Sonia to have played, if she had been clever enough to foresee it all. Too late, once the words were spoken, of course, but if she could have warned Boy what was likely to happen and then rubbed in about how that would finish him for ever in the eyes of society I think she might have stopped it. After all, he's frightfully social, poor chap. He would hate to be ostracised. As a matter of fact, though I didn't say so to him, people will come round in no time once they are married."

"But you don't really think they will marry?" said Aunt Sadie.

"My dear Sadie, after ten days in the same house with Polly I don't doubt it for one single instant. What's more, Boy knows he's in for it, all right, whether he likes it or not—and of course he half likes it very much indeed. But he dreads the consequences, not that there'll be any. People have no memory about that sort of thing and, after all, there's nothing to forget except bad taste."

"*Détournement de jeunesse?*"

"It won't occur to the ordinary person that Boy could have made a pass at Polly when she was little. We would never have thought of it, except for what he did to Linda. In a couple of years nobody outside the family will even remember what all the fuss was about."

"I'm afraid you're right," said my aunt. "Look at the Bolter! Ghastly scandal after ghastly scandal, elopements, horse whippings, puts herself up as a prize in a lottery, cannibal kings—I don't know what all—headlines in the papers, libel actions, and yet she only has to appear in London and her friends queue up to give parties for her. But don't encourage Boy by telling him. Did you suggest he might chuck it and go abroad?"

"Yes, I did, but it's no good. He misses Sonia. He is horrified, in a way, by the whole thing, hates the idea of his money being stopped, though he's not penniless himself, you know. He's got an awful cold and is down in the dumps, but at the same time you can see that the prospect dazzles him and as long as Polly makes all the running I bet you he'll play. Oh, dear, fancy taking on a new young wife at our age—how exhausting! Boy, too, who is cut out to be a widower, I do pity him."

"Pity him, indeed! All he had to do was to leave little girls alone."

"You're so implacable, Sadie. It's a heavy price to pay for a bit of cuddling. I wish you could see the poor chap . . . !"

"Whatever does he do with himself all the time?"

"He's embroidering a counterpane," said Davey. "It's his wedding present for Polly. He calls it a bedspread."

"Oh, really!" Aunt Sadie shuddered. "He is the most dreadful man! Better not tell Matthew. In fact, I wouldn't tell him you've been over at all. He nearly has a fit every time he thinks of Boy now, and I don't blame him. Bedspread, indeed!"

15

S O O N after this, Polly announced to Aunt Sadie that she would like to go to London the following day as she had an appointment there with Boy. We were sitting alone with Aunt Sadie in her little room. Although it was the first time that Polly had mentioned her uncle's name to anybody at Alconleigh, except me, she brought it out not only without a tremor of self-consciousness but as though she spoke of him all and every day. It was an admirable performance. There was a pause. Aunt Sadie was the one who blushed and found it difficult to control her voice, and when at last she replied it did not sound natural at all, but hard and anxious.

"Would you care to tell me what your plans are, Polly?"

"Please—to catch the 9.30, if it's convenient."

"No, I don't mean your plans for tomorrow, but for your life."

"You see, that's what I must talk about, with Boy. Last time I saw him we made no plans, we simply became engaged to be married."

"And this marriage, Polly dear—your mind is made up?"

"Yes, quite. So I don't see any point in all this waiting. As we are going to be married whatever happens, what can it matter when? In fact, there is every reason why it should be very soon now. It's out of the question for me to go and live with my mother again, and I can't foist myself on you indefinitely. You've been much too kind as it is."

"Oh, my darling child, don't give that a thought. It never matters having people here, so long as Matthew likes them. Look at Davey and Fanny, they're in no hurry to go. They know quite well we love having them."

"Oh, yes, I know, but they are family."

"So are you, almost, and quite as welcome as if you were. I have got to go to London in a few weeks, as you know, for Linda's baby, but that needn't make any difference to you, and you must stay on for as long as ever you like. There'll be Fanny, and when Fanny goes there are the children—they worship you, you are their heroine, it's wonderful for them having you here. So don't think about that again. Don't, for heaven's sake, rush into marriage because you think you have nowhere to live, because for one thing it's not the case at all, since you can live here, and, anyhow, it could never be a sufficient reason for taking such a grave step."

"I'm not rushing," said Polly. "It's the only marriage

I could ever have made, and if it had continued to be impossible I should have lived and died a spinster."

"Oh, no, you wouldn't," said Aunt Sadie. "You've no idea how long life goes on and how many, many changes it brings. Young people seem to imagine that it's over in a flash, that they do this thing, or that thing, and then die, but I can assure you they are quite wrong. I suppose it's no good saying this to you, Polly, as I can see your mind is made up, but since you have the whole of your life before you as a married woman, why not make the most of being a girl? You'll never be one again. You're only twenty. Why be in such a hurry to change?"

"I hate being a girl. I've hated it ever since I grew up," said Polly. "And besides, do you really think a lifetime is too long for perfect happiness? I don't. . . ."

Aunt Sadie gave a profound sigh.

"I wonder why it is that all girls suppose the married state to be one of perfect happiness? Is it just clever old Dame Nature's way of hurrying them into the trap?"

"Dear Lady Alconleigh, don't be so cynical."

"No, no, you are quite right, I mustn't be. You've settled upon your future, and nothing anybody can say will stop you, I'm sure, but I must tell you that I think you are making a terrible mistake. There, I won't say another word about it. I'll order the car for the 9.30, and will you be catching the 4.45 back or the 6.10?"

"4.45 please. I told Boy to meet me at the Ritz at one. I sent him a postcard yesterday."

And by a miracle the said postcard had lain about all day on the hall table without either Jassy or Victoria spotting it. Hunting had begun again, and although they were only allowed out three times a fortnight the sheer physical exhaustion which it induced did a great deal towards keeping their high spirits within bounds. As for Uncle Matthew, who went out four days a week, he hardly opened an eye after tea time, but nodded away, standing up in his business room, with the gramophone blaring his favourite tunes. Every few minutes he gave a great jump and rushed to change the needle and the disc.

That evening, before dinner, Boy rang up. We were all in the business room listening to *Lakmè* on the gramophone, new records which had just arrived from the Army and Navy Stores. My uncle ground his teeth when the temple bells were interrupted by a more penetrating peal, and gnashed them with anger when he heard Boy's voice asking for Polly, but he handed her the receiver and pushed up a chair for her with the old-fashioned courtesy which he used towards those he liked. He never treated Polly as if she were a very young person, and I believe he was really rather in awe of her.

Polly said, "Yes? Oh? Very well. Good-bye." and hung up the receiver. Even this ordeal had done nothing to shake her serenity.

She told us that Boy had changed the rendezvous, saying he thought it was pointless to go all the way to London, and suggesting the Mitre in Oxford as a more convenient meeting place.

"So perhaps we could go in together, Fanny darling."

I was going, anyhow, to visit my house.

"Ashamed of himself," said Davey, when Polly had gone upstairs. "Doesn't want to be seen. People are beginning to talk. You know how Sonia can never keep a secret, and once the Kensington Palace set gets hold of something it is all round London in a jiffy."

"Oh, dear," said Aunt Sadie. "But if they are seen at the Mitre it will look far worse. I feel rather worried. I only promised Sonia they shouldn't meet here, but ought I to tell her? What do you think?"

"Shall I go over to Silkin and shoot the sewer?" said Uncle Matthew, half-asleep.

"Oh, no, darling, please don't. What do you think, Davey?"

"Don't you worry about the old she-wolf. Good Lord, who cares a brass button for her?"

If Uncle Matthew had not hated Boy so much, he would have been quite as eager as his daughters were to aid and abet Polly in any enterprise that would fly in the face of Lady Montdore.

Davey said, "I wouldn't give it a thought. It so happens that Polly has been perfectly open and above board about the whole thing—but suppose she hadn't told you? She's always going in to Oxford with Fanny, isn't she? I should turn the blind eye."

So in the morning Polly and I motored to Oxford together, and I lunched, as I often did, with Alfred at the George. (If I never mention Alfred in this story, it is because he is so totally uninterested in other human beings and their lives that I think he was hardly aware of what was going on. He certainly did not enter into it with fascination like the rest of us. I suppose that I and his children and, perhaps, an occasional clever pupil seem real to him, but otherwise he lives in a world of shadows and abstract thought.)

After luncheon I spent a freezing, exhausting and

discouraging hour in my little house, which seemed hopelessly haunted by builders. I noted, with something like despair, that they had now made one of the rooms cosy, a regular home from home, with blazing fire, stewing tea and film stars on the walls. As far as I could see, they never left it at all to ply their trade and, indeed, I could hardly blame them for that, so terrible were the damp and cold in the rest of the house. After a detailed inspection with the foreman, which merely revealed more exposed pipes and fewer floor boards than last time I had been there, I went to the window of what was supposed to be my drawing room, to fortify myself with the view of Christ Church, so beautiful against the black clouds. One day, I thought (it was an act of faith), I would sit by that very window, open wide, and there would be green trees and a blue sky behind the college. I gazed on, through glass which was almost opaque with dirt and white-wash, forcing myself to imagine that summer scene, when, battling their way down the street, the East wind in their faces, Polly and the Lecturer appeared to view. It was not a happy picture, but that may have been the fault of the climate. No aimless dalliance hand in hand beneath warm skies for poor English lovers who, if circumstances drive them to making love out of doors, are obliged to choose between the sharp brisk walk and the stupefying stuffiness of the cinema. They stumped on out of my sight, hands in pockets, heads bowed, plunged, one would have said, in gloom.

Before going home, I paid a visit to Woolworth, having been enjoined by Jassy to get her a goldfish bowl for her frog spawn. She had broken hers the day

before and had only got the precious jelly to the spare-
room bath just in time, she said, to save it. Alfred and
I were obliged to use the nursery bathroom until Jassy
got a new bowl. "So you see how it's to your own advantage, Fanny, not to forget."

Once inside Woolworth I found other things that I
needed, as one always does, and presently I ran into
Polly and Boy. He was holding a mouse trap, but I
think it was really shelter from the wind that they
sought.

"Home soon?" said Polly.

"Now, d'you think?" I was dead tired.

"Do let's."

So we all three went to the Clarendon Yard where
our respective motor cars were waiting. The Lecturer
still had a terrible cold, which made him most unap-
petizing, I thought, and he seemed very grumpy. When
he took my hand to say good-bye he gave it no extra
squeeze, nor did he stroke and tickle our legs when
tucking us up in the rug, which he would certainly
have done had he been in a normal state, and when we
drove off he just walked gloomily away with no backward glance, jaunty wave or boyish shake of the curls.
He was evidently at a low ebb.

Polly leaned forward, wound up the window between
us and the chauffeur and said, "Well, everything's settled, thank goodness. A month from to-day if I can get
my parents' consent. I shall still be under age, you see.
So the next thing is a tussle with Mummy. I'll go over
to Hampton tomorrow if she's there and point out that
I shall be of age in May, after which she won't be able
to stop me, so hadn't she better swallow the pill and

have done with it. They won't be wanting to have birthday celebrations for me now, since, in any case, Daddy is cutting me off without a shilling."

"Do you think he really will?"

"As if I cared! The only thing I mind about is Hampton, and he can't leave me that even if he wants to. Then I shall say, 'Do you intend to put a good face on it and let me be married in the chapel (which Boy terribly wants for some reason, and I would rather like it, I must say) or must we sneak off and be done in London?' Poor Mummy—now I'm out of her clutches I feel awfully sorry for her, in a way. I think the sooner it's over the better for everybody."

Boy, it was clear, was still leaving all the dirty work to Polly. Perhaps his cold was sapping his will power, or perhaps the mere thought of a new young wife at his age was exhausting him already.

So Polly rang up her mother and asked if she could lunch at Hampton the following day and have a talk. I thought it would have been more sensible to have had the talk without the additional strain imposed by a meal, but Polly seemed unable to envisage a country house call which did not centre round food. Perhaps she was right, since Lady Montdore was very greedy and therefore more agreeable during and after meals than at other times. In any case, this is what she suggested; she also told her mother to send a motor as she did not like to ask the Alconleighs for one two days running. Lady Montdore said very well, but that she must bring me, Lord Montdore was still in London and I suppose she felt she could not bear to see Polly alone. Anyhow, she was one of those people who always avoid a tête-à-tête, if possible, even with their intimates. Polly said to me that she herself had just been going to ask if I could come too.

"I want a witness," she added. "If she says yes in front of you she won't be able to wriggle out of it again later."

Poor Lady Montdore, like Boy, was looking very much down. Not only old and ill (also like Boy, she was still afflicted with Lady Patricia's funeral cold which seemed to have been a specially virulent germ), but positively dirty. The fact that she had never, at the best of times, been very well groomed, had formerly been off-set by her flourish and swagger, radiant health, enjoyment of life, and the inward assurance of superiority bestowed upon her by "all this." These supports had been cut away by her cold as well as by the simultaneous defection of Polly, which must have taken much of the significance out of "all this" and of Boy, her constant companion, the last lover, surely, that she would ever have. Life, in fact, had become sad and meaningless.

We began luncheon in silence. Polly turned her food over with a fork. Lady Montdore refused the first dish, while I munched away rather self-consciously alone, enjoying the change of cooking. Aunt Sadie's food, at that time, was very plain. After a glass or two of wine, Lady Montdore cheered up a bit and began to chat. She told us that the dear Grand Duchess had sent her such a puddy postcard from Cap d'Antibes where she was staying with other members of the Imperial family. She remarked that the Government really ought to make more effort to attract such important visitors to England.

"I was saying so only the other day to Ramsay," she complained. "And he quite agreed with me but, of course, one knows nothing will be done; it never is in this hopeless country. So annoying. All the Rajahs are at Survretta House again. . . . The King of Greece has gone to Nice. . . . The King of Sweden has gone to Cannes and the young Italians are doing winter sports. Perfectly ridiculous not to get them all here."

"Whatever for," said Polly, "when there's no snow?"

"Plenty in Scotland. Or teach them to hunt. They'd love it. They only want encouraging a little."

"No sun," I said.

"Never mind. Make it the fashion to do without sun, and they'll all come here. They came for my ball and Queen Alexandra's funeral—they love a binge, poor dears. The Government really ought to pay one to give a ball every year. It would restore confidence and bring important people to London."

"I can't see what good all these old royalties do when they are here," said Polly.

"Oh, yes, they do, they attract Americans, and so on," said Lady Montdore, vaguely. "Always good to have influential people around, you know. Good for a private family and also good for a country. I've always gone in for them myself and I can tell you it's a very great mistake not to. Look at poor dear Sadie, I've never heard of anybody important going to Alconleigh."

"Well," said Polly, "and what harm has it done her?"

"Harm! You can see the harm all round. First of all, the girls' husbands." On this point Lady Montdore did not lean, suddenly remembering, no doubt, her own situation in respect of daughters' husbands, but continued, "Poor Matthew has never got anything, has he? I don't only mean jobs, but not even a V.C. in the war and, goodness knows, he was brave enough. He may not be quite cut out to be a Governor, I grant you that, especially not where there are black people, but you don't tell me there's nothing he could have got, if Sadie had been a little cleverer about it. Something at Court, for instance. It would have calmed him down."

The idea of Uncle Matthew at Court made me choke into my pancake, but Lady Montdore took no notice and went on.

"And now I'm afraid it will be the same story with the boys. I'm told they were sent to the very worst house at Eton because Sadie had nobody to advise her or help her at all when the time came for them to go there. One must be able to pull strings in life. Everything depends on that in this world, I'm afraid. It's the only way to be successful. Luckily for me, I like important people best, and I get on with them like a house on fire, but even if they bored me I should have thought it my duty to cultivate them, for Montdore's sake."

When we had finished our meal we installed ourselves in the Long Gallery. The butler brought in a coffee tray which Lady Montdore told him to leave. She always had several cups of strong black coffee. As soon as he had gone she turned to Polly and said sharply, "So what is it you want to say to me?"

I made a half-hearted attempt to go, but they both insisted on me staying. I knew they would.

"I want to be married in a month from now," said Polly. "And to do that I must have your consent as I'm not of age until May. It seems to me that as it is only a question of nine weeks, when I shall marry anyhow, you might as well agree and get it over, don't you think?"

"I must say that's very puddy—your poor aunt—when the breath has hardly left her body."

"It doesn't make the slightest difference to Aunt

Patricia whether she has been dead three months or three years, so let's leave her out of it. The facts are what they are. I can't live at Alconleigh much longer. I can't live here with you. Hadn't I better start my new life as soon as possible?"

"Do you quite realize, Polly, that the day you marry Boy Dougdale your father is going to alter his will?"

"Yes, yes, yes," said Polly impatiently. "The times you've told me!"

"I've only told you once before."

"I've had a letter about it. Boy has had a letter about it. We know."

"I wonder whether you also know that Boy Dougdale is a very poor man? They lived, really, on Patricia's allowance, which, of course, in the ordinary way your father would have continued during Boy's lifetime. That will also stop if he marries you."

"Yes. It was all in the letters."

"And don't count on your father changing his mind, because I've no intention of allowing him to."

"I'm quite sure you haven't."

"You think it doesn't matter being poor, but I wonder if you realize what it is like."

"The one who doesn't realize," said Polly, "is you."

"Not from experience, I'm glad to say, but from observation I do. One's only got to look at the hopeless, dreary expression on the faces of poor people to see what it must be."

"I don't agree at all. But anyhow we shan't be poor like poor people. Boy has £800 a year, besides what he makes from his books."

"The parson here and his wife have £800 a year," said Lady Montdore. "And look at their faces . . . !"

"They were born with those. I did better, thanks to you. In any case, Mummy, it's no good going on and on arguing about it, because everything is as much settled as if we were married already, so it's just pure waste of time."

"Then why have you come? What do you want me to do?"

"First, I want to have the wedding next month, for which I need your consent and then I also want to know what you and Daddy prefer about the actual marriage ceremony itself. Shall we be married here in the chapel or shall I go off without you to London for it? We naturally don't want anybody to be there except Fanny and Lady Alconleigh, and you, if you'd care to come. I must say, I would love to be given away by Daddy. . . ."

Lady Montdore thought for awhile and finally said, "I think it is quite intolerable of you to put us in this position and I shall have to talk it over with Montdore, but frankly I think that if you intend to go through with this indecent marriage at all costs, it will make the least talk if we have it here, and before your birthday. Then I shan't have to explain why there are to be no coming-of-age celebrations. The tenants have begun asking about that already. So I think you may take it that you can have the marriage here, and next month, after which, you incestuous little trollop, I never want to set eyes on either you or your uncle again, as long as I live. And please don't expect a wedding present from me."

Tears of self-pity were pouring down her cheeks. Perhaps she was thinking of the magnificent parure in its glass case against which, had things been otherwise, so many envious noses would have been pressed during the wedding reception at Montdore House. "From the Bride's Parents." Her dream of Polly's wedding, long and dearly cherished, had ended in a sad awakening indeed.

"Don't cry, Mummy, I'm so very, very happy."

"Well, I'm not," said Lady Montdore, and rushed furiously from the room.

EXACTLY one month later Davey, Aunt Sadie and I drove over to Hampton together for the wedding, our ears full of the lamentations of Jassy and Victoria, who had not been invited.

"Polly is a horrible Counter Hon and we hate her," they said. "After we made our fingers bleed over that rope ladder, not to speak of all the things we would have done for her, smuggling the Lecturer up to the Hons' cupboard—sharing our food with him—no risk we wouldn't have taken to give them a few brief moments of happiness together, only they were too cold-blooded to want it, and she doesn't even ask us to the wedding. Do admit, Fanny."

"I don't blame her for a single minute," I said. "A wedding is a very serious thing. Naturally she doesn't want gusts of giggles the whole way through it."

"And did we gust at yours?"

"I expect so, only it was a bigger church, and more people, and I didn't hear you."

Uncle Matthew, on the other hand, was asked and said that nothing would induce him to accept.

"Wouldn't be able to keep my hands off the sewer," he said. "Boy!" he went on, scornfully. "There's one thing, you'll hear his real name at last. Just note it down for me, please. I've always wanted to know what it is, to put in a drawer."

It was a favourite superstition of Uncle Matthew's that if you wrote somebody's name on a piece of paper and put it in a drawer, that person would die within the year. The drawers at Alconleigh were full of little slips bearing the names of those whom my uncle wanted out of the way, private hates of his and various public figures, such as Bernard Shaw, de Valera, Gandhi, Lloyd George and the Kaiser, while every single drawer in the whole house contained the name Labby, Linda's old dog. The spell hardly ever seemed to work, even Labby having lived far beyond the age usual in Labradors, but he went hopefully on, and if one of the characters did happen to be carried off in the course of nature he would look pleased, but guilty, for a day or two.

"I suppose we must all have heard his name when he married Patricia," Aunt Sadie said, looking at Davey. "But I can't remember it, can you? Such a thousand, thousand years ago. Poor Patricia, what can she be thinking now?"

"Was she married in the chapel at Hampton, too?" I said.

"No, in London, and I'm trying to remember where. Lord Montdore and Sonia were married in the Abbey, of course. I well remember that because Emily was a bridesmaid and I was so furiously jealous, and my Nanny took me, but outside, because Mamma thought we would see more like that than if we were stuck away behind a tomb. It was like a royal wedding, almost. Of course I was out by the time Patricia married. St. Margaret's, Westminster, I think—yes, I'm nearly sure it was. I know we all thought she was awfully old for a white wedding, thirty, or something terrible."

"But she was beautiful," said Davey.

"Very much like Polly, of course, but she never had that something extra, whatever it is, that makes Polly such a radiant beauty. I only wish I knew why these lovely women have both thrown themselves away on that old Lecturer—so unnatural."

"Poor Boy," said Davey, with a deeply sympathetic sigh.

Davey, who had been in Kent with Aunt Emily since finishing his cure, had come back to Alconleigh in order to be best man. He had accepted, so he said, for poor Patricia's sake, but really I think because he longed to go to the wedding. He also very much enjoyed the excuse it gave him to bustle about between Silkin and Hampton and see for himself all that was going on in those two stricken homes.

Polly had gone back to Hampton. She had taken no steps whatever towards getting a trousseau and, as the engagement and wedding were to be announced simultaneously in the *Times*, "took place very quietly, owing to deep mourning, at Hampton Park" (all these little details arranged by Davey), she had no letters to write, no presents to unpack and none of the business that usually precedes a wedding. Lord Montdore had insisted that she should have an interview with his lawyer, who came all the way from London to explain to her formally that everything hitherto set aside in her father's will, for her and her children, that is to say, Montdore House, Craigside Castle and their contents, the property in Northumberland, with its coal mines, the valuable and extensive house property in London, one or two docks and about two million pounds sterling would now all go to her father's only male heir, Cedric Hampton. In the ordinary course of events he would merely have inherited Hampton itself and Lord Montdore's titles, but as the result of this new will, Cedric Hampton was destined to be one of the five or six richest men in England.

"And how is Lord Montdore taking it?" Aunt Sadie asked Davey when he brought back this news from Hampton, via a visit to Boy at Silkin.

"Quite impossible to say. Sonia is wretched, Polly is nervous, but Montdore is just as usual, you couldn't guess that anything out of the ordinary was happening to him."

"I always knew he was an old stick. Had you realized he was so rich, Davey?"

"Oh, yes, one of the very richest."

"Funny when you think how stingy Sonia is, in little ways. How long d'you imagine he'll keep it up, cutting off Polly, I mean?"

"As long as Sonia is alive. I bet you she won't forgive, and, as you know, he is entirely under her thumb."

"Yes. So what does Boy say to living with a wife, on £800 a year?"

"Doesn't like it. He talks of letting Silkin and going to live somewhere cheap, abroad. I told him he'll have to write more books. He doesn't do so badly with them, you know, but he is very low, poor old fellow, very."

"I expect it will do him good to get away," I said.

"Well, yes," said Davey expressively. "But . . ."

"I do wonder what Cedric Hampton is like."

"So do we all. Boy was talking about it just now. It seems they don't really know where he is, even. The father was a bad lot. He went to Nova Scotia, fell ill there and married his nurse, an elderly Canadian woman, who had this one child, but he (the father) is dead and nothing more is known except the bare fact that there is this boy. Montdore gives him some small allowance, paid into a Canadian bank every year. Don't you think it's very odd he hasn't taken more interest in him, considering he will have his name, and is the only hope of this ancient family being carried on?"

"Probably he hated the father."

"I don't believe he ever knew him. They are quite a different generation—second cousins, once removed—something like that. No, I put it down to Sonia. I expect she couldn't bear the idea of Hampton going away from Polly, and so pretended to herself that this Cedric did not really exist. You know what a one she is for shutting her eyes to things she doesn't like. I should imagine she'll be obliged to face up to him now, Montdore is sure to want to see him, under these new circumstances."

"Sad, isn't it, the idea of some great lumping colonial at Hampton!"

"Simply tragic!" said Davey. "Poor Montdores, I do feel for them."

Somehow, the material side of the business had never been fully born in upon me until Davey went into these facts and figures, but now I realized that "all this" was indeed something tremendous, to be so carelessly thrown into the lap of a total stranger.

When we arrived at Hampton, Aunt Sadie and I were shown straight into the chapel, where we sat alone. Davey went off to find Boy. The chapel was a Victorian building among the servants' quarters. It had been constructed by the "old lord," and contained his marble effigy, in Garter robes, with that of Alice, his wife. There was some bright stained glass, a family pew designed like a box at the opera, all red plush with curtains, and a very handsome organ. Davey had engaged a first-class organist from Oxford, who now regaled us with Bach preludes. None of the interested parties seemed to have bothered to take a hand in any of the arrangements, Davey had chosen all the music, and the gardener had evidently been left to himself with the flowers, which were quite overwhelming in their magnificence—the exaggerated hot-house flowers beloved of all gardeners and, it must be said, of Lady Montdore too, arranged with typical florist's taste. I began to feel dreadfully sad. The Bach and the flowers induced melancholy; besides, look at it as you would, this marriage was a depressing business.

Boy and Davey came up the aisle, and Boy shook hands with us. He had evidently got rid of his cold, at last, and was looking quite well; his hair, I noticed, had received the attention of a damp comb to induce little waves and a curl or two, and his figure, not bad at all, especially from behind, was set off by his wedding clothes. He wore a white carnation, and Davey a red one. But though he was in the costume of a bridegroom, he had not the spirit to add this new part to his repertory and his whole attitude was more appropriate to a chief mourner. Davey even had to show him where to stand, by the altar steps. I never saw a man look so hopeless.

The clergyman took up his position, a very disapproving expression on his face. Presently a movement at our left indicated that Lady Montdore had come into the family pew, which had its own entrance. It was impossible to stare, but I could not resist a glance and saw that she looked as if she were going to be sick. Boy also glanced, after which his back view became eloquent of a desire to slink in beside her and have a good, long gossip. It was the first time he had seen her since they had read the Infanta's letter together.

The organist from Oxford stopped playing Bach, which he had been doing with less and less interest during the last few minutes, and paused. Looking around, I saw that Lord Montdore was standing at the entrance to the chapel. He was impassive, well-preserved, a cardboard Earl, and might have been about to lead his daughter up the aisle of Westminster Abbey to marry the King of England for all that could be read into his look.

"Oh Perfect Love, all Human Thought Transcending" rang out, sung by an invisible choir in the gallery. And then, up the aisle, one large white hand on her father's arm, dispelling the gloomy embarrassment which hung like a fog in the chapel, came Polly, calm, confident and noble, radiating happiness. Somehow she had got herself a wedding dress (Did I recognize a ball dress of last season? No matter.) and was in a cloud of white tulle, and lilies of the valley, and joy. Most brides have difficulty with their expression as they go to the altar, looking affected, or soulful, or, worst of all, too eager, but Polly simply floated along on waves of bliss, creating one of the most beautiful moments I have ever experienced.

There was a dry, choking sound on our left, the door of the family pew was slammed, Lady Montdore had gone.

The clergyman began to intone the wedding service. "For-as-much," and so on, "Who giveth this woman to be married to this man?" Lord Montdore bowed, took Polly's bouquet from her and went into the nearest pew.

"Please say after me, 'I, Harvey, take thee, Leopoldina . . .'" A look from Aunt Sadie.

It was soon over. One more hymn, and I was left alone while they all went behind a screen to sign the register. Then the burst of Mendelssohn and Polly in her cloud of joy floated out again as she had come in, only on the arm of a different well-preserved old man.

While Polly and Boy changed into their going-away things, we waited in the Long Gallery to say good-bye and see them off. They were motoring to the Lord Warden at Dover for the night, and going abroad the following day. I half-expected that Polly would send for me to go upstairs and chat, but she did not, so I stayed with the others. I think she was so happy that she hardly noticed if people were with her or she was alone. Perhaps she really preferred the latter. Lady Montdore put in no further appearance. Lord Montdore talked to Davey, congratulating him upon an anthology he had recently published, called *In Sickness and in Health*. I heard him say that, to his mind, there was not quite enough Browning, but that apart from that it would all have been his own choice.

"But Browning was so healthy," objected Davey. The stress throughout the book was upon sickness.

A footman handed round glasses of champagne. Aunt Sadie and I settled down, as one always did, somehow, at Hampton, to a prolonged scrutiny of *Tatler, Sketch* and *Bystander,* and Polly took so long that I even got on to *Country Life* before she appeared. Aunt Sadie also loved these papers dearly, though it never would have occurred to her to buy them for herself.

Through my happy haze of Baronets' wives, their children, their dogs, their tweeds and their homes, or just their huge faces, wave of hair on the forehead held by a diamond clip, I was conscious that the atmosphere in the Long Gallery, like that in the chapel, was one of embarrassment and gloom.

When Boy reappeared, I saw him give a puzzled glance at the mutilated fire screen, and then, realizing what had happened to it, he turned his back on the room and stood gazing out of the window. Nobody spoke to him. Lord Montdore and Davey sipped champagne, having exhausted the topic of the anthology, in silence.

At last Polly came in, wearing her last year's mink coat and a tiny brown hat. Though the cloud of tulle had gone, the cloud of joy still enveloped her. She was perfectly unselfconscious, hugged her father, kissed us all, including Davey, took Boy by the arm and led him to the front door. We followed. The servants, looking sad, and the elder ones sniffing were gathered in the hall. She said good-bye to them, had some rice thrown over her, rather half-heartedly, by the youngest house-maid, got into the big Daimler, followed, very half-heartedly, by Boy, and was driven away.

We said good-bye politely to Lord Montdore and followed suit. As we went up the drive I looked back. The footmen had already shut the front door, and it seemed to me that beautiful Hampton, between the pale spring green of its lawns and the pale spring blue of the sky, lay deserted, empty and sad. Youth had gone from it and henceforward it was to be the home of two lonely old people.

About a mile from Alconleigh the children met us and crammed into the motor car.

"So come on, tell what it was?"

"What was what?"

"The Lecturer's real name, of course. We've come all this way to hear."

"Harvey."

"Like Hervey the Handsome," said Jassy, "who married the beautiful Molly Lepel."

"If you call a dog Hervey I shall love him," said Victoria.

"No," said Davey, "AR. I specially looked on the register."

"Yes, I see," said Jassy. "More like Boy Nichols?"

PART II

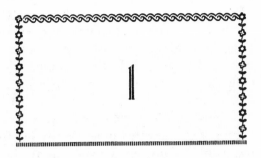

MY REAL life as a married woman, that is to say, life with my husband in our own house, now began. One day I went to Oxford and a miracle seemed to have taken place. There was paper on all the walls of my house, the very paper I had chosen, too, and looking even prettier than I had hoped it would, the smell of cheap cigarettes, cement, stewed tea and dry rot had gone, and in its place there was a heavenly smell of new paint and cleanliness, the floor boards were all smooth and solid, and the windows so clean that they seemed to be glassless. The day was perfect. Spring had come and my home was ready; I felt too happy for words. To set the seal upon this happiness, the wife of a Professor had called, her card and her husband's two cards had carefully been put by the workmen on a chimney piece: Professor and Mrs. Cozens, 209 Banbury Road. Now, at last I was a proper, grown-up married lady, on whom people called. It was very thrilling.

I had at this time a romantic but very definite picture in my mind of what life was going to be like in Oxford. I imagined a sort of Little Gidding, a community of delightful, busy, cultivated people, bound together by shared intellectual tastes and by their single-minded exertions on behalf of the youth entrusted to their care. I supposed that the other wives of dons would be beautiful, quiet women, versed in all the womanly arts but that of coqueterie, a little worn with the effort of making a perfection of their homes at the same time as rearing large families of clever little children, and keeping up with things like Kafka, but never too tired or too busy for long, serious discussions on subjects of importance, whether intellectual or practical. I saw myself, in the day-time, running happily in and out of the houses of these charming creatures, old houses, with some important piece of architecture framed in the windows, as Christ Church was in mine, passionately sharing every detail of their lives, while the evenings would be spent listening to grave and scholarly talk between our husbands. In short, I saw them as a tribe of heavenly new relations, more mature, more intellectual Radletts. This happy intimacy seemed to be heralded by the cards of Professor and Mrs. Cozens. For one moment the fact that they lived in the Banbury Road struck a note of disillusionment, but then it occurred to me that of course the clever Cozens must have found some little old house in that unpromising neighbourhood, some nobleman's folly, sole reminder of long vanished pleasure grounds, and decided to put up with the Banbury Road for the sake of its doorways and cornices, the rococo detail of its ceilings and the excellent proportions of its rooms.

I never shall forget that happy, happy day. The house at last was mine, the workmen had gone, the Cozens had come, the daffodils were out in the garden, and a blackbird was singing fit to burst its lungs. Alfred looked in and seemed to find my sudden rush of high spirits quite irrational. He had always known, he said, that the house would be ready sooner or later, and had not, like me, alternated between faith and black moods of scepticism. As for the Cozens, in spite of the fact that I realized by now that one human being, in Alfred's eyes, was exactly the same as another, I did find his indifference with regard to them and their cards rather damping.

"It's so terrible," I wailed, "because I can't return the call, our cards haven't come yet. Oh, yes, they are promised for next week, but I long to go now, this very minute, don't you see?"

"Next week will do quite well," Alfred said, shortly.

Soon an even more blissful day dawned. I woke up in my own bed in my own bedroom, done up in my own taste and arranged entirely to suit me. True, it was freezing cold and pouring with rain on this occasion, and, since I had as yet no servant, I was obliged to get up very early and cook Alfred's breakfast, but I did not mind. He was my own husband, and the cooking took place in my own kitchen. It all seemed like heaven to me.

And now, I thought, for the happy sisterhood on which I had pinned my hopes. But alas, as so often happens in life, this turned out rather differently from what I had expected. I found myself landed with two sisters indeed, but they were very far removed from the charming companions of my dream. One was Lady

Montdore and the other was Norma Cozens. At this time I was not only young, barely twenty, but extremely simple. Hitherto, my human relationships had been with members of my family or with other girls (school-fellows and debutantes) of my own age. They had been perfectly easy and straightforward and I had no idea that anything more complicated could exist. Even love, with me, had followed an exceptionally level path. I supposed, in my simplicity, that when people liked me I ought to like them back as much, and that whatever they expected of me, especially if they were older people, I was morally bound to perform. In the case of these two, I doubt if it ever occurred to me that they were eating up my time and energy in a perfectly shameless way. Before my children were born, I had time on my hands and I was lonely. Oxford is a place where social life, contrary to what I had imagined, is designed exclusively for celibate men; all the good talk, good food and good wine being reserved for those gatherings where there are no women; the whole tradition is in its essence monastic, and, as far as society goes, wives are quite superfluous.

I should never have chosen Norma Cozens to be an intimate friend, but I suppose that her company must have seemed preferable to hours of my own, while Lady Montdore did at least bring a breath of air which, though it could not have been described as fresh, had its origins in the great world outside our cloister, a world where women count for something.

Mrs. Cozen's horizon also extended beyond Oxford, though in another direction. Her maiden name was Boreley, and the Boreley family was well known to me, since her grandfather's huge 1890 Elizabethan house was situated not far from Alconleigh, and they were the new rich of the neighbourhood. This grandfather, now Lord Driersley, had made his money in foreign railroads. He had married into the landed gentry and produced a huge family, all the members of which, as they grew up and married, he settled on estates within easy motoring distance of Driersley Manor. They, in their turns, all became notable breeders, so that the Boreley tentacles had spread by now over a great part of the West of England and there seemed to be absolutely no end of Boreley cousins, aunts, uncles, brothers and sisters and their respective in-laws. There was very little variety about them; they all had the same cross, white guinea-pig look, thought alike, and led the same sort of lives, sporting country lives, they seldom went to London. They were respected by their neighbours for the conformity, to the fashion of the day, of their morals, for their wealth and for their excellence at all kinds of sport. They did everything that they ought to do in the way of sitting on Benches and County Councils, walking hound puppies and running Girl Guides, one was an M.P., another an M.F.H. In short, they were the backbone of England. Uncle Matthew, who encountered them on local business, loathed them all, and they were collectively in many drawers under the one name, Boreley, I never quite knew why. However, like Gandhi, Bernard Shaw and Labby the Labrador, they continued to flourish, and no terrible Boreley holocaust ever took place.

My first experience of Oxford society, as the wife of a junior don, was a dinner party given in my honour by the Cozens. The Waynflete Professor of Pastoral Theol-

ogy was the professor of Alfred's subject, and was, therefore, of importance in our lives and an influence upon
Alfred's career. I understood this to be so without Alfred exactly putting it into words. In any case, I was, of
course, anxious that my first Oxford appearance should
be a success, anxious to look nice, make a good impression, and be a credit to my husband. My mother had
given me an evening dress from Mainbocher which
seemed specially designed for such an occasion. It had
a white pleated chiffon skirt, and black silk jersey top
with a high neck and long sleeves, which was tucked
into a wide, black, patent-leather belt. Wearing this,
and my only jewel, a diamond clip sent by my father, I
thought I was not only nicely, but also suitably dressed.
My father, incidentally, had turned a deaf ear to Lady
Montdore's suggestion that he should buy me a place,
declaring himself to be too utterly ruined even to in-
crease my allowance on my marriage. He did, however,
send a cheque and this pretty jewel.

The Cozens' house was not a nobleman's folly. It
was the very worst kind of Banbury Road house, depressing, with laurels. The front door was opened by a slut.
I had never seen a slut before but recognized the genus
without difficulty as soon as I set eyes on this one. Inside
the hall, Alfred and I and the slut got rather mixed up
with a large pram, however we sorted ourselves out and
put down our coats, and then she opened a door and
shot us, without announcing our names, into the terrible Cozens' drawing room. All this to the accompaniment of shrill barking from four Border Terriers.

I saw at once that my dress would not do. Norma told
me afterwards, when pointing out the many fearful
gaffes which I was supposed to have made during the

course of the evening, that as a bride I would have been expected to wear my wedding dress at our first dinner party. But, even apart from that blunder, a jersey top, however Parisian, was obviously unacceptable for evening wear in high Oxford society. The other women present were either in lace or marocain, décolleté to the waist, behind, and with bare arms. Their dresses were in shades of biscuit, and so were they. It was a cold evening following upon a chilly day, the Cozens' hearth was not laid for a fire, but had a piece of pleated paper in the grate, and yet these naked ladies did not seem to be cold. They were not blue and goosey as I should have been, nor did they shiver. I was soon to learn that in donnish circles the Oxford summer is considered to be horribly hot, and the Oxford winter nice and bracing, but that no account is taken of the between seasons or of the findings of the thermometer; cold is never felt. Apart from there being no fire, the room was terribly cheerless. The hard little sofa, the few and hard little armchairs were upholstered in a cretonne of so dim and dismal a pattern that it was hard to imagine anybody, even a Boreley, actually choosing it, to imagine them going into a shop, and taking a seat, and having cretonnes thrown over a screen one after another, and suddenly saying, all excited, "That's the very thing for me —stop!" The lights were unshaded and held in chromium-plated fittings. There was no carpet on the floor, just a few slippery rugs; the walls were of shiny cream paint, and there were no pictures, objects or flowers to relieve the bareness.

Mrs. Cozens, whose cross, creased Boreley face I recognized from my hunting days, greeted us heartily enough, and the Professor came forward with a shadow of Lord

Montdore's manner, an unctuous geniality which may have orginated with the Church, though his version of it was as that of a curate to Lord Montdore's cardinal. There were three other couples to whom I was introduced, all dons and their wives. I was perfectly fascinated to see these people among whom I was henceforward to live. They were ugly and not specially friendly, but no doubt, I supposed, very brilliant.

The food at dinner, served by the slut in a gaunt dining room, was so terrible that I felt deeply sorry for Mrs. Cozens, thinking that something must have gone wrong. I have had so many such meals since then that I do not remember exactly what it was, I guess, however, that it began with tinned soup and ended with dry sardines on dry toast, and that we drank a few drops of white wine. I do remember that the conversation was far from brilliant, a fact which, at the time, I attributed to the horrible stuff we were trying to swallow, but which I now know was more likely to have been due to the presence of females; dons are quite used to bad food but become paralized in mixed company. As soon as the last sardine tail had been got down, Mrs. Cozens rose to her feet, and we went into the drawing room, leaving the men to enjoy the one good item of the whole menu, excellent vintage port. They only re-appeared just before it was time to go home.

Over the coffee, sitting round the pleated paper in the fireplace, the other women talked of Lady Montdore and Polly's amazing marriage. It seemed that, while their husbands all knew Lord Montdore slightly, none of them knew Lady Montdore, not even Norma Cozens, though, as a member of an important county family, she had been inside Hampton once or twice to various big functions. They all spoke, however, not only as if they knew her quite well, but as if she had done each of them personally some terrible wrong. Lady Montdore was not popular in the county, and the reason was that she turned up her nose at the local squires and their wives as well as at the local tradesmen and their wares, ruthlessly importing both her guests and her groceries from London.

It is always interesting, and usually irritating, to hear what people have to say about somebody whom they do not know but we do. On this occasion I positively squirmed with interest and irritation. Nobody asked for my opinion, so I sat in silence, listening. The dominant thought of the discussion was that Lady Montdore, wicked as hell, had been envious of Polly, her youth and her beauty, ever since she grew up, had snubbed her and squashed her and kept her out of sight as much as possible, and that, furthermore, as soon as Polly got an admirer, Lady Montdore had somehow managed to send him about his business, finally driving her into the arms of her uncle as the only escape from an un-happy home.

"Now I happen to know for a fact that Polly," (they all called her Polly, though none of them knew her) "was on the point of getting engaged to Joyce Fleet-wood, only just the other day too, he stayed at Hampton for Christmas and it was all going like a house on fire. His own sister told me. Well, Lady Montdore got rid of him in double quick time, you see."

"Yes, and wasn't it just the same with John Con-ingsby? Polly was madly in love with him, and no doubt he'd have come up to scratch in the end, but when Lady Montdore twigged what was going on she had him out on his ear."

"And in India too it happened several times. Polly only had to fancy a young man for him to vanish mysteriously." They spoke as if Lady Montdore were an enchantress in a fairy tale.

"She was jealous, you know, of her being supposed to be such a beauty (never could see it myself, don't admire that flat fish look)."

"You'd think she'd want to get her off all the quicker."

"You can't tell how jealousy is going to take people."

"But I've always heard that Dougdale was Lady Montdore's own lover."

"Of course he was, and that's exactly why she never imagined there could be anything between him and Polly. Serves her jolly well right, she ought to have let the poor girl marry all those others when she wanted to."

"What a sly little thing though, under the very noses of her mother and her aunt like that."

"I don't expect there's much to choose between them. The one I'm sorry for is poor old Lord Montdore, he's such a wonderful old man and she's led him the most awful dance, you know, for years, ever since they married. Daddy says she utterly ruined his career, and if it hadn't been for her he could have been Prime Minister or anything."

"Well, but he was Viceroy," I said, putting in my oar at last. I felt thoroughly on Lady Montdore's side against these hideous people.

"Yes, he was, and everybody knows she nearly lost us India. I believe the harm she did there was something terrible. Daddy has a great friend, an Indian judge, you should hear his stories! Her rudeness . . . !"

"Of course lots of people say Polly isn't Lord Montdore's child at all. King Edward, I've heard."

"It doesn't seem to make much difference now, whose child she is, because he's cut her out of his will and some American gets it all."

"And the whole thing is that old woman's fault, the old tart. That's all she is when you come to think of it. Needn't give herself such airs. . . ."

I suddenly became very furious. I was well aware of Lady Montdore's faults, I knew that she was deplorable in many ways, but it seemed to me wrong of people who had never even met her and knew nothing at first hand, to speak of her like this. I had a feeling that they did so out of an obscure jealousy, and that she only had to take any of these women up and bestow a flicker of her charm upon them for them to become her grovelling toadies.

"I hear she made a ghastly scene at the wedding," said the don's wife whose Daddy knew an Indian judge. "Screamed and yelled and had hysterics."

"She didn't," I said.

"Why, how do you know?"

"Because I was there."

They looked at me curiously and rather angrily, as though I ought to have spoken up sooner, and changed the subject to the eternal ones of children's illnesses and servants' misdeeds.

I hoped that at my next dinner party I should be meeting the noble, thoughtful, intellectual women of my Oxford dream, if, indeed, they existed.

After this Norma Cozens took a fancy to me for some reason, and used to drop into my house on her way to or from the huge walks she went for every day with the Border Terriers. I think she was the crossest person I ever met, nothing was ever right for her, and her conversation, which consisted of lectures, advice and criticism, was punctuated with furious sighs, but she was not a bad old thing, good-natured at heart, and often did me little kindnesses. I came to like her in the end the best of all the dons' wives. She was at least natural and unpretentious and brought her children up in an ordinary way. Those I found impossible to get on with were the arty-crafty ones with modern ideas, and ghastly children who had never been thwarted or cleaned up by the hand of a nanny. Norma was a type with which I was more familiar, one of those women in brown with whom the English countryside teems, who possess no talents, and especially not those it is nice for a woman to have, such as for housekeeping and dress, and no sense of humour, but who, nevertheless, are not exactly stupid and not at all nasty. Anyhow, there she was, self-constituted part of my new life, and accepted by me as such without question.

2

A MORE difficult and exacting relationship was the one which now developed between me and Lady Montdore. She haunted my house, coming at much odder and more inconvenient times than Norma (who was very conventional in such ways), and proceeded to turn me into a lady in waiting. It was quite easy. Nobody has ever sapped my will power as she did, and, like Lord Montdore, but unlike Polly, I was completely under her thumb. Even Alfred lifted his eyes for a moment from pastoral theology and saw what was going on. He said he could not understand my attitude, and that it made him impatient.

"You don't really like her, you're always complaining about her, why not say you are out when she comes?"

Why not, indeed? The fact was that I had never got over the physical feeling of terror which Lady Montdore had inspired in me from childhood, and though with my reason I knew now what she was, and did not care for what I knew, though the idol was down from its pedestal, the bullfighter back in his ready-made suit, and she was revealed as nothing more or less than a selfish old woman, still I remained in awe of her. When Alfred told me to pretend to be out when she came I knew that this would be impossible for me.

"Oh no, darling, I don't think I could do that."

He shrugged his shoulders and said no more. He never tried to influence me, and very rarely commented on, or even appeared to notice, my behaviour and the conduct of my life.

Lady Montdore's plan was to descend upon me without warning, either on her way to or from London, or on shopping expeditions to Oxford, when she would take me round with her to fetch and carry and check her list. She would engage all my attention for an hour or two, tiring me out, exactly as small children can, with the demands she made of concentration upon her, and then vanish again, leaving me dissatisfied with life. As she was down on her own luck, but would have considered it a weakness to admit it, even to herself, she was obliged to bolster up "all this," to make it seem a perfect compensation for what she had lost, by denigrating the circumstances of other people. It was even a help to her, I suppose, because otherwise I cannot account for her beastliness, to run down my poor little house, so unpretentious, and my dull little life, and she did so with such conviction that, since I am easily discouraged, it often took days before everything seemed all right again.

Days, or a visit from some member of the Radlett family. The Radletts had the exactly opposite effect, and always made me feel wonderful, owing to a habit known in the family as "exclaiming."

"Fanny's shoes . . . ! Where? Lilley and Skinner? I must dash. And the lovely new skirt! Not a new suit, let's see—not lined with silk—Fanny! You are lucky, it is unfair!"

"Oh, dear, why doesn't my hair curl like that? Oh, the bliss of Fanny altogether—her eyelashes! You are lucky, it is unfair!"

These exclamations, which I remember from my very earliest childhood, now also embraced my house and household arrangements.

"The wallpaper! Fanny! Your bed—it can't be true! Oh, look at the darling little bit of Belleek—where did you find it? No! Do let's go there. And a new cushion! Oh, it is unfair, you are lucky to be you."

"I say, Fanny's food! Toast at every meal! Not Yorkshire pudding! Why can't we live with Fanny always—the heaven of it here! Why can't I be you?"

Fortunately for my peace of mind Jassy and Victoria came to see me whenever there was a motor car going to Oxford, which was quite often, and the elder ones always looked in if they were on their way to Alconleigh.

As I got to know Lady Montdore more intimately, I began to realize that her selfishness was monumental. She had no thoughts except in relation to herself, could discuss no subject without cleverly edging it round to something directly pertaining to her. The only thing she ever wanted to know about people was what impression did she make on them, and she would do anything to find this out, sometimes digging traps for the unwary, into which, in my innocence, I was very apt to tumble.

"I suppose your husband is a clever man, at least so Montdore tells me. Of course it's a thousand pities he is so dreadfully poor, I hate to see you living in this horrid little hovel—so unsuitable—and not more important, but Montdore says he has the reputation of being clever."

She had dropped in just as I was having my tea, which consisted of a few rather broken digestive biscuits with a kitchen pot on a tray and without a plate. I was so busy that afternoon, and Mrs. Heathery, my maid of all work, was so busy too, that I had dashed into the kitchen and taken the tray myself, like that. Unfortunately, it never seemed to be chocolate cake and silver tea-pot day when Lady Montdore came, though, such were the vagaries of my housekeeping while I was a raw beginner, that these days did quite often, though quite unaccountably, occur.

"Is that your tea? All right dear, yes, just a cup, please. How weak you have it! No, no, this will do quite well. Yes, as I was saying, Montdore spoke of your husband to-day at luncheon, with the Bishop. They had read something of his and seem to have been quite impressed, so I suppose he really is clever, after all."

"Oh, he is the cleverest man I ever met," I said, happily. I loved to talk about Alfred, it was the next best thing to being with him.

"So of course I suppose he thinks I'm a very stupid person." She looked with distaste at the bits of digestives, and then took one.

"Oh, no, he doesn't," I said, inventing, because Alfred had never put forward any opinion on the subject one way or another.

"I'm sure he must, really. You don't mean to tell me he thinks I'm clever?"

"Yes, very clever. He p'raps doesn't look upon you as an intellectual. . . ."

Crash! I was in the trap.

"Oh, indeed! Not an intellectual!"

I could see at once that she was terribly offended and thrashed about unhappily in my trap trying to extricate myself, to no avail, however. I was in it up to the neck.

"You see, he doesn't believe that women ever are intellectuals, hardly, hardly ever, perhaps one in ten million. . . . Virginia Woolf, perhaps . . ."

"I suppose he thinks I never read. Many people think that, because they see me leading this active life, wearing myself out for others. Perhaps I might prefer to sit in a chair all day and read some book, very likely I would, but I shouldn't think it right, in my position, to do so. I can't only be thinking of myself, you see. I never do read books in the daytime, that's perfectly true, I simply haven't a moment, but your husband doesn't know, and nor do you, what I do at night. I don't sleep well, not well at all, and at night I read volumes."

Old volumes of the *Tatler*, I guessed. She had them all bound up from the beginning, and very fascinating they were.

"You know, Fanny," she went on, "it's all very well for funny little people like you to read books the whole time. You only have yourselves to consider, whereas Montdore and I are public servants, in a way, we have something to live up to, tradition and so on, duties to perform, you know. It's a very different matter. A great deal is expected of us, I think and hope not in vain. It's a hard life, make no mistake about that; hard and tiring, but occasionally we have our reward—when people get a chance to show how they worship us. For instance, when we came back from India and the dear villagers pulled our motor car up the drive. Really touching! Now all you intellectual people never have moments like that. Well," she rose to leave, "one lives and learns. I know now that I am outside the pale, intellectually. Of course, my dear child, we must remember that all those women students probably give your husband a very funny notion of what the female sex is really like. I wonder whether he realizes that it's only the ones who can't hope for anything better that come here. Perhaps he finds them very fascinating—one never sees him in his own home, I notice." She was working herself up into a tremendous temper now. "And if I might offer you a little advice, Fanny, it would be to read fewer books, dear, and make your house slightly more comfortable. That is what a man appreciates, in the long run."

She cast a meaning look at the plateless digestives, and went away without saying good-bye.

I was really upset to have annoyed her so stupidly and tactlessly, and felt certain that she would never come and see me again; funnily enough, instead of being relieved by this thought, I minded.

I had no time to brood over it however, for hardly was she out of the house than Jassy and Victoria bundled in.

"Not digestives! Vict—look, digestives! Isn't Fanny wonderful? You can always count on something heavenly—weeks since I tasted digestives, my favourite food too."

Mrs. Heathery, who adored the children and had heard their shrieks as they came in, brought up some fresh tea and a Fuller's cake, which elicited more exclamations.

"Oh, Mrs. Heathery, you angel on earth, not Fuller's walnut? How can you afford it, Fanny? We haven't had it at home since Fa's last financial crisis. But things are better, you know. We are back to Bromo again now and the good writing paper. When the loo paper gets thicker and the writing paper thinner it's always a bad sign, at home."

"Fa had to come about some harness, so he brought us in to see you, only ten minutes, though. The thing is, we've got a funny story about Sadie for you, so are you listening? Well, Sadie was telling how some people, before their babies are born, gaze at Greuze so that the babies shall look like it, and she said, 'You never know about these things, because when I was a little girl in Suffolk a baby was born in the village with a bear's head. And what do you think? Exactly nine months before a dancing bear had been in that neighbourhood.' So Vict said, 'But I can quite understand that. I always think bears are simply terribly attractive,' and Sadie gave the most tremendous jump I ever saw and said, 'You awful child, that's not what I mean at all.' So are you shrieking, Fanny?"

"We saw your new friend Mrs. Cozens just now and her blissful Borders. You are so lucky to have new friends. It is unfair—we never do. Really, you know, we are the Lady of Shalott with our pathetic lives we lead. Even Davey never comes, now horrible Polly's marriage is over. Oh, by the way, we had a postcard from horrible Polly, but it's no use her bombarding us with these postcards—we can never, never forgive."

"Where was it from?"

"Seville. That's in Spain."

"Did she sound happy?"

"Do people ever sound unhappy on postcards, Fanny? Isn't it always lovely weather and everything wonderful, on postcards? This one was a picture of a glorious girl called La Macarena, and the funny thing is this La Macarena is the literal image of horrible Polly herself. Do you think Lady Montdore gazed a bit before H. P. was born?"

"You mustn't say horrible Polly to me when I love her so much."

"Well, we'll have to see. We love her in a way, in spite of all, and in a few years, possibly, we might forgive, though I doubt if we can ever forget her deep, base treachery. Has she written to you?"

"Only postcards," I said. "One from Paris and one from St. Jean de Luz."

Polly had never been much of a letter writer.

"I wonder if it's as nice as she thought, being in bed with that old Lecturer."

"Marriage isn't only bed," I said, primly. "There are other things."

"You go and tell that to Sadie. There's Fa's horn, we must dash or he'll never bring us again if we keep him waiting, and we promised we would the very second he blew. Oh, dear, back to the fields of barley and of rye. You are so lucky to live in this sweet little house in a glamorous town. Good-bye Mrs. Heathery—the cake!"

They were still cramming it into their mouths as they went downstairs.

"Come in and have some tea," I said to Uncle Matthew, who was at the wheel of his new big Wolseley. When my uncle had a financial crisis he always bought a new motor car.

"No, thank you, Fanny. Very kind of you, but there's

a perfectly good cup of tea waiting for me at home, and you know I never go inside other people's houses if I can possibly avoid it. Good-bye."

He put on his green hat, called a bramble, which he always wore, and drove away.

My next caller was Norma Cozens, who came in for a glass of sherry, but her conversation was so dull that I have not the heart to record it. It was a compound of an abscess between the toes of the mother Border Terrier, the things the laundry does to sheets, how it looked to her as if the slut had been at her store cupboard, so she was planning to replace her by an Austrian at 2/– a week cheaper wages, and how lucky I was to have Mrs. Heathery, but I must look out because new brooms sweep clean and Mrs. Heathery was sure not to be nearly as nice as she seemed.

I was very much mistaken if I thought that Lady Montdore was now out of my life for good. In less than a week she was back again. The door of my house was always kept on the latch, like a country-house door, and she never bothered to ring but just stumped upstairs. On this occasion it was five minutes to one and I plainly saw that I would have to share the little bit of salmon I had ordered for myself, as a treat, with her.

"And where is your husband to-day?"

She showed her disapproval of my marriage by always referring to Alfred like this and never by his name. He was still Mr. Thing in her eyes.

"Lunching in college."

"Ah, yes? Just as well, so he won't be obliged to endure my unintellectual conversation."

I was afraid it would all start over again, including

the working herself up into a temper, but apparently she had decided to treat my unlucky remark as a great joke.

"I told Merlin," she said, "that in Oxford circles I am not thought an intellectual, and I only wish you could have seen his face!"

When Mrs. Heathery offered the fish to Lady Montdore she scooped up the whole thing. No tiresome inhibitions caused her to ask what I would eat, and, in fact, I had some potatoes and salad. She was good enough to say that the quality of the food in my house seemed to be improving.

"Oh, yes, I know what I wanted to ask you," she said. "Who is this Virginia Woolf you mentioned to me? Merlin was talking about her, too, the other day at Maggie Greville's."

"She's a writer," I said. "A novelist, really."

"Yes, I see. And as she's so intellectual, no doubt she writes about nothing but stationmasters."

"Well, no," I said, "she doesn't."

"I must confess that I prefer books about society people, not being myself a highbrow."

"She did write a fascinating book about a society person," I said, "called *Mrs. Dalloway*."

"Perhaps I'll read it, then. Oh, of course I'd forgotten—I never read, according to you—don't know how. Never mind. In case I have a little time this week, Fanny, you might lend it to me, will you? Excellent cheese—don't tell me you get this in Oxford?"

She was in an unusually good temper that day. I believe the fall of the Spanish throne had cheered her up. She probably foresaw a perfect swarm of Infantas winging its way towards Montdore House, besides, she was greatly enjoying all the details from Madrid. She said that the Duke of Barbarossa (this may not be the name, but it sounded like it) had told her the inside story, in which case he must also have told it to the *Daily Express,* where I had read word for word what she now kindly passed on to me, and several days before. She remembered to ask for *Mrs. Dalloway* before leaving, and went off with the book in her hand, a first edition. I felt sure that I had seen the last of it, but she brought it back the following week, saying that she really must write a book herself, as she knew she could do much better than that.

"Couldn't read it," she said. "I did try, but it is too boring. And I never got to that society person you told me of. Now, have you read the Grand Duchess' *Memoirs?* I won't lend you mine, you must buy them for yourself, Fanny, and that will help the dear Duchess with another guinea. They are wonderful. There is a great deal, nearly a whole chapter, about Montdore and me in India—she stayed with us at Viceroy's House, you know. She has really captured the spirit of the place quite amazingly. She was only there a week, but one couldn't have done it better oneself. She describes a garden party I gave, and visits to the Ranees in their harems, and she tells what a lot I was able to do for those poor women of India, and how they worshipped me. Personally, I find memoirs so very much more interesting than any novel because they are true. I may not be an intellectual, but I do like to read the truth about things. Now in a book like the Grand Duchess' you can see history in the very making, and if you love history as I do (but don't tell your husband I said so, dear, he would never believe it), if you love history, you must be interested to know the inside story, and it's only people like the Grand Duchess who are in a position to tell us that. And this reminds me, Fanny dear, will you put a call through to Downing Street for me, please, and get hold of the P.M. or his secretary? I will speak myself when he is on the line. I'm arranging a little dinner for the Grand Duchess, to give her book a good start. Of course I don't ask you, dear—it wouldn't be intellectual enough—just a few politicians and writers, I thought. Here is the number, Fanny."

I was trying at this time to economize in every direction, having overspent myself on doing up the house, and I had made a rule never to telephone, even to Aunt Emily's house or Alconleigh, if a letter would do as well, so it was most unwillingly that I did as she asked. There was a long wait on the line before I got the Prime Minister himself, after which Lady Montdore spoke for ages, the pip-pip-pips going at least five times —I could hear them—every pip an agony to me. First of all, she fixed a date for her dinner party; this took a long time, with many pauses while he consulted his secretary, and two pip-pip-pips. Then she asked if there were anything new from Madrid.

"Yes," she said. "Badly advised, poor man (pip-pip-pip), I fear. I saw Freddy Barbarossa last night (they are being so brave about it, by the way, quite stoical. Yes, at Claridge's), and he told me . . ." Here a flood of *Daily Express* news and views. "But Montdore and I are very much worried about our own special Infanta—yes, a close friend of ours—oh, Prime Minister, if you could hear anything I should be so more than grateful. Will you, really? You know, there is a whole chapter on Madrid in the Grand Duchess' book. It makes it very topical, rather splendid for her. Yes, a near relation. She describes the view (pip-pip-pip) from the Royal Palace —yes, very bleak—I've been there, wonderful sunsets, though. I know, poor woman. Oh, she hated them at first, she had special opera glasses with black spots for the cruel moments. Have you heard where they are going? Yes, Barbara Barbarossa told me that too, but I wonder they don't come here. You ought to try and persuade them. Yes, I see. Well, we'll talk about all that. Meanwhile, dear Prime Minister, I won't keep you any longer (pip-pip-pip), but we'll see you on the tenth. So do I. I'll send your secretary a reminder, of course. Good-bye."

She turned to me, beaming, and said, "I have the most wonderful effect on that man, you know. It's quite touching how he dotes on me. I really think I could do anything with him, anything at all."

She never spoke of Polly. At first I supposed that the reason why she liked to see so much of me was that I was associated in her mind with Polly, and that sooner or later she would unburden herself to me, or even try and use me as go-between in a reconciliation. I soon realized, however, that Polly and Boy were dead to her. She had no further use for them, since Boy could never be her lover again, and Polly could never now, it seemed, do her credit in the eyes of the world. She simply dismissed them from her thoughts. Her visits to me were partly the outcome of loneliness and partly due to the fact that I was a convenient halfway house between London and Hampton, and that she could use me as restaurant, cloakroom and telephone booth when in Oxford.

She was horribly lonely, you could see that. She filled

Hampton every week end with important people, with smart people, even just with people, but, although so great is the English predilection for country life, she generally managed to get these visits extended from Friday to Tuesday, even so she was left with two empty days in the middle of the week. She went less and less to London. She had always preferred Hampton, where she reigned alone, to London where she faced a certain degree of competition, and life there without Polly to entertain for and without Boy to help her plot the social game, had evidently become meaningless and dull.

3

IT WAS no doubt the dullness of her life which now deflected her thoughts towards Cedric Hampton, Lord Montdore's heir. They still knew nothing about him beyond the mere fact of his existence, which had hitherto been regarded as extremely superfluous since but for him the whole of "all this," including Hampton, would have gone to Polly, and, although the other things she had been going to inherit were worth more money, it was Hampton they all loved so much. I have never made out his exact relationship to Lord Montdore, but I know that when Linda and I used to "look him up" to see if he was the right age for us to marry, it always took ages to find him, breathing heavily over the peerage, pointing, and going back and back.

. . . having had issue,
♦ Henry, b. 1875, who m. Dora, dau. of Stanley Booter Esq. of Annapolis, Nova

Scotia, and d. 1913 leaving issue,
♦ Cedric, heir pres., b. 1907.

Just the right age, but what of Nova Scotia? An atlas, hastily consulted, showed it to be horribly marine. "A transatlantic Isle of Wight," as Linda put it. "No, thanks." Sea breezes, in so far as they are good for the complexion, were regarded by us as a means and not an end, for at that time it was our idea to live in capital cities and go to the opera alight with diamonds—"Who is that lovely woman?"—and Nova Scotia was clearly not a suitable venue for such doings. It never seemed to occur to us that Cedric could perhaps have been transplanted from his native heath to Paris, London or Rome. Colonial, we thought, ignorantly. It ruled him out. I believe Lady Montdore knew very little more about him than we did. She had never felt interest or curiosity towards those unsuitable people in Canada. They were one of the unpleasant things of life and she preferred to ignore them. Now, however, left alone with an "all this" which would one day, and one day fairly soon, by the look of Lord Montdore, be Cedric's, she thought and spoke of him continually, and presently had the idea that it would amuse her to see him.

Of course no sooner had she conceived this idea than she wanted him to be there the very next minute, and was infuriated by the delays that ensued. For Cedric could not be found.

I was kept informed of every stage in the search for him, as Lady Montdore could now think of nothing else.

"That idiotic woman has changed her address," she told me. "Montdore's lawyer has had the most terrible time getting in touch with her at all. Now, fancy moving in Canada. You'd think one place there would be exactly the same as another, wouldn't you? Sheer waste of money, you'd think. Well, they've found her at last, and now it seems that Cedric isn't with her at all, but somewhere in Europe. Very odd of him not to have called on us, in that case. So now, of course, there'll be more delays. Oh, dear, people are too inconsiderate! It's nothing but self, self, self, nowadays, nothing . . . !"

In the end, Cedric was traced to Paris ("Simply extraordinary," she said. "Whatever could a Canadian be doing in Paris? I don't quite like it."), and an invitation to Hampton was given and accepted.

"He comes next Tuesday, for a fortnight. I wrote out the dates very carefully indeed. I always do when it is a question of a country-house visit, then there is no awkwardness about the length of it. People know exactly when they are expected to leave. If we like him he can come again, now we know that he lives in Paris, such an easy journey. But what do you suppose he is doing there, dear? I hope he's not an artist. Well, if he is, we shall simply have to get him out of it—he must learn to behave suitably, now. We are sending to Dover for him, so that he'll arrive just in time for dinner. Montdore and I have decided not to dress that evening, as most likely he has no evening clothes, and one doesn't wish to make him feel shy at the very beginning of his visit, poor boy."

This seemed most unlike Lady Montdore, who usually loved making people feel shy, it was well known to be one of her favourite diversions. No doubt Cedric was to be her new toy, and until such time as, inevitably, I felt, just as Norma felt about Mrs. Heathery, disillusionment set in, nothing was to be too good for him, and no line of conduct too much calculated to charm him.

I began to think a great deal about Cedric. It was such an interesting situation and I longed to know how he would take it, this young man from the West suddenly confronted with aristocratic England in full decadence, the cardboard Earl, with his empty nobility of look and manner, the huge luxurious houses, the terrifying servants, the atmosphere of bottomless wealth. I remembered how exaggerated it had all seemed to me as a child, and supposed that he would see it with very much the same eyes and find it equally overpowering.

I thought, however, that he might feel at home with Lady Montdore, especially as she desired to please, there was something spontaneous and almost childlike about her which could accord with a transatlantic outlook. It was the only hope, otherwise, if he were at all timid, I thought he would find himself submerged. Words dimly associated with Canada kept on occurring to me, the word lumber, the word shack, staking a claim. (Uncle Matthew had once staked a claim, I knew, in Ontario, in his wild young poker-playing days, with Harry Oakes.) How I wished I could be present at Hampton when this lumberjack arrived to stake his claim to that shack. Hardly had I formed the wish than it was granted, Lady Montdore ringing up to ask if I would go over for the night. She thought it would make things easier to have another young person there when Cedric arrived.

This was a wonderful reward, as I duly remarked to Alfred, for having been a lady-in-waiting.

Alfred said, "If you have been putting yourself out

all this time with a reward in view, I don't mind at all. I objected because I thought you were drifting along in the wake of that old woman merely from a lazy good-nature, and with no particular motive. That is what I found degrading. Of course, if you were working for a wage it is quite a different matter, so long, of course," he said, with a disapproving look, "as the wage seems to you worth while."

It did.

The Montdores sent a motor car to Oxford for me. When I arrived at Hampton I was taken straight upstairs to my room, where I had a bath and changed, according to instructions brought me by Lady Montdore's maid, into a day dress. I had not spent a night at Hampton since my marriage. Knowing that Alfred would not want to go, I had always refused Lady Montdore's invitations, but my bedroom there was still deeply familiar to me. I knew every inch of it by heart. Nothing in it ever changed, the very books, between their mahogany book-ends, were the same collection that I had known and read there now for twelve years, or more than half my life: novels by Robert Hitchens and W. J. Locke, Napoleon, *The Last Phase* by Lord Rosebery, *The House of Mirth* by Edith Wharton, Hare's *Two Noble Lives, Dracula,* and a book on dog management. In front of them on a mahogany tall-boy was a Japanese bronze tea-kettle with embossed water lilies. On the walls, besides the two country-house old masters, despised of Davey, were a Morland print "The Higglers Preparing for Market," a Richmond water colour of the "old lord" in a kilt, and an oil painting of Toledo either by Boy or Lady Montdore, whose styles were indistinguishable. It was in their early manner, and had probably hung there for twenty years. This room had a womb-like quality in my mind, partly because it was so red and warm and velvety and enclosed, and partly because of the terror with which I always used to be assailed by the idea of leaving it and venturing downstairs. This evening as I dressed I thought how lovely it was to be grown-up, a married woman, and no longer frightened of people. Of Lord Merlin a little, of the Warden of Wadham perhaps, but these were not panicky, indiscriminate social terrors. They could rather be classed as wholesome, awe inspired by gifted elders.

When I was ready I went down to the Long Gallery, where Lord and Lady Montdore were sitting in their usual chairs one on each side of the chimney piece, but not at all in their usual frame of mind. They were both, and especially Lady Montdore, in a twitter of nerves, and looked up quite startled when I came into the room, relaxing again when they saw that it was only me. I thought that from the point of view of a stranger, a backwoodsman from the American continent, they struck exactly the right note. Lord Montdore, in an informal green-velvet smoking jacket, was impressive with his white hair and carved unchanging face, while Lady Montdore's very dowdiness was an indication that she was too grand to bother about clothes, and this too would surely impress. She wore printed black-and-white crepe-de-chine, her only jewels the enormous half-hoop rings which flashed from her strong old woman's fingers, and sat, as she always did, her knees well apart, her feet in their large buckled shoes firmly planted on the ground, her hands folded in her lap.

"We lit this little fire," she said, "thinking that he

may feel cold after the journey." It was unusual for her to refer to any arrangement in her house, people being expected to like what they found there, or else to lump it. "Do you think we shall hear the motor when it comes up the drive? We generally can if the wind is in the west."

"I expect I shall," I said, tactlessly. "I hear everything."

"Oh, we're not stone deaf ourselves. Show Fanny what you have got for Cedric, Montdore."

He held out a little book in green morocco, Gray's *Poems*.

"If you look at the fly leaf," he said, "you will see that it was given to my grandfather by the late Lord Palmerston the day that Cedric's grandfather was born. They evidently happened to be dining together. We think that it should please him."

I did so hope it would. I suddenly felt very sorry for these two old people, and longed for Cedric's visit to be a success and cheer them up.

"Canadians," he went on, "should know all about the poet Gray, because General Woolf, at the taking of Quebec . . ."

There were footsteps now in the red drawing room, so we had not heard the motor, after all. Lord and Lady Montdore got up and stood together in front of the fireplace as the butler opened the door and announced, "Mr. Cedric Hampton."

There was a glitter of blue and gold across the parquet, and a human dragon-fly was kneeling on the fur rug in front of the Montdores, one long white hand extended towards each. He was a tall, thin young man, supple as a girl, dressed in rather a bright blue suit;

his hair was the gold of a brass bed knob, and his insect appearance came from the fact that the upper part of the face was concealed by blue goggles set in gold rims quite an inch thick.

He was flashing a smile of unearthly perfection. Relaxed and happy, he knelt there bestowing this smile upon each Montdore in turn.

"Don't speak," he said, "just for a moment. Just let me go on looking at you—wonderful, wonderful people!"

I could see at once that Lady Montdore was very highly gratified. She beamed with pleasure. Lord Montdore gave her a hasty glance to see how she was taking it, and when he saw that beaming was the note he beamed too.

"Welcome," she said, "to Hampton."

"The beauty," Cedric went on, floating jointlessly to his feet. "I can only say that I am drunk with it. England, so much more beautiful than I had imagined (I have never had very good accounts of England, somehow), this house, so romantic, such a repository of treasures, and, above all, you—the two most beautiful people I have ever seen!"

He spoke with rather a curious accent, neither French nor Canadian, but peculiar to himself, in which every syllable received rather more emphasis than is given by the ordinary Englishman. Also he spoke, as it were, through his smile, which would fade a little, then flash out again, but which never altogether left his face.

"Won't you take off your spectacles?" said Lady Montdore. "I should like to see your eyes."

"Later, dear Lady Montdore, later. When my dreadful, paralyzing shyness (a disease with me) has quite worn off. They give me confidence, you see, when I am dreadfully nervous, just as a mask would. In a mask one can face anything. I should like my life to be a perpetual *bal masqué*, Lady Montdore, don't you agree? I long to know who the Man in the Iron Mask was, don't you, Lord Montdore? Do you remember when Louis XVIII first saw the Duchesse d'Angoulême after the Restoration? Before saying anything else, you know —wasn't it all awful, or anything?—he asked if poor Louis XVI had ever told her who the Man in the Iron Mask was? I love Louis XVIII for that—so like *one*."

Lady Montdore indicated me. "This is our cousin —and a distant relation of yours, Cedric—Fanny Wincham."

He took my hand and looked long into my face, saying, "I am enchanted to meet you," as if he really was. He turned again to the Montdores, and said, "I am so happy to be here."

"My dear boy, we are so happy to have you. You should have come before. We had no idea—we thought you were always in Nova Scotia, you see."

Cedric was gazing at the big French map table. "Riesener," he said. "This is a very strange thing, Lady Montdore, and you will hardly believe it, but where I live in France we have its pair. Is that not a coincidence? Only this morning, at Chèvres, I was leaning upon that very table."

"What is Chèvres?"

"Chèvres—Fontaine, where I live, in the Seine et Oise."

"But it must be quite a large house," said Lady Montdore, "if that table is in it?"

"A little larger, in every dimension, than the central

block at Versailles, and with much more water. At Versailles there only remain seven hundred *bouches*. (how is *bouche* in English? Jets?) At Chèvres we have one thousand five hundred, and they play all the time."

Dinner was announced. As we moved towards the dining room, Cedric stopped to examine various objects and touched them lovingly.

"Weisweiller—Boule—Riesener—Jacob . . . How is it you come to have these marvels, Lord Montdore, such important pieces?"

"My great-grandfather (your great-great-grandfather), who was himself half-French, collected it all his life. Some of it he bought during the great sales of royal furniture after the Revolution and some came to him through his mother's family, the Montdores."

"And the *boiseries!*" said Cedric. "First quality Louis XV. There is nothing to equal this at Chèvres. It's like jewellery when it is so fine."

We were now in the little dining room.

"He brought them over too, and built the house round them." Lord Montdore was evidently much pleased by Cedric's enthusiasm. He loved French furniture himself but seldom found anybody in England to share his taste.

"Porcelain with Marie Antoinette's cypher—delightful. At Chèvres we have the Meissen service she brought with her from Vienna. We have many relics of Marie Antoinette, poor dear, at Chèvres."

"Who lives there?" asked Lady Montdore.

"I do," he replied carelessly, "when I wish to be in the country. In Paris I have a pavilion of all beauty, *one's* idea of heaven." Cedric made great use of the word "one," which he pronounced with peculiar emphasis. Lady Montdore had always been a one for one, but she said it quite differently—"w'n." "It stands between courtyard and garden. It was built for Madame du Barry. Tiny, you know, but all one needs, that is to say, a bedroom and a bed-ballroom. You must come and stay with me there, dear Lady Montdore. You will live in my bedroom, which has comfort, and I in the bed-ballroom. Promise me that you will come."

"We shall have to see. Personally, I have never been very fond of France. The people are so frivolous. I greatly prefer the Germans."

"Germans!" said Cedric earnestly, leaning across the table and gazing at her through his goggles. "The frivolity of the Germans terrifies even one. I have a German friend in Paris, and a more frivolous creature, Lady Montdore, does not exist. This frivolity has caused me many a heartache, I must tell you."

"I hope you will make some suitable English friends now, Cedric."

"Yes, yes, that is what I long for. But please, can my chief English friend be you, dear, dearest Lady Montdore?"

"I think you should call us Aunt Sonia and Uncle Montdore."

"May I, really? How charming you are to me! How happy I am to be here. You seem, Aunt Sonia, to shower happiness around you."

"Yes, I do. I live for others, I suppose that's why. The sad thing is that people have not always appreciated it. They are so selfish themselves."

"Oh, yes, aren't they selfish? I too have been a victim to the selfishness of people all my life. This German

friend I mentioned just now, his selfishness passes com-
prehension. How one does suffer!"

"It's a he, is it?" Lady Montdore seemed glad of this.

"A boy called Klugge. I hope to forget all about him
while I am here. Now, Lady Montdore—dearest Aunt
Sonia—after dinner I want you to do me a great, great
favour. Will you put on your jewels so that I can see
you sparkling in them? I do so long for that."

"Really, my dear boy, they are down in the strong
room. I don't think they've been cleaned for ages."

"Oh, don't say no, don't shake your head! Ever since
I set eyes on you I have been thinking of nothing else,
you must look so truly glorious in them. Mrs. Wincham
(you are Mrs. I hope, aren't you? Yes, yes, I can tell
that you are not a spinster), when did you last see Aunt
Sonia laden with jewels?"

"It was at the ball for . . ." I stopped awkwardly,
jibbing at the name, which was never now mentioned,
but Cedric saved me from embarrassment by exclaiming, "A ball! Aunt Sonia, how I would love to see you
at a ball. I can so well imagine you at all the great
English functions, coronations, Lords, balls, Ascot,
Henley. What is Henley? No matter . . . And I can
see you, above all, in India, riding on your elephant
like a goddess. How they must have worshipped you
there."

"Well, you know, they did," said Lady Montdore,
delighted. "They really worshipped us. It was quite
touching. And, of course, we deserved it. We did a very
great deal for them. I think I may say we put India on
the map. Hardly any of one's friends in England had
ever even heard of India before we went there, you
know."

"I'm sure. What a wonderful and fascinating life you lead, Aunt Sonia. Did you keep a journal when you were in the East? Oh! please say yes, I would so love to read it."

This was a very lucky shot. They had indeed filled a huge folio, whose morocco label, surmounted by an earl's coronet, announced "Pages from Our Indian Diary. M. and S. M."

"It's really a sort of scrapbook," Lord Montdore said. "Accounts of our journeys up-country, photographs, sketches by Sonia and our brother-in . . . That is to say, a brother-in-law we had then, letters of appreciation from rajahs . . ."

"And Indian poytry translated by Montdore . . . 'Prayer of a Widow before Suttee,' 'Death of an Old Mahout,' and so on, touching, it makes you cry."

"Oh, I must read it all, every word, I can hardly wait."

Lady Montdore was radiant. How many and many a time had she led her guests to "Pages from Our Indian Diary," like horses to water, and watched them straying off after one half-hearted sip. Never before, I guess, had anybody so eagerly demanded to read it.

"Now, you must tell us about your life, my dear boy," said Lady Montdore. "When did you leave Canada? Your home is in Nova Scotia, is it not?"

"I lived there until I was eighteen."

"Montdore and I have never been in Canada. The States, of course—we spent a month once in New York and Washington and we saw Niagara Falls, but then we were obliged to come home. I only wish we could have gone on, they were quite touchingly anxious to have us, but Montdore and I cannot always do as we should like. We have our duties. Of course that was a long time ago, twenty-five years, I should think, but I daresay Nova Scotia doesn't alter much?"

"I am very very happy to say that kindly Nature has allowed a great sea-fog of oblivion to rise between me and Nova Scotia, so that I hardly remember one single thing about it."

"What a strange boy you are!" she said indulgently, but she was very well suited by the fact of the sea-fog, since the last thing she wanted would have been long-winded reminiscences of Cedric's family life in Canada. It was all, no doubt, much better forgotten, and especially the fact that Cedric had a mother. "So you came to Europe when you were eighteen?"

"Paris. Yes, I was sent to Paris by my guardian, a banker, to learn some horrid sort of job, I quite forget what, as I never had to go near it. It is not necessary to have jobs, in Paris. One's friends are so very, very kind."

"Really, how funny. I always thought the French were so mean."

"Certainly not to *one*. My needs are simple, admittedly, but such as they are they have all been satisfied over and over again."

"What are your needs?"

"I need a very great deal of beauty round me, beautiful objects wherever I look, and beautiful people who see the point of *one*. And speaking of beautiful people, Aunt Sonia, after dinner, the jewels? Don't, don't, please, say no!"

"Very well then," she said. "But now, Cedric, won't you take off your glasses?"

"Perhaps I could. Yes, I really think the last vestige of my shyness has gone."

He took them off, and the eyes which were now dis-
closed, blinking a little in the light, were the eyes of
Polly, large, blue, and rather blank. They quite startled
me, but I do not think the Montdores were specially
struck by the resemblance, though Lady Montdore said,
"Anybody can tell that you are a Hampton, Cedric.
Please never let's see those horrid spectacles again."

"My goggles? Specially designed by Van Cleef for
one?"

"I hate spectacles," said Lady Montdore firmly.

Lady Montdore's maid was now sent for, given the
key of the safe from Lord Montdore's key ring and told
to bring up all the jewel cases. When dinner was over
and we got back to the Long Gallery, leaving Lord
Montdore to his port, but accompanied by Cedric, who
was evidently unaware of the English custom which
keeps the men in the dining room after dinner, and
who followed Lady Montdore like a dog, we found the
map table covered with blue velvet trays, each of which
contained a parure of large and beautiful jewels. Cedric
gave a cry of happiness and got down to work at once.

"In the first place, dear Aunt Sonia," he said, "this
dress won't do. Let me see . . . ah, yes . . ." He took
a piece of red brocade off the piano and draped her in
it very cleverly, pinning it in place on one shoulder
with a huge diamond brooch. "Have you some maquil-
lage in this bag, dear? And a comb?"

Lady Montdore rummaged about and produced a
cheap lipstick and a small green comb with a tooth out.

"Naughty, naughty you," he said, carefully painting
her face. "It cakes! Never mind, that will do for now.
Not pulling your hair, am I? We've got to show the
bone structure, so beautiful on you. I think you'll have

to find a new coiffeur, Aunt Sonia. We'll see about
that. . . . Anyway it must go up—up—like this. Do
you realize what a difference that makes? Now, Mrs.
Wincham, will you please put out the top lights for
me, and bring the lamp from that bureau over here.
Thank you."

He placed the lamp on the floor at Lady Montdore's
feet and began to hang her with diamonds, so that the
brocade was covered with them to her waist, finally
poising the crown of pink diamonds on the top of her
head.

"Now," he said. "Look!" and he led her to a looking
glass on the wall. She was entranced by the effect, which
was indeed very splendid.

"My turn," he said.

Although Lady Montdore seemed to be almost solid
with diamonds, the cases on the table still held many
huge jewels. He took off his coat, his collar and tie,
pulled open his shirt and clasped a great necklace of
diamonds and sapphires round his neck, wound up
another piece of silk into a turban, stuck a diamond
feather in it and put it on his head. He went on talking
all the time.

"You really must pat your face more, Aunt Sonia."

"Pat?"

"With nourishing creams. I'll show you. Such a
wonderful face, but uncultivated, neglected and starved.
We must feed it up, exercise it and look after it better
from now on. You'll soon see what a lot can be done.
Twice a week you must sleep in a mask."

"A mask?"

"Yes, back to masks, but this time I mean the sort
you paint on at night. It goes quite hard, so that you

look like Commandeur in Don Juan, and in the morning you can't smile, not a glimmer, so you mustn't telephone until you've removed it with the remover, because you know how if you telephone smilelessly you sound cross, and if it happened to be *one* at the other end, *one* couldn't bear that."

"Oh, my dear boy, I don't know about this mask. What would Griffith say?"

"If Griffith is your maid, she won't notice a thing, they never do. We shall notice, though, your great new beauty. Those cruel lines!"

They were absorbed in each other and themselves, and when Lord Montdore came in from the dining room they did not even notice. He sat for a while in his usual attitude, the fingers of both hands pressed together, looking into the fire, and very soon crept off to bed. In the months which had passed since Polly's marriage he had turned into an old man. He was smaller, his clothes hung sadly on him, his voice quavered and complained. Before he went, he gave the little book of poems to Cedric, who took it with a charming show of appreciation and looked at it until Lord Montdore was out of sight, when he quickly turned back to the jewels.

I was pregnant at this time and began to feel sleepy very soon after dinner. I had a look at the picture papers, and then followed Lord Montdore's example.

"Good night," I said, making for the door. They hardly bothered to answer. They were now standing each in front of a looking glass, a lamp at their feet, happily gazing at their own images.

"Do you think it is better like that?" one would say.

"Much better," the other would reply, without looking.

From time to time they exchanged a jewel ("Give me the rubies, dear boy." "May I have the emeralds, if you've finished with them?"), and he was now wearing the pink tiara, jewels lay all around them, tumbled onto the chairs and tables, even on the floor.

"I have a confession to make to you, Cedric," she said, as I was leaving the room. "I really rather like amethysts."

"Oh, but I love amethysts," he replied, "so long as they are nice, large, dark stones, set in diamonds. They suit *one* so well."

The next morning when I went to Lady Montdore's room to say good-bye, I found Cedric, in a pale mauve silk dressing gown, sitting on her bed. They were both rubbing cream into their faces out of a large pink pot. It smelt delicious, and certainly belonged to him.

"And after that," he was saying, "until the end of her life she wore a thick black veil."

"And what did he do?"

"He left cards on all Paris, on which he had written *'mille regrets.'* "

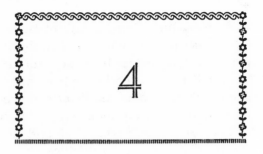

4

FROM the moment that the Montdores first set eyes
on Cedric, there was no more question of his having
come to Hampton for a fortnight. He was obviously
there for good and all. They both took him to their
hearts and loved him, almost at once, better than they
had loved Polly for years, ever since she was a small
child. The tremendous vacuum created by her departure was happily filled again, and filled by somebody
who was able to give more than Polly had ever given
in the way of companionship. Cedric could talk intelligently to Lord Montdore about the objects of art at
Hampton. He knew an enormous amount about such
things, though in the ordinary sense of the word he was
uneducated, ill-read, incapable of the simplest calcula-
tion, and curiously ignorant of many quite elementary
subjects. He was one of those people who take in the
world through eye and ear, his intellect was probably

worth very little, but his love of beauty was genuine. The librarian at Hampton was astounded at his bibliographical knowledge. It seemed, for instance, that he could tell at a glance whom a book had been bound for and by whom, and he said that Cedric knew much more than he did himself about eighteenth-century French editions. Lord Montdore had seldom seen his own cherished belongings so intelligently appreciated, and it was a great pleasure to him to spend hours with Cedric going over them. He had doted on Polly, she had been the apple of his eye, in theory, but in practice she had never been in any respect a companion to him.

As for Lady Montdore, she became transformed with happiness during the months that followed, transformed, too, in other ways, Cedric taking her appearance in hand with extraordinary results. Just as Boy (it was the hold he had over her) had filled her days with society and painting, Cedric filled them with the pursuit of her own beauty, and to such an egotist this was a more satisfactory hobby. Facial operations, slimming cures, exercises, massage, diet, make-up, new clothes, jewels reset, a blue rinse for her grey hair, pink bows and diamond daisies in the blue curls; it kept her very busy. I saw her less and less, but each time I did she looked more unnaturally modish. Her movements, formerly so ponderous, became smart, spry and birdlike. She never sat now with her two legs planted on the ground, but threw one over the other, legs which, daily massaged and steamed, gradually lost their flesh and became little more than bone. Her face was lifted, plucked and trimmed, and looked as tidy as Mrs. Chaddesley Corbett's, and she learnt to flash a smile brilliant as Cedric's own.

"I make her say 'brush' before she comes into a room," he told me. "It's a thing I got out of an old book on deportment and it fixes at once this very gay smile on one's face. Somebody ought to tell Lord Alconleigh about it."

Since she had never hitherto made the smallest effort to appear younger than she was, but had remained fundamentally Edwardian-looking, as though conscious of her own superiority to the little smart ephemeral types, the Chaddesley Corbetts and so on, Cedric's production of her was revolutionary. In my opinion it was not successful, for she made the sacrifice of a grand and characteristic appearance without really gaining in prettiness, but no doubt the effort which it involved made her perfectly happy.

Cedric and I became great friends and he visited me constantly in Oxford, just as Lady Montdore used to before she became so busy, and I must say that I greatly preferred his company to hers. During the later stages of my pregnancy, and after the baby was born, he would come and sit with me for hours on end, and I felt completely at my ease with him. I could go on with my sewing, or mending, without bothering about what I looked like, exactly as if he were one of my Radlett cousins. He was kind and thoughtful and affectionate, like a charming woman friend, better, because our friendship was marred by no tinge of jealousy.

Later on, when I had got my figure back after the baby, I began to dress and make myself up with a view to gaining Cedric's approbation, but I soon found that, with the means at my disposal, it was not much use. He knew too much about women and their accessories to be impressed by anything I could manage. For instance, if I made a great effort and changed into silk stockings when I expected him, he could see at once that they were Elliston, 5/11, all I could afford, and it really seemed more sensible to stick to lisle. Indeed, he once said to me, "You know, Fanny, it doesn't matter a bit that you're not able to dress up in expensive clothes, there'd be no point in it anyway. You are like the Royal Family, my darling, whatever you wear you look exactly the same, just as they do."

I was not very much pleased, but I knew that he was right. I could never look fashionable, even if I tried as hard as Lady Montdore, with my heather-hair and round salubrious face.

I remember that my mother, during one of her rare visits to England, brought me a little jacket in scarlet cloth from Schiaparelli. It seemed to me quite plain and uninteresting, except for the label in its lining, and I longed to put this on the outside so that people would know where it came from. I was wearing it, instead of a cardigan, in my house when Cedric happened to call, and the first thing he said was, "Aha! so now we dress at Schiaparelli, I see! Whatever next?"

"Cedric! How can you tell?"

"My dear, one can always tell. Things have a signature, if you use your eyes, and mine seem to be trained over a greater range of objects than yours, Schiaparelli —Reboux—Fabergé—Viollet le Duc—I can tell at a glance, literally a glance. So your wicked mother, the Bolter, has been here since last I saw you?"

"Might I not have bought it for myself?"

"No, no, my love, you are saving up to educate your twelve brilliant sons, how could you possibly afford £25 for a little jacket?"

"Don't tell me!" I said. "£25 for this?"

"Quite that, I should guess."

"Simply silly. Why, I could have made it myself."

"But could you? And if you had, would I have come into the room and said Schiaparelli?"

"There's only a yard of stuff in it, worth a pound, if that," I went on, horrified by the waste of money.

"And how many yards of canvas in a Fragonard? And how much do planks of wood cost, or the skin of a darling goat before some clever person turns them into commodes and morocco? Art is more than yards, just as *one* is more than flesh and bones. By the way, I must warn you that Sonia will be here in a minute, in search of strong tea. I took the liberty of having a word with Mrs. Heathery, the love of whose life I am, on my way up, and I also brought some scones from the Cadena which I deposited with her."

"What is Lady Montdore doing now?" I said, beginning to tidy up the room.

"Now this very minute? She is at Parkers, buying a birthday present for me. It is to be a great surprise, but I went to Parkers and prepared the ground and I shall be greatly surprised if the great surprise is not Ackerman's *Repository*."

"I thought you turned up your nose at English furniture?" I said.

"Less and less. Provincial but charming is now my attitude, and Ackerman's *Repository* is such an amusing book. I saw a copy the other day when Sonia and I went over to Lord Merlin's, and I long to possess it. I expect it will be all right. Sonia loves to give me these large presents, impossible to carry about. She thinks they anchor me to Hampton. I don't blame her, her life there must have been too dull for words, without me."

"But are you anchored?" I said. "It always seems to me that the place where you really belong is Paris. I can't imagine you staying here for ever."

"I can't imagine it, either, but the fact is, my darling, that the news from Paris is not too good. I told you, didn't I, that I left my German friend Klugge to look after my pavilion and keep it warm for me? Now what do I hear? The Baron came last week with a *camion* and took all the furniture, every stick, leaving poor Klugge to sleep on bare boards. I daresay he doesn't notice, he is always quite drunk by bedtime, but for waking up it can't be very nice, and meanwhile I am mourning my commodes. Louis XV—a pair—such *marqueterie*, such bronzes, really important pieces, *objets de musée*—well, often have I told you about them. Gone! The Baron, during one fatal afternoon, took everything. Bitter work!"

"What Baron?" I asked.

I knew all about Klugge, how hideous and drunken and brutal and German and unlettered he was, so that Cedric never could explain why he put up with his vagaries for a single moment, but the Baron was a new figure to me. Cedric was evasive, however. He was better than anybody I have ever known at not answering questions if he did not want to.

"Just another friend. The first night I was in Paris I went to the Opera, and I don't mind telling you, my darling, that all eyes were upon me, in my box, the poor *artistes* might just as well not have been on the stage at all. Well, one of the eyes belonged to the Baron."

"Two of the eyes, you mean," I said.

"No, dear, one. He wears a patch to make himself look sinister and fascinating. Nobody knows how much I hate barons. I feel exactly like King John whenever I think of them."

"But, Cedric, I don't understand. How could he take your furniture away?"

"How could he? How, indeed? Alas, he has, and that is that. My Savonnerie, my Sèvres, my sanguines, all my treasures gone, and I confess I am very low about it, because, although they cannot compare in quality with what I see every day round me at Hampton, one does so love one's own things which one has bought and chosen oneself. I must say the Boule at Hampton is the best I have ever seen—even at Chèvres we had no Boule like that. Sensational. Have you been over since we began to clean the bronzes? Oh, you must come. I have taught my friend Archie how to unscrew the bits, scrub them with ammonia, and pour boiling water on them from a kettle so that they dry at once with no moisture left to turn them green. He does it all day, and when he has finished it glitters like the cave of Aladdin."

This Archie was a nice handsome boy, a lorry driver, whom Cedric had found with his lorry broken down near the gates of Hampton.

"For your ear alone, my darling, it was a stroke of thunder when I saw him. What one does so love about love is the time before they find out what *one* is like."

"And it's also very nice," I said, disloyally, "before *one* finds out what they are like."

Archie had now left his lorry for ever, and gone to live at Hampton to do odd jobs. Lady Montdore was enthusiastic about him.

"So willing," she would say. "So clever of Cedric to think of having him. Cedric always does such original things."

Cedric went on, "But I suppose you would think it more hideous than ever, Fanny. I know that you like a room to sparkle with freshness, whereas I like it to glitter with richness. That is where we differ at present, but you'll change. Your taste is really good, and it is bound to mature one day."

It was true that my taste at this time, like that of the other young people I knew who cared at all about their houses, favoured pickled or painted furniture with a great deal of white, and upholstery in pale cheerful colours. French furniture with its finely chiselled ormolu (what Cedric called bronzes), its severe lines and perfect proportions was far above my head in those days, while Louis XIV needlework, of which there was a great amount at Hampton, seemed dark and stuffy, I frankly preferred a cheerful chintz.

Cedric's word with Mrs. Heathery had excellent results, and even Lady Montdore showed no signs of despising the tea which arrived at the same time as she did. In any case, now that she was happy again, she was much more good-natured about the attempts of the humble, such as myself, to regale her.

Her appearance still gave me quite a jump, though by now I really should have been getting accustomed to her flashing smile, her supple movements, and the pale-blue curls, a little sparse upon the head, not un-attractively so, but like a baby's curls. To-day she was hatless, and wore a tartan ribbon to keep her hair in place. She was dressed in a plain but beautifully made grey coat and skirt, and as she came into the room, which was full of sun, she took her coat off with a curious, swift, double-jointed movement, revealing a piqué blouse and a positively girlish waistline. It was warm spring weather just then, and I knew that she and Cedric did a lot of sun bathing in a summer house specially designed by him, as a result of which her skin had gone rather a horrid yellow, and looked as if it had to be soaked in oil to prevent it from falling into a thousand tiny cracks. Her nails were varnished dark red, and this was an improvement, since formerly they had been furrowed and not always quite clean. The old-fashioned hoops of enormous diamonds set in gold which used so stiffly to encircle her stiff fingers were replaced by square-cut diamonds in clusters of cabuchon emeralds and rubies, her diamond earrings too had been reset, in the shape of cockle shells, and more large diamonds sparkled in a fashionable pair of clips, at her throat. The whole thing was stunning.

But although her aspect was so much changed, her personality remained the same, and the flashing (brush) smile was followed by the well-known up and down look.

"Is that your baby, making that horrid noise, Fanny?"

"Yes. He never cries, as a rule, but his teeth are upsetting him."

"Poor thing," said Cedric. "Couldn't he go to the dentist?"

"Well, I've got your birthday present, Cedric. It can't be a surprise though, because it's all over the floor of the motor. They seemed to think, at Parker's, that you would like it—a book called Ackerman's *Suppository*, or something."

"Not Ackerman's *Suppository*—not really!" said

Cedric, clasping his hands under his chin in a very characteristic gesture. "How kind you are to me! How could you have guessed? Where did you find it? But, dearest, it's bad about the surprise. Birthday presents really ought to be surprises. I can't get Sonia to enter into the true spirit of birthdays, Fanny, what can *one* do about it?"

I thought *one* had done pretty well. Lady Montdore was famous for never giving presents at all, either for birthdays or at Christmas, and had never even relaxed this rule in favour of the adored Polly, though Lord Montdore used to make up for that by giving her several. But she showered presents, and valuable presents too, on Cedric, snatching at the smallest excuse to do so, and I quite saw that with somebody so intensely appreciative this must be a great pleasure.

"But I have got a surprise for you, as well as the books, something I bought in London," she said, looking at him fondly.

"No!" said Cedric. I had the feeling he knew all about that, too. "I shan't have one moment's peace until I've wormed it out of you—how I wish you hadn't told me."

"You've only got to wait until to-morrow."

"Well, I warn you I shall wake you up for it at six. Now finish your tea, dear, and come, we ought to be getting back. I'm in a little bit of a fuss to see what Archie has been up to with all those bronzes. He's doing the Boule to-day and I have had a horrid idea—suppose he has re-assembled it into a lorry by mistake? What would dearest Uncle Montdore say if he suddenly came upon a huge Boule lorry in the middle of the Long Gallery?"

No doubt, I thought, but that both Lord and Lady Montdore would happily have got into it and been taken for a ride by Cedric. He had completely mesmerized them, and nothing that he could do ever seemed otherwise to them than perfection.

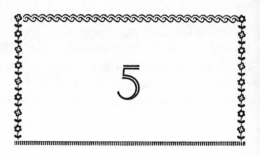

5

CEDRIC'S advent at Hampton naturally created quite a stir in the world outside. London society was not at first given the chance to form an opinion on him, because this was the year following the Financial Crisis. In fact, Cedric and the Crisis had arrived at about the same time, and Lady Montdore, though herself unaffected by it, thought that as there was no entertaining in London it was hardly worth while to keep Montdore House open, she had it shrouded in dust sheets except for two rooms where Lord Montdore could put up if he wanted to go to the House of Lords.

Lady Montdore and Cedric never stayed there. They sometimes went to London, but only for the day. She no longer invited large house parties to Hampton. She said people could talk about nothing but money any more and it was too boring, but I thought there was another reason, and that she really wanted to keep Cedric to herself.

The county, however, hummed and buzzed with Cedric, and little else was talked of. I need hardly say that Uncle Matthew, after one look, found that the word sewer had become obsolete and inadequate. Scowling, growling, flashing of eyes and grinding of teeth, to a degree hitherto reserved for Boy Dougdale, were intensified a hundredfold at the mere thought of Cedric, and accompanied by swelling veins and apoplectic noises. The drawers at Alconleigh were emptied of the yellowing slips of paper on which my uncle's hates had mouldered all these years, and each now contained a clean new slip with the name, carefully printed in black ink, Cedric Hampton. There was a terrible scene on Oxford platform one day. Cedric went to the bookstall to buy *Vogue*, having mislaid his own copy. Uncle Matthew, who was waiting there for a train, happened to notice that the seams of his coat were piped in a contrasting shade. This was too much for his self-control. He fell upon Cedric and began to shake him like a rat. Just then, very fortunately, the train came in, whereupon my uncle, who suffered terribly from train fever, dropped Cedric and rushed to catch it. "You'd never think," as Cedric said afterwards, "that buying *Vogue* magazine could be so dangerous. It was well worth it though, lovely Spring modes."

The children, however, were in love with Cedric and furious because I would not allow them to meet him in my house. But Aunt Sadie, who seldom took a strong line about anything, had solemnly begged me to keep them apart, and her word with me was law. Besides, from my pinnacle of sophistication as wife and mother, I also considered Cedric to be unsuitable company for the very young, and when I knew he was coming to see me I took great care to shoo away any undergraduates who might happen to be sitting about in my drawing room.

Uncle Matthew and his neighbours seldom agreed on any subject. He despised their opinions, and they, in their turn, found his violent likes and dislikes quite incomprehensible, taking their cue as a rule from the balanced Boreleys. Over Cedric, however, all were united. Though the Boreleys were not haters in the Uncle Matthew class, they had their own prejudices, things they "could not stick," foreigners, for example, well-dressed women and the Labour Party. But the thing they could stick least in the world were "Aesthetes—you know—those awful effeminate creatures—pansies." When, therefore, Lady Montdore, whom anyhow they could not stick much, installed the awful effeminate pansy Cedric at Hampton, and it became borne in upon them that he was henceforth to be their neighbour for ever, quite an important one at that, the future Lord Montdore, hatred really did burgeon in their souls. At the same time they took a morbid interest in every detail of the situation, and these details were supplied to them by Norma, who got her facts, I am ashamed to say, from me. It tickled me so much to make Norma gasp and stretch her eyes with horror that I kept back nothing that might tease her and infuriate the Boreleys.

I soon found out that the most annoying feature of the whole thing to them was the radiant happiness of Lady Montdore. They had all been delighted by Polly's marriage, even those people who might have been expected wholeheartedly to take Lady Montdore's side over it, such as the parents of pretty young daughters,

having said with smug satisfaction "Serve her right."
They hated her and were glad to see her downed. Now,
it seemed, the few remaining days of this wicked
woman, who never invited them to her parties, were
being suitably darkened with a sorrow which must soon
bring her grey hairs to the grave. The curtain rises for
the last act and the stalls are filled with Boreleys all
agog to witness the agony, the dissolution, the muffled
drum, the catafalque, the procession to the vault, the
lowering to the tomb, the darkness. But what is this?
Onto the stage in a dazzling glare, springs Lady Montdore, supple as a young cat and her grey hair now a
curious shade of blue, with a partner, a terrible creature
from Sodom, from Gomorrah, from Paris, and with
him proceeds to dance a wild fandango of delight. No
wonder they were cross.

On the other hand, I thought the whole thing simply
splendid, since I like my fellow-beings to be happy and
the new state of affairs at Hampton had so greatly increased the sum of human happiness. An old lady, a
selfish old creature admittedly, who deserved nothing
at the end but trouble and sickness (but which of us
will deserve better?) is suddenly presented with one
of life's bonuses, and is rejuvenated, occupied, and
amused; a charming boy with a great love of beauty and
of luxury, a little venal, perhaps (but which of us is
not if we get the opportunity to be?), whose life hitherto
depended upon the whims of Barons, suddenly and
respectably acquires two doting parents and a vast
heritage of wealth, another bonus; Archie, the lorry
driver, taken from long cold nights on the road, long
oily hours under his lorry, and put to polish ormolu in
a warm and scented room; Polly married to the love of

her life; Boy married to the greatest beauty of the age, five bonuses, five happy people, and yet the Boreleys were disgusted. They must indeed be against the human race, I thought, so to hate happiness.

I said all this to Davey, and he winced a little.

"I wish you needn't go on about Sonia being an old, old woman on the brink of the grave," he said. "She is barely sixty, you know, only about ten years older than your Aunt Emily."

"Davey, she's forty years older than I am; it must seem old to me. I bet people forty years older than you are seem old to you, now do admit."

Davey admitted. He also agreed that it is nice to see people happy, but made the reservation that it is only very nice if you happen to like them, and that although he was, in a way, quite fond of Lady Montdore, he did not happen to like Cedric.

"You don't like Cedric?" I said, amazed. "How couldn't you, Dave? I absolutely love him."

He replied that, whereas to an English rosebud like myself Cedric must appear as a being from another, darkly glamorous world, he, Davey, in the course of his own wild cosmopolitan wanderings, before he had met and settled down with Aunt Emily, had known too many Cedrics.

"You are lucky," I said. "I couldn't know too many. And if you think I find him darkly glamorous you've got hold of the wrong end of the stick, my dear Dave. He seems to me like a darling Nanny."

"Darling Nanny! Polar bear—tiger—puma—something that can never be tamed. They always turn nasty in the end. Just you wait, Fanny, all this ormolu radiance will soon blacken, and the last state of Sonia will be worse than her first, I prophesy. I've seen this sort of thing too often."

"I don't believe it. Cedric loves Lady Montdore."

"Cedric," said Davey, "loves Cedric, and, furthermore, he comes from the jungle, and just as soon as it suits him he will tear her to pieces and slink back into the undergrowth—you mark my words."

"Well," I said, "if so, the Boreleys will be pleased."

Cedric himself now sauntered into the room and Davey prepared to leave. I think after all the horrid things he had just been saying he was afraid of seeming too cordial to him in front of me. It was very difficult not to be cordial to Cedric, he was so disarming.

"I shan't see you again, Fanny," Davey said, "until I get back from my cruise."

"Oh, are you going for a cruise? How delicious! Where?"

"In search of a little sun. I give a few lectures on Minoan things and go cheap."

"I do wish Aunt Emily would go too," I said. "It would be so good for her."

"She'll never move until after Siegfried's death," said Davey. "You know what she is."

When he had gone I said to Cedric, "What d'you think, he may be able to go and see Polly and Boy in Sicily—wouldn't it be interesting?"

Cedric of course was deeply fascinated by anything to do with Polly. "The absent influence, so boring and so overdone in literature, but I see now that in real life it can eat you with curiosity."

"When did you last hear from her, Fanny?" he said.

"Oh, months ago, and then it was only a postcard. I'm so delighted about Dave seeing them because he's always so good at telling. We really shall hear how they are getting on, from him."

"Sonia has still never mentioned her to me," said Cedric, "never once."

"That's because she never thinks of her then."

"I'm sure she doesn't. This Polly can't be much of a personality, to have left such a small dent where she used to live?"

"Personality . . ." I said. "I don't know. The thing about Polly is her beauty."

"Describe it."

"Oh, Cedric I've described it to you hundreds of times." It rather amused me to do so though, because I knew that it teased him.

"Well," I said, "as I've often told you before, she is so beautiful that it's difficult to pay much attention to what she is saying, or to make out what she's really like as a person, because all you want to do is just gaze and gaze."

Cedric looked sulky, as he always did when I talked like this.

"More beautiful than *one*?" he said.

"Very much like you, Cedric."

"So you say, but I don't find that you gaze and gaze at *one*. On the contrary, you listen intently, with your eye out of the window."

"She is very much like you, but all the same," I said firmly, "she must be more beautiful because there is that thing about the gazing."

This was perfectly true, and not said to annoy poor Cedric or make him jealous. He was like Polly, and very good-looking, but not an irresistible magnet to the eye as she was.

"I know exactly why," he said. "It's my beard, all that horrible shaving. I shall send to New York this very day for some wax—you can't conceive the agony it is, but if it will make you gaze, Fanny, it will be worth it."

"Don't bother to do that," I said. "It's not the shaving. You do look like Polly, but you are not as beautiful. Lady Patricia also looked like her, but it wasn't the same thing. It's something extra that Polly has, which I can't explain, I can only tell you that it is so."

"What extra can she possibly have except beardlessness?"

"Lady Patricia was quite beardless."

"You are horrid. Never mind, I shall try it and you'll see. People used to gaze before my beard grew, like mad, even in Nova Scotia. You are so fortunate not to be a beauty, Fanny, you'll never know the agony of losing your looks."

"Thank you," I said.

"And as talking about pretty Polly makes us both so disagreeable let's get onto the subject of Boy."

"Ah, now, nobody could say that Boy was pretty. No gazing there. Boy is old and grizzled and hideous."

"Now, Fanny, that's not true, dear. Descriptions of people are only interesting if they happen to be true, you know. I've seen many photographs of Boy. Sonia's books are full of them, from Boy playing diabolo, Boy in puttees for the war, to Boy with his bearer Boosee. After India I think she lost her Brownie, in the move, perhaps, because 'Pages from Our Indian Diary' seems to be the last book, but that was only three years ago and Boy was still ravishing then, the kind of looks I adore, stocky and with deep attractive furrows all over his face—dependable."

"Dependable!"

"Why do you hate him so much, Fanny?"

"Oh, I don't know, he gives me the creeps. He's such a snob, for one thing."

"I like that," said Cedric. "I am one myself."

"Such a snob that living people aren't enough for him, he has to get to know the dead, as well—the titled dead, of course, I mean. He dives about in their memoirs so that he can talk about his 'dear Duchesse de Dino,' or 'as Lady Bessborough so truly says.' He can reel off pedigrees; he always knows just how everybody was related, Royal families and things I mean. Then he writes books about all these people, and, after that, anybody would think they were his own personal property. Ugh!"

"Exactly as I had supposed," said Cedric. "A handsome, cultivated man, the sort of person I like the best. Gifted too. His needlework is marvellous and the dozens of *toiles* by him in the squash court are worthy of the Douanier himself, landscapes with gorillas. Original and bold."

"Gorillas! Lord and Lady Montdore, and anybody else who would pose."

"Well, it is original and bold to depict my aunt and uncle as gorillas. I wouldn't dare. I think Polly is a very lucky girl."

"The Boreleys think you will end by marrying Polly, Cedric." Norma had propounded this thrilling theory to me the day before. They thought that it would be a deathblow to Lady Montdore, and longed for it to happen.

"Very silly of them, dear, I should have thought they only had to look at *one* to see how unlikely that is. What else do the Boreleys say about me?"

"Cedric, do come and meet Norma one day—I simply long to see you together."

"I think not, dear, thank you."

"But why? You're always asking what she says and she's always asking what you say, you'd much better ask each other and do without the middleman."

"The thing is, I believe she would remind me of Nova Scotia, and when that happens my spirits go down, down, past *grande pluie* to *tempête*. The house carpenter at Hampton reminds me, don't ask me why, but he does, and I have to rudely look away every time I meet him. I believe that's why Paris suits me so well, there's not a shade of Nova Scotia there, and perhaps it's also why I put up with the Baron all those years. The Baron could have come from many a land of spices, but from Nova Scotia he could not have come. Whereas Boreleys abound there. But though I don't want to meet them I always like hearing about them, so do go on with what they think about *one*."

"Well, so then Norma was full of you just now, when I met her out shopping, because it seems you travelled down from London with her brother Jock yesterday, and now he can literally think of nothing else."

"Oh, how exciting. How did he know it was me?"

"Lots of ways. The goggles, the piping, your name on your luggage. There is nothing anonymous about you, Cedric."

"Oh, good!"

"So according to Norma he was in a perfect panic, sat with one eye on you and the other on the communication cord, because he expected you to pounce at any minute."

"Heavens! What does he look like?"

"You ought to know. It seems you were quite alone together after Reading."

"Well, darling, I only remember a dreadful moustachio'd murderer sitting in a corner. I remember him particularly, because I kept thinking, 'Oh, the luck of being *one* and not somebody like that.'"

"I expect that was Jock. Sandy and white."

"That's it. Oh, so that's a Boreley, is it? And do you imagine people often make advances to him, in trains?"

"He says you gave him hypnotic stares through your glasses."

"The thing is he did have rather a pretty tweed on."

"And then apparently you made him get your suitcase off the rack at Oxford, saying you are not allowed to lift things."

"No, and nor I am. It was very heavy, not a sign of a porter, as usual. I might have hurt myself. Anyway it was all right because he terribly sweetly got it down for me."

"Yes, and now he's simply furious that he did. He says you hypnotised him."

"Oh, poor him, I do so know the feeling."

"Whatever had you got in it, Cedric? He says it simply weighed a ton."

"*Complets,*" Cedric said. "And a few small things for my face. I have found a lovely new resting cream, by the way. Very little, really."

"And now they are all saying, 'There you are—if he even fixed old Jock, no wonder he has got round the Montdores.'"

"But why on earth should I want to get round the Montdores?"

"Wills and things. Living at Hampton."

"My dear, come to that, Chèvres-Fontaine is twenty times more beautiful than Hampton."

"But could you go back there now, Cedric?" I said.

Cedric gave me rather a nasty look and went on, "But in any case, I wish people would understand that there's never much point in hanging about for wills. It's just not worth it. I have a friend who used to spend months of every year with an old uncle in the Sarthe so as to stay in his will. It was torture to him, because he knew the person he loved was being unfaithful to him in Paris, and anyhow the Sarthe is utterly lugubrious, you know. But all the same he went pegging away at it. Then what occurs? The uncle dies, my poor friend inherits the house in the Sarthe, and now he feels obliged to live a living death there so as to make himself believe that there was some point after all in having wasted months of his youth in the Sarthe. You see my argument? It's a vicious circle, and there is nothing vicious about me. The thing is, I love Sonia, that's why I stay."

I believed him, really. Cedric lived in the present, it would not be like him to bother about such things as wills. If ever there were a grasshopper, a lily of the field, it was he.

When Davey got back from his cruise he rang me up and said he would come over to luncheon and tell me about Polly. I thought Cedric might as well come and hear it at first hand. Davey was always better with an audience even if he did not much like its component parts, so I rang up Hampton, and Cedric accepted to lunch with pleasure, and then said could he possibly stay with me for a night or two?

"Sonia has gone for this orange cure—yes, total starvation, except for orange juice, but don't mind too much for her, I know she'll cheat, and Uncle Montdore is in London for the House and I feel sad, all alone here. I'd love to be with you and to do some serious Oxford sightseeing, which there's never time for when I've got Sonia with me. That will be charming, Fanny, thank you, dear. One o'clock then."

Alfred was very busy just then and I was delighted to think I should have Cedric's company for a day or two. I cleared the decks by warning Aunt Sadie that he would be there, and telling my undergraduate friends that I should not be wanting them around for the present.

"Who is that spotty child?" Cedric had once said, when a boy who had been crouching by my fireplace got up and vanished at a look from me.

"I see him as the young Shelley," I answered, sententiously, no doubt.

"And *I* see him as the young Woodley."

Davey arrived first.

"Cedric is coming," I said, "so you mustn't begin without him." I could see he was bursting with his news.

"Oh, Cedric—I never come without finding that monster here. He seems to live in your house. What does Alfred think of him?"

"Doubt if he knows him by sight, to tell you the truth. Come and see the baby, Dave."

"Sorry if I'm late, darlings," Cedric said, floating in. "One has to drive so slowly in England, because of the walking *Herrschaften*. Why are the English roads always so covered with these tweeded stumpers?"

"They are colonels," I said. "Don't French colonels go for walks?"

"Much too ill. They have always lost a leg or two and been terribly gassed. I can see that French wars must have been far bloodier than English ones, though I do know a colonel, in Paris, who walks to the antique shops sometimes."

"How do they take their exercise?" I asked.

"Quite another way, darling. You haven't started about Boy, have you? Oh, how loyal. I was delayed by Sonia, too, on the telephone. She's in a terrible do. . . . It seems they've had her up for stealing the nurses' breakfast—well, had her up in front of the principal, who spoke quite cruelly to her, and said that if she does it again, or gets one more bite of illicit food, he'll give her the sack. Just imagine, no dinner, one orange juice at midnight, and woken up by the smell of kippers. So naturally the poor darling sneaked out and pinched one, and they caught her with it under her dressing gown. I'm glad to say she'd eaten most of it before they got it away from her. The thing is she started off demoralized by finding your name in the visitors' book, Davey, apparently she gave a scream and said, 'But he's a living skeleton, whatever was he doing here?' and they said you had gone there to put on weight. What's the idea?"

"The idea," said Davey, impatiently, "is health. If you are too fat you lose and if you are too thin you gain. I should have thought a child could understand that. But Sonia won't stick it for a day. No self-discipline."

"Just like *one*," said Cedric. "But then what are we to do to get rid of those kilos? Vichy, perhaps?"

"My dear, look at the kilos she's lost already," I said. "She's really so thin, ought she to get any thinner?"

"It's just that little extra round the hips," said Cedric. "A jersey and skirt is the test, and she doesn't look quite right in that yet. And there's a weeny roll round her ribs. Besides, they say the orange juice clears the skin. Oh, I do hope she sticks it for a few more days, for her own sake, you know. She says another patient told her of a place in the village where you can have Devonshire teas, but I begged her to be careful. After what happened this morning they're sure to be on the look-out and one more slip may be fatal. What d'you think, Davey?"

"Yes, they're madly strict," said Davey. "There'd be no point, otherwise."

We sat down to our luncheon and begged Davey to begin his story.

"I may as well start by telling you that I don't think they are at all happy."

Davey, I knew, was never a one for seeing things through rose-coloured spectacles, but he spoke so definitely and with so grave an emphasis, that I felt I must believe him.

"Oh, Dave, don't say that. How dreadful!"

Cedric, who, since he did not know and love Polly, was rather indifferent as to whether she was happy or not, said, "Now, Davey dear, you're going much too fast. New readers begin here. You left your boat . . ."

"I left my ship at Syracuse, having wired them from Athens that I would be arriving for one night, and they met me on the quay with a village taxi. They have no motor car of their own."

"Every detail. They were dressed?"

"Polly wore a plain blue-cotton frock and Boy was in shorts."

"Wouldn't care to see Boy's knees," I said.

"They're all right," said Davey, standing up for Boy, as usual.

"Well then, Polly? Beautiful?"

"Less beautiful" (Cedric looked delighted to hear this news) "and peevish. Nothing right for her. Hates living abroad, can't learn the language, talks Hindustanee to the servants, complains that they steal her stockings . . ."

"You're going much too fast, we're still in the taxi. You can't skip to stockings like this—how far from Syracuse?"

"About an hour's drive, and beautiful beyond words —the situation, I mean. The villa is on a south-easterly slope looking over olive trees, umbrella pines and vineyards to the sea—you know, the regular Mediterranean view that you can never get tired of. They've taken the house, furnished, from Italians and complain about it ceaselessly. It seems to be on their minds, in fact. I do see that it can't be very nice in winter—no heating, except open fireplaces which smoke, bath water never hot, none of the windows fit, and so on, you know. Italian houses are always made for the heat, and of course it can be jolly cold in Sicily. The inside is hideous, all khaki and bog oak, depressing, if you had to be indoors much. But at this time of year it's ideal, you live on a terrace, roofed-in with vines and bougainvillaea —I never saw such a perfect spot—huge tubs of geraniums everywhere—simply divine."

"Oh, dear, as I seem to have taken their place in life I do wish we could swop over sometimes," said Cedric. "I do so love Sicily."

"I think they'd be all for it," said Davey. "They struck me as being very homesick. Well, we arrived in time for luncheon and I struggled away with the food (Italian cooking, so oily)."

"What did you talk about?"

"Well, you know, really, it was one long wail from them about how difficult everything is, more expensive than they thought it would be and how the people— village people, I mean—don't really help but say yes, yes, the whole time and nothing gets done, and how they are supposed to have vegetables out of the garden in return for paying the gardener's wages but actually they have to buy everything and as they are sure he sells the vegetables in the village they suppose that it's their own that they buy back again; how when they first came there wasn't a kettle in the place and the blankets were as hard as boards, and none of the electric-light switches worked and no lamps by the beds—you know, the usual complaints of people who take furnished houses. I've heard them a hundred times. After luncheon it got very hot, which Polly doesn't like, and she went off to her room with everything drawn and I had a session with Boy on the terrace, and then I really saw how the land lay. Well, all I can say is, I know it is wrong, not right, to arouse the sexual instincts of little girls so that they fall madly in love with you, but the fact is, poor old Boy is taking a fearful punishment. You see, he has literally nothing to do from morning to night, except water his geraniums, and you know how bad it is for them to have too much water. Of course they are all leaf as a result, I told him so. He has nobody to talk to, no club, no London Library, no neighbours, and, of course, above all, no Sonia to keep him on the run. I don't expect he ever realized what a lot of his time used to be taken up by Sonia. Polly's no company for him, really. You can see that, and in many ways she seems dreadfully on his nerves. She's so insular, you know, nothing is right for her, she hates the place, hates the people, even hates the climate. Boy, at least, is very cosmopolitan, speaks beautiful Italian, prepared to be interested in the local folklore, and things like that, but you can't be interested quite alone and Polly is so discouraging. Everything seems rot to her and she only longs for England."

"Funny," I said, "that she should be quite so narrow-mindedly English when you think that she spent five years in India."

"Oh, my dear child, the butler was grander and the weather was hotter but otherwise there wouldn't be much to choose between Hampton and Viceroy's House. If anything, Viceroy's House was the less cosmopolitan of the two, I should say, and certainly it was no preparation for Sicilian housekeeping. No, she simply loathes it. So there is the poor fellow, shut up month after month with a cross little girl he has known from a baby. Not much cop, you must admit."

"I thought," said Cedric, "that he was so fond of dukes? Sicily is full of heavenly dukes, you know."

"Fairly heavenly, and they're nearly always away. Anyhow, he doesn't count them the same as French or English dukes."

"Well, that's nonsense, nobody could be grander than Monte Pincio. But if he doesn't count them (I do see some of the others are a bit unreal), and if he's got to live abroad, I can't imagine why he doesn't choose Paris. Plenty of proper dukes there—fifty, to be exact—Souppes told me so once. You know how they can only talk about each other, in that trade."

"My dear Cedric, they are very poor—they can't afford to live in England, let alone Paris. That's why they are still in Sicily. If it wasn't for that they'd come home now like a shot. Boy lost money in the crash last autumn, and he told me that if he hadn't got a very good let for Silkin they would really be almost penniless. Oh, dear, and when you think how rich Polly would have been . . ."

"No cruel looks at *one*," said Cedric. "Fair's fair, you know."

"Anyway it's a shocking business and only shows where dear old sex can land a person. I never saw anybody so pleased as he was when I appeared—like a dog let off a lead. Wanted to hear every single thing that's been going on. You could just see how lonely and bored he feels, poor chap."

But I was thinking of Polly. If Boy was bored and lonely, she was not likely to be very happy, either. The success or failure of all human relationships lies in the atmosphere each person is aware of creating for the other. What atmosphere could a disillusioned Polly feel that she was creating for a bored and lonely Boy? Her charm, apart from her beauty, and husbands, we know, get accustomed to the beauty of their wives so that it ceases to strike them at the heart, her charm used to derive from the sphinx-like quality which came from her secret dream of Boy. In the early days of that dream coming true, at Alconleigh, happiness had made her irresistible. But I quite saw that with the riddle solved, and with the happiness dissolved, Polly, without her own little daily round of Madame Rita, Debenhams and the hairdresser to occupy her, and too low in vitality to invent new interests for herself, might easily sink into sulky dumps. She was not at all likely to find consolation in Sicilian folklore, I knew, and probably not, not yet anyhow, in Sicilian noblemen.

"Oh, dear," I said. "If Boy isn't happy I don't suppose Polly can be, either. Oh, poor Polly."

"Poor Polly—m'm—but at least it was her idea," said Davey. "My heart bleeds for poor Boy. Well, he can't say I didn't warn him, over and over again."

"What about a baby?" I asked. "Any signs?"

"None that I could see, but, after all, how long have they been married? Eighteen months? Sonia was eighteen years before she had Polly."

"Oh, goodness!" I said. "I shouldn't imagine the Lecturer, in eighteen years time, will be able . . ."

I was stopped by a well-known hurt look on Davey's face.

"Perhaps that is what makes them sad," I ended rather lamely.

"Possibly. Anyhow I can't say that I formed a happy impression."

At this point Cedric was called to the telephone, and Davey said to me in a lowered voice, "Entirely between you and me, Fanny, and this is not to go any further, I think Polly is having trouble with Boy."

"Oh, dear," I said, "kitchen maids?"

"No," said Davey, "not kitchen maids."

"Don't tell me!" I said, horrified.

Cedric came back and said that Lady Montdore had

been caught red-handed having elevenses in the Devonshire tea-rooms and had been given the sack. She told him that the motor would call for him on its way, so that she would have a companion for the drive home.

"There now," he said gloomily. "I shan't have my little visit to you, after all, and I had so been looking forward to it."

It struck me that Cedric had arranged the orange cure less with a view to getting rid of kilos than to getting rid of Lady Montdore for a week or two. Life with her must be wearing work, even to Cedric, with his unflagging spirits and abounding energy, and he may well have felt that he had earned a short holiday after nearly a year of it.

6

CEDRIC HAMPTON and Norma Cozens met at last, but though the meeting took place in my garden it was none of my arranging—a pure chance. I was sitting, one afternoon of Indian summer, on my lawn, where the baby was crawling about stark naked and so brown that he looked like a little Topsy, when Cedric's golden head appeared over the fence, accompanied by another head, that of a thin and ancient horse.

"I'm coming to explain," he said, "but I won't bring my friend. I'll attach him to your fence, darling. He's so sad and good, he won't do any harm, I promise."

A moment later he joined me in the garden. I put the baby back in its pram and was turning to Cedric to ask what this was all about, when Norma came up the lane which passes my garden, on her afternoon trudge with her dogs. Now the Boreley family consider that they have a special mandate, bestowed from on high, to deal with everything that regards the horse. They feel it to be their duty, no less than their right, and therefore the moment she saw Cedric's friend, sad and good, standing by my fence, Norma unhesitatingly came into the garden to see what she could do about it. I introduced Cedric to her.

"I don't want to interrupt you," she said, her eye upon the famous piping of the seams, brown to-day upon a green linen coat, vaguely Tyrolean in aspect, "but there's a very old mare, Fanny, tied up to your fence. Do you know anything about it? Whom does she belong to?"

"Don't, dear Mrs. Cozens, tell me that the first horse I have ever owned is a female!" said Cedric, with a glittering (brush) smile.

"The animal is a mare," said Norma, "and if she is yours I must tell you that you ought to be ashamed of yourself for keeping her in that dreadful condition."

"Oh, but I only began keeping her ten minutes ago. My intention is to build her up. I hope that when you see her again, in a few months time, you simply won't know her."

"Do you mean to say that you bought that creature? She ought to go straight away to the kennels."

"The kennels? But why? She's not a dog!"

"The knacker, the horse butcher," said Norma impatiently, "she must be put down immediately, or I shall ring up the R.S.P.C.A."

"Oh, please don't do that. I'm not being cruel to her, I'm being kind. That horrid man I bought her from, he was being beastly, he was taking her to the knacker. My plan was to save her from him. I couldn't bear to see the expression on her poor face."

"Well, but what are you going to do with her, my dear boy?"

"I thought—set her free."

"Set her free? She's not a bird, you know, you can't go setting horses free like that—not in England anyway."

"Yes, I can. Not in Oxford, perhaps, but where I live there is a *vieux parc, solitaire et glacé*, and it is my intention to set her free there, to have happy days away from knackers. Isn't knacker a hateful word, Mrs. Cozens?"

"The grazing at Hampton is let," said Norma. It was the kind of detail the Boreleys could be counted on to tell you.

Cedric, however, took no notice and went on, "She was being driven down the street in a van with her head sticking out at the back, and I could see at once that she was longing for some nice person to get her out of the fix she was in, so I stopped the van and bought her. You could see how relieved she felt."

"How much?"

"Well, I offered the man forty pounds. It was all I had on me, so he let me have her for that."

"Forty pounds!" cried Norma, aghast. "Why, you could get a hunter for less than forty pounds."

"But, my dearest Mrs. Cozens, I don't want a hunter. It's the last thing. I'd be far too frightened. Besides, look at the time you have to get up—I heard them the other morning in the woods, half-past six. Well, you know, I'm afraid it's 'up before seven *dead* before eleven' with *one*. No, I just wanted this special old clipper-clopper. She's not the horse to make claims on a chap. She won't want to be ridden all the time, as a younger horse might, and there she'll be, if I feel like having a few words with her occasionally. But the great question now, which I came to tease practical Fanny with, is how to get her home?"

"And if you go buying up all the horses that are fit for the kennels, however do you imagine hounds are going to be fed?" said Norma, in great exasperation. She was related to several Masters of fox-hounds and her sister had a pack of beagles, so no doubt she was acquainted with all their problems.

"I shan't buy up all the horses," said Cedric, soothingly, "only this one, which I took a liking for. Now, dear Mrs. Cozens, do stop being angry and just tell me how I can get her home, because I know you can help if you want to and I simply can't get over the luck of meeting you here at the very moment when I needed you so badly."

Norma began to weaken, as people so very often did with Cedric. It was extraordinary how fast he could worm his way through a thick crust of prejudice, and, just as in the case of Lady Montdore, the people who hated him the most were generally those who had seen him from afar but never met him. But whereas Lady Montdore had "all this" to help in her conquest of disapproval, Cedric relied upon his charm, his good looks and his deep inborn knowledge of human, and especially female, nature.

"Please," he said, his eyes upon her, blinking a little.

I could see that he had done the trick, Norma was considering.

"Well," she said at last, "there are two ways of doing it. I can lend you a saddle and you can ride her over. I'm not sure she's up to it, but you could see . . ."

"No, Mrs. Cozens, no. I have some literary sense—

Fauntleroy on his pony, gallant little figure, the wind in his golden curls, all right, and if my uncle had had the sense to get me over from Canada when I was younger we should have seen that very thing, I've no doubt. But the gloomy old Don on Rosinante is quite another matter, and I can't face it."

"Which gloomy old don?" asked Norma with interest. "But it makes no odds, she'd never get there. Twenty miles, now I come to think of it—and I expect she's as lame as a cat."

She went to the fence and peered over.

"Those hocks . . . ! You know, it honestly would be kinder—oh, very well, very well. If nothing I can say will make you understand that the animal would be far happier dead, you'll have to get the horse box. Shall I ring up Stubby now, on Fanny's telephone and see if he can come round at once?"

"No! You wouldn't do that for me? Oh, dearest Mrs. Cozens I can only say—angel! What a miracle that I met you!"

"Lie down," she said, to the Borders, and went indoors.

"Sexually unsatisfied, poor her," said Cedric, when she had gone.

"Really, Cedric, what nonsense! She's got four children."

"I can't help it. Look at all those wrinkles. She could try patting in muscle oil, of course, and I shall suggest it as soon as I get to know her a little better, but I'm afraid the trouble is more deep-seated. Of course, I feel certain the Professor must be a secret queer—nobody but a queer would ever marry Norma, to begin with."

"Why? She's not at all boyish."

"No, dearest, it isn't that; but there is a certain type of Norma-ish lady which appeals to queers, don't ask me why, but so it is. Now, supposing I arranged for her to come over every Tuesday and share a facial with Sonia, what do you think? The competition would be good for both of them, and it would cheer Sonia up to see a woman so much younger, so much more deeply haggard."

"I wouldn't," I said. "Norma always says she can't stick Lady Montdore."

"Does she know her? Of course, I doubt if anything short of a nice lift would fix Mrs. Cozens, but we could teach her 'brush' and a little charm to help the Waynflete Prof to do his work a bit better, or, failing that, and I fear it's rather a desperate hope, some nice Woodley might come to the rescue. No, darling, not *one*," he added, in response to a meaning look from me. "The cuticles are too desperately anaphrodisiac."

"I thought you never wanted to see her because she reminded you of Nova Scotia?"

"Yes, I thought she would, but she is too English. She fascinates me for that reason; you know how very, very pro-English I am becoming. The cuticles are rather Nova Scotian, but her soul is the soul of Oxfordshire and I shall cultivate her after this like mad."

Some half an hour later, as Cedric went off, sitting by the driver of the horse box, Norma, panting a little from her efforts with the mare, who had stubbornly refused at first to get into it, said, "You know, that boy has some good in him, after all. What a shame he couldn't have gone to a decent public school instead of being brought up in those shocking colonies."

To my amazement, and great secret annoyance,

Cedric and Norma now became extremely friendly, and he went to see her, when he was in Oxford, quite as often as he did me.

"Whatever do you talk about?" I said to him crossly.

"Oh, we have cosy little chats about this and that. I love Englishwomen; they are so restful."

"Well, I'm fairly fond of old Norma, but I simply can't imagine what you see in her, Cedric."

"I suppose I see whatever you see," he replied carelessly.

After a bit, he persuaded her to give a dinner party, to which he promised to bring Lady Montdore. Lord Montdore never went out now, and was sinking happily into old age. His wife being provided with a companion for every hour of the day, he was not only allowed but encouraged to have a good long nap in the afternoon, and he generally either had his dinner in bed or shuffled off there immediately after dinner. The advent of Cedric must have proved a blessing to him in more ways than one. People very soon got into the habit of asking Cedric with Lady Montdore instead of her husband, and it must be said that he was much better company. They were going out more now than when Cedric first arrived, the panic caused by the financial crisis was subsiding and people had begun to entertain again. Lady Montdore was too fond of society to keep away from it for long, and Cedric, firmly established at Hampton, weighed down with many large expensive gifts, could surely now be shown to her friends without danger of losing him.

In spite of the fact that she was by way of being unable to stick Lady Montdore, Norma got into a perfect state over this dinner party, dropping in on me at all hours to discuss the menu and the fellow guests, and finally imploring me to come on the morning of the day to make a pudding for her. I said that I would do so on one condition: she must buy a quart of cream. She wriggled like an eel not to have to do this, but I was quite firm. Then she said would the top of the milk do? No, I said, it must be thick rich unadulterated cream. I said I would bring it with me and let her know how much I had paid for it, and she reluctantly agreed. Although she was, I knew, very wealthy, she never spent a penny more than she could help on her house, her table or her clothes (except her riding clothes, for she was always beautifully turned out in the hunting field and I am sure her horses lived on an equine substitute for cream). So I went round, and, having provided myself with the suitable ingredients, I made her a crême Chantilly. As I got back to my own house the telephone bell was pealing away. Cedric.

"I thought I'd better warn you, my darling, that we are chucking poor Norma to-night."

"Cedric, you simply can't, I never heard anything so awful. She has bought cream!"

He gave an unkind laugh and said, "So much the better for those weedy tots I see creeping about her house."

"But why should you chuck, are you ill?"

"Not the least bit ill, thank you, love. The thing is that Merlin wants us to go over there for dinner. He has got fresh foie gras, and a fascinating Marquesa with eyelashes two inches long—he measured—do you see how *one* can't resist it?"

"*One* must resist it," I said frantically. "You simply cannot chuck poor Norma now. You'll never know the trouble she's taken. Besides, do think of us, you miserable boy, we can't chuck, only think of the dismal evening we shall have without you."

"I know, poor you—lugubrious."

"Cedric, all I can say is you are a sewer."

"Yes, darling, *mea culpa*. But it's not so much that I want to chuck as that I absolutely know I shall. I don't even intend to, I fully intend not to, it is that something in my body will make me. When I've rung off from speaking to you, I know that my hand will creep back to the receiver again of its own accord, and I shall hear my voice, but quite against my will, mind you, asking for Norma's number, and then I shall be really horrified to hear it breaking this dreadful news to Norma. So much worse, now I know about the cream, too. But there it is. But what I rang you up to say is, don't forget you are on *one's* side—no disloyalty, Fanny, please, I absolutely count, dear, on you not to egg Norma on to be furious. Because so long as you don't do that you'll find she won't mind a bit, not a bit. So, solidarity between working girls, and I'll promise to come over tomorrow and tell about the eyelashes."

Oddly enough, Cedric was right and Norma was not in the least put out. His excuse, and he had told the truth, merely adding a touch of embroidery by saying that Lady Montdore had been at school with the Marquesa, was considered quite a reasonable one, since dinner with Lord Merlin was recognized at Oxford as being the very pinnacle of human happiness. Norma rang me up to say that her dinner party was postponed, in the voice of a society hostess who postpones dinner parties every day of the week. Then, lapsing into more normal Oxford parlance she said:

"It's a bore about the cream, because they are coming on Wednesday now and it will never keep in this weather. Can you come back and make another pudding on Wednesday morning, Fanny? All right, and I'll pay you for both lots together, if that suits you. Everybody is free and I think the flowers may last over, so see you then, Fanny."

But on Wednesday Cedric was in bed with a high temperature, and on Thursday he was rushed to London by ambulance and operated upon for peritonitis, lying between life and death for several days, and in the end it was quite two months before the dinner party could take place.

At last, however, the date was fixed again, another pudding was made, and, at Norma's suggestion, I invited my Uncle Davey to come and stay for it, to pair off with her beagling sister. Norma looked down on dons quite as much as Lady Montdore did, and, as for undergraduates, although of course she must have known that such things existed, since they provided her husband and mine with a livelihood, she certainly never thought of them as human beings and possible diners out.

It would never formerly have occurred to me that "touching," a word often on Lady Montdore's lips (it was very much of her day) could come to have any relation to herself, but on the occasion of Norma's dinner, the first time I had seen Lady Montdore with Cedric since his illness, there was really something touching about her attitude towards him. It was touching to see this hitherto redoubtable and ponderous personage, thin now as a rake, in her little-girl dress of dark-blue tulle over pink taffeta, with her little-girl head of pale-blue curls, dark-blue ribbons and a swarm of diamond bees, as she listened through her own conversation to whatever Cedric might be saying, as she squinted out of the corner of her eye to see if he was happy and amused, perhaps even just to be quite sure that he was actually there, in the flesh, touching to see with what reluctance she left the dining room after dinner, touching to watch her as she sat with the rest of us in the drawing room waiting for the men to return, silent, or speaking at random, her eyes fixed upon the door like a spaniel waiting for its master. Love, with her, had blossomed late and strangely, but there could be no doubt that it had blossomed, and that this thorny old plant had very much altered in character to accord with the tender flowers and springtime verdure which now so unexpectedly adorned it. During the whole of the evening there was only one respect in which she behaved as she would have done in her pre-Cedric days, she piled wood and coal, without so much as a by-your-leave, onto the tiny fire, Norma's concession to the fact that winter had begun, so that by the end of the evening we sat in a mellow warmth such as I had never known in that room before.

The men, as they always do in Oxford, remained an inordinate length of time over their port, so long, in fact, that Lady Montdore, with growing impatience, suggested to Norma that they might be sent for. Norma, however, looked so absolutely appalled at the idea that Lady Montdore did not press it any further, but went on with her self-appointed task as stoker, one spaniel eye on the door.

"The only way to make a good fire," she said, "is to

put on enough coal. People have all kinds of theories about it, but it's really very simple. Perhaps we could ask for another scuttle, Mrs. Cozens? Very kind. Cedric mustn't get a chill, whatever happens."

"Dreadful," I said, "him being so ill, wasn't it?"

"Don't speak of it. I thought I should die. Yes, well, as I was saying. It's exactly the same with coffee, you know. People have these percolators and things and get the Bolter to buy them special beans in Kenya. Perfectly pointless. Coffee is good if it is made strong enough and nasty if it is not. What we had just now would have been quite all right if your cook had put in three times the amount, you know. What can they be talking about in the dining room? It's not as if any of them were interested in politics."

At last the door opened. Davey came in first, looking bored and made straight for the fire, Cedric, the Professor and Alfred followed in a bunch, still pursuing a conversation which seemed to be interesting them deeply.

"Just a narrow edging of white . . ." I heard Cedric say, through the open door, as they came down the passage.

Later on I remembered to ask Alfred what could have led up to this remark, so typical of Cedric but so un-typical of the conversation in that house, and he replied that they had been having a most fascinating talk on burial customs in the High Yemen.

"I fear," he said, "that you bring out the worst in Cedric Hampton, Fanny. He is really a most intelligent young man, interested in a large range of subjects, though I have no doubt at all that when he is with you he confines himself, as you do, to remarks in the nature of 'And did you notice the expression on her face when she saw who was there?' because he knows that general subjects do not amuse you, only personalities. With those whose horizon is a little wider he can be very serious, let me tell you."

The fact was that Cedric could bring out edgings of white to suit all tastes.

"Well, Fanny, how do you like it?" he asked me, giving a twitch to Lady Montdore's tulle skirt. "We ordered it by telephone when we were at Craigside —don't you die for television? Mainbocher simply couldn't believe that Sonia had lost so much weight."

Indeed she was very thin.

"I sit in a steam barrel," she said, looking fondly at Cedric, "for an hour or two, and then that nice Mr. Wixman comes down twice a week when we are at Hampton and he beats and beats me and the morning is gone in a flash. Cedric sees the cook for me nowadays. I find I can't take very much interest in food, in my barrel."

"But, my dear Sonia," said Davey, "I hope you consult Dr. Simpson about all this? I am horrified to see you in such a state. Really much too thin, nothing but skin and bones. You know, at our age, it's most dangerous to play about with one's weight, a terrible strain on the heart."

It was generous of Davey to talk about "our age," since Lady Montdore was certainly fourteen years older than he was.

"Dr. Simpson!" she said derisively. "My dear Davey, he's terribly behind the times. Why, he never even told me how good it is to stand on one's head, and Cedric says in Paris and Berlin they've been doing it for ages now. I must say I feel younger every day since I learnt. The blood races through your glands, you know, and they love it."

"How d'you know they love it?' said Davey with considerable irritation. He always scorned any regime for health except the one he happened to be following himself, regarding all others as dangerous superstitions imposed on gullible fools by unscrupulous quacks. "We understand so very little about our glands," he went on. "Why should it be good for them? Did Dame Nature intend us to stand on our heads? Do animals stand on their heads, Sonia?"

"The sloth," said Cedric, "and the bat hang upside down for hours on end—you can't deny that, Davey."

"Yes, but do sloths and bats feel younger every day? I doubt it. Bats may, but I'm sure sloths don't."

"Come on, Cedric," said Lady Montdore, very much put out by Davey's remarks, "we must be going home."

Lady Montdore and Cedric now installed themselves at Montdore House for the winter and were seen no more by me. London society, having none of the prejudices against the abnormal which still exist among Boreleys and Uncle Matthews in country places, simply ate Cedric up, occasional echoes of his great success even reaching Oxford. It seemed that such an arbiter of taste, such an arranger of festivities, had not been known since the days of the beaux, and that he lived in a perfect welter of parties, dragging Lady Montdore along in his wake.

"Isn't she wonderful? You know she's seventy—eighty —ninety . . ." Her age went up by leaps and bounds.

So Cedric had transformed her from a terrifying old idol of about sixty into a delicious young darling of about a hundred. Was anything beyond his powers?

I remember one icy day of late Spring I ran into Mrs. Chaddesley Corbet, walking down the Turl with an undergraduate, perhaps her son, I thought, chinless, like her.

"Fanny!" she said. "Oh, of course, darling, you live here, don't you? I'm always hearing about you from Cedric. He dotes on you, that's all."

"Oh," I said, pleased. "And I'm so very fond of him."

"Couldn't like him more, could you? So gay, so cosy, I think he's a perfect poppet. As for Sonia, it's a transformation, isn't it? Polly's marriage seems to have turned out to be a blessing in disguise for her. Do you ever hear from Polly now? What a thing to have done, poor sweet. But I'm mad about Cedric, that's all—everybody in London is—tiny Lord Fauntleroy. They're both dining with me this evening. I'll give them your love, shall I? See you very soon, darling, good-bye."

I saw Mrs. Chaddesley Corbett perhaps once a year. She always called me darling and said she would see me very soon, and this always left me feeling quite unreasonably elated.

I got back to my house and found Jassy and Victoria sitting by the fire. Victoria was looking very green.

"I must do the talking," Jassy said. "Fa's new car makes poor Vict sick and she can't open her mouth for fear of letting the sick out."

"Go and let it out in the loo," I said. Victoria shook her head vehemently.

"She hates being," said Jassy. "Anything rather. We hope you're pleased to see us."

I said that I was, very.

"And we hope you've noted how we never do come nowadays."

"Yes, I have noted. I put it down to the hunting."

"Stupid, you are. How could one hunt, in this weather?"

"This weather only began yesterday, and I've heard of you from Norma, hunting away like anything up to now."

"We don't think you quite realize how bitterly offended we feel over your behaviour to us the last year or two."

"Now, now, children, we've had this out a thousand times," I said firmly.

"Yes, well, it's not very nice of you. After all, when you married we rather naturally expected that your home would open up all the delights of civilized society to us, and that sooner or later we should meet, in your salon, the brilliant wealthy titled men destined to become our husbands. 'I loved her from the first moment I saw her, the leggy little girl with the beautiful sensitive face, who used to sprawl about Mrs. Wincham's drawing room at Oxford.' Well, then, what happens? One of the richest parties in Western Europe becomes an *habitué de la maison* and are we thrown at his head by our cousin, naturally ambitious for our future? Does she move heaven and earth to further this splendid match? Not even asked to meet him. Spoil sport."

"Go on," I said, wearily.

"No, well, we're only bringing it up . . ." Victoria here fled the room, Jassy took no notice, ". . . in order to show our great magnanimity of soul. The fact is, that we know a very interesting piece of news, and in spite of your counter-honnish behaviour we are going to tell it to you. But we want you to realize that it is pretty noble of us, when you take everything into account, his flashing eyes, his floating hair, only seen in the distance. It is such a shame, and I must wait for Vict to come back or it would be too unfaithful, and can we have some tea? She's always starving after."

"Does Mrs. Heathery know you're here?"

"Yes, she held Vict's head."

"You don't mean to say she's been sick already?"

"It's always thrice—once in the car and twice when we get there."

"Well, if Mrs. Heathery knows, tea will appear."

It appeared simultaneously with Victoria.

"Fanny's loo! The bliss! It's got a carpet, Jassy, and it's boiling warm, one could stay there all day. Crumpets! Oh, Fanny!"

"What's this news you know?" I asked, pouring out milk for the children.

"I like tea now, please," said Jassy. "Which shows how long since you saw us. I like tea and I almost like coffee. So the news is, Napoleon has left Elba and is on his way back."

"Say it again."

"Dense. Nobody would think that you were a hostess to the younger cosmopolitan intellectual set, noted for her brilliant repartee."

"Do you mean Polly?" I said, light suddenly dawning.

"Very bright of you, dear. Josh was out exercising this morning and he stopped at the Blood Arms for a quick one, and that's what he heard. So we came dashing over to tell you, Fanny, in sickness and in health. So does one good turn not deserve another, Fanny?"

"Oh, do stop being such a bore," I said, "and go on telling. When?"

"Any day now. The tenants have gone and the house is being got ready. Lady Patricia's sheets and things, you know. She's going to have a baby."

"Who is, Polly?"

"Well, dear, who do you think? Not Lady Patricia. So that's what she's coming back for. So are you admitting that it was handsome of us to come over and tell you?"

"Very handsome," I said.

"So will you invite us to luncheon one day soon?"

"Any day you like. I'll make chocolate profiteroles with real cream."

"And what about closing our eyes with holy dread?"

"Cedric, if that's what you mean, is in London, but you can close them at Jock Boreley," I said.

"Oh, Fanny, you brute. Can we go upstairs and see dear little David?"

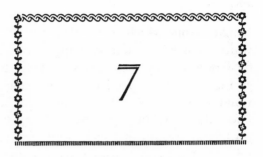

7

THE weather now became intensely cold, and much snow fell. The newspapers came out every day with horror stories of sheep buried in snowdrifts, of songbirds frozen to the branches on which they perched, of fruit trees hopelessly nipped in the bud, and the situation seemed dreadful to those who, like Mrs. Heathery, believe all they see in print without recourse to past experience. I tried to cheer her up by telling her, what, in fact, proved to be the case, that in a very short time the fields would be covered with sheep, the trees with birds and the barrows with fruit just as usual. But, though the future did not disturb me I found the present most disagreeable, that winter should set in again so late in the Spring, at a time when it would not be unreasonable to expect delicious weather, almost summer-like, warm enough to sit out of doors for an hour or two. The sky was overcast with a thick yellow blanket from which an endless pattern of black-and-white snowflakes came swirling down, and this went on day after day. One morning I sat by my window gazing idly at the pattern and thinking idle thoughts, wondering if it would ever be warm again, thinking how like a child's snowball Christ Church looked through a curtain of flakes, thinking, too, how cold it was going to be at Norma's that evening without Lady Montdore to stoke the fire, and how dull without Cedric and his narrow edging of white. Thank goodness, I thought, that I had sold my father's diamond brooch and installed central heating with the proceeds. Then I began to remember what the house had been like two years before when the workmen were still in it, and how I had looked out through that very same pane of glass, filthy dirty then, and splashed with whitewash, and seen Polly struggling into the wind with her future husband. I half wanted and half did not want Polly in my life again. I was expecting another baby and felt tired, really, not up to much.

Then, suddenly, the whole tempo of the morning completely altered because here in my drawing room, heavily pregnant, beautiful as ever, in a red coat and hat, was Polly, and, of course, all feelings of not wanting her melted away and were forgotten. In my drawing room, too, was the Lecturer, looking old and worn.

When Polly and I had finished hugging and kissing and laughing and saying, "Lovely to see you," and "Why did you never write?" she said,

"Can I bend you to my will?"

"Oh, yes you can. I've got simply nothing to do. I was just looking at the snow."

"Oh, the heaven of snow," she said, "and clouds,

after all those blue skies. Now the thing is, Fanny, can I bend you until late this afternoon, because Boy has got an utter mass of things to do and I can't stand about much, as you see. But you must frankly tell me if I shall be in your way, because I can always go to Elliston's waiting room. The blissful bliss of Elliston after those foreign shops! I nearly cried for happiness when we passed their windows just now—the bags! the cretonnes! The horror of abroad!"

"But that's wonderful," I said, "then you'll both lunch here?"

"Boy has to lunch with someone on business," said Polly, quickly. "You can go off then, darling, if you like, as Fanny says she can keep me. Don't bother to wait any more. Then come back for me here when you've finished?"

Boy, who had been rubbing his hands together in front of the fire, went off, rather glum, wrapping a scarf round his throat.

"And don't hurry a bit," she called after him, opening the door again and shouting down the stairs. "Now, darling Fanny, I want to do one final bend and make you lunch with me at Fuller's. Don't speak! You're going to say 'look at the weather,' aren't you? but we'll ring up for a taxi. Fullers! You'll never know how much I used to long for Dover sole and walnut cake and just this sort of a day in Sicily. Do you remember how we used to go there from Alconleigh when you were getting your house ready? I can't believe this is the same house, can you? Or that we are the same people, come to that. Except I see you're the same darling Fanny, just as you were the same when I got back from India. Why is it that I, of all people, keep

on having to go abroad? I do think it's too awful, don't
you?"

"I only went just that once," I said. "It's very light,
isn't it?"

"Yes, horrible glare. Just imagine if one had to live
there for ever. You know we started off in Spain. And
you'll never believe this, but they are two hours late
for every meal—two hours, Fanny—(can we lunch at
half past twelve to-day?) so of course by then you've
stopped feeling hungry and only feel sick. Then, when
the food comes, it is all cooked in rancidol. I can smell
it now, it's on everybody's hair, too, and to make it
more appetizing there are pictures all round you of
some dear old bull being tortured to death. They think
of literally nothing all day but bulls and the Virgin.
Spain was the worst of all, I thought. Of course Boy
doesn't mind abroad a bit, in fact, he seems to like it,
and he can talk all those terribly affected languages
(darling, Italian! you'd die!) but I truly don't think I
could have borne it much longer. I should have pined
away with homesickness. Anyway, here I am."

"What made you come back?" I said, really wondering how they could afford it, poor as Davey said they
were. Silkin was not a big house, but it would require
three or four servants.

"Well, you remember my Auntie Edna at Hampton
Court? The good old girl died and left me all her
money—not much, but we think we can just afford to
live at Silkin. Then Boy is writing a book and he had
to come back for that, London Library and Paddington."

"Paddington?" I said, thinking of the station.

"Duke Muniment room. Then there's this baby.

Fancy, if one had to have a baby abroad, poor little thing, not a cow in the place. All the same, Boy doesn't much want to settle down here for good. I think he's still frightened of Mummy, you know. I am a bit, myself—not frightened exactly, but bored at the idea of scenes. But there's really nothing more she can do to us, is there?"

"I don't think you need worry about her a bit," I said. "Your mother has altered completely in the last two years."

I could not very well say my real thought, which was that Lady Montdore no longer cared a rap for Boy or for Polly, and that she would most likely be quite friendly to them. It all depended upon Cedric's attitude, everything did, nowadays, as far as she was concerned.

Presently, when we were settled at our table at Fullers, among the fumed oak and the daintiness ("Isn't everything clean and lovely? Aren't the waitresses fair? You can't think how dark the waiters always are, abroad.") and had ordered our Dover soles, Polly said that now I must tell her all about Cedric.

"Do you remember," she said, "how you and Linda used to look him up to see if he would *do*."

"Well, he wouldn't have *done*," I said. "That's one thing quite certain."

"So I imagine," said Polly.

"How much do you know about him?"

I suddenly felt rather guilty at knowing so much myself and hoped that Polly would not think I had gone over to the enemy's camp. It is so difficult if you are fond of sport to resist running with the hare and hunting with the hounds.

"Boy made friends, in Sicily, with an Italian duke called Monte Pincio. He is writing about a former Pincio in his new book, and this wop knew Cedric in Paris, so he told us a lot about him. He says he is very pretty."

"Yes, that's quite true."

"How pretty, Fan? Prettier than me?"

"No. One doesn't have to gaze and gaze at him like one does with you."

"Oh, darling, you are so kind. Not any longer though, I fear."

"Just exactly the same. But he is very much like you. Didn't the Duke say that?"

"Yes. He said we were Viola and Sebastian. I must say I die for him."

"He dies for you, too. We must arrange it."

"Yes, after the baby—not while I'm such a sight. You know how sissies hate pregnant ladies. Poor Monte would do anything to get out of seeing me, lately. Go on telling more about Cedric and Mummy."

"I really think he loves your mother, you know. He is such a slave to her, never leaves her for a moment, always in high spirits. . . . I don't believe anybody could put it on to that extent, it must be love."

"I'm not surprised," said Polly. "I used to love her before she began about the marrying."

"There!" I said.

"There what?"

"Well, you told me once that you'd hated her all your life, and I knew it wasn't true."

"The fact is," said Polly, "when you hate somebody you can't imagine what it's like not hating them. It's just the same as with love. But of course with Mummy, who is such excellent company, so lively, you do love her before you find out how wicked she can be. And I don't suppose she's in all that violent hurry to get Cedric off that she was with me."

"No hurry," I said.

Polly's blank blue look fell upon my face. "You mean she's in love with him herself?"

"In love? I don't know. She loves him like anything. He makes such fun for her, you see, her life has become so amusing. Besides, she must know quite well that marriage isn't his thing exactly, poor Cedric."

"Oh, no," said Polly. "Boy agrees with me that she knows nothing, nothing whatever about all that. He says she once made a fearful gaffe about Sodomites, mixing them up with Dolomites. It was all over London. No, I guess she's in love. She's a great, great faller in love, you know. I used to think at one time that she rather fancied Boy, though he says not. Well, it's all very annoying because I suppose she doesn't miss me one little bit, and I miss her, often. And now tell me, how's my dad?"

"Very old," I said. "Very old, and your mother so very young. You must be prepared for quite as much of a shock when you see her as when you see him."

"No, really? How d'you mean, very young? Dyed hair?"

"Blue. But what one chiefly notices is that she has become so thin and supple, quick little movements, flinging one leg over the other, suddenly sitting on the floor, and so on. Quite like a young person."

"Good gracious," said Polly. "And she used to be so very stiff and solid."

"It's Mr. Wixman, Cedric's and her masseur. He pounds and pulls for an hour every morning, then she has another hour in a hay-box—full-time work, you know, what with the creaming and splashing and putting on a mask and taking it off again and having her nails done and her feet and then all the exercises, as well as having her teeth completely re-arranged and the hairs zipped off her arms and legs—I truly don't think I could be bothered."

"Operations on her face?"

"Oh, yes, but that was ages ago. All the bags and wrinkles gone, eyebrows plucked, and so on. Her face is very tidy now."

"Of course it may seem odd here," said Polly, "but you know there are hundreds and hundreds of women like that abroad. I suppose she stands on her head and lies in the sun? Yes, they all do. She must be a sight. Scene or no scene, I utterly can't wait for her, Fanny. When can we arrange it?"

"Not for the moment. They're in London now, fearfully busy with the Longhi ball they are giving at Montdore House. Cedric came to see me the other day and could talk of nothing else—he says they won't be going to Hampton again until it's over."

"What is a Longhi ball?"

"You know, Venetian. Real water, with real gondolas floating on it, in the ballroom. *O sole mio* on a hundred guitars, all the footmen in masks and capes, no light except from candles in Venetian lanterns until the guests get to the ballroom, when a searchlight will be trained on Cedric and your mother, receiving from a gondola. Fairly different from your ball, Polly. Oh, yes, and I know, Cedric won't allow any Royalties to be asked at all, because he says they ruin everything, in London. He says they are quite different in Paris where they know their place."

"Goodness!" said Polly. "How times have changed! Not even old Super-Ma'am?"

"No, not even your mother's new Infanta. Cedric was adamant."

"Fanny, it's your duty to go to it. You will, won't you?"

"Oh, darling, I can't. I feel so sleepy after dinner when I am pregnant, you know. I really couldn't drag myself. We shall hear about it all right, from Cedric."

"And when does it take place?"

"Under a month from now, the sixteenth, I believe."

"Why that's the very day I'm expecting my baby. How convenient. Then when everything's all over we can meet, can't we? You will fix it, promise."

"Oh, don't worry. We shan't be able to hold Cedric back. He's fearfully interested in you. You're Rebecca to him."

Boy came back to my house just as we were finishing our tea. He looked perished with cold and very tired but Polly would not let him wait while some fresh tea was made. She allowed him to swallow a tepid cup and dragged him off.

"I suppose you've lost the key of the car as usual," she said unkindly on their way downstairs.

"No no, here it is, on my key ring."

"Miracle," said Polly. "Well, then, good-bye, my darling. I'll telephone and we'll do some more benders."

When Alfred came in later on I said to him, "I've seen Polly! Just imagine, she spent the whole day here, and oh, Alfred, she's not a bit in love any more!"

"Do you never think of anything but who is or is

not in love with whom?" he said in tones of great exasperation.

Norma, I knew, would be just as uninterested, and I longed very much for Davey or Cedric to pick it all over with.

8

SO POLLY now settled into her aunt's house at
Silkin. It had always been Lady Patricia's house more
than Boy's, as she was the one who lived there all the
time, while Boy flitted about between Hampton and
London with occasional visits to the Continent, and it
was arranged inside with a very feminine form of taste-
lessness, that is to say, no taste and no comfort, either.
It was a bit better than Norma's house, but not much,
the house itself being genuinely old instead of Banbury
Road old and standing in the real country instead of
an Oxford suburb. It contained one or two good pieces
of furniture, and where Norma would have had cretonnes the Dougdales had Boy's needlework. But there
were many similarities, especially upstairs, where lino-
leum covered the floors, and every bathroom, in spite
of the childlessness of the Dougdales, was a nursery
bathroom, smelling strongly of not very nice soap.

Polly did not attempt to alter anything. She just flopped into Lady Patricia's bed, in Lady Patricia's bedroom whose windows looked out onto Lady Patricia's grave. "Beloved wife of Harvey Dougdale," said the gravestone, which had been erected some weeks after poor Harvey Dougdale had acquired a new beloved wife. "She shall not grow old as we that are left grow old."

I think Polly cared very little about houses, which, for her, consisted of Hampton and the rest, and that if she could no longer live at Hampton she could not take much interest in any other house. Whatever it was in life that Polly did care for, and time had yet to disclose the mystery, it was certainly not her home. She was in no sense what the French call a *"femme d'intérieur,"* and her household arrangements were casual to the verge of chaos. Nor, any longer, alas, was it Boy. Complete disillusion had set in, as far as he was concerned, and she was behaving towards him with exactly the same off-hand coldness that had formerly characterized her attitude towards her mother, the only difference being that whereas she had always been a little frightened of Lady Montdore it was Boy, in this case, who was a little frightened of her.

Boy was busily occupied with his new book. It was to be called *Three Dukes,* and the gentlemen it portrayed were considered by Boy to be perfect examples of nineteenth-century aristocracy in their three countries. The Dukes in question were Paddington, Souppes and Monte Pincio, all three masters, it seemed, of the arts of anecdote, adultery and gourmandise, members of the Jockey Club, gamblers and sportsmen. He had a photograph, the frontispiece for his book, of all three together, taken at a shoot at Landçut, standing in front of an acre of dead animals; with their tummies, their beards, their deerstalker's hats and white gaiters they looked like nothing so much as three King Edwards all in a row. Polly told me that he had finished Pincio while they were in Sicily, the present man having put the necessary documents at his disposal, and was now engaged upon Paddington with the assistance of the Duke's librarian, motoring off to Paddington Park every morning, notebook in hand. The idea was that when that was finished he should go to France in pursuit of Souppes. Nobody ever had the least objection to Boy "doing" their ancestors: he always made them so charming and endowed them with such delightful vices, besides which it gave a guarantee, a hallmark of ancient lineage, since he never would take on anybody whose family did not go back to well before the Conquest, in England, or, who, if foreign, could not produce at least one Byzantine Emperor, Pope or pre-Louis XV Bourbon in their family tree.

The day of the Montdore House ball came and went, but there was no sign of Polly's baby. Aunt Sadie always used to say that people unconsciously cheat over the dates when babies are expected in order to make the time of waiting seem shorter, but if that is so it certainly makes the last week or two seem endless. Polly depended very much on my company and would send a motor car most days to take me over to Silkin for an hour or two. The weather was heavenly at last, and we were able to go for little walks and even to sit in a sheltered corner of the garden, wrapped in rugs.

"Don't you love it," Polly said, "when it's suddenly like this after the winter and all the goats and hens look so happy?"

She did not seem very much interested in the idea of having a baby, though she once said to me, "Doesn't it seem funny to have talcum powder and things and boring old Sister waiting about, and all for somebody who doesn't exist?"

"Oh, I always think that," I said. "And yet the very moment they are there they become such an integral part of your life that you can't imagine what it was like without them."

"I suppose so. I wish they'd hurry up. So what about the ball—have you heard anything? You really ought to have gone, Fanny."

"I couldn't have. The Warden of Wadham and Norma went—not together, I don't mean, but they are the only people I've seen so far. It seems to have been very splendid, Cedric changed his dress five times. He started with tights made of rose petals and a pink wig and ended as Doris Keane in *Romance* and a black wig. He had real diamonds on his mask. Your mother was a Venetian youth, to show off her new legs, and they stood in a gondola giving away wonderful prizes to everybody—Norma got a silver snuffbox—and it went on till seven. Oh, how badly people do describe balls."

"Never mind, there'll be the *Tatler*."

"Yes, they said it was flash, flash all night. Cedric is sure to have the photographs to show us."

Presently Boy strolled up and said, "Well, Fanny, what d'you hear of the ball?"

"Oh, we've just had the ball," said Polly. "Can't begin all over again. What about your work?"

"I could bring it out here, if you like."

"You know I don't count your silly old embroidery as work."

Boy's face took on a hurt expression and he went away.

"Polly, you are awful," I said.

"Yes, but it's for his own good. He pretends he can't concentrate until after the baby now, so he wanders about getting on everybody's nerves when he ought to be getting on with Paddington. He must hurry, you know, if the book is to be out for Christmas. Have you ever met Geoffrey Paddington, Fanny?"

"Well, I have," I said, "because Uncle Matthew once produced him for a house party at Alconleigh. Old."

"Not the least bit old," said Polly, "and simply heavenly. You've no idea how nice he is. He came first to see Boy about the book and now he comes quite often, to chat. Terribly kind of him, don't you think? Mamma is his chief hate, so I never saw him before I married. I remember she was always trying to get him over to Hampton and he never would come. Perhaps he'll be here one day when you are. I'd love you to meet him."

I did meet him after that, several times, finding his shabby little Morris Cowley outside Silkin when I arrived. He was a poor man, since his ancestor, the great Duke, left much glory but little cash, and his father, the old gentleman in spats, had lavished most of what there was on La Païva and ladies of the kind. I thought him rather nice and very dull, and could see that he was falling in love with Polly.

"Don't you think he's terribly nice?" said Polly, "and so kind of him to come when I look like this."

"Your face is the same," I said.

"I really quite long for him to see me looking ordinary—if I ever do. I'm losing hope in this baby being born at all."

It was born, though, that very evening, took one look, according to the Radletts, at its father, and quickly died again.

Polly was rather ill and the Sister would not allow any visitors for about ten days after the baby was born, but as soon as she did I went over. I saw Boy for a moment in the hall. He looked even more gloomy than usual. Poor Boy, I thought, left with a wife who now so clearly disliked him and not even a baby to make up for it.

Polly lay in a bower of blossoms. The Sister was very much in evidence and there should have been a purple-faced wailing monster in a Moses basket to complete the picture. I really felt its absence as though it were that of a person well known to me.

"Oh, poor . . ." I began. But Polly had inherited a great deal of her mother's talent for excluding what was disagreeable, and I saw at once that any show of sympathy would be out of place and annoy her, so, instead, I exclaimed, Radlett fashion, over two camellia trees in full bloom which stood on each side of her bed.

"Geoffrey Paddington sent them," she said. "Do admit that he's a perfect love, Fanny. You know Sister was with his sister when she had her babies."

But then whom had Sister not been with? She and Boy must have had some lovely chats, I thought, the first night or two when Polly was feverish and they had sat up together in his dressing room. She kept on coming into the room while I was there, bringing a tray, taking away an empty jug, bringing some more flowers, any excuse to break in on our talk and deposit some nice little dollop of gossip. She had seen my condition at a glance, she had also realized that I was too small a fish for her net, but she was affability itself and said that she hoped I would come over every day now and sit with Lady Polly.

"Do you ever see Jeremy Chaddesley Corbett at Oxford?" she asked. "He is one of my favourite babies."

Presently she came in empty-handed and rather pink, almost, if such a thing were possible with her, rattled, and announced that Lady Montdore was downstairs. I felt that, whereas she would have bundled any of us into our coffins with perfect calm, the advent of Lady Montdore had affected even her nerves of iron. Polly, too, was thrown off her balance for a moment and said faintly, "Oh! Is Mr.—I mean my—I really mean is Boy there?"

"Yes, he's with her now. He sent word to say, will you see her? If you don't want to, Lady Polly, I can say quite truthfully that you may not have another visitor to-day. You really ought not to, the first day, in any case."

"I'll go," I said, getting up.

"No, no, no, Fanny, you mustn't, darling. I'm not sure I will see her, but I couldn't possibly be left alone with her. Sit down again at once, please."

There were voices in the garden outside.

"Do go to the window," said Polly. "Is it them?"

"Yes, and Cedric is there, too," I said. "And they're all three walking round the garden together."

"No! But I must I must see Cedric! Sister, do be a darling, go down and tell them to come up at once."

"Now, Lady Polly, no. And please don't work yourself up, you must avoid any excitement. It's absolutely out of the question for you to see a stranger to-day. Close relations was what Dr. Simpson said, and one at a time. I suppose your mother must be allowed up for a few minutes if you want her, but nobody else and certainly not a strange young man."

"I'd better see Mummy," Polly said, to me "or else this silly feud will go on for ever, besides, I really can't wait to see her hair and her legs. Oh, dear, though, the one I long for is Cedric."

"She seems to be in a very friendly mood," I said, still looking at them out of the window. "Laughing and chatting away. Very smart in navy blue with a sailor hat. Boy is being wonderful. I thought he might be knocked groggy by her appearance, but he's pretending not to notice. He's looking at Cedric all the time. They are getting on like mad."

Most astute of him, I thought privately, if he hit it off with Cedric he would, very soon, be back in Lady Montdore's good graces, and then, perhaps, there could be a little modification of Lord Montdore's will.

"I die for the sailor hat. Come on, let's get it over. All right then, Sister, ask her to come up—wait—give me a comb and a glass first, will you? Go on with the running commentary, Fanny."

"Well, Cedric and Boy are chatting away like mad. I think Boy is admiring Cedric's suit, a sort of coarse blue tweed, very pretty, piped with scarlet. Lady Montdore is all smiles, having a good look round. You know the way she does."

"I can just see it," said Polly, combing her hair.

I did not quite like to say that Lady Montdore at this very moment was peering over the churchyard wall at her sister-in-law's grave. Boy and Cedric had left her there and were wandering off together towards the wrought-iron gates which led to the kitchen garden, laughing, talking and gesticulating.

"Go on," said Polly, "keep it up, Fanny."

"There's Sister, she is floating up to your mother, who is simply beaming—they both are—I never saw such smiles. Goodness, how Sister is enjoying it! Here they come. Your mother looks so happy, I feel quite sentimental, you can see how she must have been missing you, really at the bottom of her heart, all this time."

"Nonsense," said Polly, but she looked rather pleased.

"Darling, I do so feel I shall be in the way. Let me escape now through Boy's dressing room."

"Oh, on no account whatever, Fanny. Fanny you'll upset me if you do that—I absolutely insist on you staying here—I can't face her alone, beams or no beams."

Perhaps it had occurred to her, as it now did to me, that Lady Montdore's beam would very likely fade at the sight of Polly in Lady Patricia's room, unchanged in almost every respect, in the very bed where Lady Patricia had breathed her last, and that her repugnance for what Polly had done would be given a new reality. Even I had found it rather unattractive until I had got used to the idea. But over-sensibility had never been one of Lady Montdore's failings, and, besides, the great flame of happiness that Cedric had lit in her heart had long since burnt up all emotions which did not directly relate to him. He was the only person in the world now who had any substance for her.

So the beam did not flicker. She positively radiated good humour as she kissed Polly first and then me. She looked round the room and said, "You've moved the dressing table. It's much better like that, more light. Lovely flowers, dear, these camellias—can I have one for Cedric's buttonhole? Oh, from Paddington, are they? Poor Geoffrey, I fear he's a bit of a megalomaniac. I haven't been over there once since he succeeded. His father, now, was very different, a charming man, great friend of ours. King Edward was very fond of him, too, and of course Loelia Paddington was perfectly lovely— people used to stand on chairs, you know. So the poor little baby died. I expect it was just as well. Children are such an awful expense, nowadays."

Sister, who came back into the room just in time to hear this remark, put her hand to her heart and nearly fainted. That was going to be something to tell her next patients about, never, in all her sister-hood, can she have heard its like from a mother to an only daughter. But Polly, gazing open-mouthed at her mother, taking in every detail of the new appearance, was quite un-moved. It was too typical of Lady Montdore's whole outlook on life for somebody who had been brought up by her to find it odd or upsetting. In any case, I doubt if she minded much about the baby, herself. She seemed to me rather like a cow whose calf has been taken away from it at birth, unconscious of her loss.

"What a pity you couldn't have come to the ball, Fanny," Lady Montdore went on. "Just only for half an hour, to have a look. It was really beautiful. A lot of Cedric's friends came from Paris for it, in most strik-ing dresses and, I am bound to say, though I have never liked the French, they were very civil indeed and so appreciative of anything one did for them. They all

said there hadn't been such a party since the days of
Robert de Montesquiou, and I can believe it. It cost
£4000, you know, the water for the gondolas was so
heavy, for one thing. Well, it shows these foreigners
that England isn't done for yet; excellent propaganda.
I wore all my diamonds and I have given Cedric a revolving diamond star (goes by clockwork) and he wore
it on his shoulder—most effective, I must say. We thoroughly enjoyed every minute and I wish you could read
the letters I've had about it, really touching, people have
had so little pleasure the last year or two and it makes
them all the more grateful, of course. Next time we
come over I'll bring the photographs. They give a
wonderful idea of what it was like."

"What was your dress, Mummy?"

"Longhi," said Lady Montdore evasively. "Veronica
Chaddesley Corbett was very good, as a prostitute (they
were called something different in those days) and
Davey was there, Fanny, have you heard from him? He
was the Black Death. Everybody made a real effort,
you know. It's a terrible pity you girls couldn't have
come."

There was a pause. She looked round the room and
said with a sigh, "Poor Patricia—well, never mind,
that's all over now. Boy was telling us about his book,
such an excellent idea—*Three Dukes*—and Cedric is
very much interested because young Souppes, the son
of the Prince des Ressources whom we used to see at
Trouville, is a friend of his and Chèvres-Fontaine,
which Cedric used to take every summer, belongs to his
first cousin. Isn't it a curious coincidence? So of course
Cedric can tell Boy a great many things he never knew

about them all, and they think later on they might go to Paris together to do some research. In fact, we might all go, wouldn't that be amusing?"

"Not me," said Polly, "no more abroad for me, ever."

At this point Boy came into the room and I discreetly left it, in spite of a furious look from the bed. I went into the garden to find Cedric. He was sitting on the churchyard wall, the pale sunshine on his golden hair, which I perceived to be tightly curled, an aftermath of the ball, no doubt, and plucking away with intense concentration at the petals of a daisy.

"He loves me, he loves me not, he loves me, he loves me not, don't interrupt, my angel, he loves me, he loves me not, oh, heaven, heaven, heaven! He loves me! I may as well tell you, my darling, that the second big thing in my life has begun."

A most sinister ray of light suddenly fell upon the future.

"Oh, Cedric," I said. "Do be careful."

I need not have felt any alarm, however. Cedric managed the whole thing quite beautifully. As soon as Polly had completely recovered her health and looks, he put Lady Montdore and Boy into the big Daimler and rolled them away to France. The field was thus left to a Morris Cowley which, sure enough, could be seen outside Silkin day after day. Before very long, Polly got into it and was driven over to Paddington Park, where she remained.

Then the Daimler rolled back to Hampton.

"So here we are, my darling, having lovely cake and eating it, too, which is *one's* great aim in life."

"The Boreleys think it simply terrible," I said.